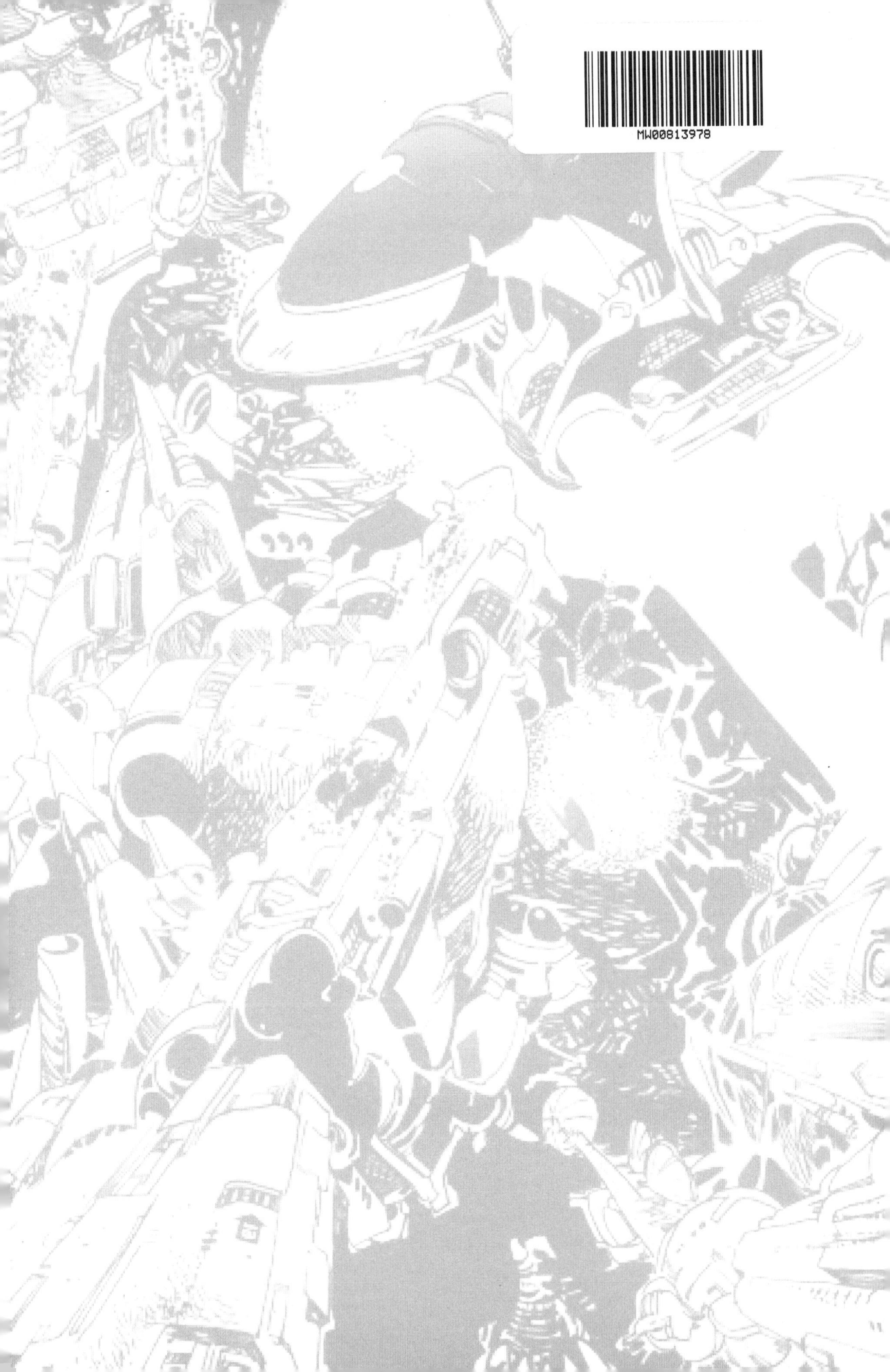

PRISON SHIP

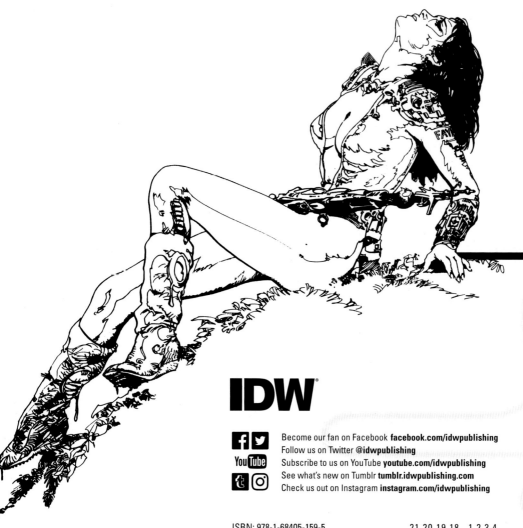

IDW

Become our fan on Facebook **facebook.com/idwpublishing**
Follow us on Twitter **@idwpublishing**
Subscribe to us on YouTube **youtube.com/idwpublishing**
See what's new on Tumblr **tumblr.idwpublishing.com**
Check us out on Instagram **instagram.com/idwpublishing**

ISBN: 978-1-68405-159-5   21 20 19 18   1 2 3 4

WRITTEN BY
BRUCE JONES

ART BY
ESTEBAN MAROTO

COVER COLORS BY
SANTI CASAS

TRANSLATION BY
ANNA ROSENWONG

LETTERING BY
FRANK CVETKOVICH

COLLECTION DESIGN BY
RON ESTEVEZ

EDITS BY
JUSTIN EISINGER AND
ALONZO SIMON

PUBLISHER:
GREG GOLDSTEIN

PRISON SHIP. APRIL 2018. FIRST PRINTING. NAVE PRISON by Esteban Maroto Copyright © Esteban Maroto, 2018. First published by Editorial Planeta SA. All Rights Reserved. © 2018 Idea and Design Works, LLC. The IDW logo is registered in the U.S. Patent and Trademark Office. IDW Publishing, a division of Idea and Design Works, LLC. Editorial offices: 2765 Truxtun Road, San Diego, CA 92106. Any similarities to persons living or dead are purely coincidental. With the exception of artwork used for review purposes, none of the contents of this publication may be reprinted without the permission of Idea and Design Works, LLC. Printed in Korea.

IDW Publishing does not read or accept unsolicited submissions of ideas, stories, or artwork.

Greg Goldstein, President & Publisher
Robbie Robbins, EVP & Sr. Art Director
Chris Ryall, Chief Creative Officer & Editor-in-Chief
Matthew Ruzicka, CPA, Chief Financial Officer
David Hedgecock, Associate Publisher
Laurie Windrow, Senior Vice President of Sales & Marketing
Lorelei Bunjes, VP of Digital Services
Eric Moss, Sr. Director, Licensing & Business Development

Ted Adams, Founder & CEO of IDW Media Holdings

For international rights, please
contact licensing@idwpublishing.com

Jones • Maroto

PRISON SHIP

INTRODUCTION

Josep Toutain has been a special character in my life since he showed up in Madrid in 1960 to convince me to come to Barcelona—which was at the time, I dare say, Europe's cultural center.

He was complex and hard to classify. An agent, editor, manager, and patron, he was at times aloof and arrogant, at others paternal and overly possessive, but always the hardworking entrepreneur. He was in love with his profession and with the special Catalonia in his head—one far from today's "nationalistic" frenzy.

In short, a novel character from a unique, creative moment in time I continue to miss to this day.

I've worked with many national and international scriptwriters, although whenever I can, I usually prefer to illustrate my own stories. When they let me, I've tried to contribute my own ideas. I think it's a good way to "enrich" the final results.

One of the scriptwriters I most love and appreciate is Roy Thomas, who I've known for over 45 years—though, oddly, we've never met in person. We have connected by phone, fax, emails, and letters, and our collaboration has always been fruitful. We've invented famous characters together: Red Sonja, Satana, Vlad the Impaler, Big Red, and more—the list is extensive. But the most famous was Red Sonja.

He and Stan Lee wanted to change the look of a character Barry Windsor Smith was drawing. She wore a long coat of armor, and they asked me to "show as much skin as possible." I chipped away at her chain mail until it became a bikini, which, over the years, has become famous.

We've laughed a lot about how a warrior could possibly head into battle wearing a bikini, although as I told Roy, Red Sonja's "weapons" were under her thong.

I've always tried to contribute ideas to the scripts I was illustrating. I think back fondly of the time when this was possible. Now, the excessive proliferation of all kinds of technology, video games, and media make this approach extremely difficult.

With fervent gratitude, I would like to dedicate this to Archie Goodwin, and his magnificent horror stories, Peter David of the Atlantic chronicles and Aquaman, Don MacGregor, Lady Rawhide, Scarlet Fever, Enrique Sánchez Abuli, Mauro Boselli, Claudio Chiaverotti, Sergio Bonelli, Bill Dubay, and many others who would make this list tediously long.

Something special happened in the case of Bruce Jones. I hadn't worked for Toutain Selecciones Ilustradas for a while. One day, he called to ask me to illustrate an eight-page story with 12 episodes, which he needed to fill the *1984* magazine. It seems some readers had asked for me to contribute again.

The story was written by someone who truly understands how graphic narrative works. Let's keep in mind that Bruce Jones is also wonderful at drawing—although for my taste, his work was a bit lacking in fantasy, but you have to consider it was the early '80s, when science fiction hadn't reached today's heights.

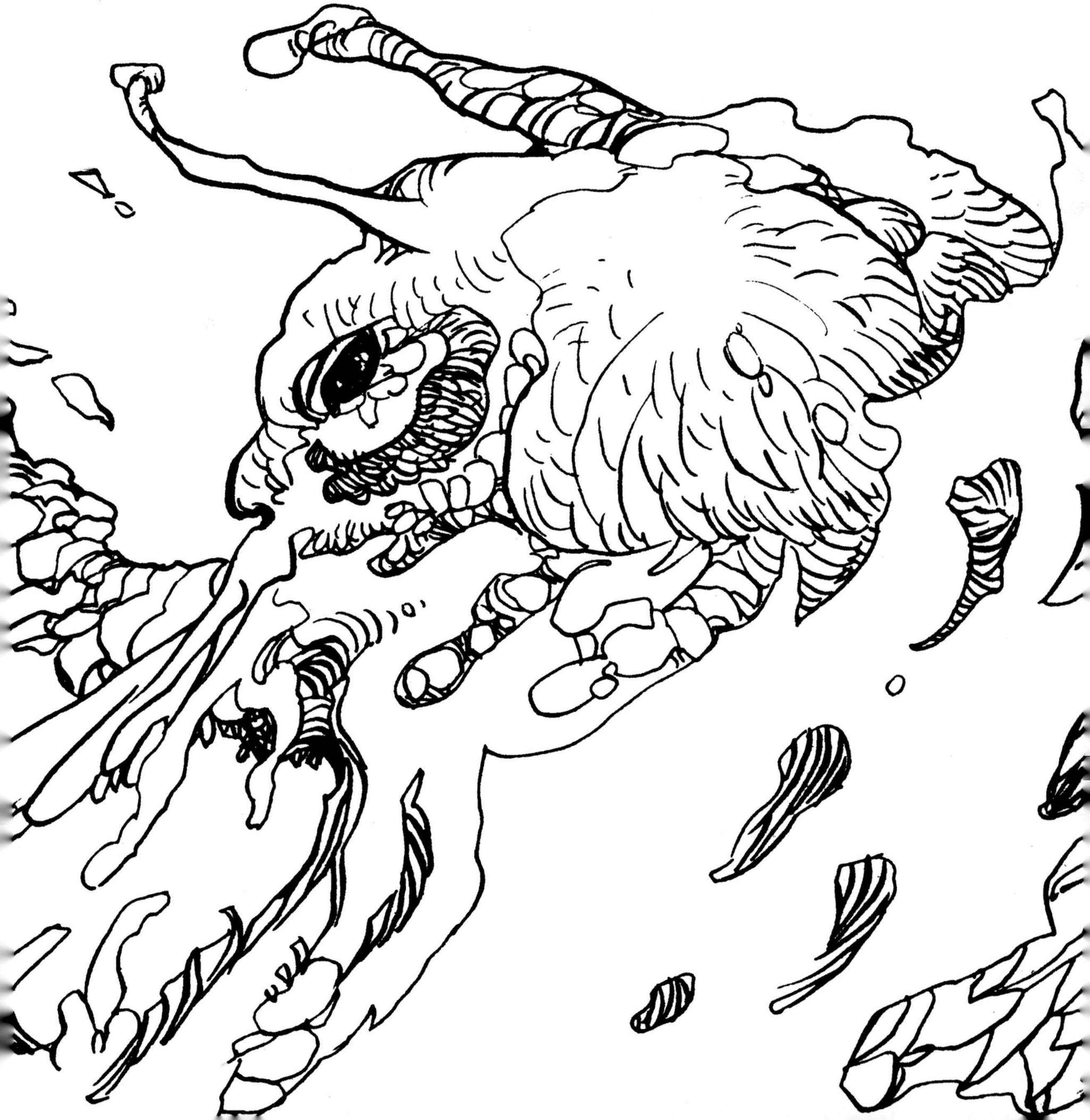

I agreed to draw the scripts, which were already finished, though I couldn't contribute any suggestions, as I usually do. I didn't even get to speak or correspond with Bruce Jones.

Later on, Warren published my drawings in one of his new magazines, which he'd wanted to give a more "erotic" tone—based on his concept of eroticism. He completely changed the script, signed it as Alabaster Redzone—which I think was Bill Dubay's pen name—and introduced one of the most surrealist elements I've ever seen in comics.

Faye, the protagonist—now called Diana Jacklighter, another one of my characters—spoke through a "penis" they'd added to the drawings to float around her.

After publishing two chapters, Warren decided to sell the publishing house to Harris Publications.

As always in our complicated business world, the workers and the artists were the ones who lost out. It was just one more episode in a long list of blunders and fraudulent manipulations.

We're so used to "losing" that we get nervous when we "win."

Many of the originals I'd drawn for Warren disappeared under mysterious circumstances. When I've tried to recover them, people at Harris have told me they'd been "burned." I seem to be in a passionate relationship with fire.

Esteban Maroto

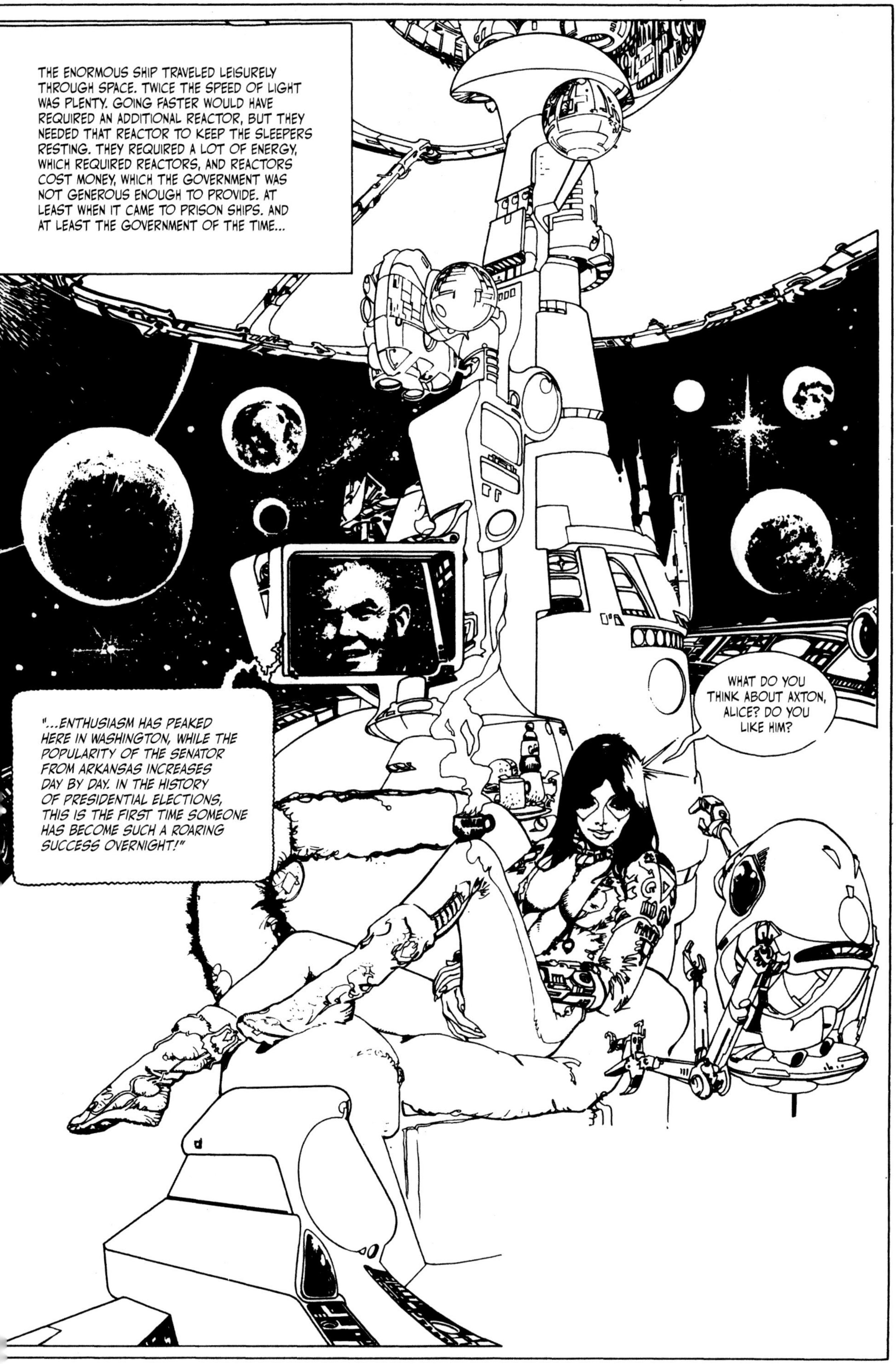
THE ENORMOUS SHIP TRAVELED LEISURELY THROUGH SPACE. TWICE THE SPEED OF LIGHT WAS PLENTY. GOING FASTER WOULD HAVE REQUIRED AN ADDITIONAL REACTOR, BUT THEY NEEDED THAT REACTOR TO KEEP THE SLEEPERS RESTING. THEY REQUIRED A LOT OF ENERGY, WHICH REQUIRED REACTORS, AND REACTORS COST MONEY, WHICH THE GOVERNMENT WAS NOT GENEROUS ENOUGH TO PROVIDE. AT LEAST WHEN IT CAME TO PRISON SHIPS. AND AT LEAST THE GOVERNMENT OF THE TIME...
"...ENTHUSIASM HAS PEAKED HERE IN WASHINGTON, WHILE THE POPULARITY OF THE SENATOR FROM ARKANSAS INCREASES DAY BY DAY. IN THE HISTORY OF PRESIDENTIAL ELECTIONS, THIS IS THE FIRST TIME SOMEONE HAS BECOME SUCH A ROARING SUCCESS OVERNIGHT!"
WHAT DO YOU THINK ABOUT AXTON, ALICE? DO YOU LIKE HIM?

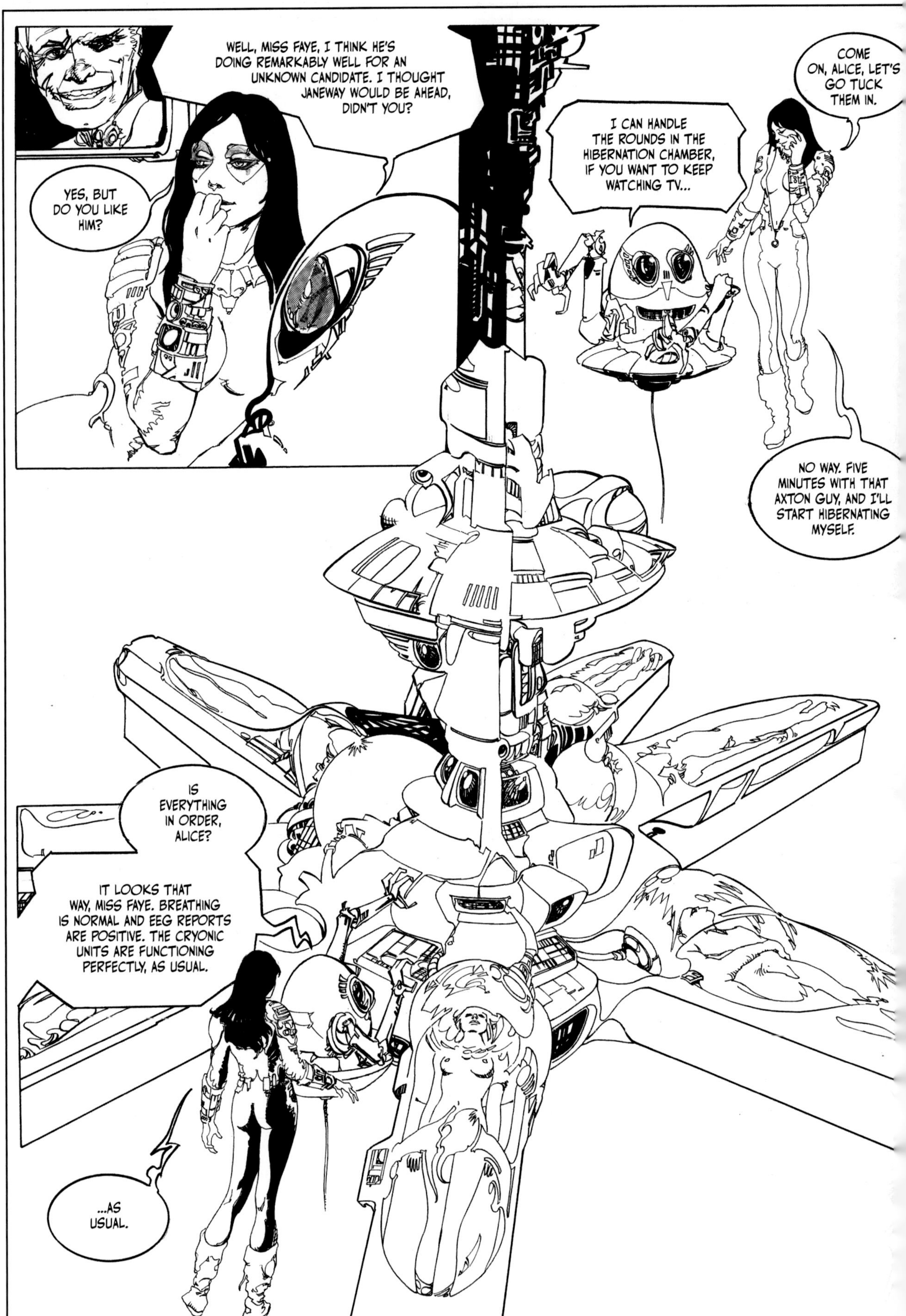

YES, BUT DO YOU LIKE HIM?
WELL, MISS FAYE, I THINK HE'S DOING REMARKABLY WELL FOR AN UNKNOWN CANDIDATE. I THOUGHT JANEWAY WOULD BE AHEAD, DIDN'T YOU?
I CAN HANDLE THE ROUNDS IN THE HIBERNATION CHAMBER, IF YOU WANT TO KEEP WATCHING TV...
COME ON, ALICE, LET'S GO TUCK THEM IN.
NO WAY. FIVE MINUTES WITH THAT AXTON GUY, AND I'LL START HIBERNATING MYSELF.
IS EVERYTHING IN ORDER, ALICE?
IT LOOKS THAT WAY, MISS FAYE. BREATHING IS NORMAL AND EEG REPORTS ARE POSITIVE. THE CRYONIC UNITS ARE FUNCTIONING PERFECTLY, AS USUAL.
...AS USUAL.

THEY DON'T LOOK LIKE CONVICTED MURDERERS WHEN THEY'RE ASLEEP WITH THEIR TEDDY BEARS, HUH? I WONDER WHAT THEY'RE DREAMING ABOUT.
THEY SAY IF AXTON IS ELECTED, HE'LL BRING BACK THE DEATH PENALTY...
WHAT DO YOU THINK ABOUT THAT, ALICE?
I'M JUST A ROBOT ATTENDANT, MISS FAYE.
I'VE HEARD THEY USED TO ELECTROCUTE OR GAS PEOPLE... LIKE STRAY DOGS. CAN YOU IMAGINE?
NO, MISS FAYE.
HOW WOULD THEY KILL THEM NOW? MAYBE THEY'D LET THEM SLEEP FOREVER IN THE REFRIGERATION CHAMBERS... THAT WOULDN'T BE SO BAD...
...UNLESS YOU HAVE A NIGHTMARE.
YES, MISS FAYE.
COME ON, ALICE. LET'S HAVE A GLASS OF WARM MILK AND GO TO BED.
3

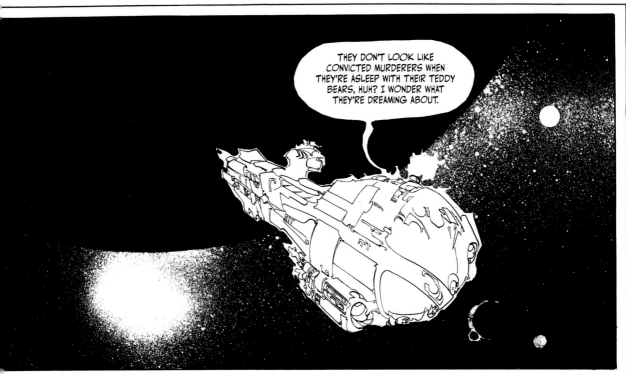

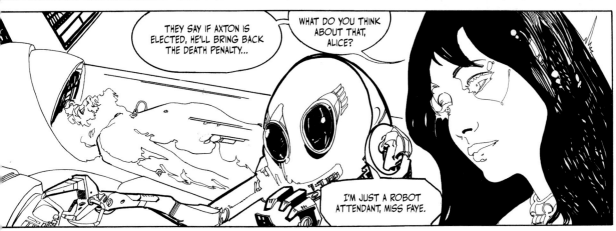

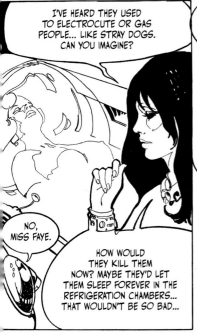

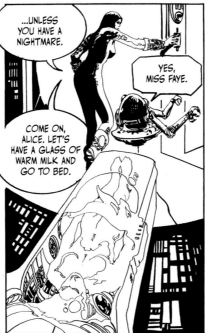

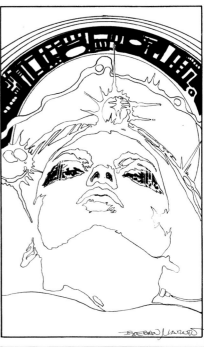

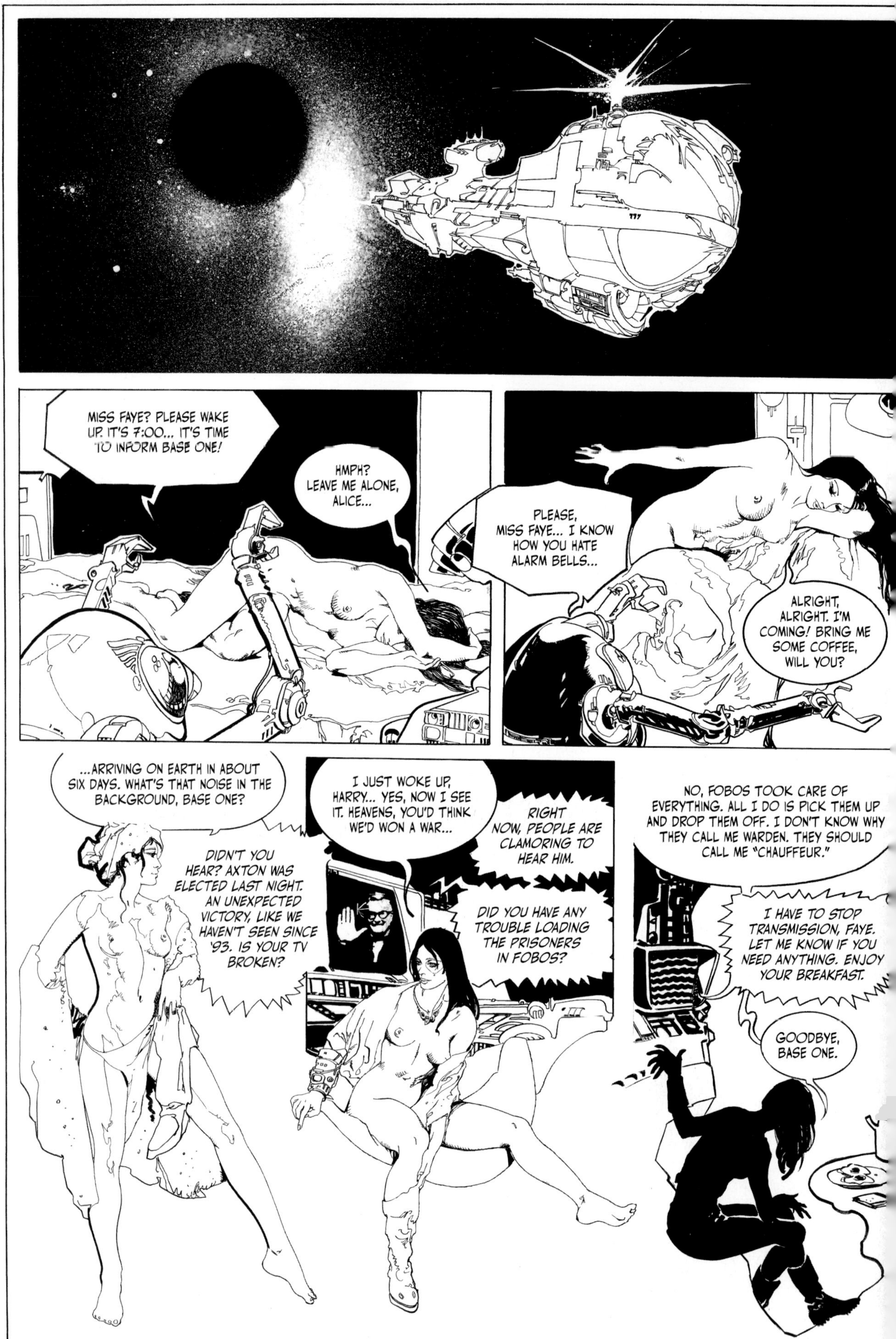
MISS FAYE? PLEASE WAKE UP. IT'S 7:00... IT'S TIME TO INFORM BASE ONE!
HMPH? LEAVE ME ALONE, ALICE...
PLEASE, MISS FAYE... I KNOW HOW YOU HATE ALARM BELLS...
ALRIGHT, ALRIGHT. I'M COMING! BRING ME SOME COFFEE, WILL YOU?
...ARRIVING ON EARTH IN ABOUT SIX DAYS. WHAT'S THAT NOISE IN THE BACKGROUND, BASE ONE?
DIDN'T YOU HEAR? AXTON WAS ELECTED LAST NIGHT. AN UNEXPECTED VICTORY, LIKE WE HAVEN'T SEEN SINCE '93. IS YOUR TV BROKEN?
I JUST WOKE UP, HARRY... YES, NOW I SEE IT. HEAVENS, YOU'D THINK WE'D WON A WAR...
RIGHT NOW, PEOPLE ARE CLAMORING TO HEAR HIM.
DID YOU HAVE ANY TROUBLE LOADING THE PRISONERS IN FOBOS?
NO, FOBOS TOOK CARE OF EVERYTHING. ALL I DO IS PICK THEM UP AND DROP THEM OFF. I DON'T KNOW WHY THEY CALL ME WARDEN. THEY SHOULD CALL ME "CHAUFFEUR."
I HAVE TO STOP TRANSMISSION, FAYE. LET ME KNOW IF YOU NEED ANYTHING. ENJOY YOUR BREAKFAST.
GOODBYE, BASE ONE.

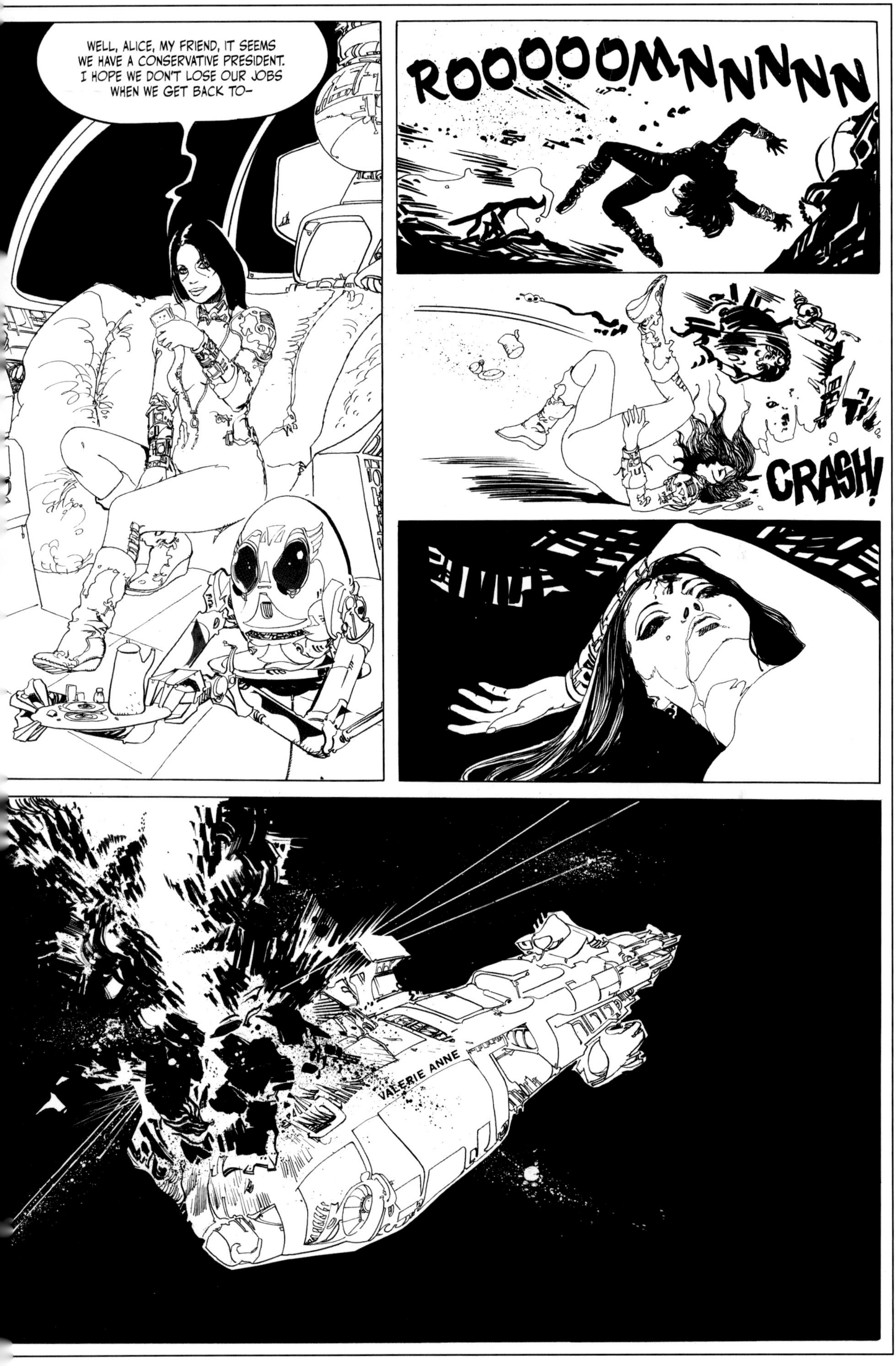
WELL, ALICE, MY FRIEND, IT SEEMS WE HAVE A CONSERVATIVE PRESIDENT. I HOPE WE DON'T LOSE OUR JOBS WHEN WE GET BACK TO–
ROOOOOMNNNNN
CRASH!
VALERIE ANNE

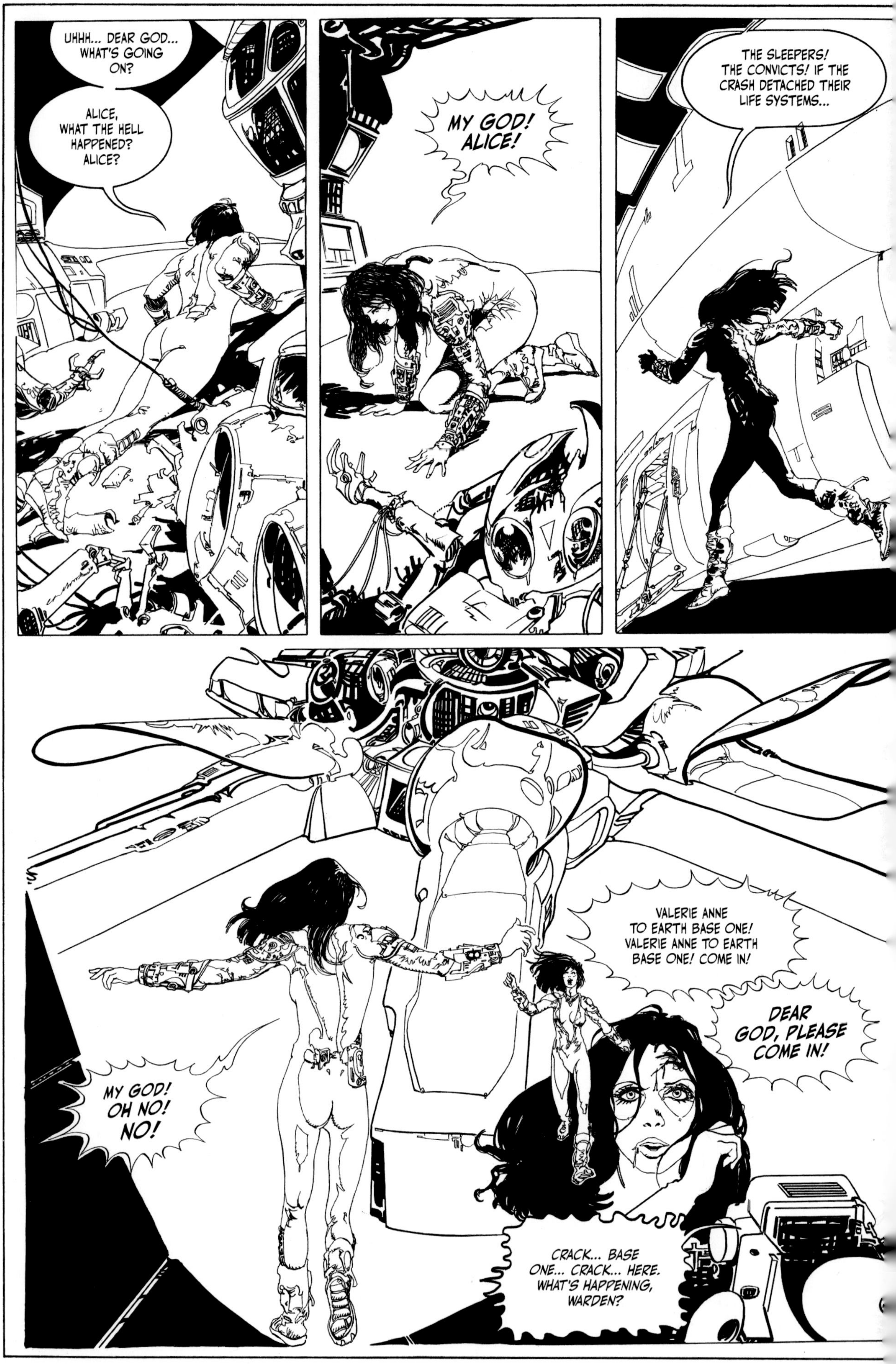
UHHH... DEAR GOD... WHAT'S GOING ON?
ALICE, WHAT THE HELL HAPPENED? ALICE?
MY GOD! ALICE!
THE SLEEPERS! THE CONVICTS! IF THE CRASH DETACHED THEIR LIFE SYSTEMS...
VALERIE ANNE TO EARTH BASE ONE! VALERIE ANNE TO EARTH BASE ONE! COME IN!
DEAR GOD, PLEASE COME IN!
MY GOD! OH NO! NO!
CRACK... BASE ONE... CRACK... HERE. WHAT'S HAPPENING, WARDEN?

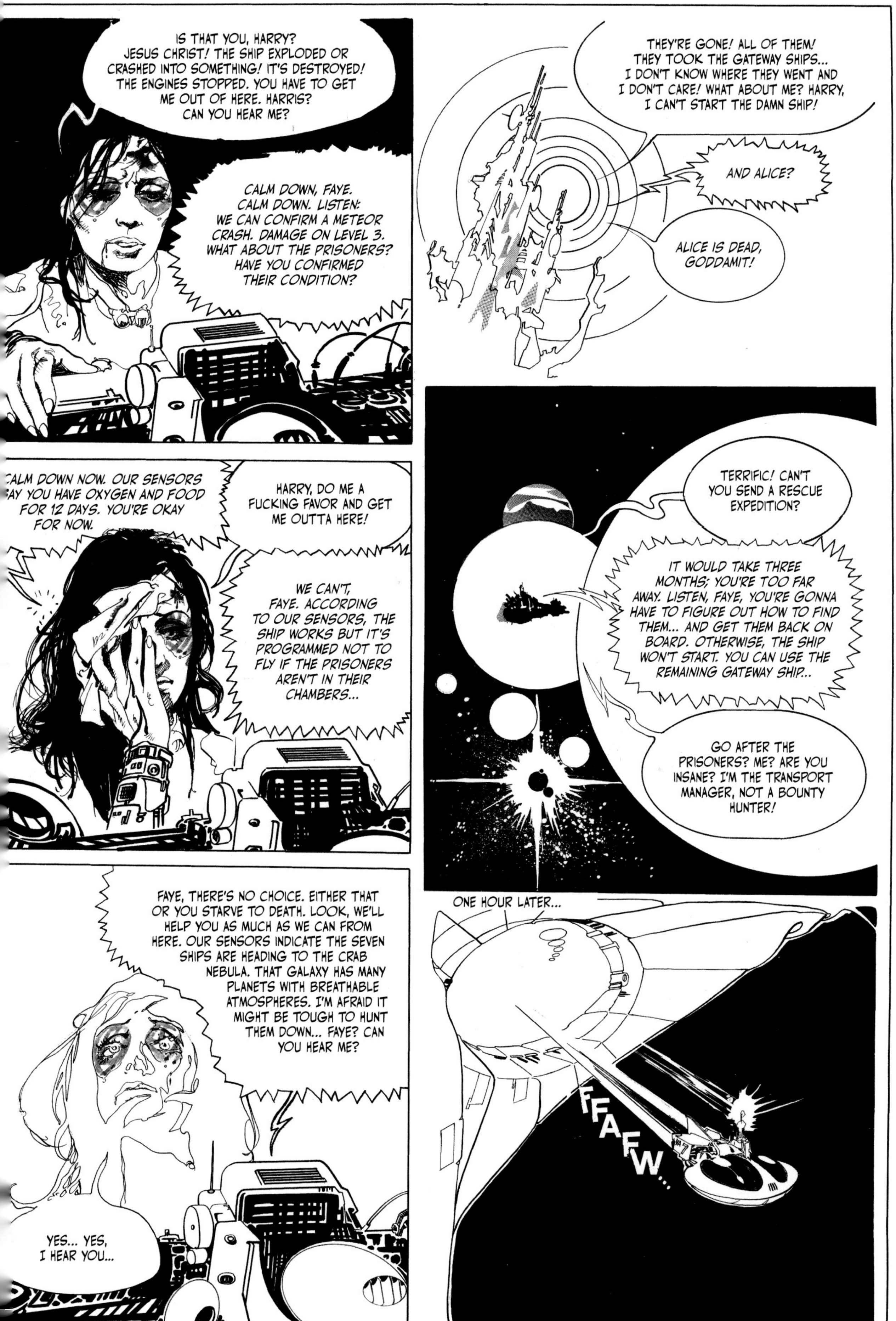
IS THAT YOU, HARRY? JESUS CHRIST! THE SHIP EXPLODED OR CRASHED INTO SOMETHING! IT'S DESTROYED! THE ENGINES STOPPED. YOU HAVE TO GET ME OUT OF HERE. HARRIS? CAN YOU HEAR ME?
CALM DOWN, FAYE. CALM DOWN. LISTEN: WE CAN CONFIRM A METEOR CRASH. DAMAGE ON LEVEL 3. WHAT ABOUT THE PRISONERS? HAVE YOU CONFIRMED THEIR CONDITION?
THEY'RE GONE! ALL OF THEM! THEY TOOK THE GATEWAY SHIPS... I DON'T KNOW WHERE THEY WENT AND I DON'T CARE! WHAT ABOUT ME? HARRY, I CAN'T START THE DAMN SHIP!
AND ALICE?
ALICE IS DEAD, GODDAMIT!
CALM DOWN NOW. OUR SENSORS SAY YOU HAVE OXYGEN AND FOOD FOR 12 DAYS. YOU'RE OKAY FOR NOW.
HARRY, DO ME A FUCKING FAVOR AND GET ME OUTTA HERE!
WE CAN'T, FAYE. ACCORDING TO OUR SENSORS, THE SHIP WORKS BUT IT'S PROGRAMMED NOT TO FLY IF THE PRISONERS AREN'T IN THEIR CHAMBERS...
TERRIFIC! CAN'T YOU SEND A RESCUE EXPEDITION?
IT WOULD TAKE THREE MONTHS; YOU'RE TOO FAR AWAY. LISTEN, FAYE, YOU'RE GONNA HAVE TO FIGURE OUT HOW TO FIND THEM... AND GET THEM BACK ON BOARD. OTHERWISE, THE SHIP WON'T START. YOU CAN USE THE REMAINING GATEWAY SHIP...
GO AFTER THE PRISONERS? ME? ARE YOU INSANE? I'M THE TRANSPORT MANAGER, NOT A BOUNTY HUNTER!
FAYE, THERE'S NO CHOICE. EITHER THAT OR YOU STARVE TO DEATH. LOOK, WE'LL HELP YOU AS MUCH AS WE CAN FROM HERE. OUR SENSORS INDICATE THE SEVEN SHIPS ARE HEADING TO THE CRAB NEBULA. THAT GALAXY HAS MANY PLANETS WITH BREATHABLE ATMOSPHERES. I'M AFRAID IT MIGHT BE TOUGH TO HUNT THEM DOWN... FAYE? CAN YOU HEAR ME?
YES... YES, I HEAR YOU...
ONE HOUR LATER...
FFAFW...

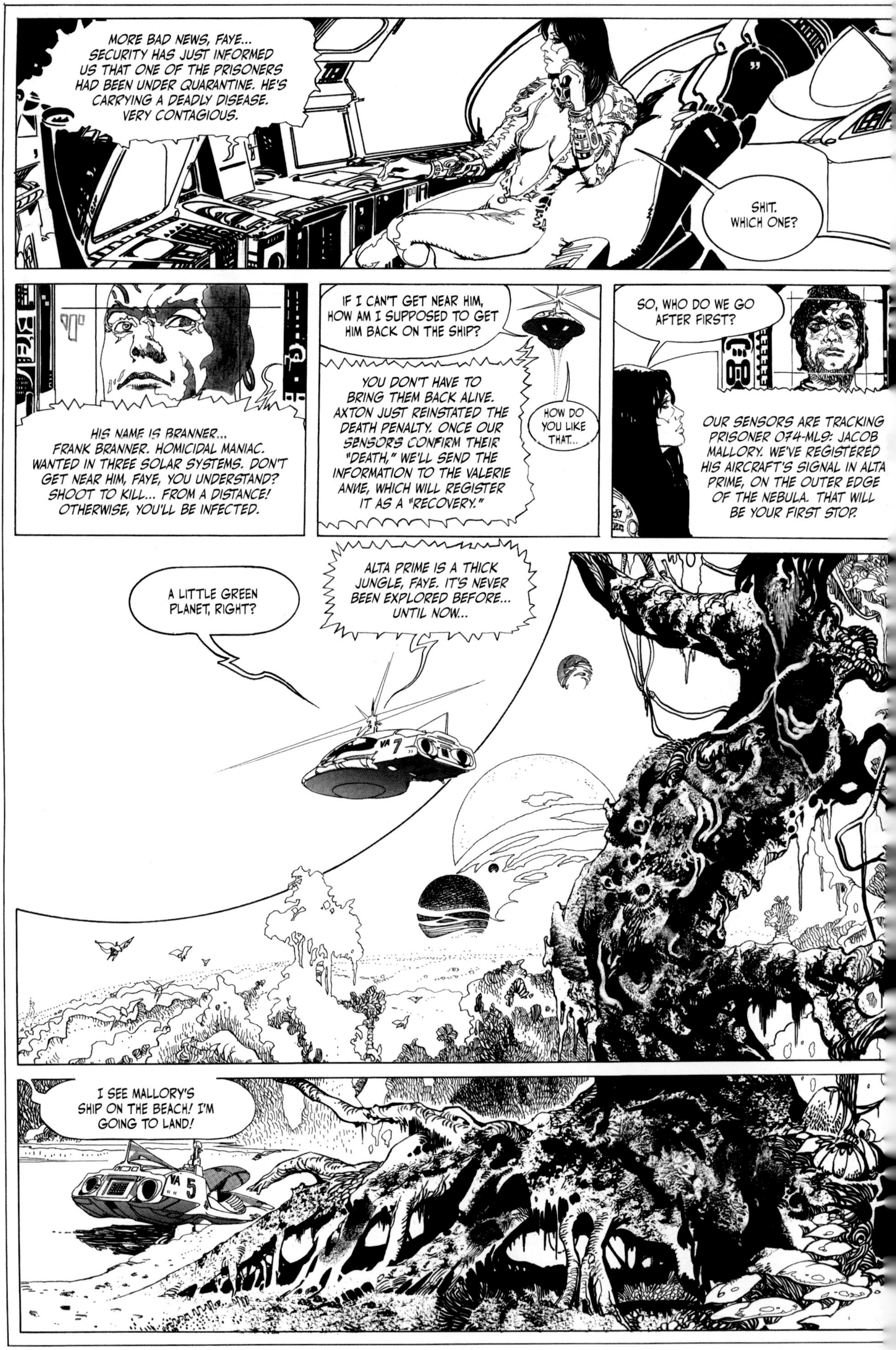
MORE BAD NEWS, FAYE... SECURITY HAS JUST INFORMED US THAT ONE OF THE PRISONERS HAD BEEN UNDER QUARANTINE. HE'S CARRYING A DEADLY DISEASE. VERY CONTAGIOUS.
SHIT. WHICH ONE?
HIS NAME IS BRANNER... FRANK BRANNER. HOMICIDAL MANIAC. WANTED IN THREE SOLAR SYSTEMS. DON'T GET NEAR HIM, FAYE, YOU UNDERSTAND? SHOOT TO KILL... FROM A DISTANCE! OTHERWISE, YOU'LL BE INFECTED.
IF I CAN'T GET NEAR HIM, HOW AM I SUPPOSED TO GET HIM BACK ON THE SHIP?
YOU DON'T HAVE TO BRING THEM BACK ALIVE. AXTON JUST REINSTATED THE DEATH PENALTY. ONCE OUR SENSORS CONFIRM THEIR "DEATH," WE'LL SEND THE INFORMATION TO THE VALERIE ANNE, WHICH WILL REGISTER IT AS A "RECOVERY."
HOW DO YOU LIKE THAT...
SO, WHO DO WE GO AFTER FIRST?
OUR SENSORS ARE TRACKING PRISONER 074-ML9: JACOB MALLORY. WE'VE REGISTERED HIS AIRCRAFT'S SIGNAL IN ALTA PRIME, ON THE OUTER EDGE OF THE NEBULA. THAT WILL BE YOUR FIRST STOP.
A LITTLE GREEN PLANET, RIGHT?
ALTA PRIME IS A THICK JUNGLE, FAYE. IT'S NEVER BEEN EXPLORED BEFORE... UNTIL NOW...
VA 7
I SEE MALLORY'S SHIP ON THE BEACH! I'M GOING TO LAND!
VA 5

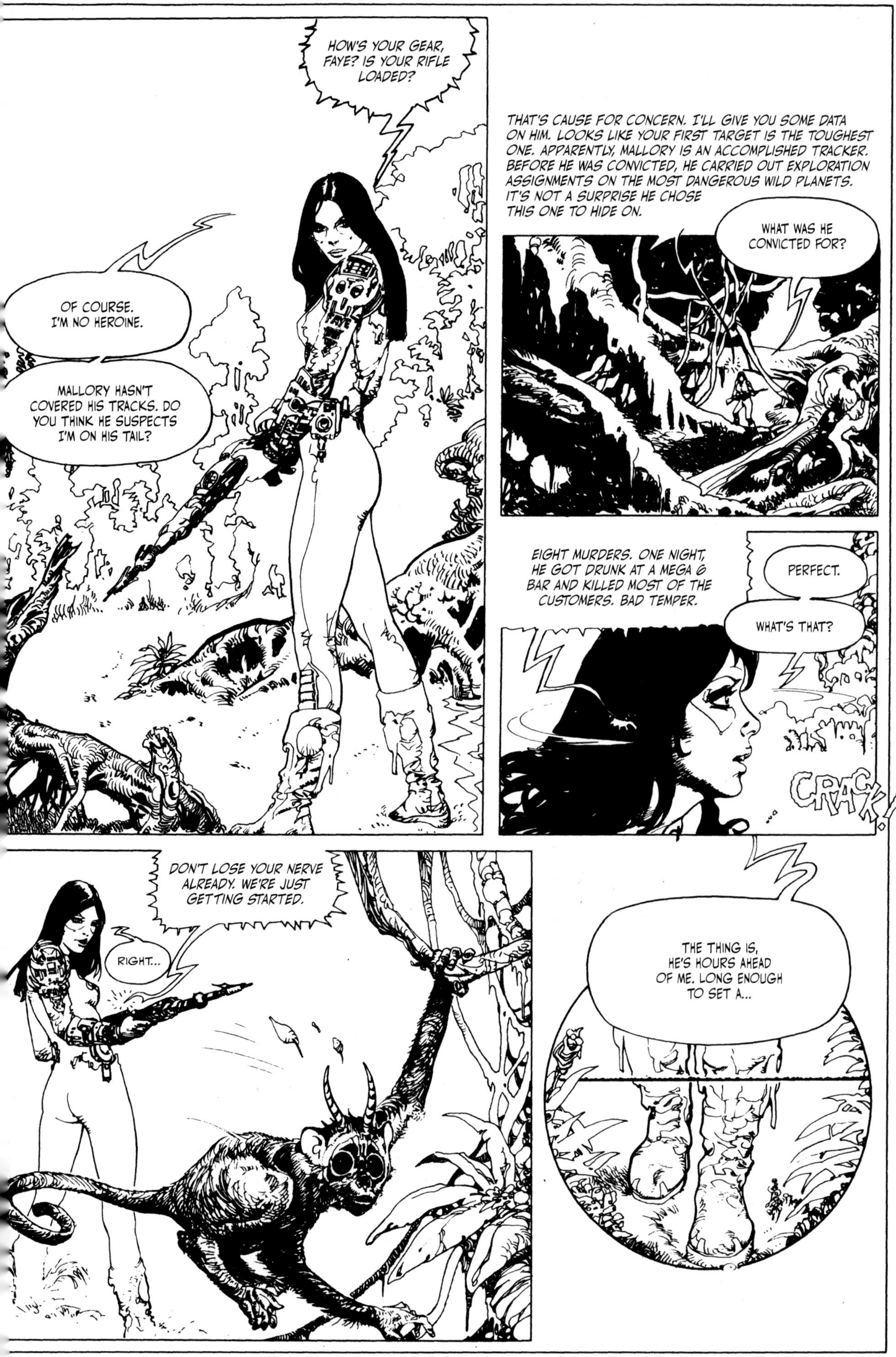
HOW'S YOUR GEAR, FAYE? IS YOUR RIFLE LOADED?
OF COURSE. I'M NO HEROINE.
MALLORY HASN'T COVERED HIS TRACKS. DO YOU THINK HE SUSPECTS I'M ON HIS TAIL?
THAT'S CAUSE FOR CONCERN. I'LL GIVE YOU SOME DATA ON HIM. LOOKS LIKE YOUR FIRST TARGET IS THE TOUGHEST ONE. APPARENTLY, MALLORY IS AN ACCOMPLISHED TRACKER. BEFORE HE WAS CONVICTED, HE CARRIED OUT EXPLORATION ASSIGNMENTS ON THE MOST DANGEROUS WILD PLANETS. IT'S NOT A SURPRISE HE CHOSE THIS ONE TO HIDE ON.
WHAT WAS HE CONVICTED FOR?
EIGHT MURDERS. ONE NIGHT, HE GOT DRUNK AT A MEGA 6 BAR AND KILLED MOST OF THE CUSTOMERS. BAD TEMPER.
PERFECT.
WHAT'S THAT?
CRACK!
DON'T LOSE YOUR NERVE ALREADY. WE'RE JUST GETTING STARTED.
RIGHT...
THE THING IS, HE'S HOURS AHEAD OF ME. LONG ENOUGH TO SET A...

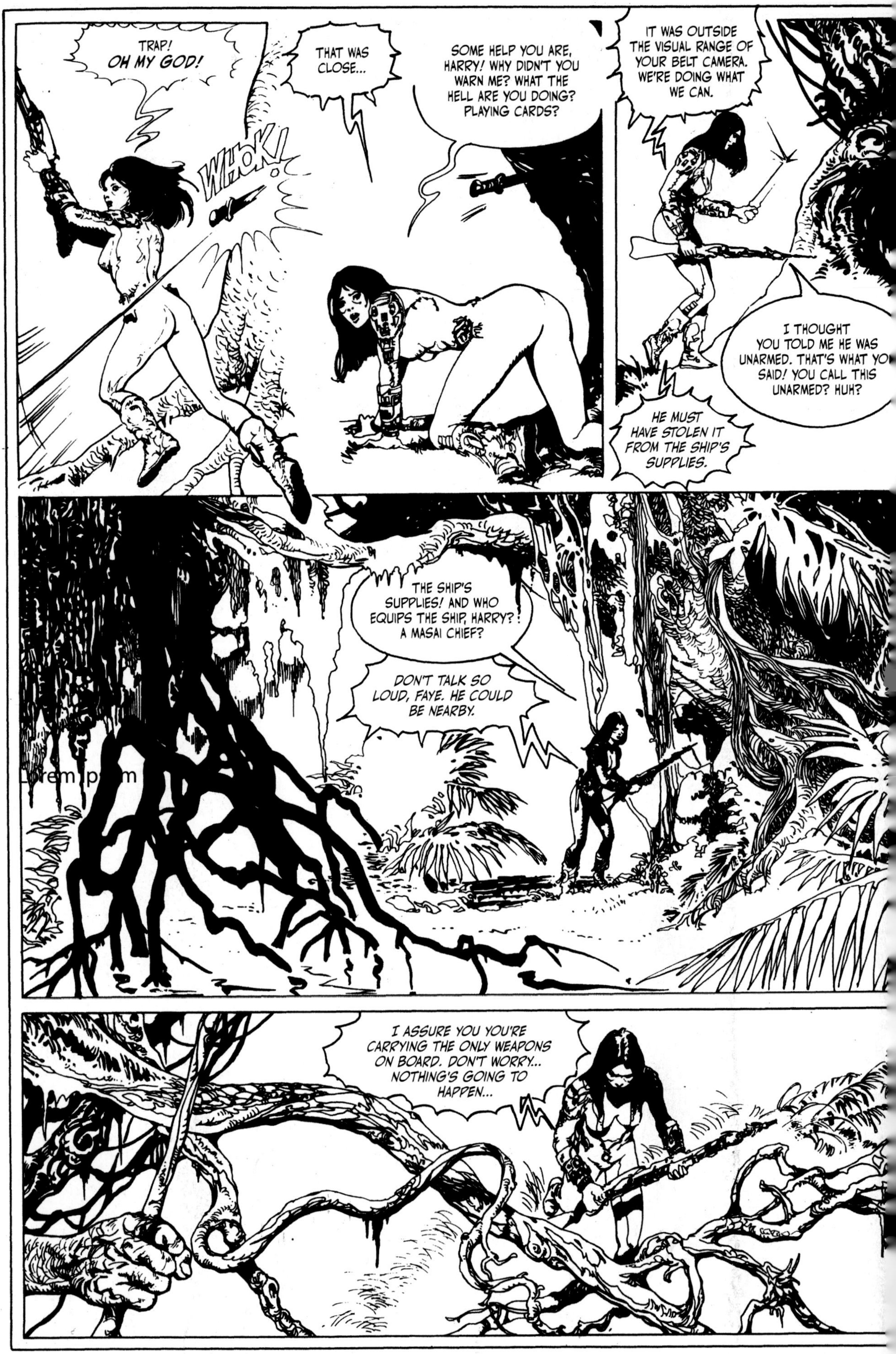
TRAP! OH MY GOD!
WHOK!
THAT WAS CLOSE...
SOME HELP YOU ARE, HARRY! WHY DIDN'T YOU WARN ME? WHAT THE HELL ARE YOU DOING? PLAYING CARDS?
IT WAS OUTSIDE THE VISUAL RANGE OF YOUR BELT CAMERA. WE'RE DOING WHAT WE CAN.
I THOUGHT YOU TOLD ME HE WAS UNARMED. THAT'S WHAT YO SAID! YOU CALL THIS UNARMED? HUH?
HE MUST HAVE STOLEN IT FROM THE SHIP'S SUPPLIES.
THE SHIP'S SUPPLIES! AND WHO EQUIPS THE SHIP, HARRY? A MASAI CHIEF?
DON'T TALK SO LOUD, FAYE. HE COULD BE NEARBY.
I ASSURE YOU YOU'RE CARRYING THE ONLY WEAPONS ON BOARD. DON'T WORRY... NOTHING'S GOING TO HAPPEN...

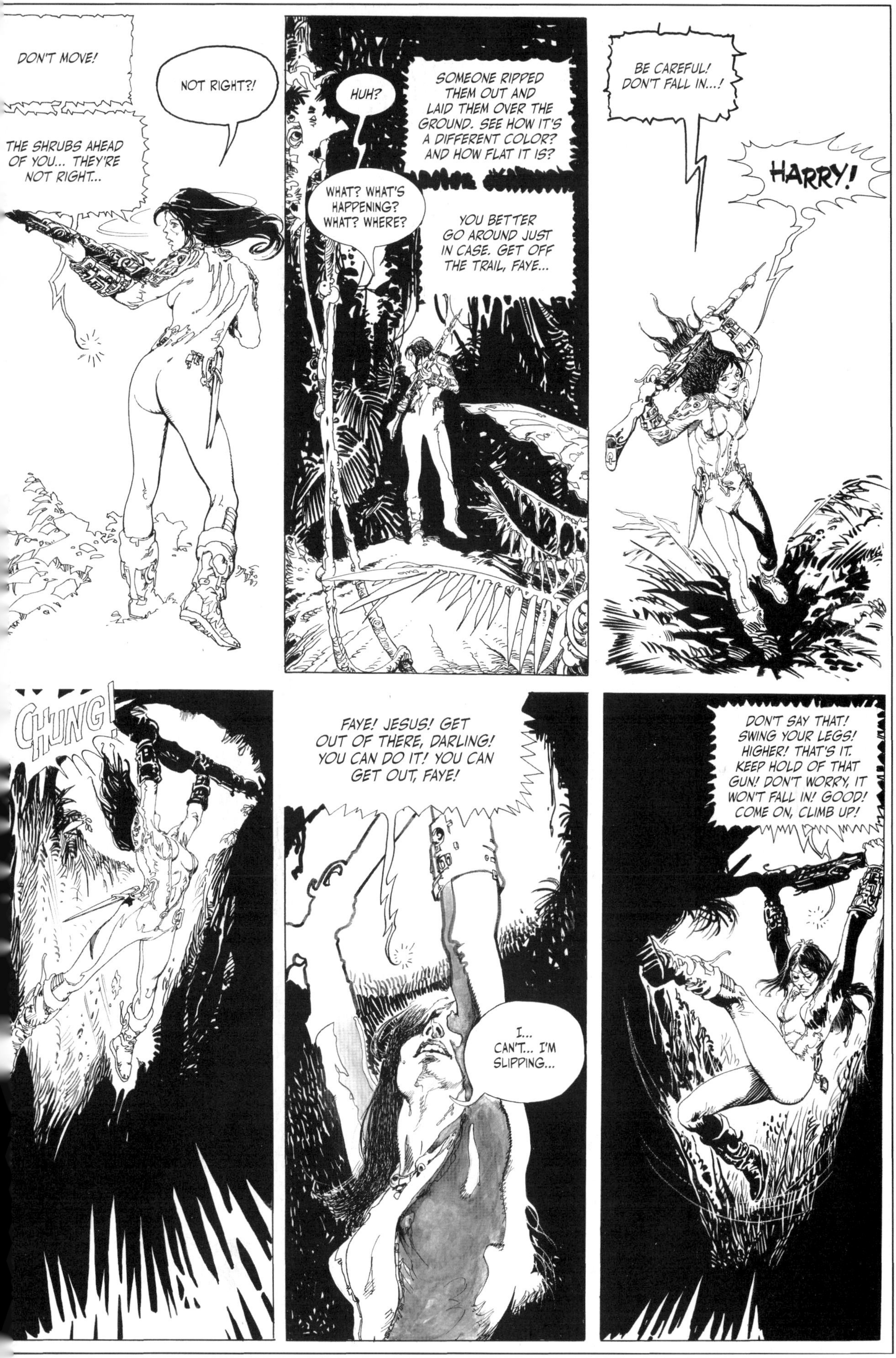

DON'T MOVE!
NOT RIGHT?!
THE SHRUBS AHEAD OF YOU... THEY'RE NOT RIGHT...
HUH?
SOMEONE RIPPED THEM OUT AND LAID THEM OVER THE GROUND. SEE HOW IT'S A DIFFERENT COLOR? AND HOW FLAT IT IS?
WHAT? WHAT'S HAPPENING? WHAT? WHERE?
YOU BETTER GO AROUND JUST IN CASE. GET OFF THE TRAIL, FAYE...
BE CAREFUL! DON'T FALL IN...!
HARRY!
CHUNG!
FAYE! JESUS! GET OUT OF THERE, DARLING! YOU CAN DO IT! YOU CAN GET OUT, FAYE!
I... CAN'T... I'M SLIPPING...
DON'T SAY THAT! SWING YOUR LEGS! HIGHER! THAT'S IT. KEEP HOLD OF THAT GUN! DON'T WORRY, IT WON'T FALL IN! GOOD! COME ON, CLIMB UP!

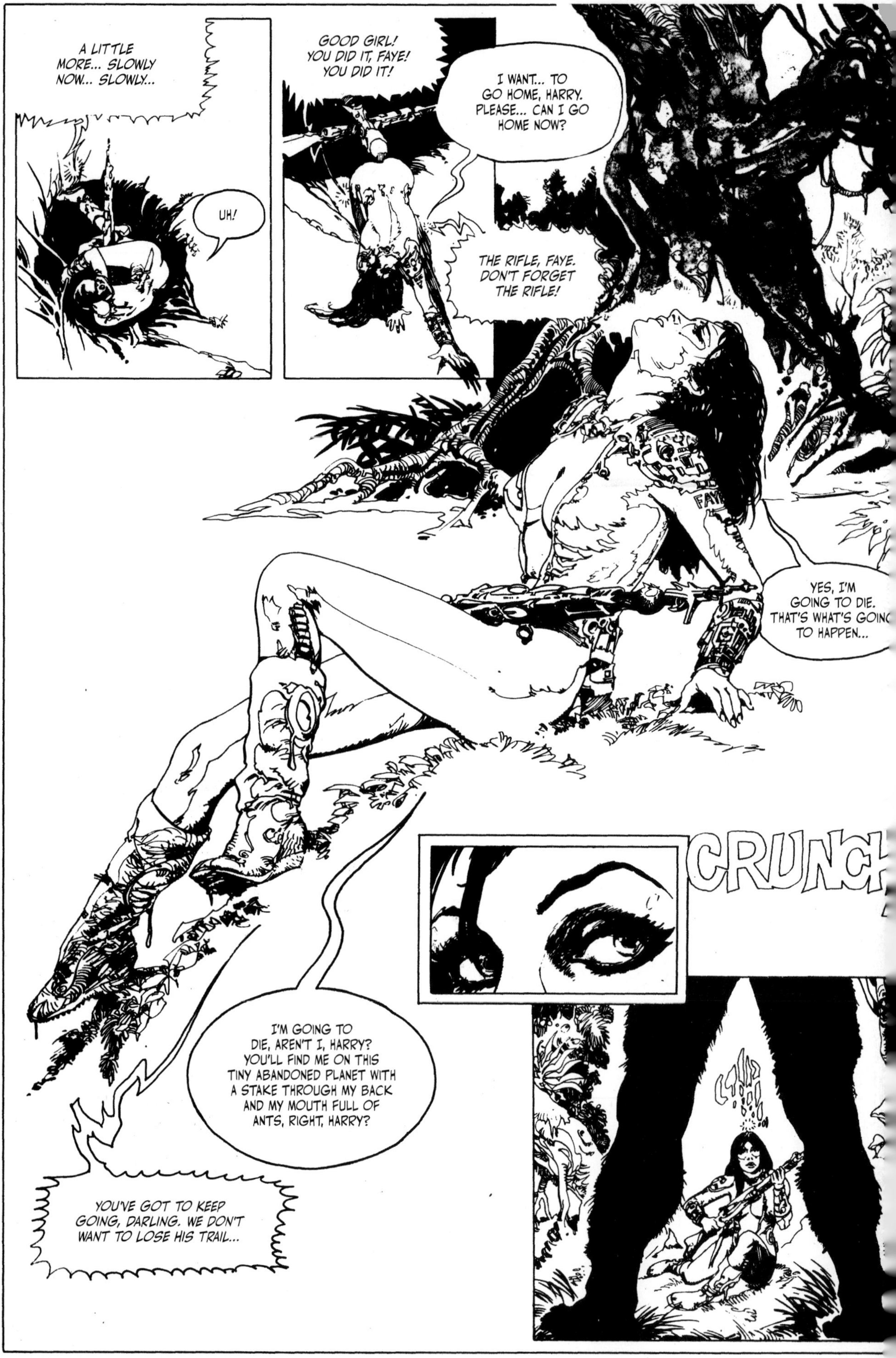

A LITTLE MORE... SLOWLY NOW... SLOWLY...
UH!
GOOD GIRL! YOU DID IT, FAYE! YOU DID IT!
I WANT... TO GO HOME, HARRY. PLEASE... CAN I GO HOME NOW?
THE RIFLE, FAYE. DON'T FORGET THE RIFLE!
FAYE
YES, I'M GOING TO DIE. THAT'S WHAT'S GOING TO HAPPEN...
CRUNCH
I'M GOING TO DIE, AREN'T I, HARRY? YOU'LL FIND ME ON THIS TINY ABANDONED PLANET WITH A STAKE THROUGH MY BACK AND MY MOUTH FULL OF ANTS, RIGHT, HARRY?
YOU'VE GOT TO KEEP GOING, DARLING. WE DON'T WANT TO LOSE HIS TRAIL...

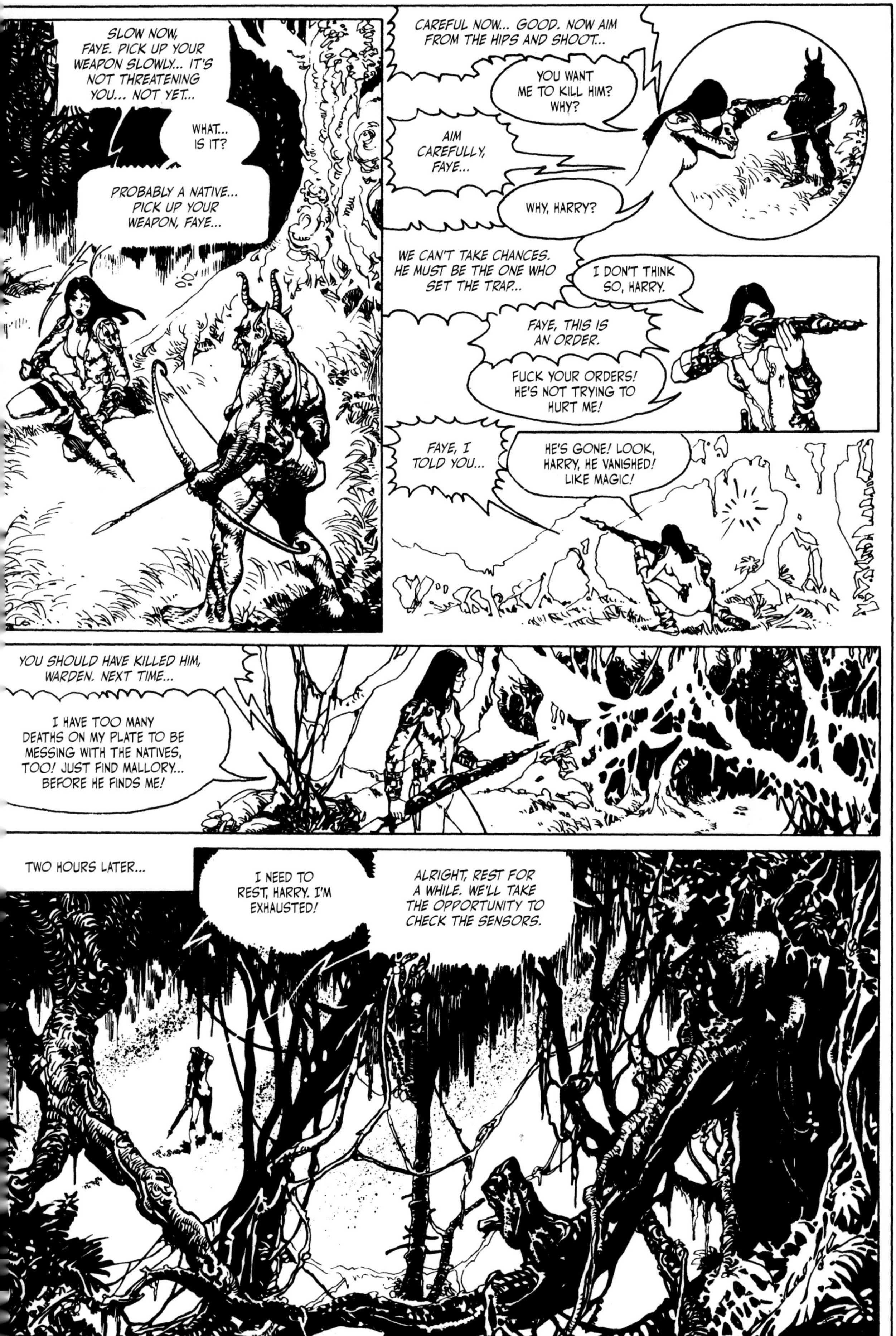

SLOW NOW, FAYE. PICK UP YOUR WEAPON SLOWLY... IT'S NOT THREATENING YOU... NOT YET...
WHAT... IS IT?
PROBABLY A NATIVE... PICK UP YOUR WEAPON, FAYE...
CAREFUL NOW... GOOD. NOW AIM FROM THE HIPS AND SHOOT...
YOU WANT ME TO KILL HIM? WHY?
AIM CAREFULLY, FAYE...
WHY, HARRY?
WE CAN'T TAKE CHANCES. HE MUST BE THE ONE WHO SET THE TRAP...
I DON'T THINK SO, HARRY.
FAYE, THIS IS AN ORDER.
FUCK YOUR ORDERS! HE'S NOT TRYING TO HURT ME!
FAYE, I TOLD YOU...
HE'S GONE! LOOK, HARRY, HE VANISHED! LIKE MAGIC!
YOU SHOULD HAVE KILLED HIM, WARDEN. NEXT TIME...
I HAVE TOO MANY DEATHS ON MY PLATE TO BE MESSING WITH THE NATIVES, TOO! JUST FIND MALLORY... BEFORE HE FINDS ME!
TWO HOURS LATER...
I NEED TO REST, HARRY. I'M EXHAUSTED!
ALRIGHT, REST FOR A WHILE. WE'LL TAKE THE OPPORTUNITY TO CHECK THE SENSORS.

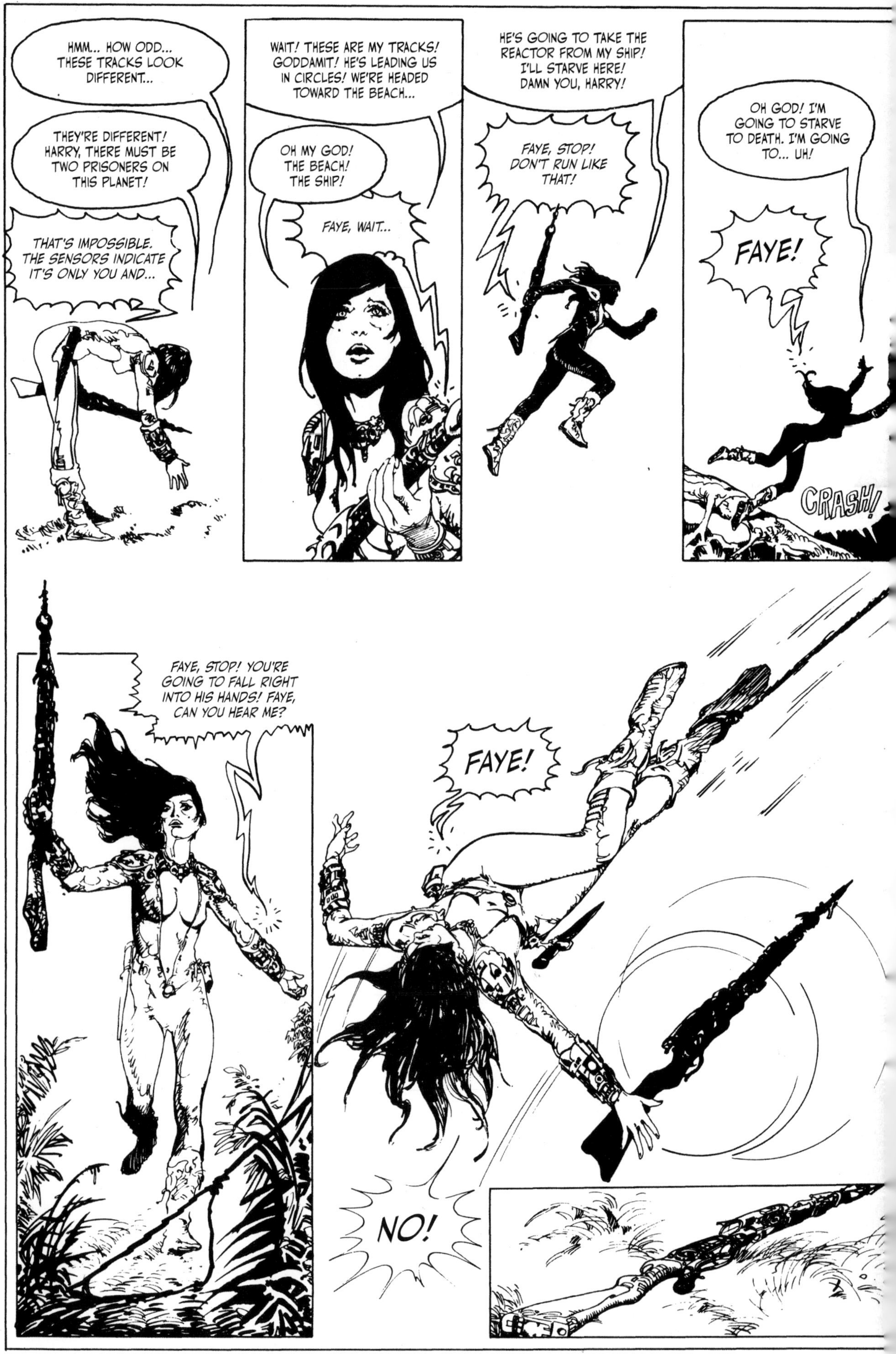
HMM... HOW ODD... THESE TRACKS LOOK DIFFERENT...
THEY'RE DIFFERENT! HARRY, THERE MUST BE TWO PRISONERS ON THIS PLANET!
THAT'S IMPOSSIBLE. THE SENSORS INDICATE IT'S ONLY YOU AND...
WAIT! THESE ARE MY TRACKS! GODDAMIT! HE'S LEADING US IN CIRCLES! WE'RE HEADED TOWARD THE BEACH...
OH MY GOD! THE BEACH! THE SHIP!
FAYE, WAIT...
HE'S GOING TO TAKE THE REACTOR FROM MY SHIP! I'LL STARVE HERE! DAMN YOU, HARRY!
FAYE, STOP! DON'T RUN LIKE THAT!
OH GOD! I'M GOING TO STARVE TO DEATH. I'M GOING TO... UH!
FAYE!
CRASH!
FAYE, STOP! YOU'RE GOING TO FALL RIGHT INTO HIS HANDS! FAYE, CAN YOU HEAR ME?
FAYE!
NO!

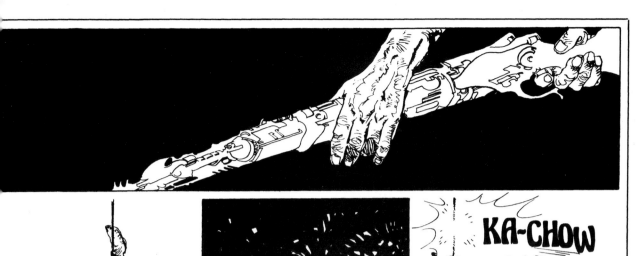

KA-CHOW

HARRY!

HARRY, DO SOMETHING! PLEASE, FOR GOD'S SAKE! HE'S GOING TO KILL ME!

HARRY, HELP ME!

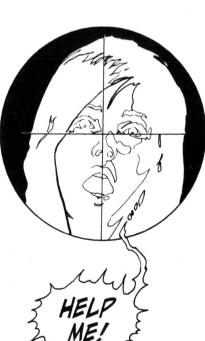

HELP ME!

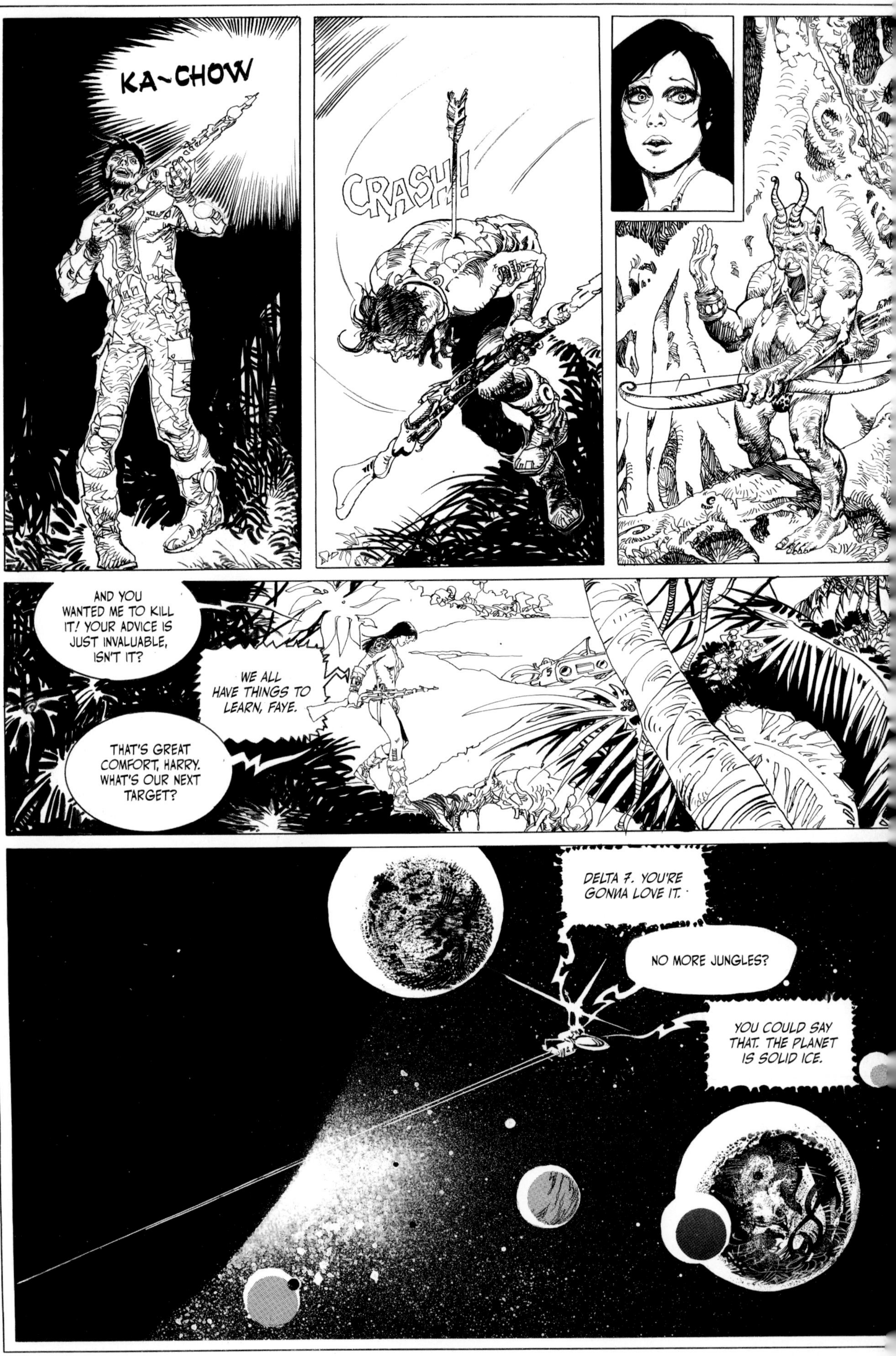
KA~CHOW
CRASH!
AND YOU WANTED ME TO KILL IT! YOUR ADVICE IS JUST INVALUABLE, ISN'T IT?
WE ALL HAVE THINGS TO LEARN, FAYE.
THAT'S GREAT COMFORT, HARRY. WHAT'S OUR NEXT TARGET?
DELTA 7. YOU'RE GONNA LOVE IT.
NO MORE JUNGLES?
YOU COULD SAY THAT. THE PLANET IS SOLID ICE.

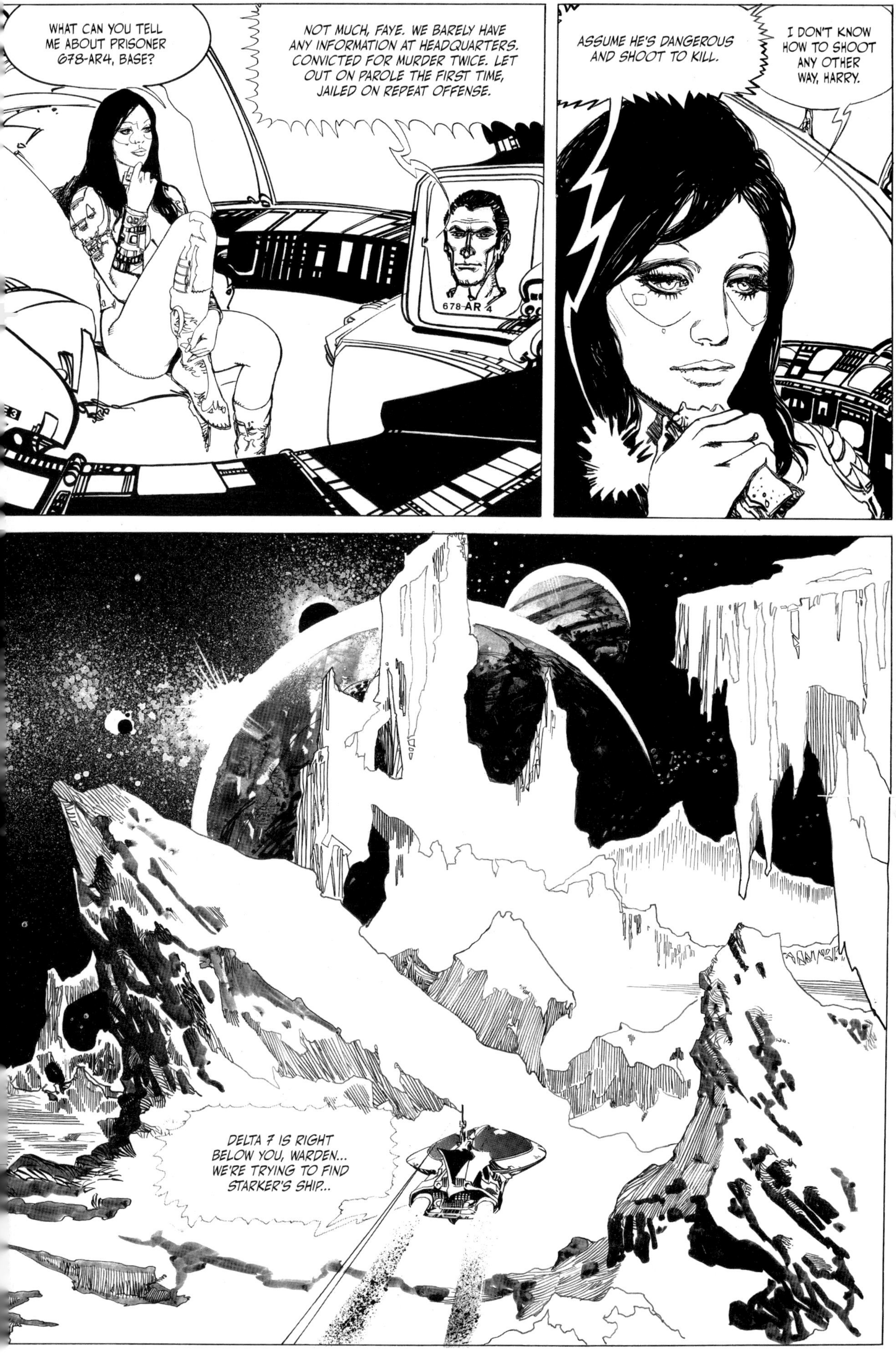
WHAT CAN YOU TELL ME ABOUT PRISONER 678-AR4, BASE?
NOT MUCH, FAYE. WE BARELY HAVE ANY INFORMATION AT HEADQUARTERS. CONVICTED FOR MURDER TWICE. LET OUT ON PAROLE THE FIRST TIME, JAILED ON REPEAT OFFENSE.
678-AR 4
ASSUME HE'S DANGEROUS AND SHOOT TO KILL.
I DON'T KNOW HOW TO SHOOT ANY OTHER WAY, HARRY.
DELTA 7 IS RIGHT BELOW YOU, WARDEN... WE'RE TRYING TO FIND STARKER'S SHIP...

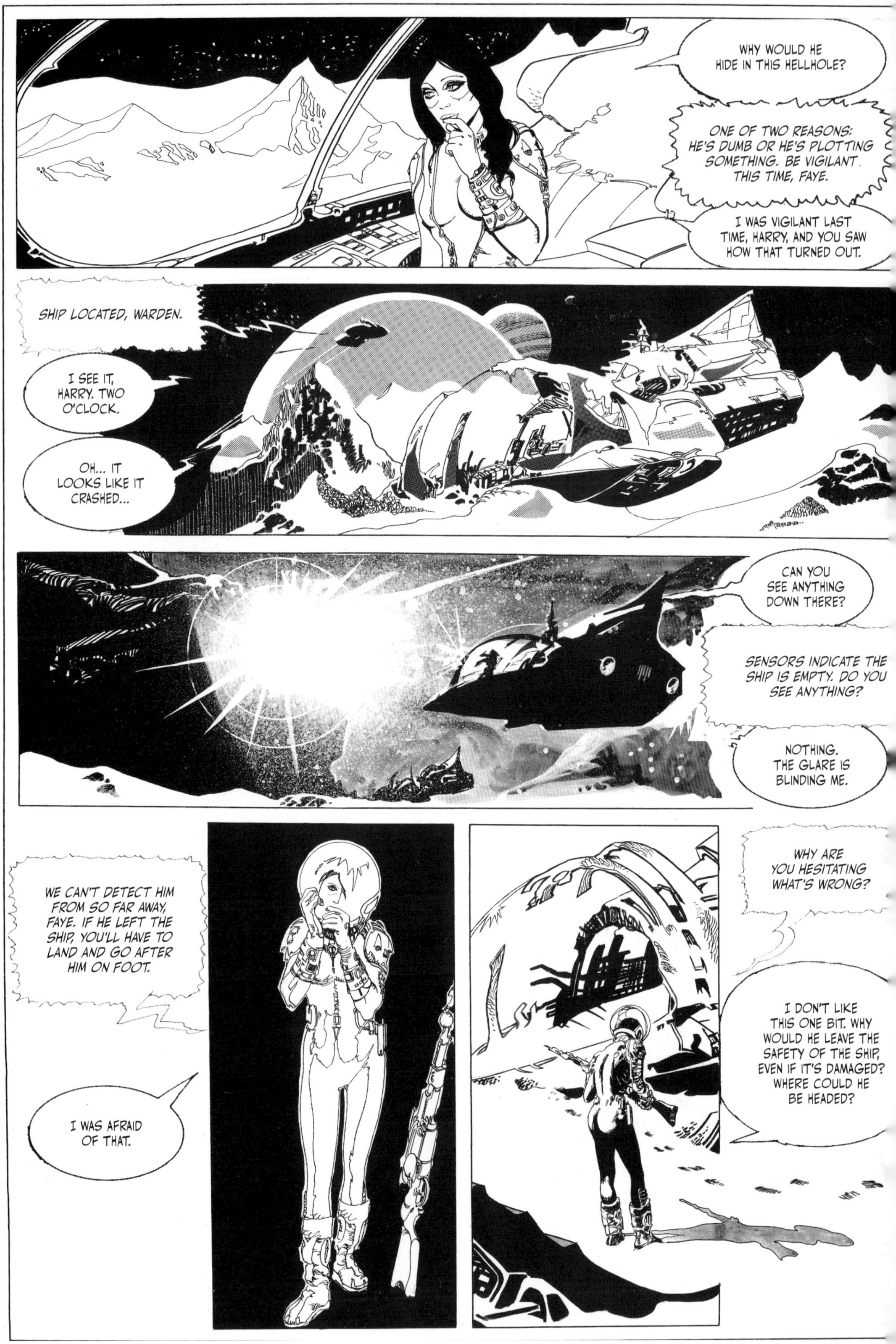
WHY WOULD HE HIDE IN THIS HELLHOLE?
ONE OF TWO REASONS: HE'S DUMB OR HE'S PLOTTING SOMETHING. BE VIGILANT THIS TIME, FAYE.
I WAS VIGILANT LAST TIME, HARRY, AND YOU SAW HOW THAT TURNED OUT.
SHIP LOCATED, WARDEN.
I SEE IT, HARRY. TWO O'CLOCK.
OH... IT LOOKS LIKE IT CRASHED...
CAN YOU SEE ANYTHING DOWN THERE?
SENSORS INDICATE THE SHIP IS EMPTY. DO YOU SEE ANYTHING?
NOTHING. THE GLARE IS BLINDING ME.
WE CAN'T DETECT HIM FROM SO FAR AWAY, FAYE. IF HE LEFT THE SHIP, YOU'LL HAVE TO LAND AND GO AFTER HIM ON FOOT.
I WAS AFRAID OF THAT.
WHY ARE YOU HESITATING WHAT'S WRONG?
I DON'T LIKE THIS ONE BIT. WHY WOULD HE LEAVE THE SAFETY OF THE SHIP, EVEN IF IT'S DAMAGED? WHERE COULD HE BE HEADED?

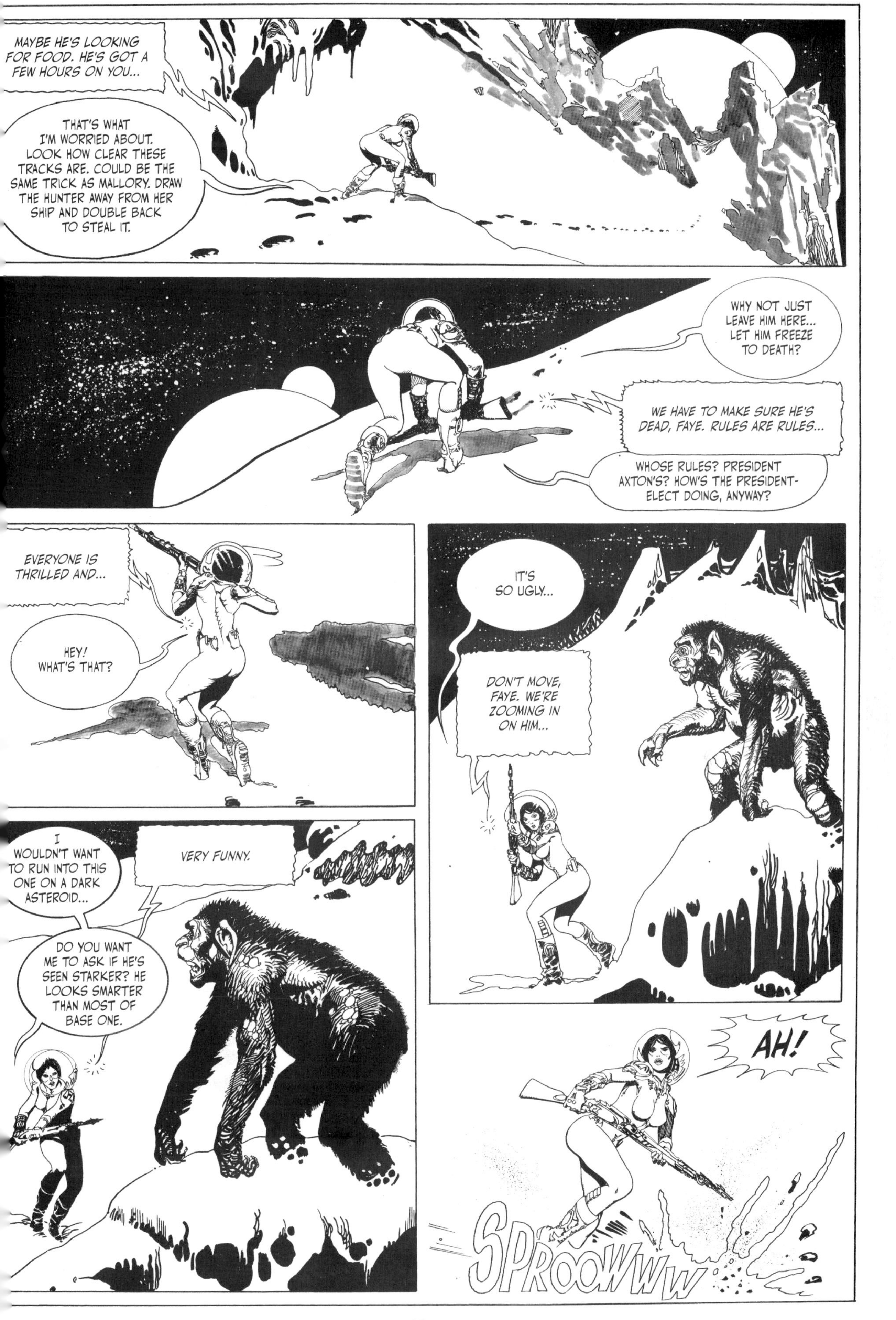

MAYBE HE'S LOOKING FOR FOOD. HE'S GOT A FEW HOURS ON YOU...
THAT'S WHAT I'M WORRIED ABOUT. LOOK HOW CLEAR THESE TRACKS ARE. COULD BE THE SAME TRICK AS MALLORY. DRAW THE HUNTER AWAY FROM HER SHIP AND DOUBLE BACK TO STEAL IT.
WHY NOT JUST LEAVE HIM HERE... LET HIM FREEZE TO DEATH?
WE HAVE TO MAKE SURE HE'S DEAD, FAYE. RULES ARE RULES...
WHOSE RULES? PRESIDENT AXTON'S? HOW'S THE PRESIDENT-ELECT DOING, ANYWAY?
EVERYONE IS THRILLED AND...
HEY! WHAT'S THAT?
IT'S SO UGLY...
DON'T MOVE, FAYE. WE'RE ZOOMING IN ON HIM...
I WOULDN'T WANT TO RUN INTO THIS ONE ON A DARK ASTEROID...
VERY FUNNY.
DO YOU WANT ME TO ASK IF HE'S SEEN STARKER? HE LOOKS SMARTER THAN MOST OF BASE ONE.
AH!
SPROOWWW

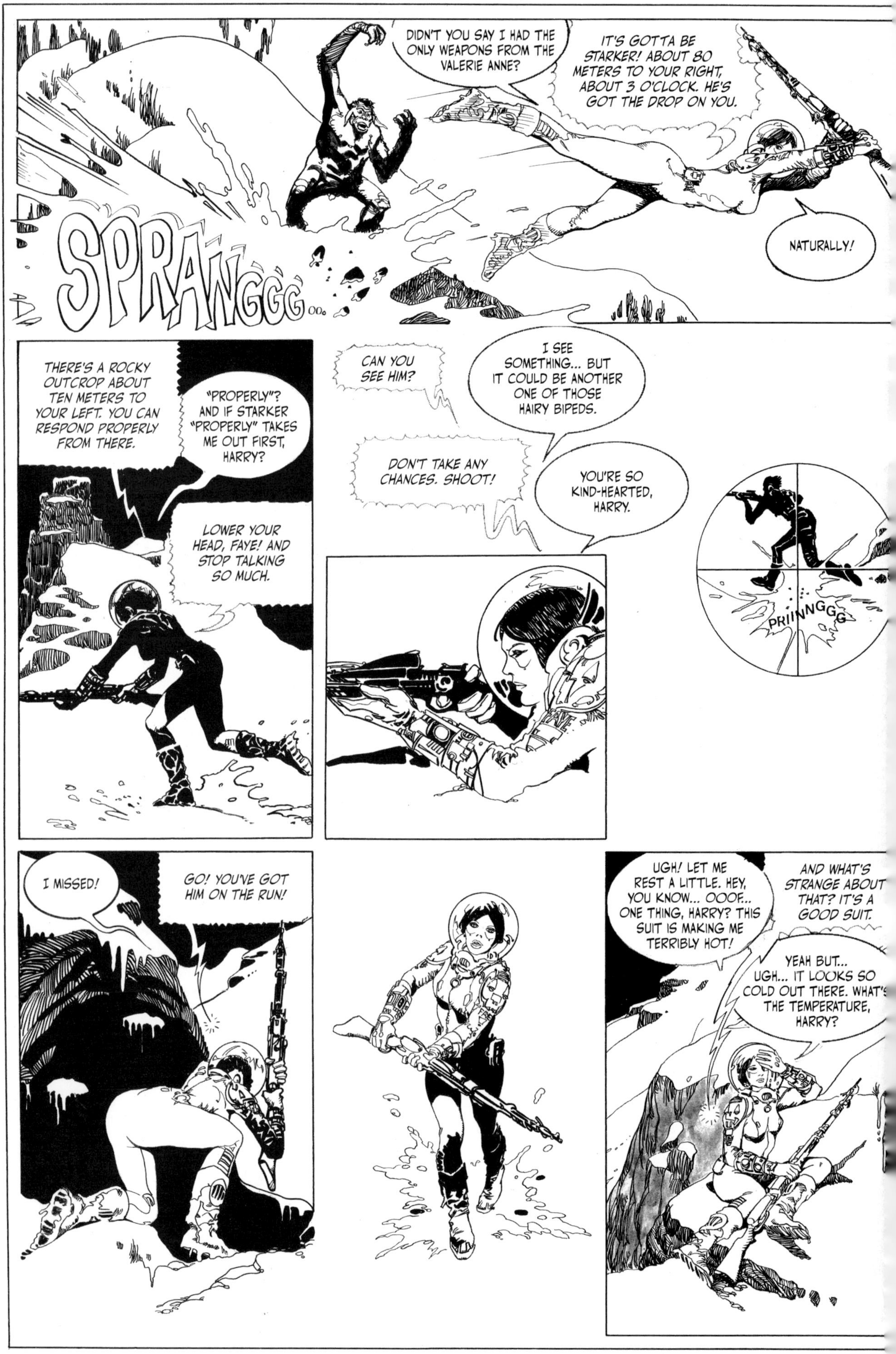

DIDN'T YOU SAY I HAD THE ONLY WEAPONS FROM THE VALERIE ANNE?
IT'S GOTTA BE STARKER! ABOUT 80 METERS TO YOUR RIGHT, ABOUT 3 O'CLOCK. HE'S GOT THE DROP ON YOU.
NATURALLY!
SPRANGGG...
THERE'S A ROCKY OUTCROP ABOUT TEN METERS TO YOUR LEFT. YOU CAN RESPOND PROPERLY FROM THERE.
"PROPERLY"? AND IF STARKER "PROPERLY" TAKES ME OUT FIRST, HARRY?
LOWER YOUR HEAD, FAYE! AND STOP TALKING SO MUCH.
CAN YOU SEE HIM?
I SEE SOMETHING... BUT IT COULD BE ANOTHER ONE OF THOSE HAIRY BIPEDS.
DON'T TAKE ANY CHANCES. SHOOT!
YOU'RE SO KIND-HEARTED, HARRY.
PRIINNGGG
I MISSED!
GO! YOU'VE GOT HIM ON THE RUN!
UGH! LET ME REST A LITTLE. HEY, YOU KNOW... OOOF... ONE THING, HARRY? THIS SUIT IS MAKING ME TERRIBLY HOT!
AND WHAT'S STRANGE ABOUT THAT? IT'S A GOOD SUIT.
YEAH BUT... UGH... IT LOOKS SO COLD OUT THERE. WHAT'S THE TEMPERATURE, HARRY?

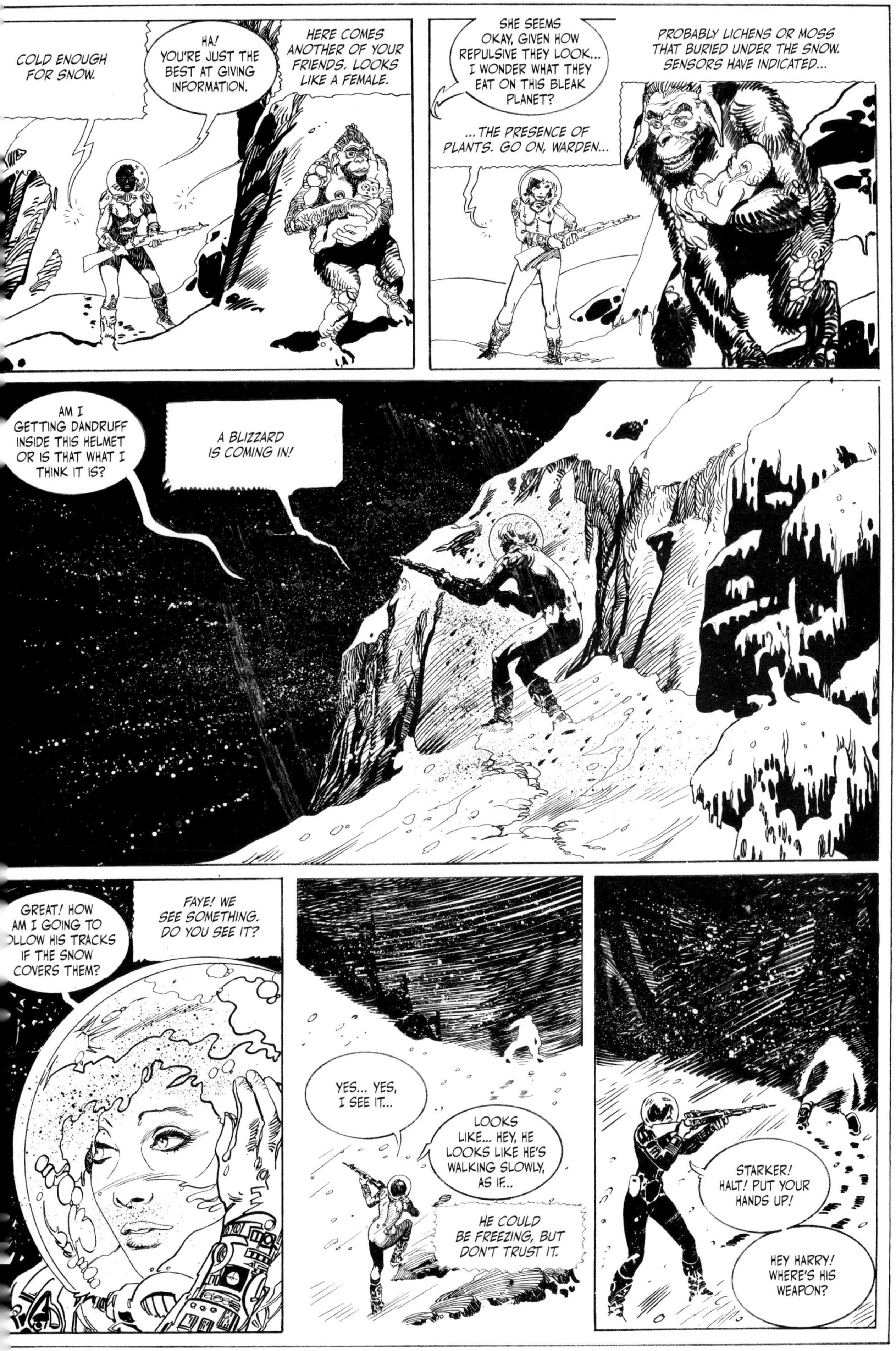
COLD ENOUGH FOR SNOW.
HA! YOU'RE JUST THE BEST AT GIVING INFORMATION.
HERE COMES ANOTHER OF YOUR FRIENDS. LOOKS LIKE A FEMALE.
SHE SEEMS OKAY, GIVEN HOW REPULSIVE THEY LOOK... I WONDER WHAT THEY EAT ON THIS BLEAK PLANET?
...THE PRESENCE OF PLANTS. GO ON, WARDEN...
PROBABLY LICHENS OR MOSS THAT BURIED UNDER THE SNOW. SENSORS HAVE INDICATED...
AM I GETTING DANDRUFF INSIDE THIS HELMET OR IS THAT WHAT I THINK IT IS?
A BLIZZARD IS COMING IN!
GREAT! HOW AM I GOING TO OLLOW HIS TRACKS IF THE SNOW COVERS THEM?
FAYE! WE SEE SOMETHING. DO YOU SEE IT?
YES... YES, I SEE IT...
LOOKS LIKE... HEY, HE LOOKS LIKE HE'S WALKING SLOWLY, AS IF...
HE COULD BE FREEZING, BUT DON'T TRUST IT.
STARKER! HALT! PUT YOUR HANDS UP!
HEY HARRY! WHERE'S HIS WEAPON?

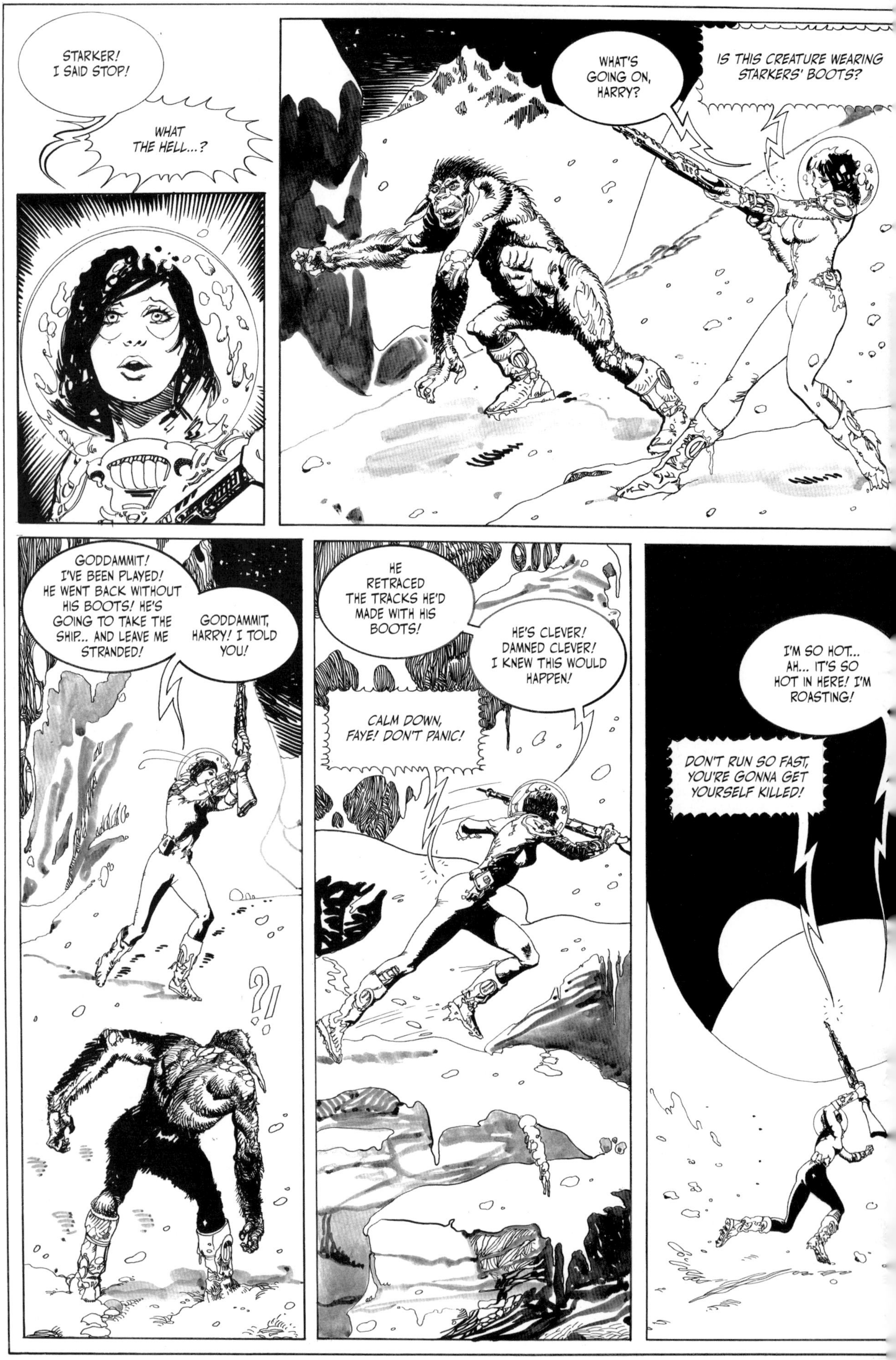
STARKER! I SAID STOP!
WHAT THE HELL...?
WHAT'S GOING ON, HARRY?
IS THIS CREATURE WEARING STARKERS' BOOTS?
GODDAMMIT! I'VE BEEN PLAYED! HE WENT BACK WITHOUT HIS BOOTS! HE'S GOING TO TAKE THE SHIP... AND LEAVE ME STRANDED!
GODDAMMIT, HARRY! I TOLD YOU!
?!
HE RETRACED THE TRACKS HE'D MADE WITH HIS BOOTS!
HE'S CLEVER! DAMNED CLEVER! I KNEW THIS WOULD HAPPEN!
CALM DOWN, FAYE! DON'T PANIC!
I'M SO HOT... AH... IT'S SO HOT IN HERE! I'M ROASTING!
DON'T RUN SO FAST, YOU'RE GONNA GET YOURSELF KILLED!

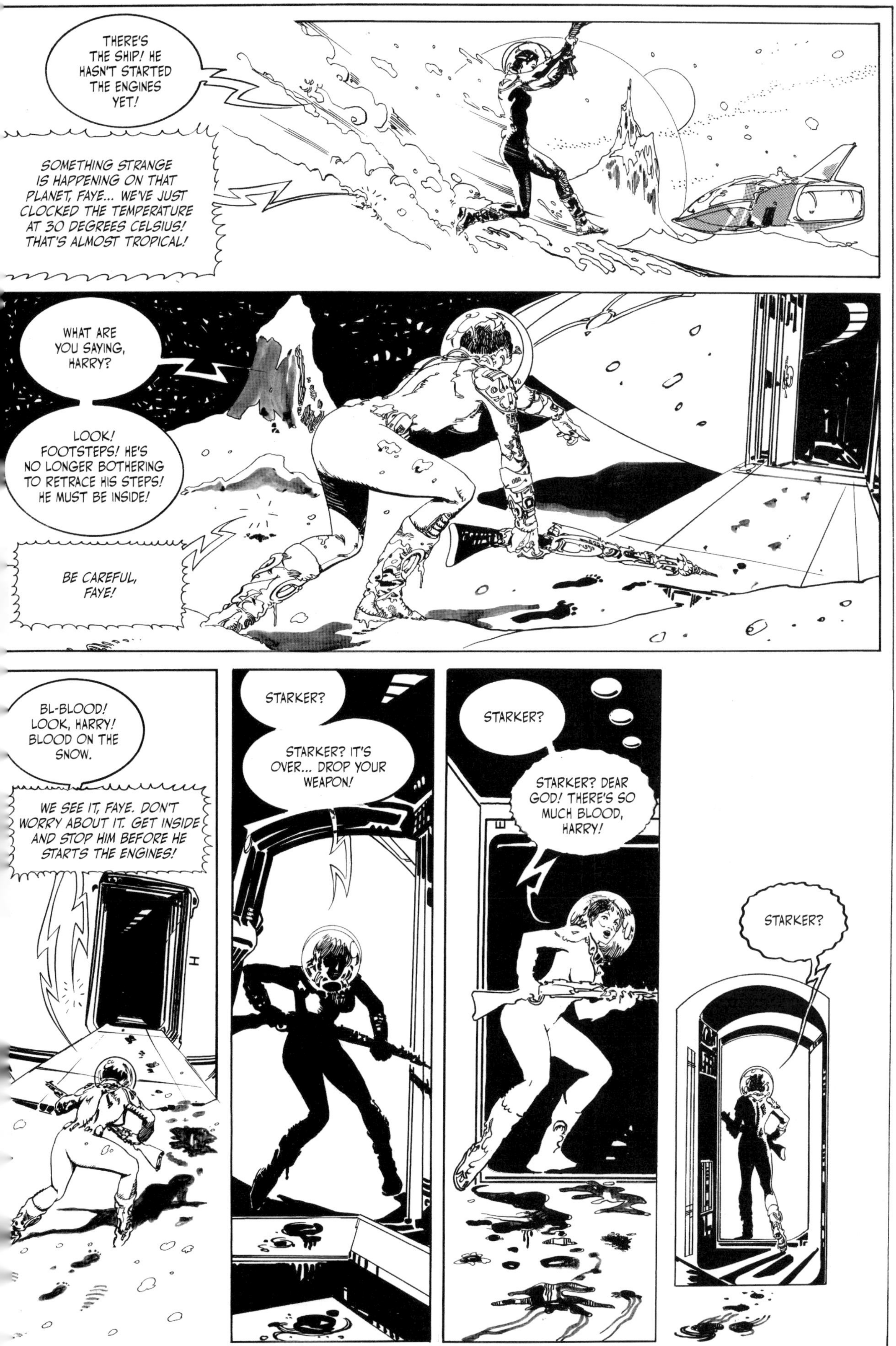
THERE'S THE SHIP! HE HASN'T STARTED THE ENGINES YET!
SOMETHING STRANGE IS HAPPENING ON THAT PLANET, FAYE... WE'VE JUST CLOCKED THE TEMPERATURE AT 30 DEGREES CELSIUS! THAT'S ALMOST TROPICAL!
WHAT ARE YOU SAYING, HARRY?
LOOK! FOOTSTEPS! HE'S NO LONGER BOTHERING TO RETRACE HIS STEPS! HE MUST BE INSIDE!
BE CAREFUL, FAYE!
BL-BLOOD! LOOK, HARRY! BLOOD ON THE SNOW.
WE SEE IT, FAYE. DON'T WORRY ABOUT IT. GET INSIDE AND STOP HIM BEFORE HE STARTS THE ENGINES!
STARKER?
STARKER? IT'S OVER... DROP YOUR WEAPON!
STARKER?
STARKER? DEAR GOD! THERE'S SO MUCH BLOOD, HARRY!
STARKER?

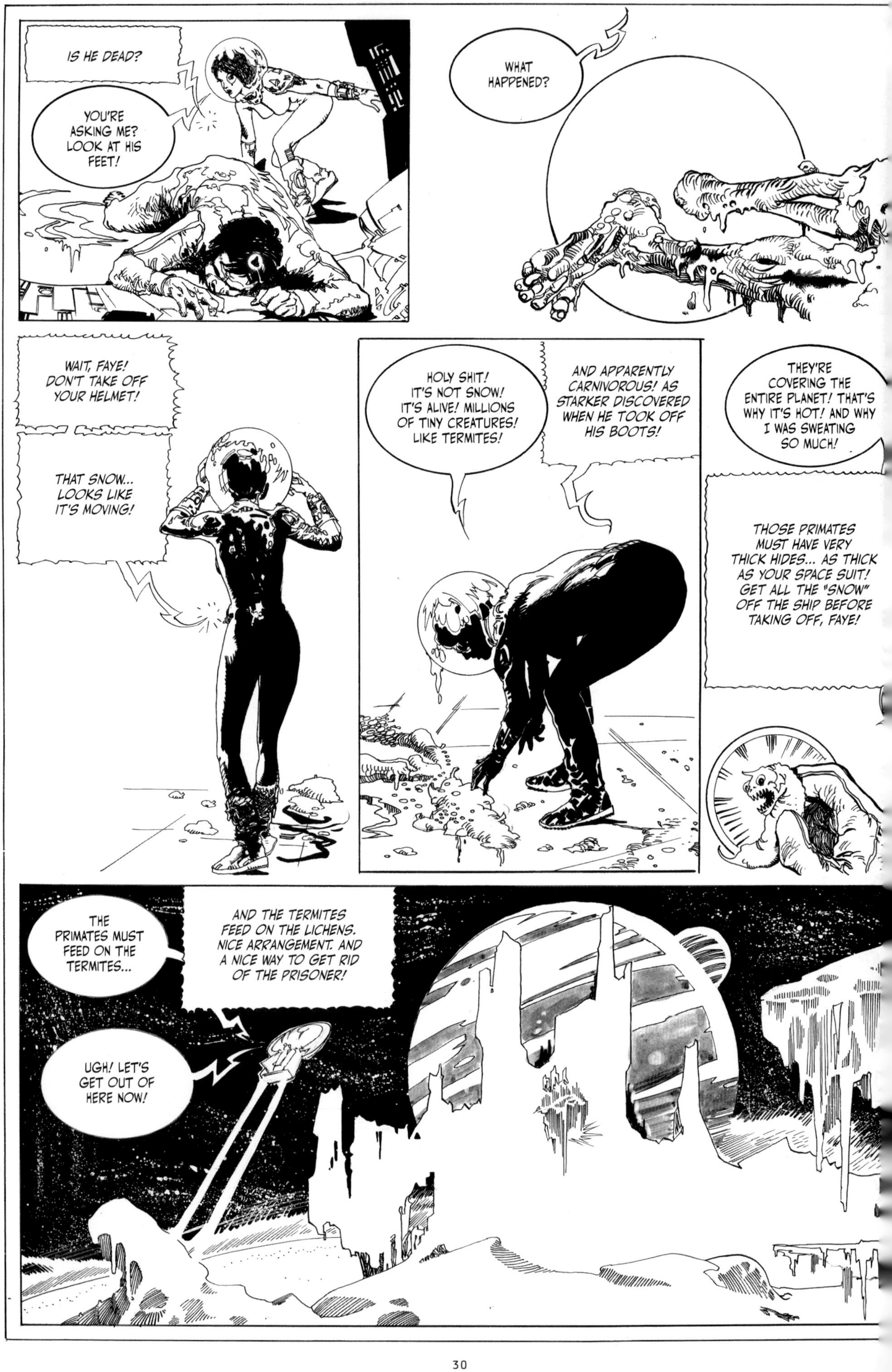
IS HE DEAD?
YOU'RE ASKING ME? LOOK AT HIS FEET!
WHAT HAPPENED?
WAIT, FAYE! DON'T TAKE OFF YOUR HELMET!
THAT SNOW... LOOKS LIKE IT'S MOVING!
HOLY SHIT! IT'S NOT SNOW! IT'S ALIVE! MILLIONS OF TINY CREATURES! LIKE TERMITES!
AND APPARENTLY CARNIVOROUS! AS STARKER DISCOVERED WHEN HE TOOK OFF HIS BOOTS!
THEY'RE COVERING THE ENTIRE PLANET! THAT'S WHY IT'S HOT! AND WHY I WAS SWEATING SO MUCH!
THOSE PRIMATES MUST HAVE VERY THICK HIDES... AS THICK AS YOUR SPACE SUIT! GET ALL THE "SNOW" OFF THE SHIP BEFORE TAKING OFF, FAYE!
THE PRIMATES MUST FEED ON THE TERMITES...
AND THE TERMITES FEED ON THE LICHENS. NICE ARRANGEMENT. AND A NICE WAY TO GET RID OF THE PRISONER!
UGH! LET'S GET OUT OF HERE NOW!

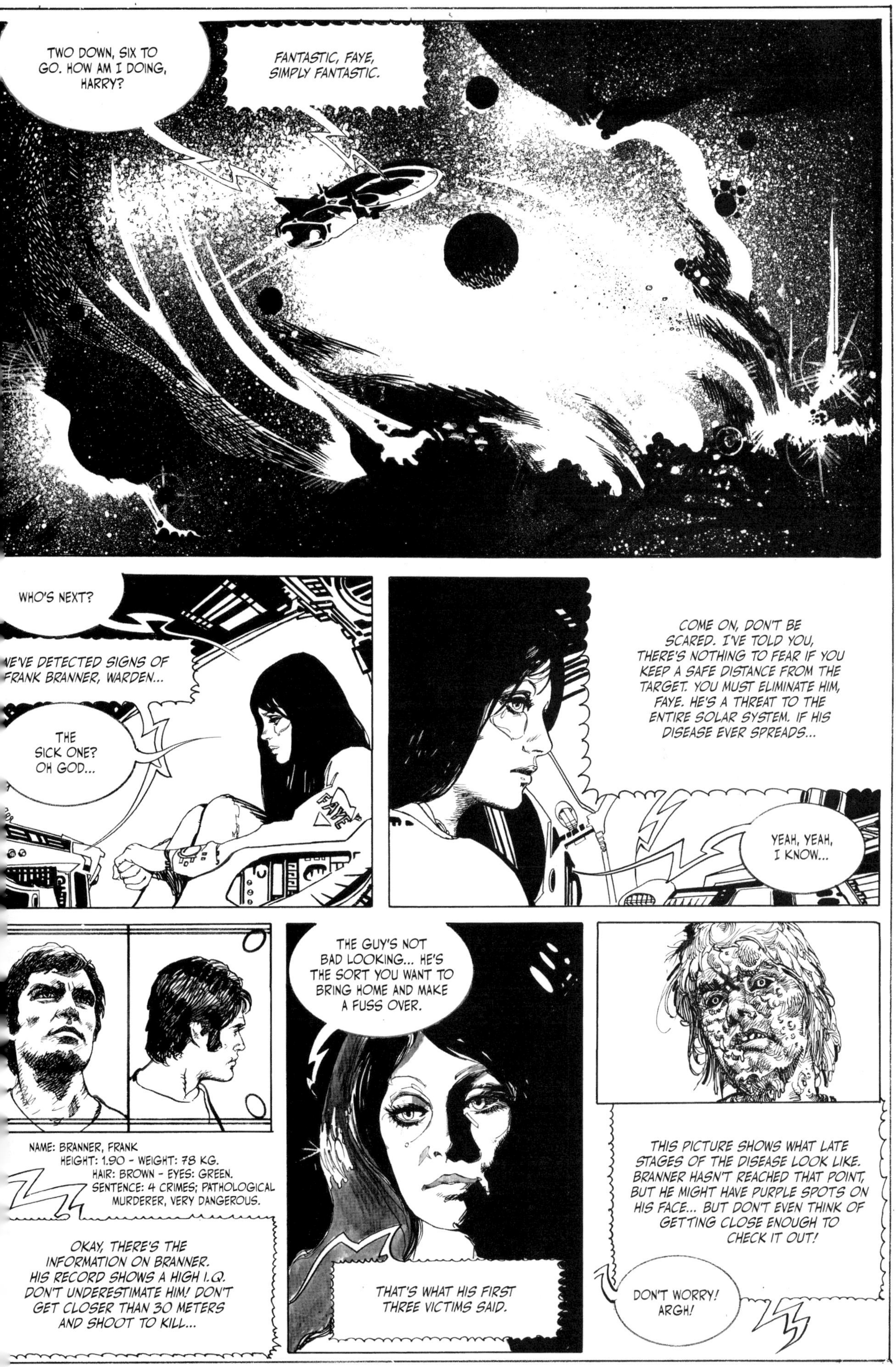

TWO DOWN, SIX TO GO. HOW AM I DOING, HARRY?
FANTASTIC, FAYE, SIMPLY FANTASTIC.
WHO'S NEXT?
WE'VE DETECTED SIGNS OF FRANK BRANNER, WARDEN...
THE SICK ONE? OH GOD...
FAYE
COME ON, DON'T BE SCARED. I'VE TOLD YOU, THERE'S NOTHING TO FEAR IF YOU KEEP A SAFE DISTANCE FROM THE TARGET. YOU MUST ELIMINATE HIM, FAYE. HE'S A THREAT TO THE ENTIRE SOLAR SYSTEM. IF HIS DISEASE EVER SPREADS...
YEAH, YEAH, I KNOW...
NAME: BRANNER, FRANK
HEIGHT: 1.90 - WEIGHT: 78 KG.
HAIR: BROWN - EYES: GREEN.
SENTENCE: 4 CRIMES; PATHOLOGICAL MURDERER, VERY DANGEROUS.
OKAY, THERE'S THE INFORMATION ON BRANNER. HIS RECORD SHOWS A HIGH I.Q. DON'T UNDERESTIMATE HIM! DON'T GET CLOSER THAN 30 METERS AND SHOOT TO KILL...
THE GUY'S NOT BAD LOOKING... HE'S THE SORT YOU WANT TO BRING HOME AND MAKE A FUSS OVER.
THAT'S WHAT HIS FIRST THREE VICTIMS SAID.
THIS PICTURE SHOWS WHAT LATE STAGES OF THE DISEASE LOOK LIKE. BRANNER HASN'T REACHED THAT POINT, BUT HE MIGHT HAVE PURPLE SPOTS ON HIS FACE... BUT DON'T EVEN THINK OF GETTING CLOSE ENOUGH TO CHECK IT OUT!
DON'T WORRY! ARGH!

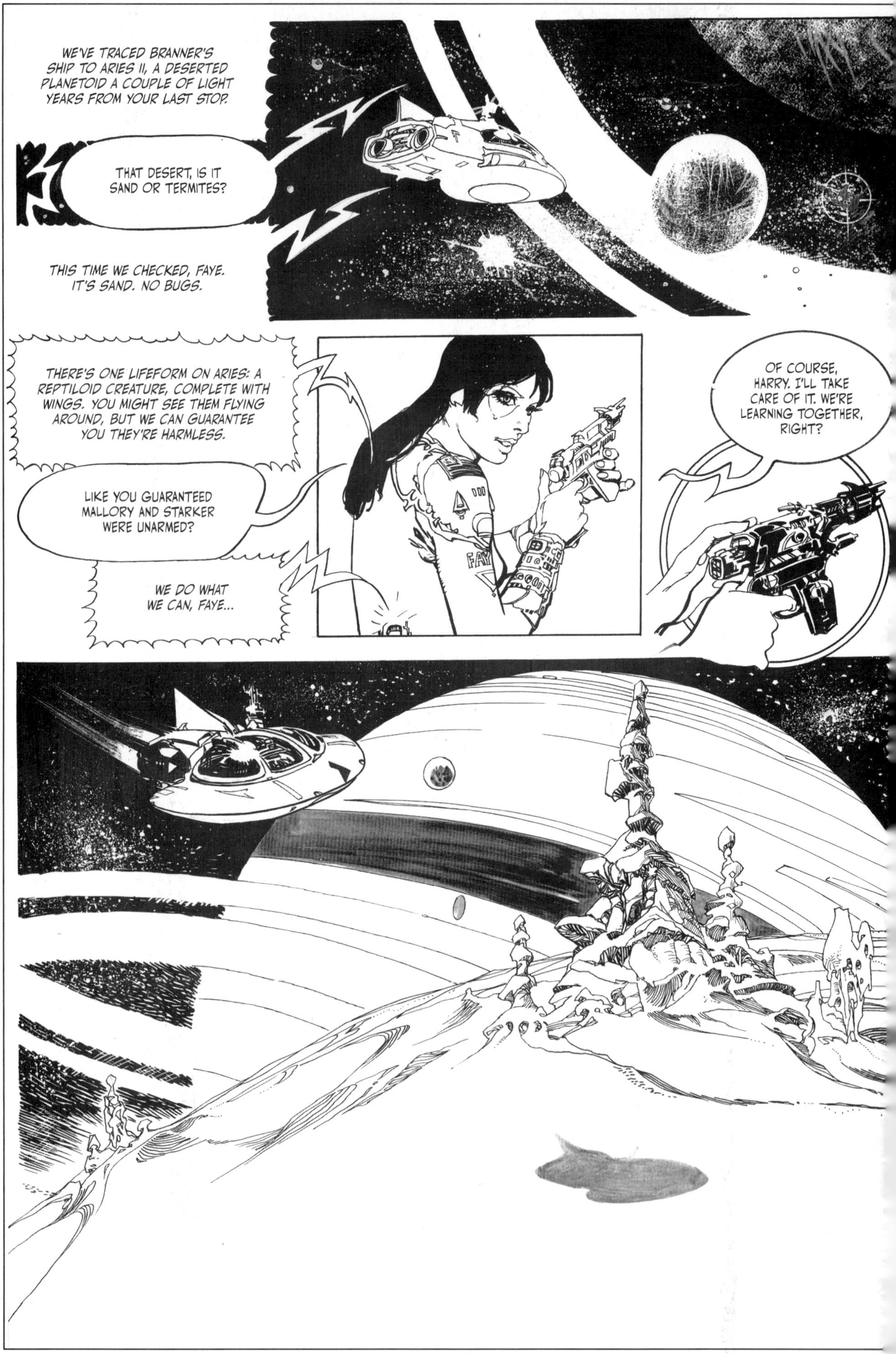

WE'VE TRACED BRANNER'S SHIP TO ARIES II, A DESERTED PLANETOID A COUPLE OF LIGHT YEARS FROM YOUR LAST STOP.
THAT DESERT, IS IT SAND OR TERMITES?
THIS TIME WE CHECKED, FAYE. IT'S SAND. NO BUGS.
THERE'S ONE LIFEFORM ON ARIES: A REPTILOID CREATURE, COMPLETE WITH WINGS. YOU MIGHT SEE THEM FLYING AROUND, BUT WE CAN GUARANTEE YOU THEY'RE HARMLESS.
LIKE YOU GUARANTEED MALLORY AND STARKER WERE UNARMED?
WE DO WHAT WE CAN, FAYE...
OF COURSE, HARRY. I'LL TAKE CARE OF IT. WE'RE LEARNING TOGETHER, RIGHT?

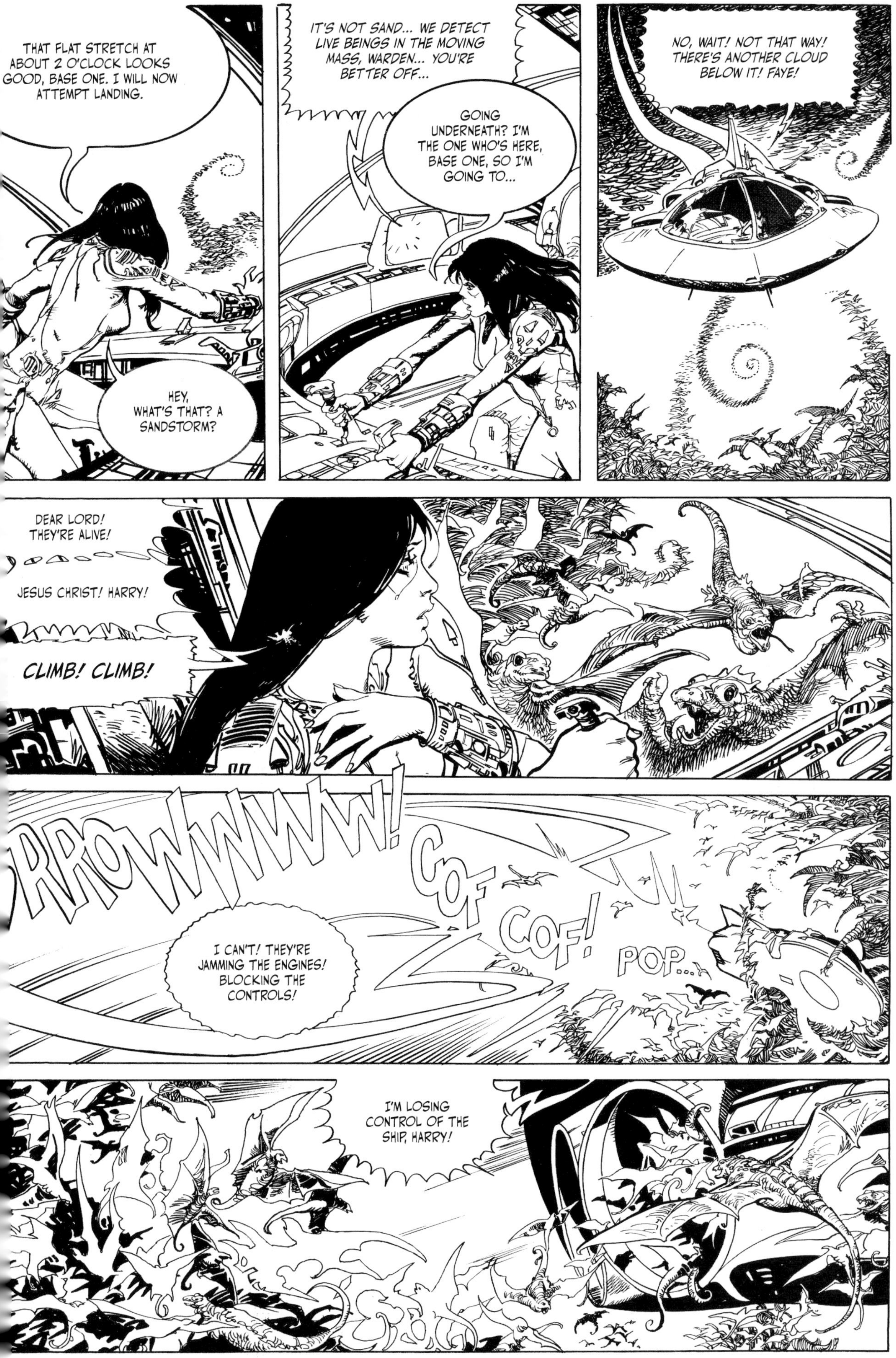
THAT FLAT STRETCH AT ABOUT 2 O'CLOCK LOOKS GOOD, BASE ONE. I WILL NOW ATTEMPT LANDING.
HEY, WHAT'S THAT? A SANDSTORM?
IT'S NOT SAND... WE DETECT LIVE BEINGS IN THE MOVING MASS, WARDEN... YOU'RE BETTER OFF...
GOING UNDERNEATH? I'M THE ONE WHO'S HERE, BASE ONE, SO I'M GOING TO...
NO, WAIT! NOT THAT WAY! THERE'S ANOTHER CLOUD BELOW IT! FAYE!
DEAR LORD! THEY'RE ALIVE!
JESUS CHRIST! HARRY!
CLIMB! CLIMB!
RROWWWWW!
COF COF!
POP...
I CAN'T! THEY'RE JAMMING THE ENGINES! BLOCKING THE CONTROLS!
I'M LOSING CONTROL OF THE SHIP, HARRY!

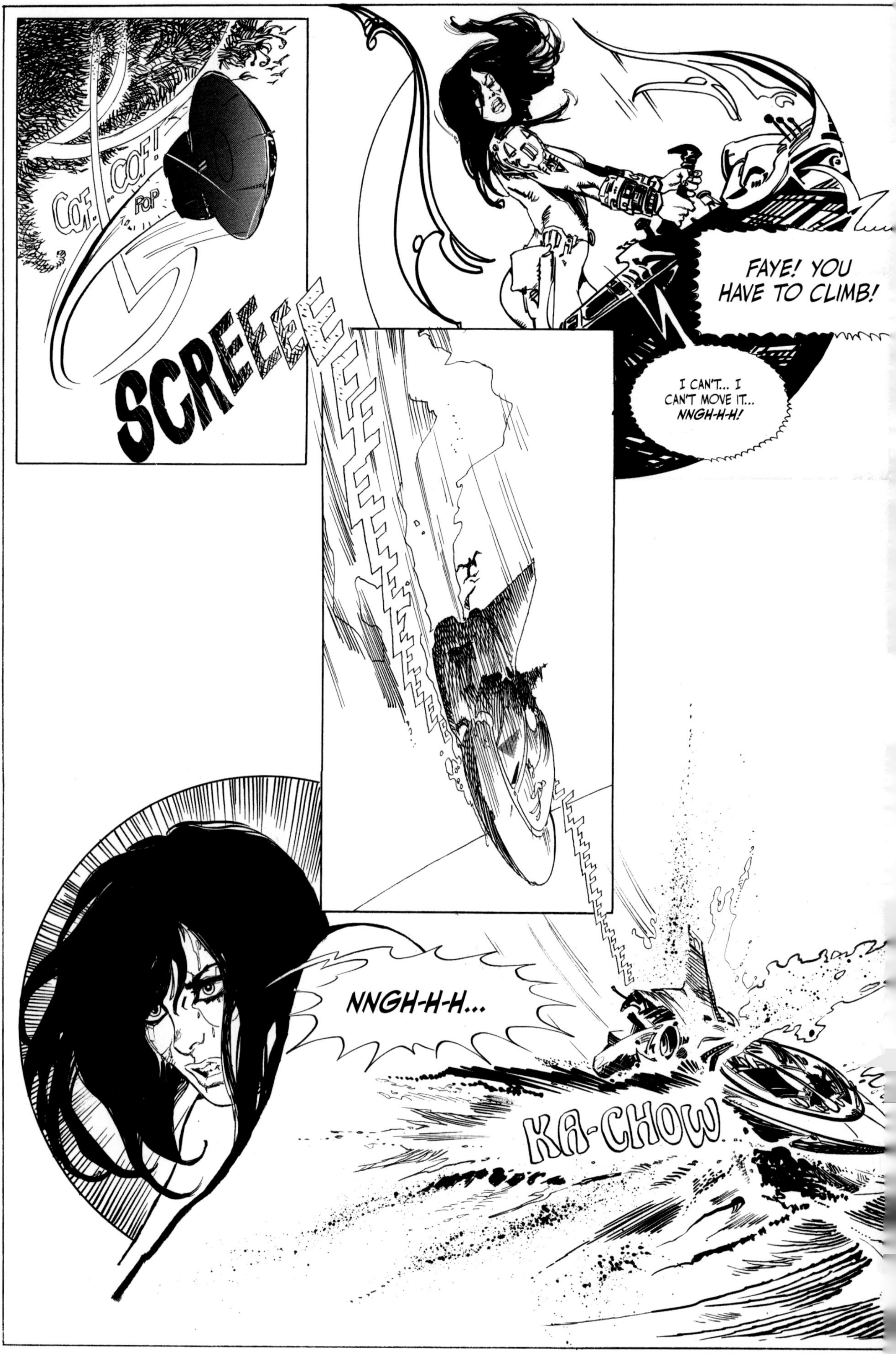
COF!.. COF!
POP
SCREEEEE
FAYE! YOU HAVE TO CLIMB!
I CAN'T... I CAN'T MOVE IT... NNGH-H-H!
NNGH-H-H...
KA-CHOW

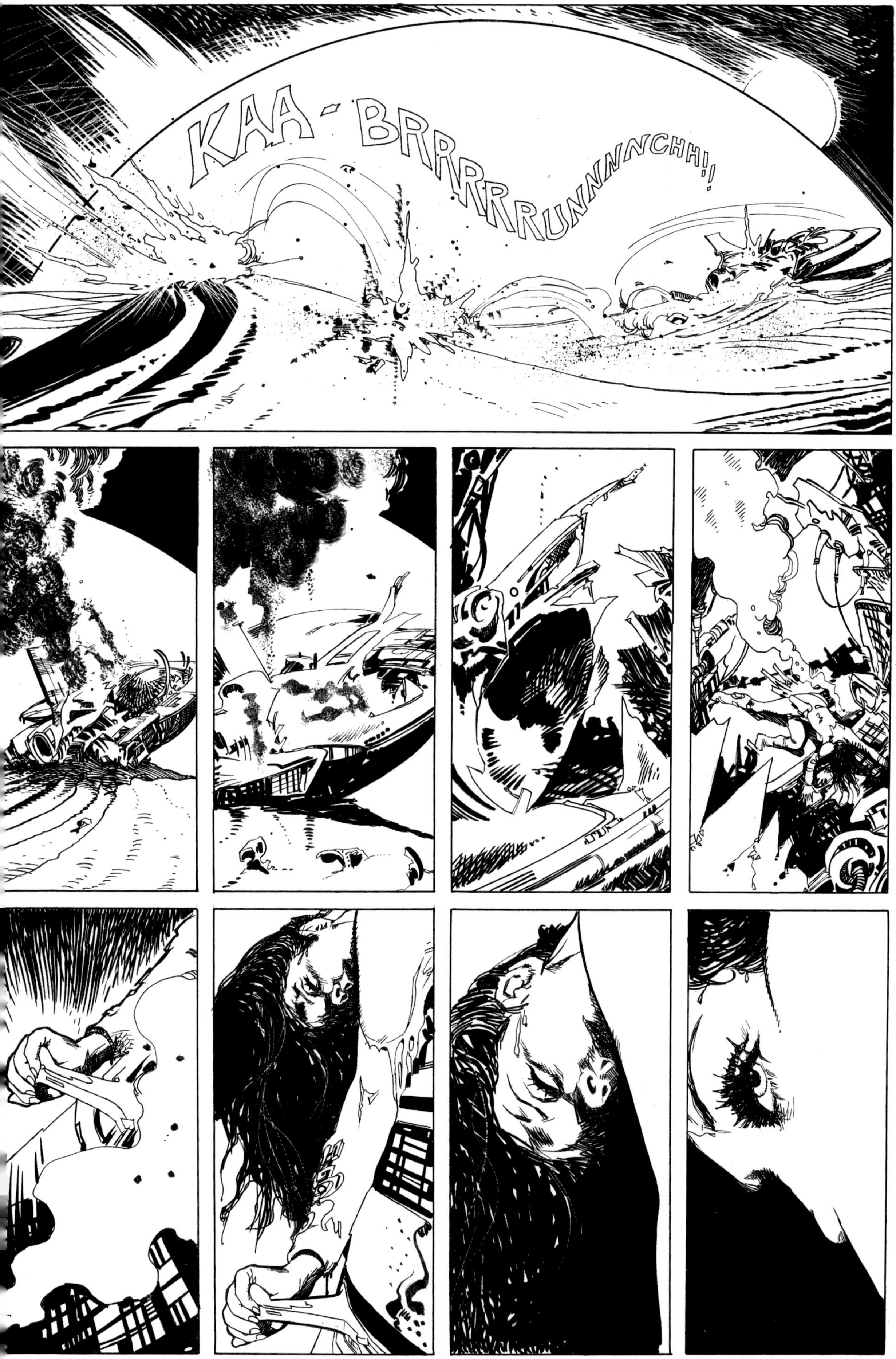
KAA-BRRRRRUNNNNNCHH!!

I DON'T SEEM TO HAVE SUSTAINED ANY SERIOUS INJURIES. BUT THERE'S NO WAY TO FIX THE RADIO AND TV TRANSMITTERS. SAME FOR THE REACTOR AND THE ENGINE ROOM. THE SHIP IS COMPLETELY DISABLED.

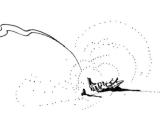

ALL THAT'S LEFT IS MY GUN, A CAN OPENER, AND THIS RECORDER. IN THIS SUN, I WON'T SURVIVE THREE WEEKS, ESPECIALLY SINCE I ONLY HAVE SUPPLIES FOR ABOUT TEN MORE DAYS AND NO WAY OF COMMUNICATING WITH BASE...

THIS IS WARDEN FAYE ROZNER. OVER AND OUT.

THE FLYING LIZARDS ARE HARMLESS, HUH? WRONG AGAIN, HARRY!

WELL, HERE I AM... LIKE THE SAYING GOES, MESS WITH THE BULL, GET THE HORNS.

NO HORNS HERE, BUT THERE'S NO SHORTAGE OF SAND.

I MIGHT MAKE IT A FEW DAYS IF I CAN KILL ONE OF THOSE FLYING LIZARDS... THAT IS, IF THEY'RE EDIBLE...

UH-H-H...

36

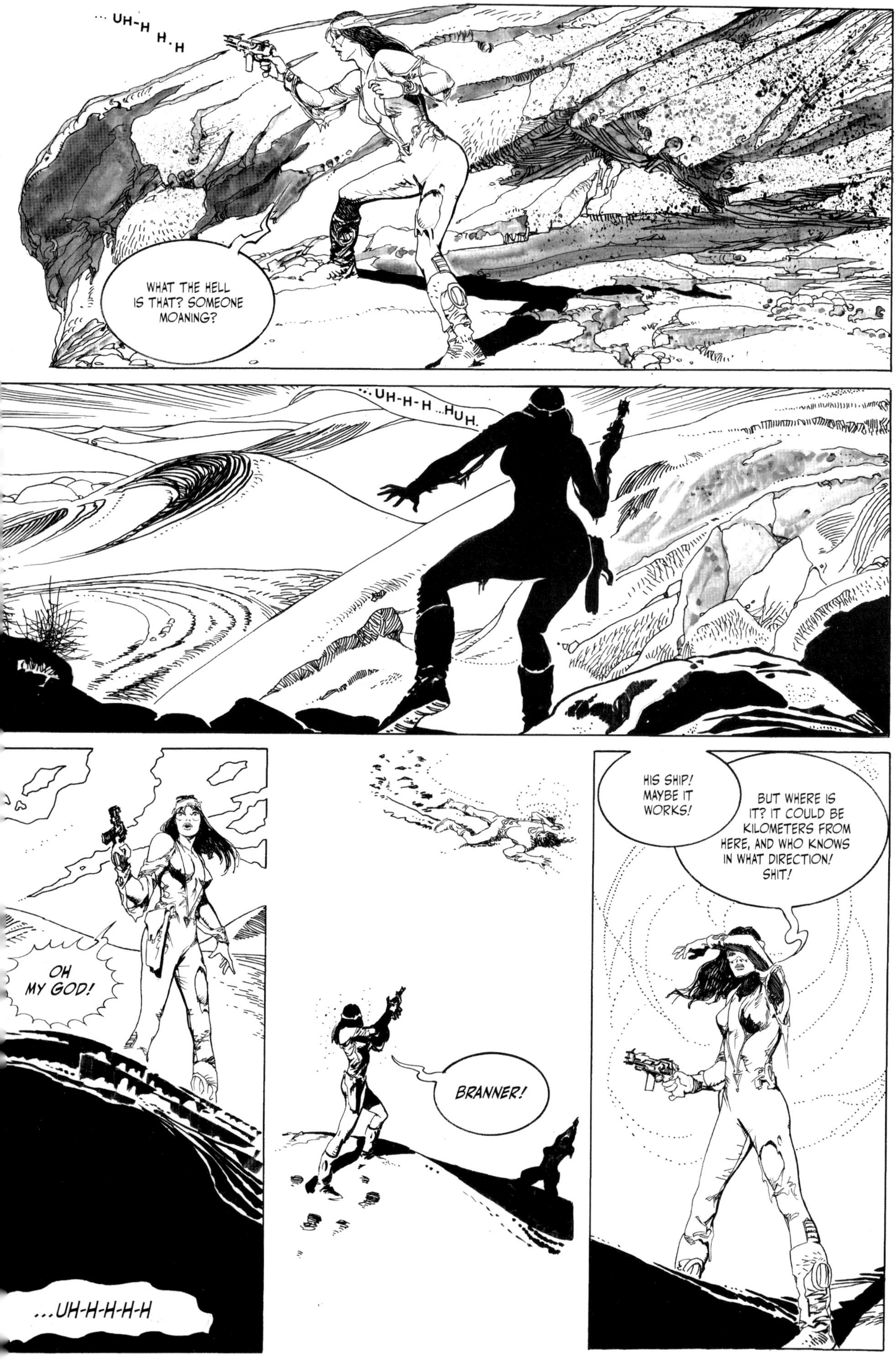

...UH-H H.H
WHAT THE HELL IS THAT? SOMEONE MOANING?
...UH-H-H ...HUH.
OH MY GOD!
...UH-H-H-H-H
BRANNER!
HIS SHIP! MAYBE IT WORKS!
BUT WHERE IS IT? IT COULD BE KILOMETERS FROM HERE, AND WHO KNOWS IN WHAT DIRECTION! SHIT!

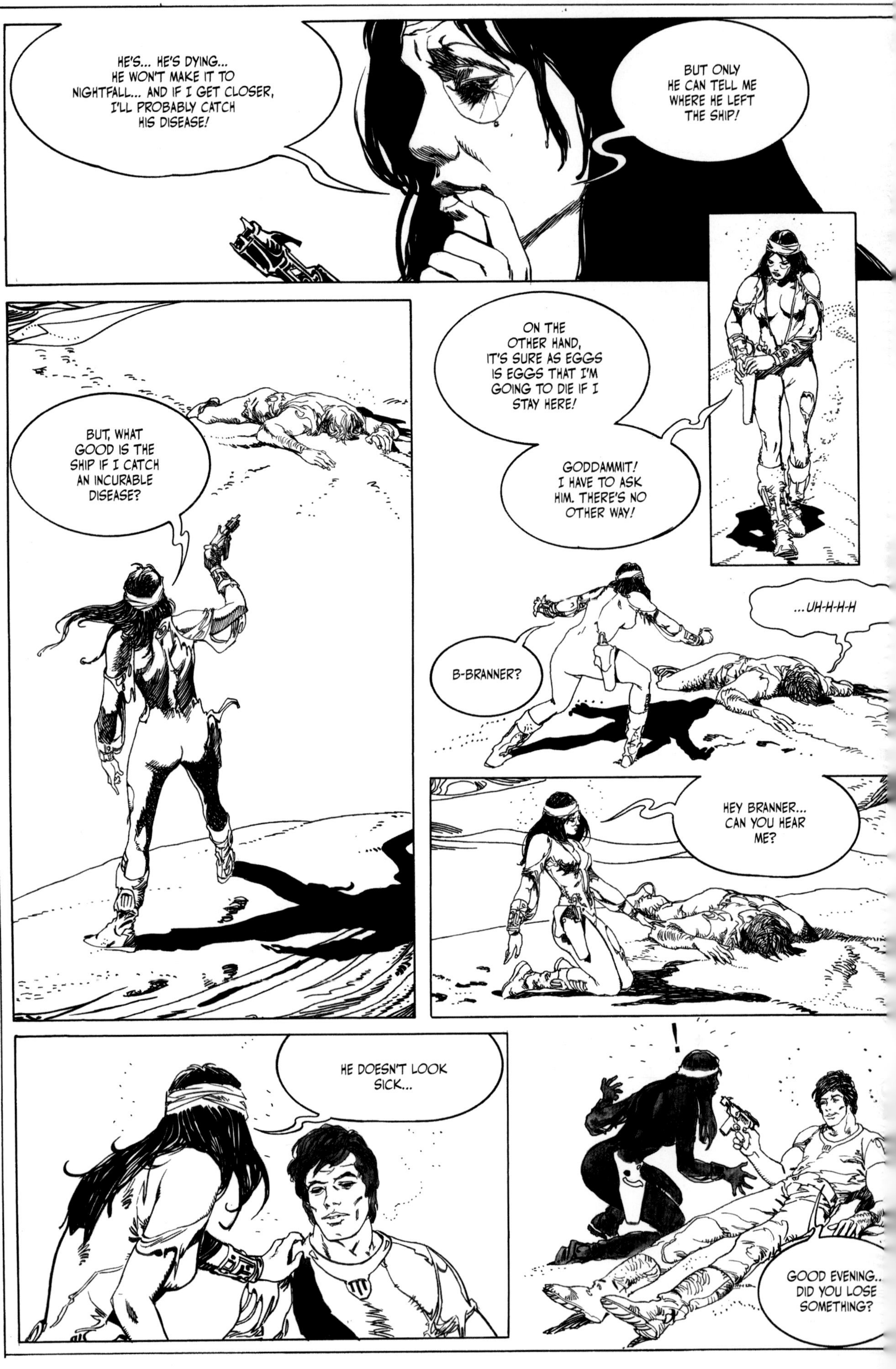

HE'S... HE'S DYING... HE WON'T MAKE IT TO NIGHTFALL... AND IF I GET CLOSER, I'LL PROBABLY CATCH HIS DISEASE!
BUT ONLY HE CAN TELL ME WHERE HE LEFT THE SHIP!
BUT, WHAT GOOD IS THE SHIP IF I CATCH AN INCURABLE DISEASE?
ON THE OTHER HAND, IT'S SURE AS EGGS IS EGGS THAT I'M GOING TO DIE IF I STAY HERE!
GODDAMMIT! I HAVE TO ASK HIM. THERE'S NO OTHER WAY!
B-BRANNER?
...UH-H-H-H
HEY BRANNER... CAN YOU HEAR ME?
HE DOESN'T LOOK SICK...
!
GOOD EVENING.. DID YOU LOSE SOMETHING?

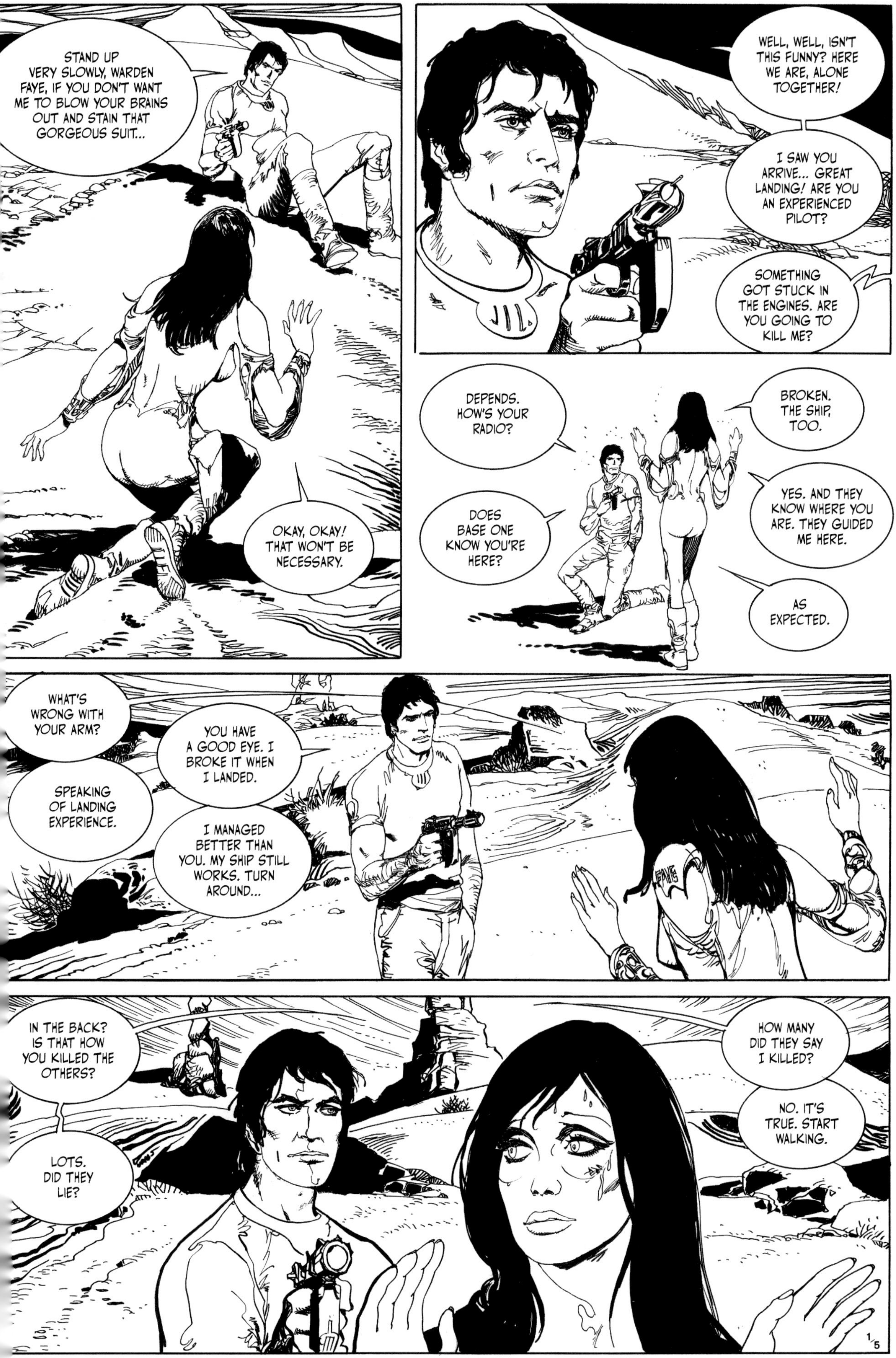

STAND UP VERY SLOWLY, WARDEN FAYE, IF YOU DON'T WANT ME TO BLOW YOUR BRAINS OUT AND STAIN THAT GORGEOUS SUIT...
OKAY, OKAY! THAT WON'T BE NECESSARY.
WELL, WELL, ISN'T THIS FUNNY? HERE WE ARE, ALONE TOGETHER!
I SAW YOU ARRIVE... GREAT LANDING! ARE YOU AN EXPERIENCED PILOT?
SOMETHING GOT STUCK IN THE ENGINES. ARE YOU GOING TO KILL ME?
DEPENDS. HOW'S YOUR RADIO?
BROKEN. THE SHIP, TOO.
DOES BASE ONE KNOW YOU'RE HERE?
YES. AND THEY KNOW WHERE YOU ARE. THEY GUIDED ME HERE.
AS EXPECTED.
WHAT'S WRONG WITH YOUR ARM?
YOU HAVE A GOOD EYE. I BROKE IT WHEN I LANDED.
SPEAKING OF LANDING EXPERIENCE.
I MANAGED BETTER THAN YOU. MY SHIP STILL WORKS. TURN AROUND...
IN THE BACK? IS THAT HOW YOU KILLED THE OTHERS?
HOW MANY DID THEY SAY I KILLED?
LOTS. DID THEY LIE?
NO. IT'S TRUE. START WALKING.

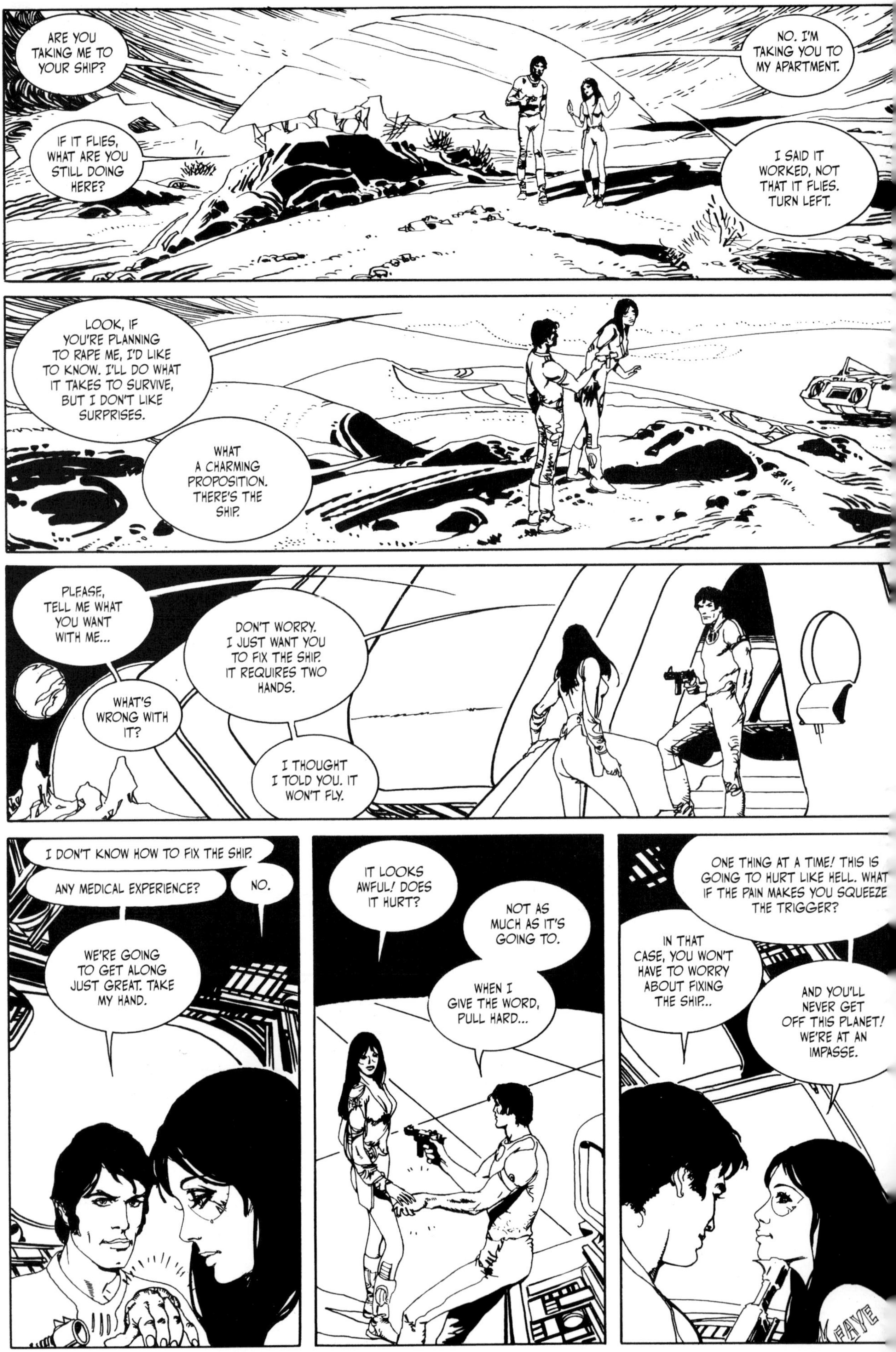
ARE YOU TAKING ME TO YOUR SHIP?
NO. I'M TAKING YOU TO MY APARTMENT.
IF IT FLIES, WHAT ARE YOU STILL DOING HERE?
I SAID IT WORKED, NOT THAT IT FLIES. TURN LEFT.
LOOK, IF YOU'RE PLANNING TO RAPE ME, I'D LIKE TO KNOW. I'LL DO WHAT IT TAKES TO SURVIVE, BUT I DON'T LIKE SURPRISES.
WHAT A CHARMING PROPOSITION. THERE'S THE SHIP.
PLEASE, TELL ME WHAT YOU WANT WITH ME...
DON'T WORRY. I JUST WANT YOU TO FIX THE SHIP. IT REQUIRES TWO HANDS.
WHAT'S WRONG WITH IT?
I THOUGHT I TOLD YOU. IT WON'T FLY.
I DON'T KNOW HOW TO FIX THE SHIP.
ANY MEDICAL EXPERIENCE?
NO.
WE'RE GOING TO GET ALONG JUST GREAT. TAKE MY HAND.
IT LOOKS AWFUL! DOES IT HURT?
NOT AS MUCH AS IT'S GOING TO.
WHEN I GIVE THE WORD, PULL HARD...
ONE THING AT A TIME! THIS IS GOING TO HURT LIKE HELL. WHAT IF THE PAIN MAKES YOU SQUEEZE THE TRIGGER?
IN THAT CASE, YOU WON'T HAVE TO WORRY ABOUT FIXING THE SHIP...
AND YOU'LL NEVER GET OFF THIS PLANET! WE'RE AT AN IMPASSE.

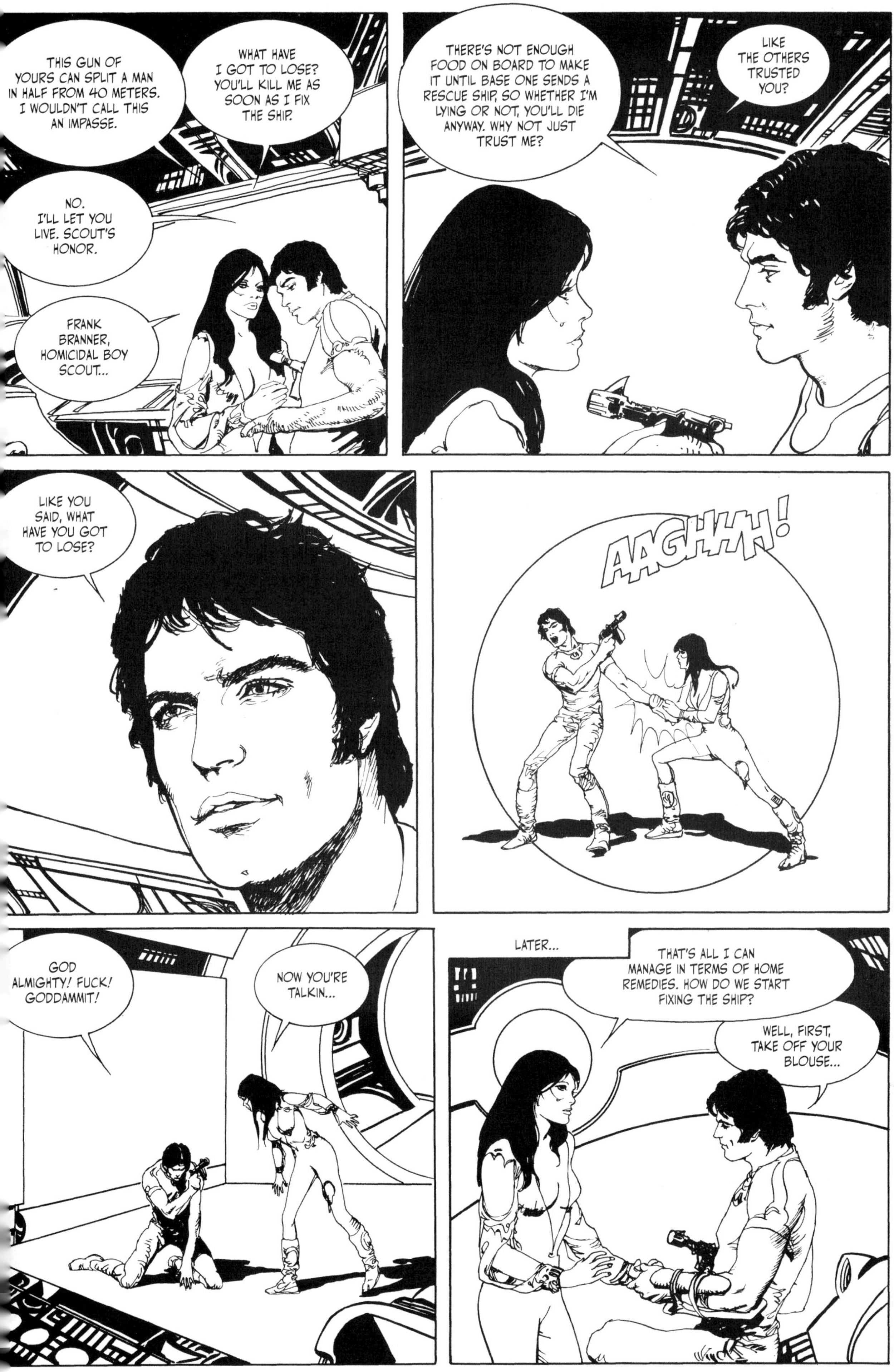
THIS GUN OF YOURS CAN SPLIT A MAN IN HALF FROM 40 METERS. I WOULDN'T CALL THIS AN IMPASSE.
WHAT HAVE I GOT TO LOSE? YOU'LL KILL ME AS SOON AS I FIX THE SHIP.
NO. I'LL LET YOU LIVE. SCOUT'S HONOR.
FRANK BRANNER, HOMICIDAL BOY SCOUT...
THERE'S NOT ENOUGH FOOD ON BOARD TO MAKE IT UNTIL BASE ONE SENDS A RESCUE SHIP, SO WHETHER I'M LYING OR NOT, YOU'LL DIE ANYWAY. WHY NOT JUST TRUST ME?
LIKE THE OTHERS TRUSTED YOU?
LIKE YOU SAID, WHAT HAVE YOU GOT TO LOSE?
AAGHHH!
GOD ALMIGHTY! FUCK! GODDAMMIT!
NOW YOU'RE TALKIN...
LATER...
THAT'S ALL I CAN MANAGE IN TERMS OF HOME REMEDIES. HOW DO WE START FIXING THE SHIP?
WELL, FIRST, TAKE OFF YOUR BLOUSE...

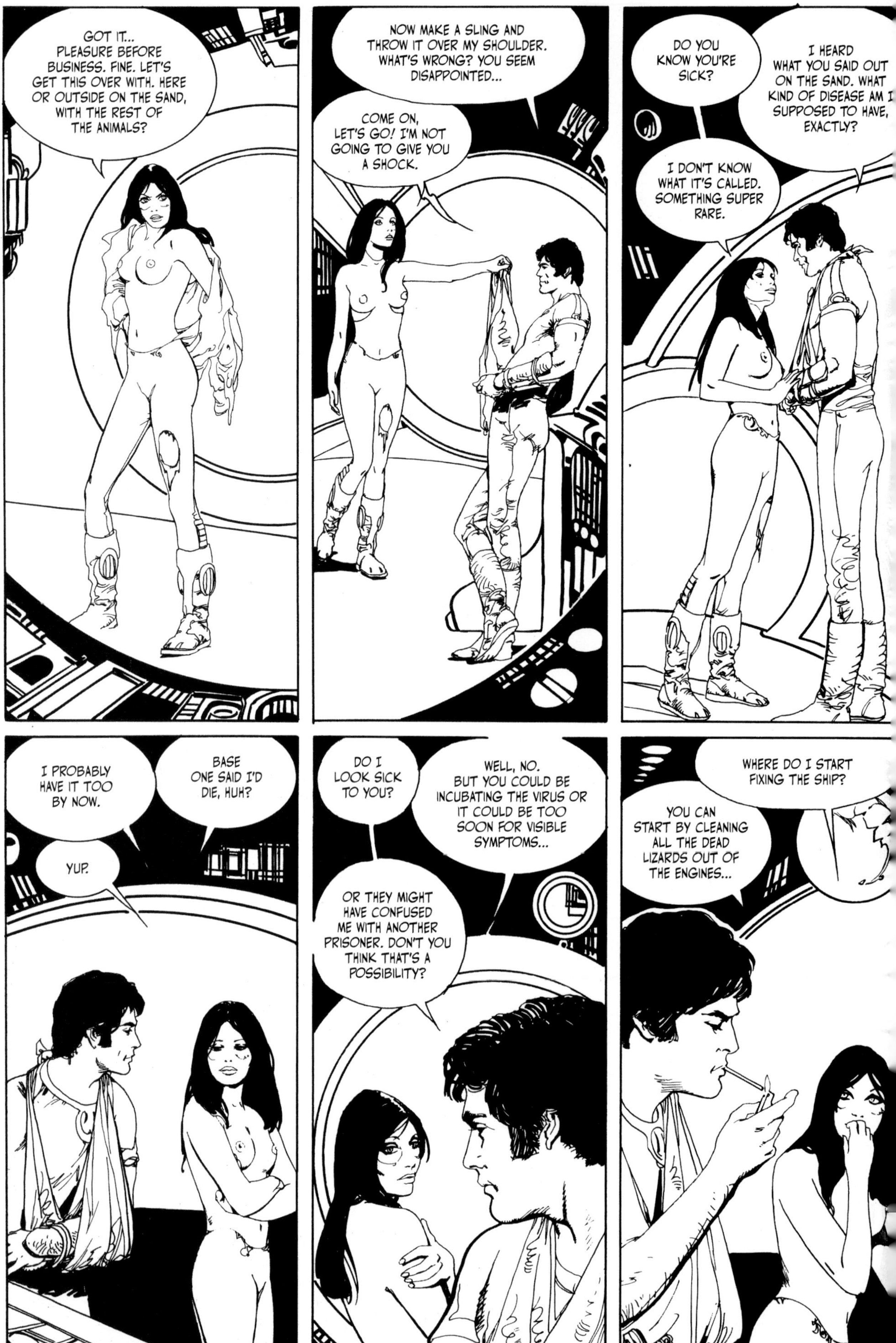
GOT IT... PLEASURE BEFORE BUSINESS. FINE. LET'S GET THIS OVER WITH. HERE OR OUTSIDE ON THE SAND, WITH THE REST OF THE ANIMALS?
NOW MAKE A SLING AND THROW IT OVER MY SHOULDER. WHAT'S WRONG? YOU SEEM DISAPPOINTED...
COME ON, LET'S GO! I'M NOT GOING TO GIVE YOU A SHOCK.
DO YOU KNOW YOU'RE SICK?
I HEARD WHAT YOU SAID OUT ON THE SAND. WHAT KIND OF DISEASE AM I SUPPOSED TO HAVE, EXACTLY?
I DON'T KNOW WHAT IT'S CALLED. SOMETHING SUPER RARE.
I PROBABLY HAVE IT TOO BY NOW.
BASE ONE SAID I'D DIE, HUH?
YUP.
DO I LOOK SICK TO YOU?
WELL, NO. BUT YOU COULD BE INCUBATING THE VIRUS OR IT COULD BE TOO SOON FOR VISIBLE SYMPTOMS...
OR THEY MIGHT HAVE CONFUSED ME WITH ANOTHER PRISONER. DON'T YOU THINK THAT'S A POSSIBILITY?
WHERE DO I START FIXING THE SHIP?
YOU CAN START BY CLEANING ALL THE DEAD LIZARDS OUT OF THE ENGINES...

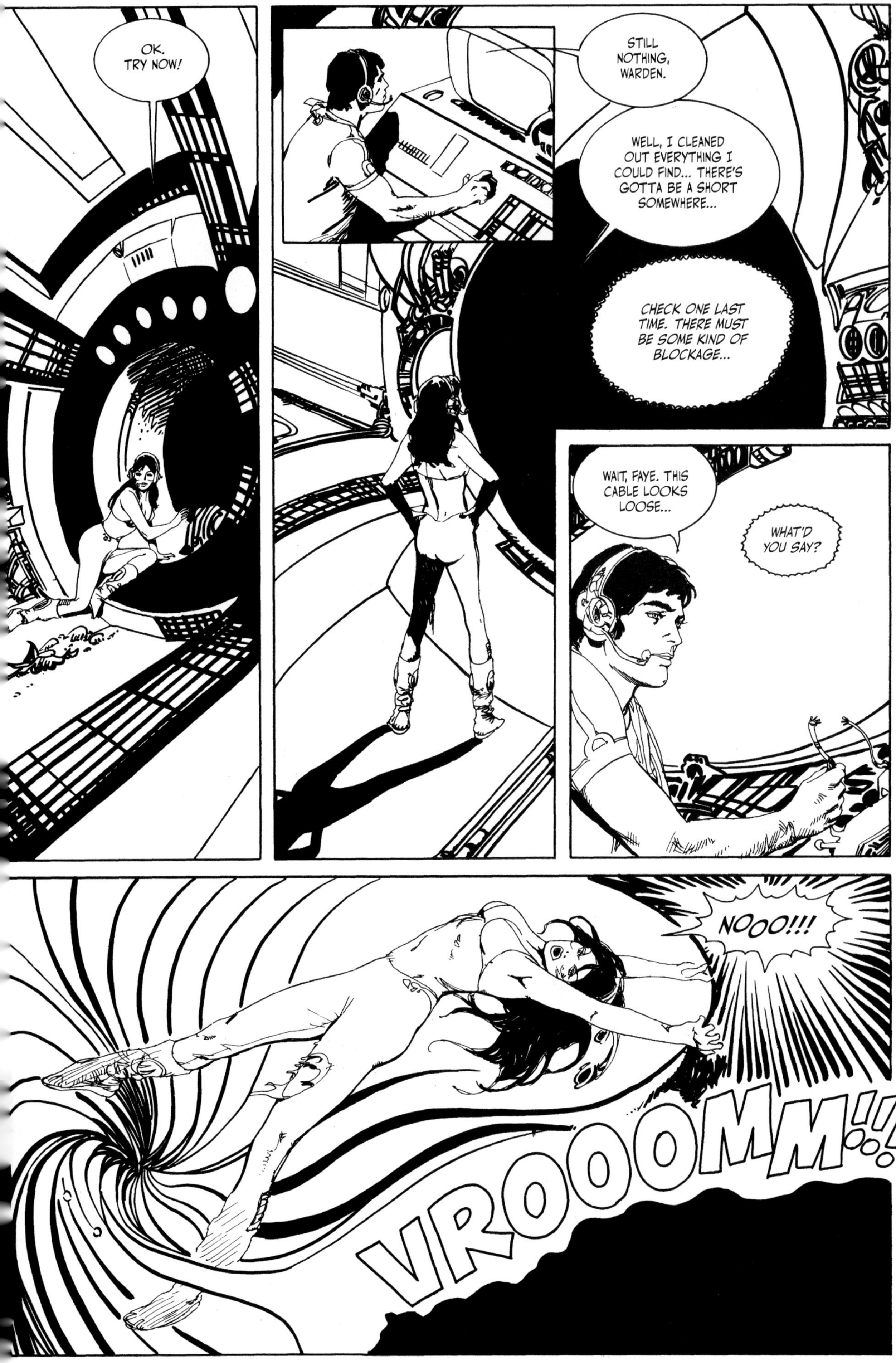
OK. TRY NOW!
STILL NOTHING, WARDEN.
WELL, I CLEANED OUT EVERYTHING I COULD FIND... THERE'S GOTTA BE A SHORT SOMEWHERE...
CHECK ONE LAST TIME. THERE MUST BE SOME KIND OF BLOCKAGE...
WAIT, FAYE. THIS CABLE LOOKS LOOSE...
WHAT'D YOU SAY?
NOOO!!!
VROOOMM!!!

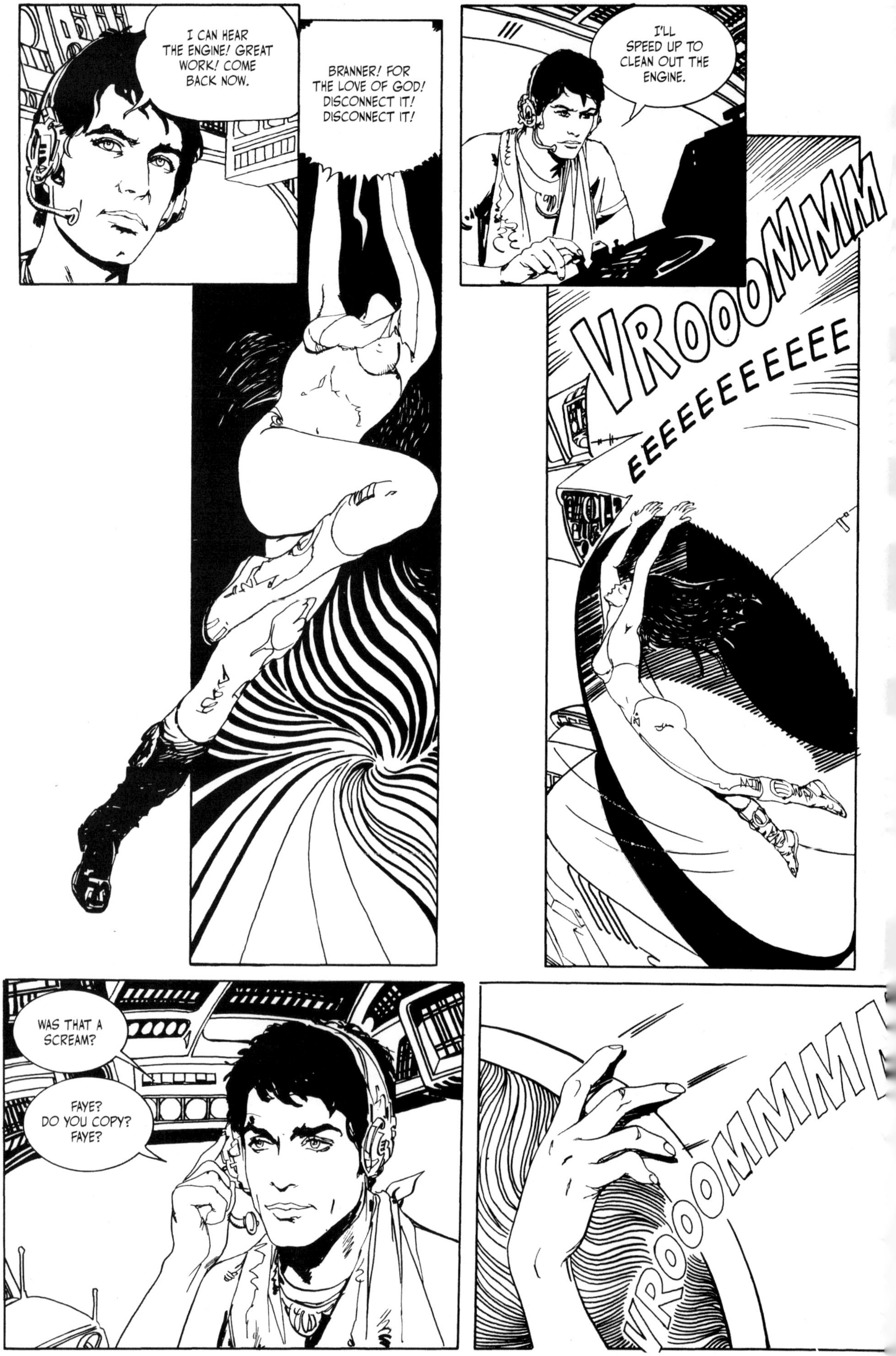
I CAN HEAR THE ENGINE! GREAT WORK! COME BACK NOW.
BRANNER! FOR THE LOVE OF GOD! DISCONNECT IT! DISCONNECT IT!
I'LL SPEED UP TO CLEAN OUT THE ENGINE.
VROOOMMM
EEEEEEEEEEE
WAS THAT A SCREAM?
FAYE? DO YOU COPY? FAYE?
VROOOMMMM

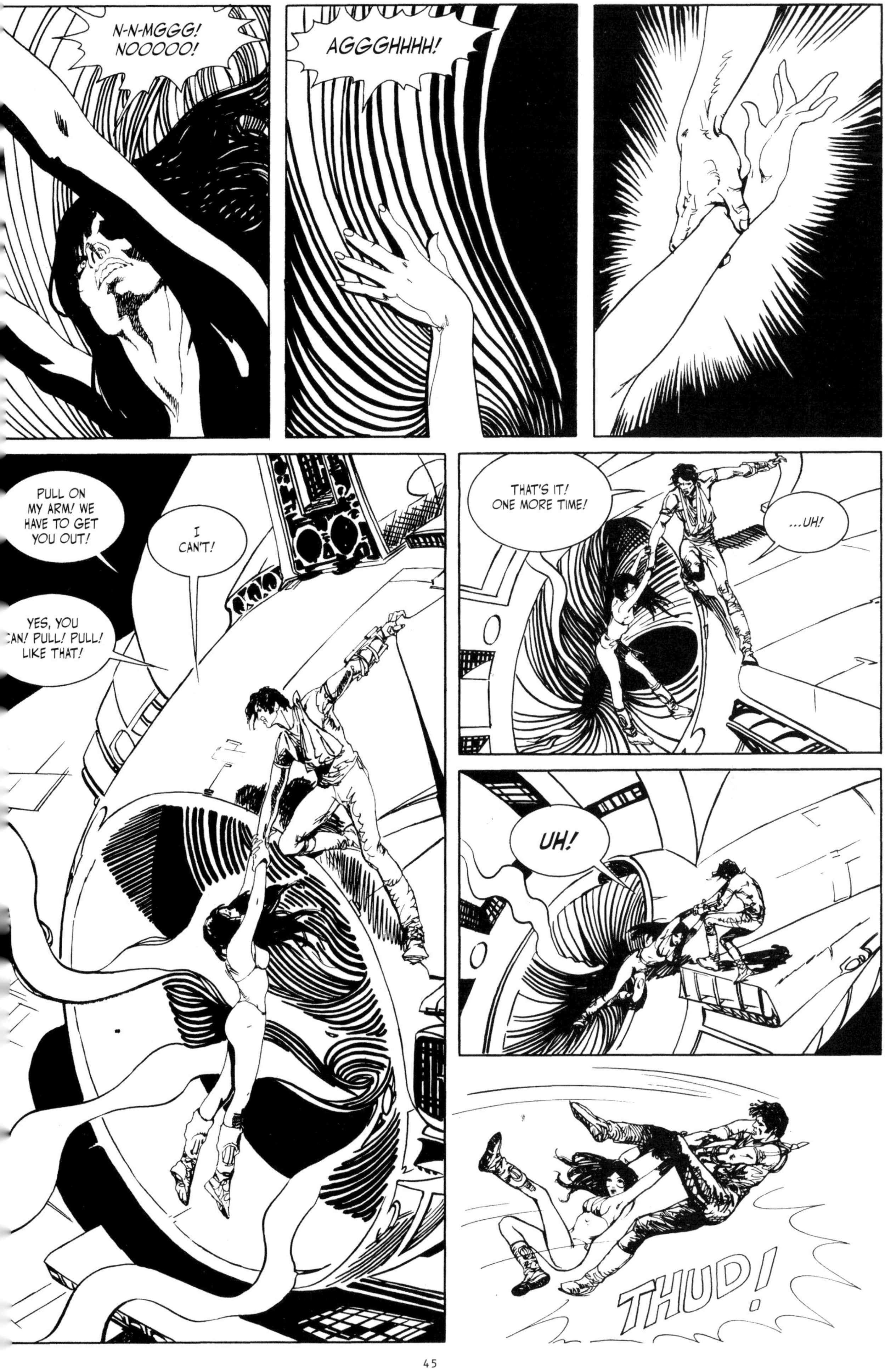
N-N-MGGG! NOOOOO!
AGGGHHHH!
PULL ON MY ARM! WE HAVE TO GET YOU OUT!
I CAN'T!
YES, YOU CAN! PULL! PULL! LIKE THAT!
THAT'S IT! ONE MORE TIME!
...UH!
UH!
THUD!

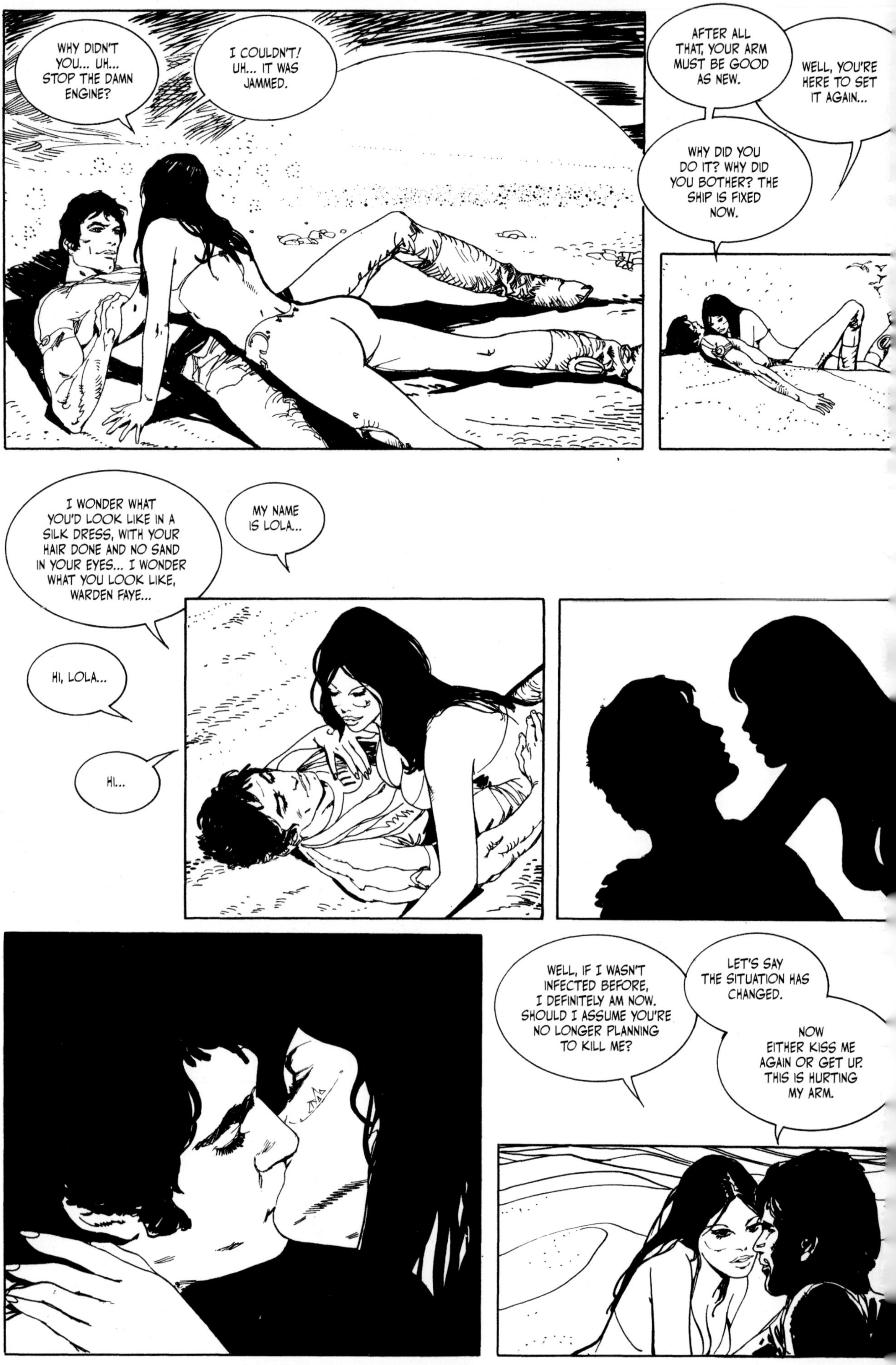
WHY DIDN'T YOU... UH... STOP THE DAMN ENGINE?
I COULDN'T! UH... IT WAS JAMMED.
AFTER ALL THAT, YOUR ARM MUST BE GOOD AS NEW.
WELL, YOU'RE HERE TO SET IT AGAIN...
WHY DID YOU DO IT? WHY DID YOU BOTHER? THE SHIP IS FIXED NOW.
I WONDER WHAT YOU'D LOOK LIKE IN A SILK DRESS, WITH YOUR HAIR DONE AND NO SAND IN YOUR EYES... I WONDER WHAT YOU LOOK LIKE, WARDEN FAYE...
MY NAME IS LOLA...
HI, LOLA...
HI...
WELL, IF I WASN'T INFECTED BEFORE, I DEFINITELY AM NOW. SHOULD I ASSUME YOU'RE NO LONGER PLANNING TO KILL ME?
LET'S SAY THE SITUATION HAS CHANGED.
NOW EITHER KISS ME AGAIN OR GET UP. THIS IS HURTING MY ARM.

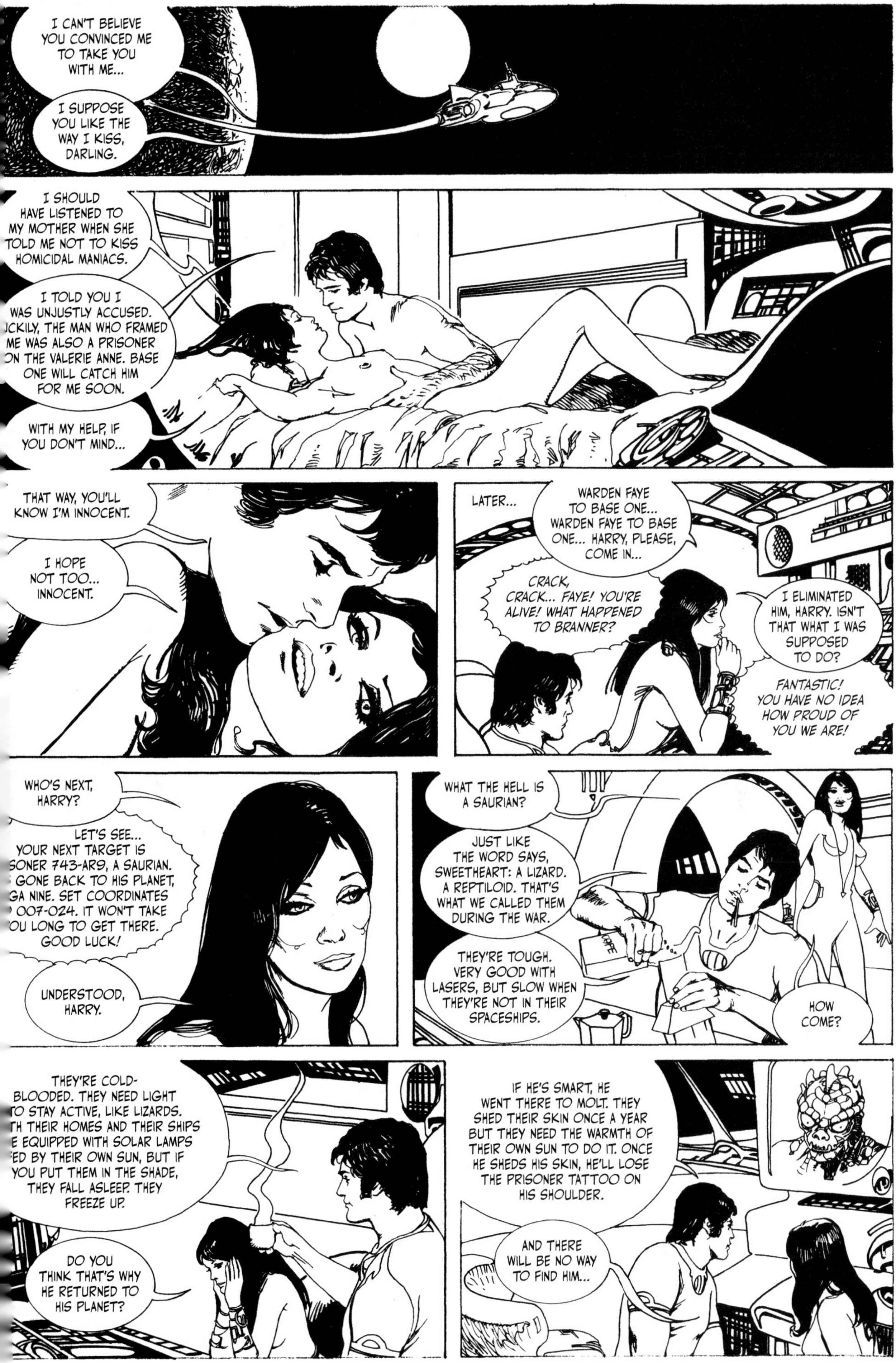
I CAN'T BELIEVE YOU CONVINCED ME TO TAKE YOU WITH ME...
I SUPPOSE YOU LIKE THE WAY I KISS, DARLING.
I SHOULD HAVE LISTENED TO MY MOTHER WHEN SHE TOLD ME NOT TO KISS HOMICIDAL MANIACS.
I TOLD YOU I WAS UNJUSTLY ACCUSED. CKILY, THE MAN WHO FRAMED ME WAS ALSO A PRISONER ON THE VALERIE ANNE. BASE ONE WILL CATCH HIM FOR ME SOON.
WITH MY HELP, IF YOU DON'T MIND...
THAT WAY, YOU'LL KNOW I'M INNOCENT.
I HOPE NOT TOO... INNOCENT.
LATER...
WARDEN FAYE TO BASE ONE... WARDEN FAYE TO BASE ONE... HARRY, PLEASE, COME IN...
CRACK, CRACK... FAYE! YOU'RE ALIVE! WHAT HAPPENED TO BRANNER?
I ELIMINATED HIM, HARRY. ISN'T THAT WHAT I WAS SUPPOSED TO DO?
FANTASTIC! YOU HAVE NO IDEA HOW PROUD OF YOU WE ARE!
WHO'S NEXT, HARRY?
LET'S SEE... YOUR NEXT TARGET IS SONER 743-AR9, A SAURIAN. GONE BACK TO HIS PLANET, GA NINE. SET COORDINATES 007-024. IT WON'T TAKE OU LONG TO GET THERE. GOOD LUCK!
UNDERSTOOD, HARRY.
WHAT THE HELL IS A SAURIAN?
JUST LIKE THE WORD SAYS, SWEETHEART: A LIZARD. A REPTILOID. THAT'S WHAT WE CALLED THEM DURING THE WAR.
THEY'RE TOUGH. VERY GOOD WITH LASERS, BUT SLOW WHEN THEY'RE NOT IN THEIR SPACESHIPS.
HOW COME?
THEY'RE COLD-BLOODED. THEY NEED LIGHT O STAY ACTIVE, LIKE LIZARDS. TH THEIR HOMES AND THEIR SHIPS E EQUIPPED WITH SOLAR LAMPS ED BY THEIR OWN SUN, BUT IF YOU PUT THEM IN THE SHADE, THEY FALL ASLEEP. THEY FREEZE UP.
DO YOU THINK THAT'S WHY HE RETURNED TO HIS PLANET?
IF HE'S SMART, HE WENT THERE TO MOLT. THEY SHED THEIR SKIN ONCE A YEAR BUT THEY NEED THE WARMTH OF THEIR OWN SUN TO DO IT. ONCE HE SHEDS HIS SKIN, HE'LL LOSE THE PRISONER TATTOO ON HIS SHOULDER.
AND THERE WILL BE NO WAY TO FIND HIM...

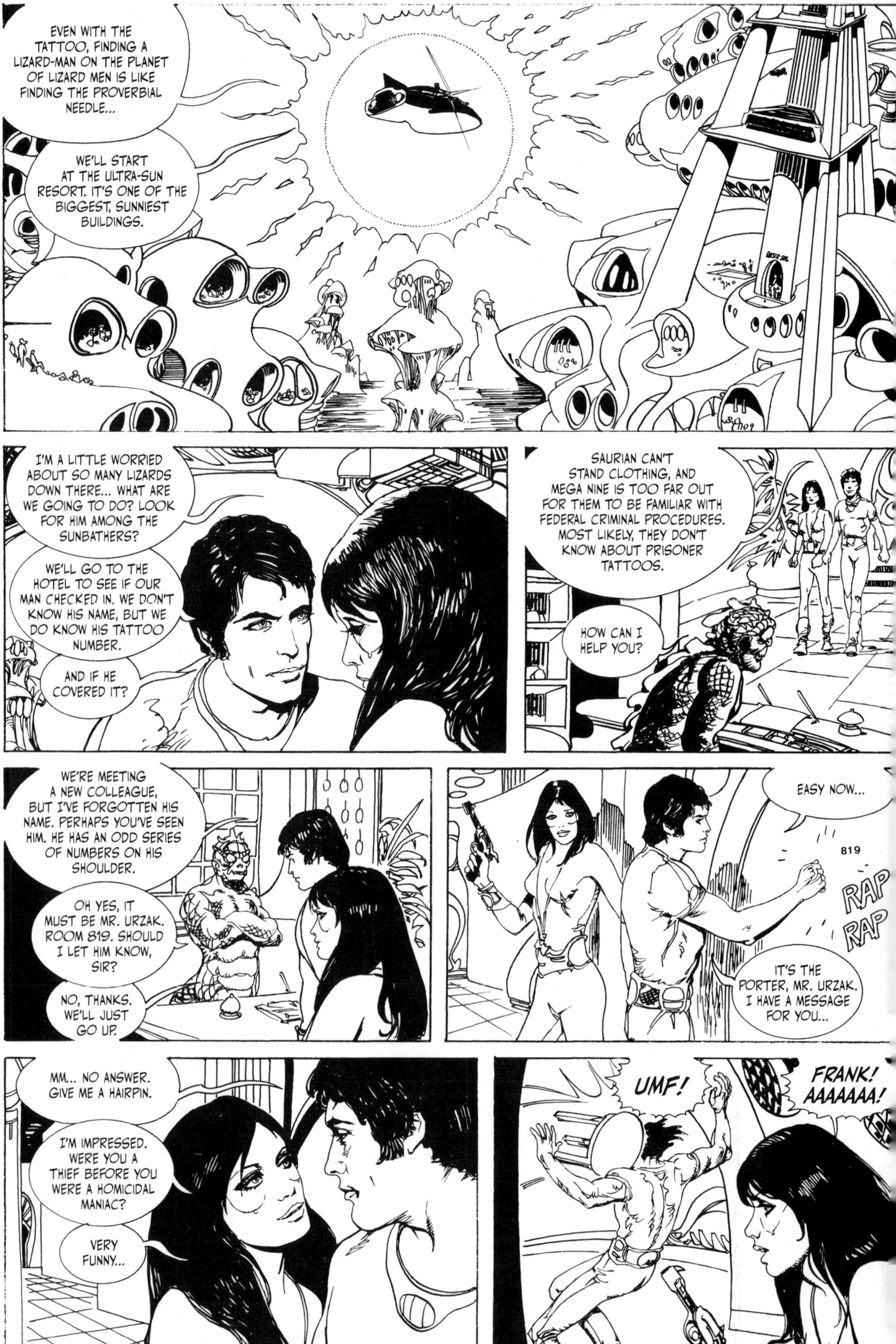

EVEN WITH THE TATTOO, FINDING A LIZARD-MAN ON THE PLANET OF LIZARD MEN IS LIKE FINDING THE PROVERBIAL NEEDLE...
WE'LL START AT THE ULTRA-SUN RESORT. IT'S ONE OF THE BIGGEST, SUNNIEST BUILDINGS.
I'M A LITTLE WORRIED ABOUT SO MANY LIZARDS DOWN THERE... WHAT ARE WE GOING TO DO? LOOK FOR HIM AMONG THE SUNBATHERS?
WE'LL GO TO THE HOTEL TO SEE IF OUR MAN CHECKED IN. WE DON'T KNOW HIS NAME, BUT WE DO KNOW HIS TATTOO NUMBER.
AND IF HE COVERED IT?
SAURIAN CAN'T STAND CLOTHING, AND MEGA NINE IS TOO FAR OUT FOR THEM TO BE FAMILIAR WITH FEDERAL CRIMINAL PROCEDURES. MOST LIKELY, THEY DON'T KNOW ABOUT PRISONER TATTOOS.
HOW CAN I HELP YOU?
WE'RE MEETING A NEW COLLEAGUE, BUT I'VE FORGOTTEN HIS NAME. PERHAPS YOU'VE SEEN HIM. HE HAS AN ODD SERIES OF NUMBERS ON HIS SHOULDER.
OH YES, IT MUST BE MR. URZAK. ROOM 819. SHOULD I LET HIM KNOW, SIR?
NO, THANKS. WE'LL JUST GO UP.
EASY NOW...
819
RAP RAP
IT'S THE PORTER, MR. URZAK. I HAVE A MESSAGE FOR YOU...
MM... NO ANSWER. GIVE ME A HAIRPIN.
I'M IMPRESSED. WERE YOU A THIEF BEFORE YOU WERE A HOMICIDAL MANIAC?
VERY FUNNY...
UMF!
FRANK! AAAAAAA!

AFTER BRANNER RECOVERED...

OOOH MY HEAD... WHAT HAPPENED?

URZAK HIT YOU WITH A CHAIR. THEN HE GRABBED MY GUN AND WENT OUT THE FIRE ESCAPE.

THERE'S HIS SKIN. DAMMIT! WE LOST HIM.

NOT YET! LOOK, HE'S STILL ON HIS WAY DOWN. LET'S GO!

FORGET IT. BY THE TIME WE'RE DOWN THERE, HE'LL BE GONE.

WAIT. DO YOU KNOW HOW TO SWIM?

NO! AND I WOULDN'T DO WHAT YOU'RE THINKING EVEN IF I COULD!

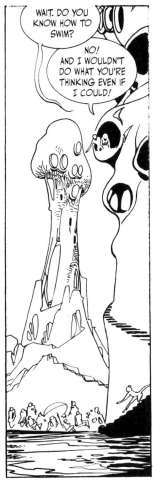

I DON'T BELIEVE YOU, WARDEN.

NO, FRANK. OH MY GOD!

SPLASSS!

YOU FUCKING PSYCHO! IRRESPONSIBLE ASSHOLE!

PLEASE FORGIVE HER. SHE HATES GETTING HER HAIR WET...

I SHOULD BREAK YOUR OTHER ARM FOR THAT...

LOOK! THE PRISONER! RUN!

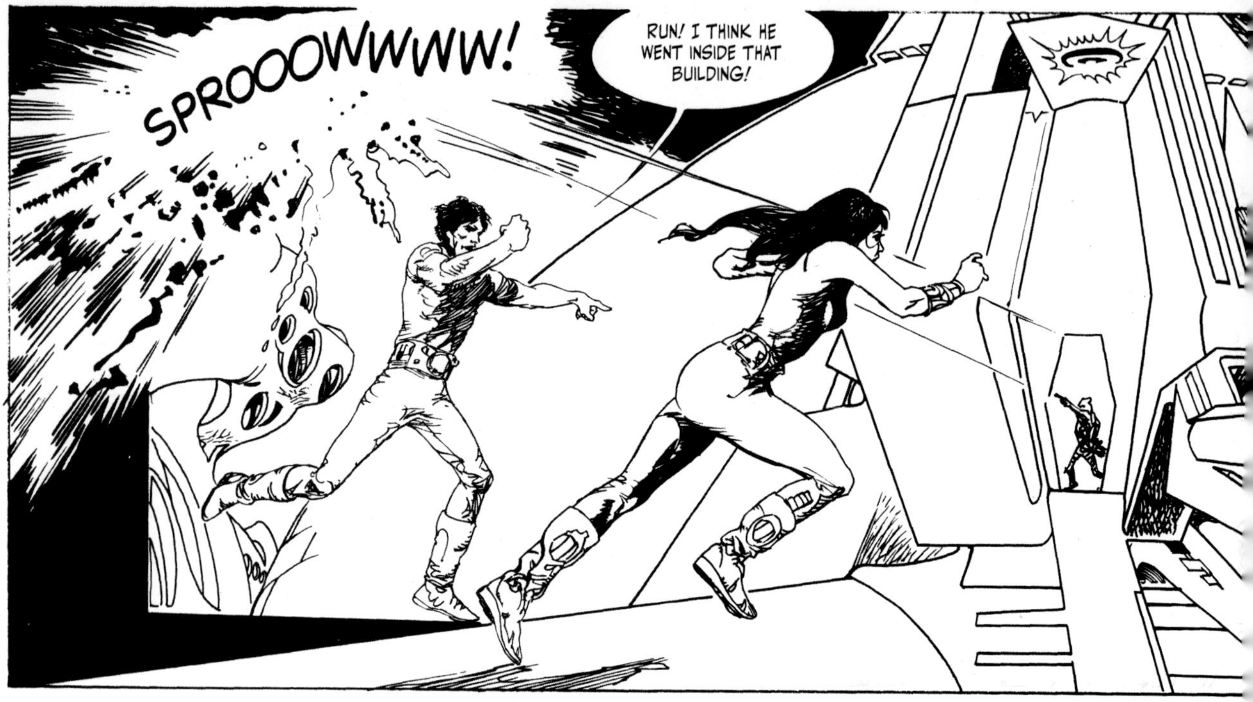
SPROOOWWWW!
RUN! I THINK HE WENT INSIDE THAT BUILDING!

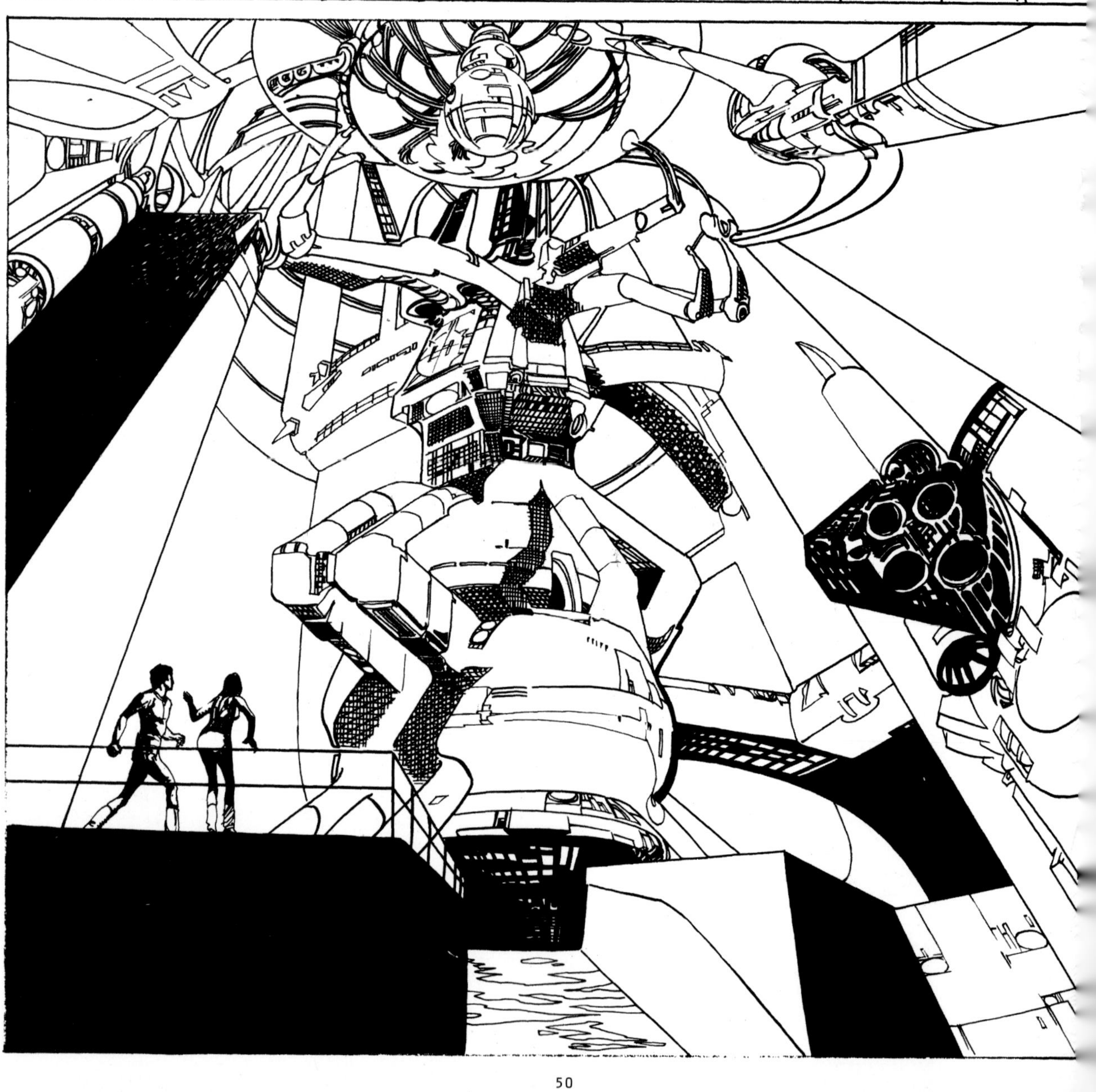

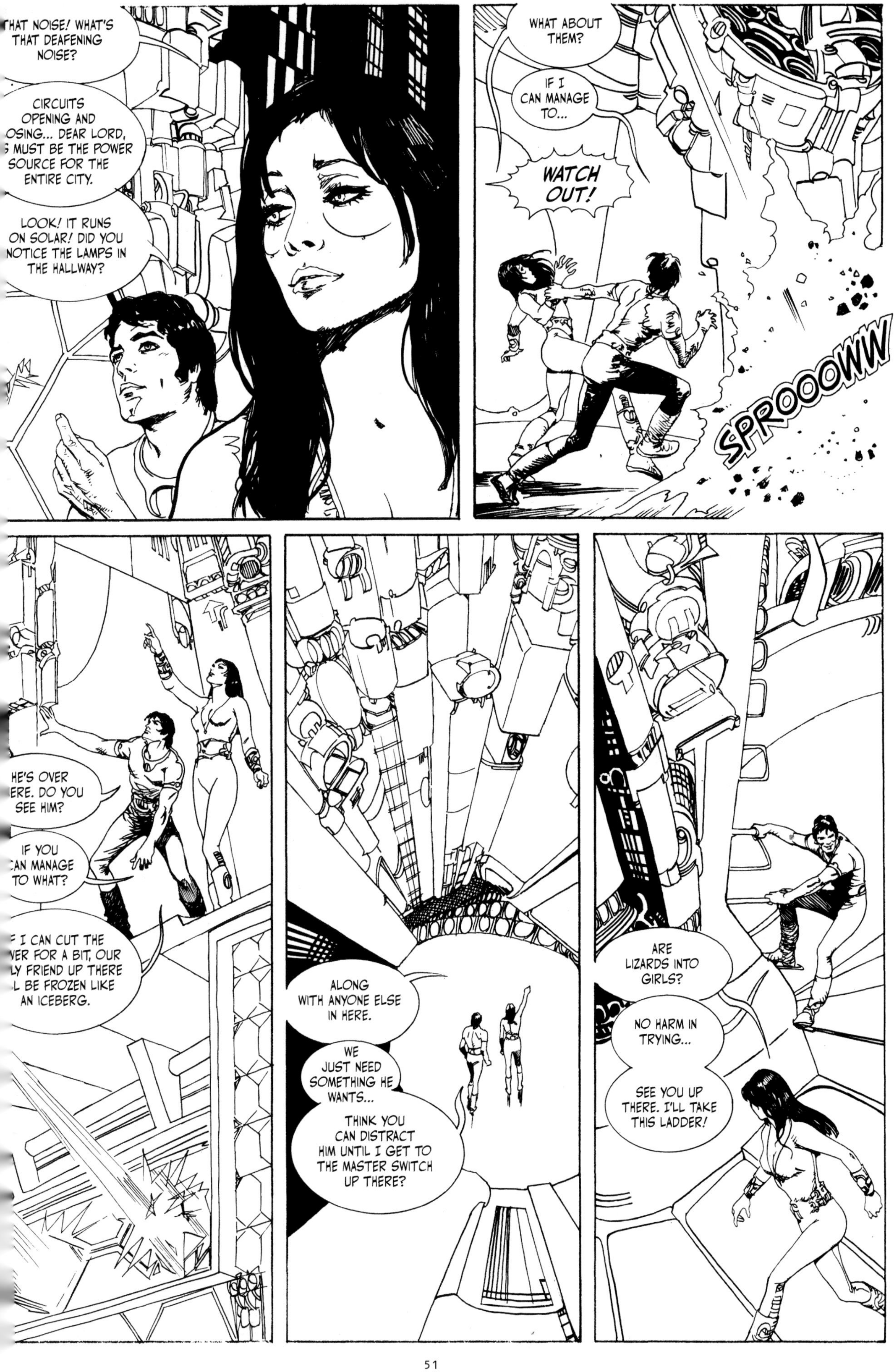

THAT NOISE! WHAT'S THAT DEAFENING NOISE?
CIRCUITS OPENING AND OSING... DEAR LORD, S MUST BE THE POWER SOURCE FOR THE ENTIRE CITY.
LOOK! IT RUNS ON SOLAR! DID YOU NOTICE THE LAMPS IN THE HALLWAY?
WHAT ABOUT THEM?
IF I CAN MANAGE TO...
WATCH OUT!
SPROOOWW
HE'S OVER ERE. DO YOU SEE HIM?
IF YOU CAN MANAGE TO WHAT?
F I CAN CUT THE WER FOR A BIT, OUR LY FRIEND UP THERE L BE FROZEN LIKE AN ICEBERG.
ALONG WITH ANYONE ELSE IN HERE.
WE JUST NEED SOMETHING HE WANTS...
THINK YOU CAN DISTRACT HIM UNTIL I GET TO THE MASTER SWITCH UP THERE?
ARE LIZARDS INTO GIRLS?
NO HARM IN TRYING...
SEE YOU UP THERE. I'LL TAKE THIS LADDER!

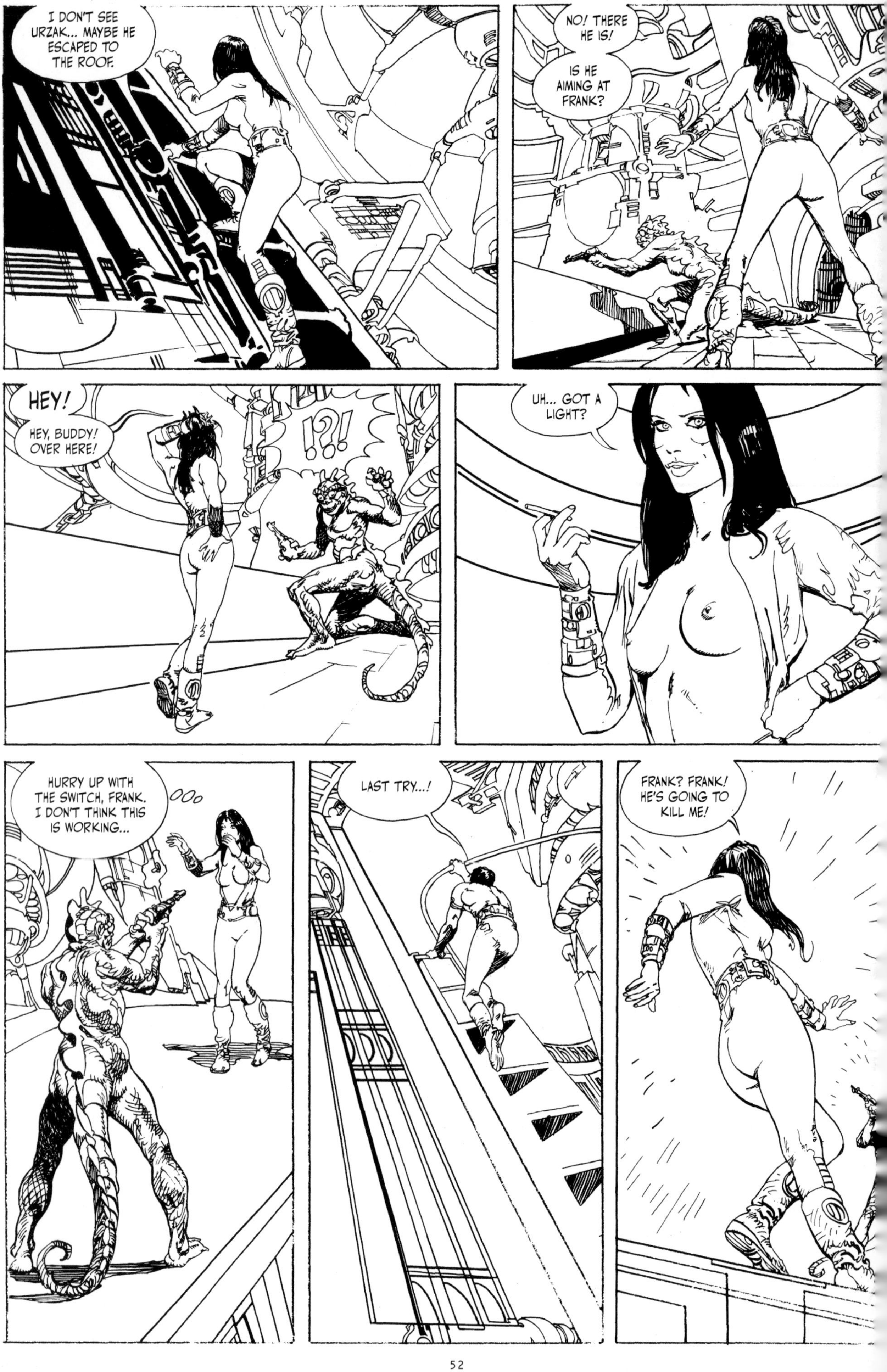
I DON'T SEE URZAK... MAYBE HE ESCAPED TO THE ROOF.
NO! THERE HE IS!
IS HE AIMING AT FRANK?
HEY!
HEY, BUDDY! OVER HERE!
!?!
UH... GOT A LIGHT?
HURRY UP WITH THE SWITCH, FRANK. I DON'T THINK THIS IS WORKING...
OOo
LAST TRY...!
FRANK? FRANK! HE'S GOING TO KILL ME!

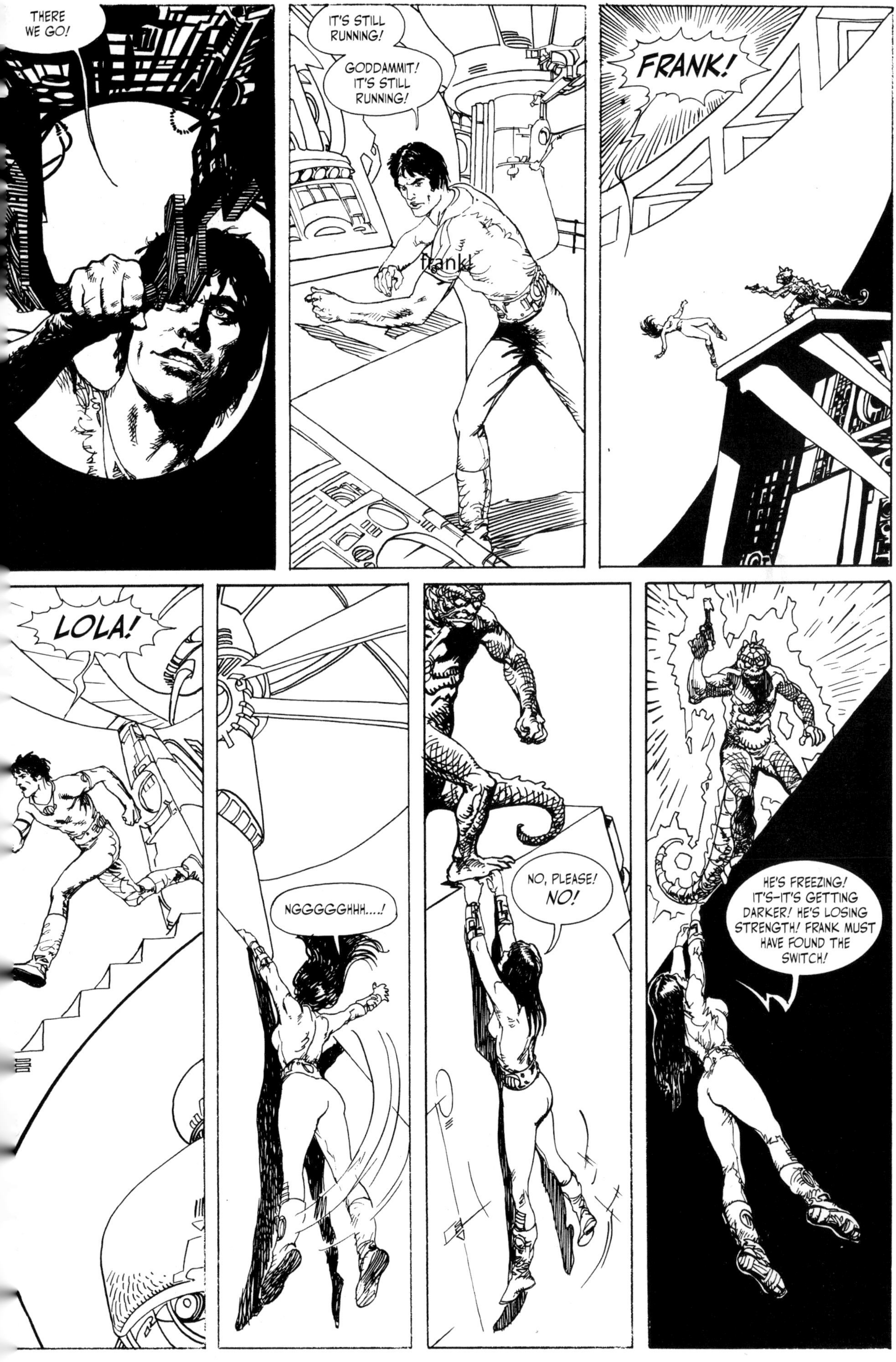
THERE WE GO!
IT'S STILL RUNNING!
GODDAMMIT! IT'S STILL RUNNING!
frank!
FRANK!
LOLA!
NGGGGGHHH....!
NO, PLEASE! NO!
HE'S FREEZING! IT'S–IT'S GETTING DARKER! HE'S LOSING STRENGTH! FRANK MUST HAVE FOUND THE SWITCH!

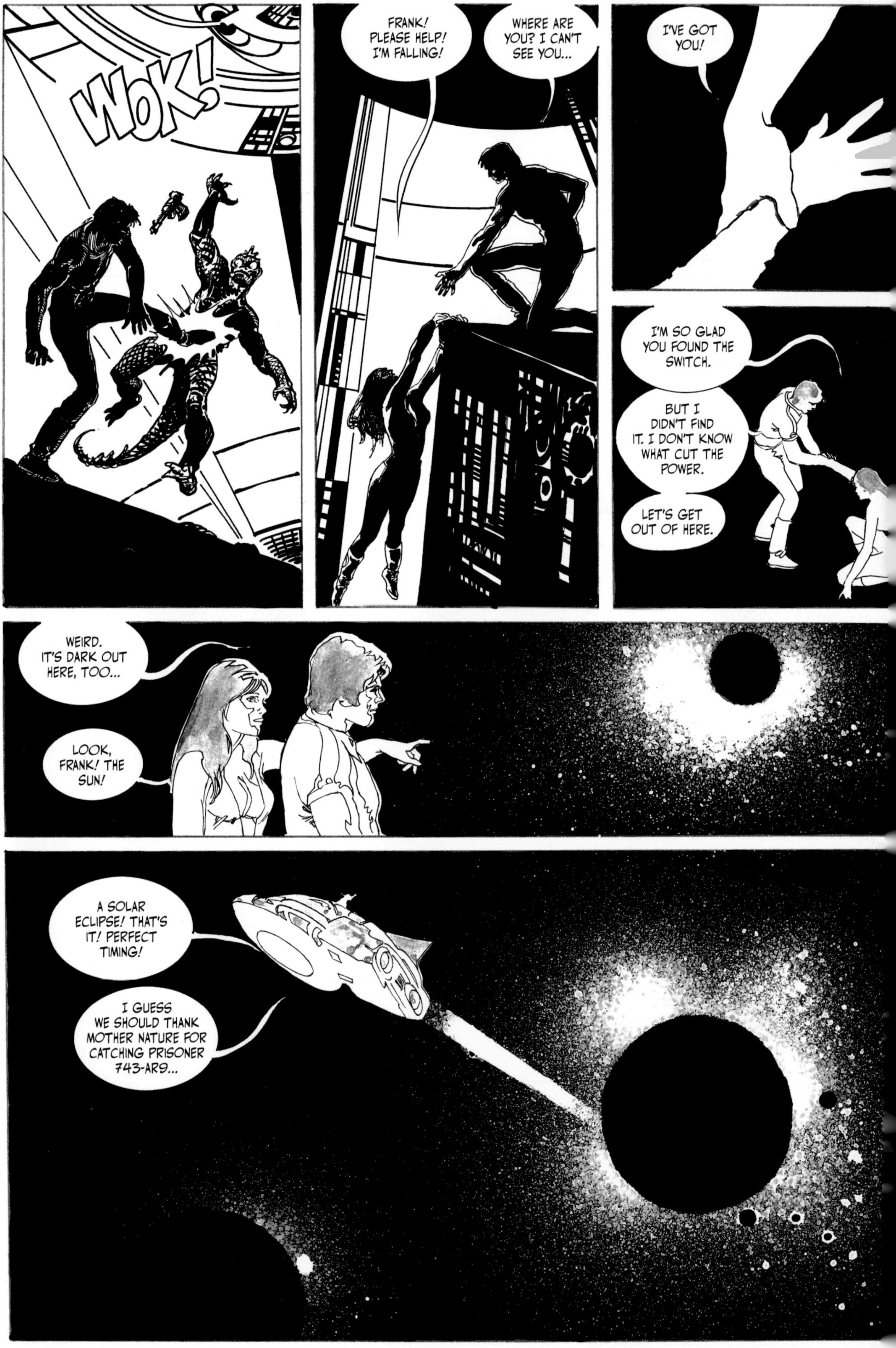
WOK!
FRANK! PLEASE HELP! I'M FALLING!
WHERE ARE YOU? I CAN'T SEE YOU...
I'VE GOT YOU!
I'M SO GLAD YOU FOUND THE SWITCH.
BUT I DIDN'T FIND IT. I DON'T KNOW WHAT CUT THE POWER.
LET'S GET OUT OF HERE.
WEIRD. IT'S DARK OUT HERE, TOO...
LOOK, FRANK! THE SUN!
A SOLAR ECLIPSE! THAT'S IT! PERFECT TIMING!
I GUESS WE SHOULD THANK MOTHER NATURE FOR CATCHING PRISONER 743-AR9...

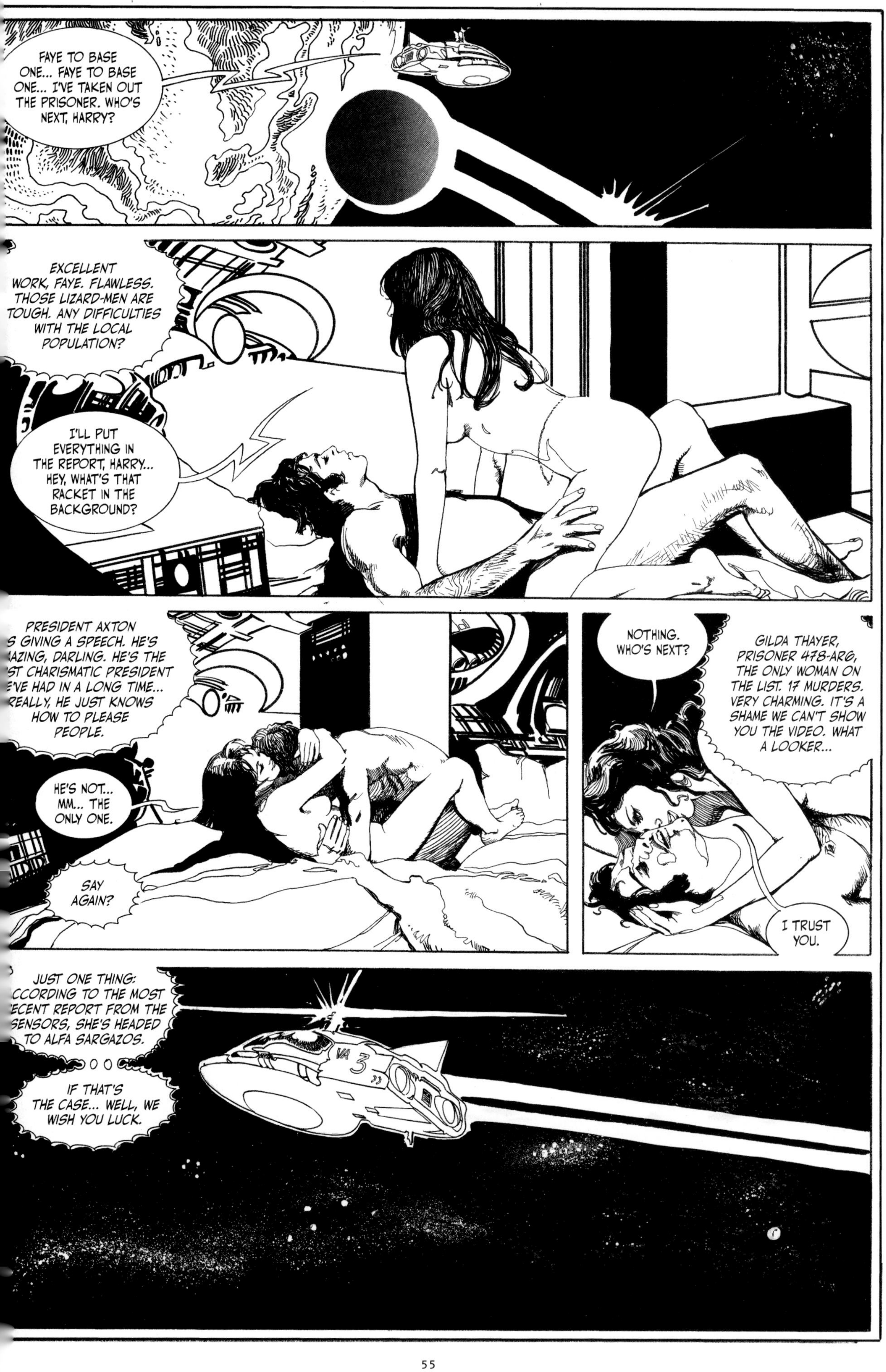
FAYE TO BASE ONE... FAYE TO BASE ONE... I'VE TAKEN OUT THE PRISONER. WHO'S NEXT, HARRY?
EXCELLENT WORK, FAYE. FLAWLESS. THOSE LIZARD-MEN ARE TOUGH. ANY DIFFICULTIES WITH THE LOCAL POPULATION?
I'LL PUT EVERYTHING IN THE REPORT, HARRY... HEY, WHAT'S THAT RACKET IN THE BACKGROUND?
PRESIDENT AXTON S GIVING A SPEECH. HE'S AZING, DARLING. HE'S THE ST CHARISMATIC PRESIDENT E'VE HAD IN A LONG TIME... REALLY, HE JUST KNOWS HOW TO PLEASE PEOPLE.
HE'S NOT... MM... THE ONLY ONE.
SAY AGAIN?
NOTHING. WHO'S NEXT?
GILDA THAYER, PRISONER 478-ARG, THE ONLY WOMAN ON THE LIST. 17 MURDERS. VERY CHARMING. IT'S A SHAME WE CAN'T SHOW YOU THE VIDEO. WHAT A LOOKER...
I TRUST YOU.
JUST ONE THING: CCORDING TO THE MOST ECENT REPORT FROM THE SENSORS, SHE'S HEADED TO ALFA SARGAZOS.
IF THAT'S THE CASE... WELL, WE WISH YOU LUCK.
VA 3

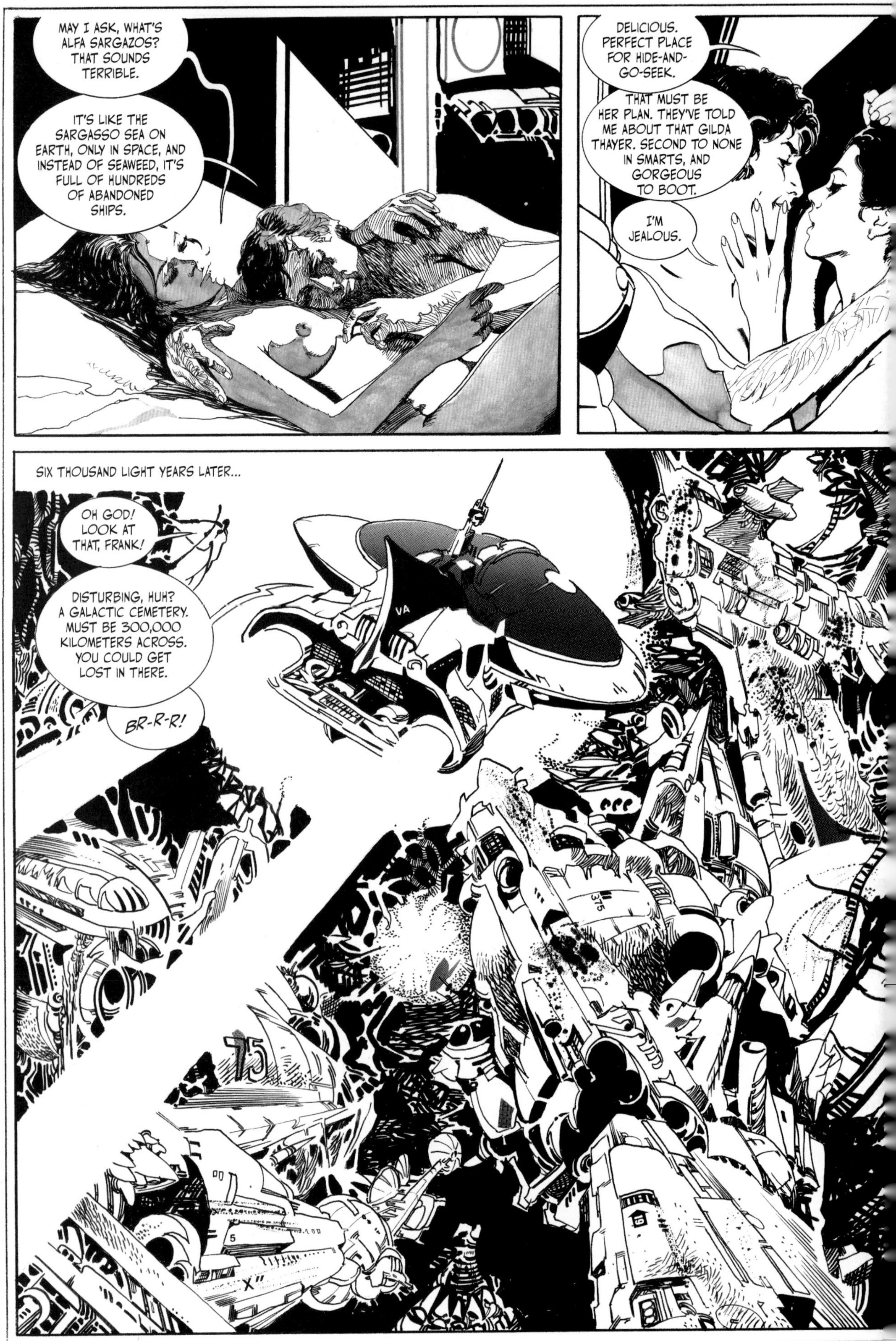
MAY I ASK, WHAT'S ALFA SARGAZOS? THAT SOUNDS TERRIBLE.
IT'S LIKE THE SARGASSO SEA ON EARTH, ONLY IN SPACE, AND INSTEAD OF SEAWEED, IT'S FULL OF HUNDREDS OF ABANDONED SHIPS.
DELICIOUS. PERFECT PLACE FOR HIDE-AND-GO-SEEK.
THAT MUST BE HER PLAN. THEY'VE TOLD ME ABOUT THAT GILDA THAYER. SECOND TO NONE IN SMARTS, AND GORGEOUS TO BOOT.
I'M JEALOUS.
SIX THOUSAND LIGHT YEARS LATER...
OH GOD! LOOK AT THAT, FRANK!
DISTURBING, HUH? A GALACTIC CEMETERY. MUST BE 300,000 KILOMETERS ACROSS. YOU COULD GET LOST IN THERE.
BR-R-R!

GOT ANYTHING FOR ME, HARRY?

NOTHING, FAYE. THOSE PILES OF SCRAP METAL ARE PARALYZING OUR SENSORS.

WAIT, WAIT, I THINK I SEE SOMETHING!

I'VE GOT IT! THAT'S HER SPACESHIP! ANY SIGNS OF LIFE, BASE ONE?

NOT INSIDE THE SHIP. BUT WE DETECTED SOMETHING ALIVE AT THE PERIMETER. GO INVESTIGATE.

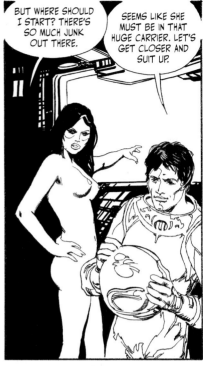

BUT WHERE SHOULD I START? THERE'S SO MUCH JUNK OUT THERE.

SEEMS LIKE SHE MUST BE IN THAT HUGE CARRIER. LET'S GET CLOSER AND SUIT UP.

WHY WOULD SHE DROP ANCHOR NEAR THAT PILE OF JUNK?

I'M SURE SHE'S DYING TO TELL US AS SOON AS WE GET IN.

HOLY SHIT!

ALL IT'S MISSING ARE BATS AND COBWEBS.

IT LOOKS ABANDONED, DON'T YOU THINK? BASE ONE SAYS THERE'S LIFE AROUND HERE SOMEWHERE...

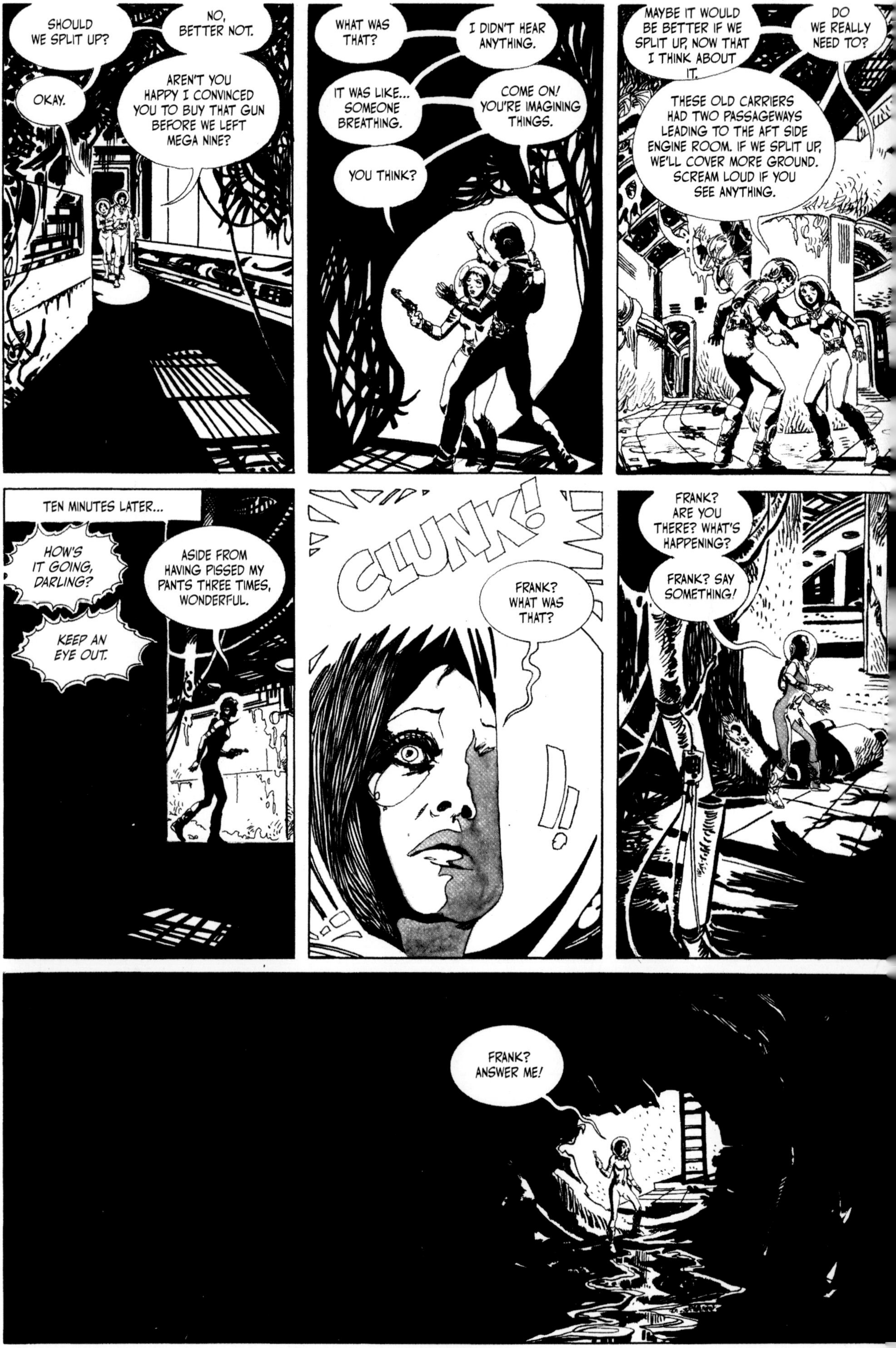
SHOULD WE SPLIT UP?
NO, BETTER NOT.
OKAY.
AREN'T YOU HAPPY I CONVINCED YOU TO BUY THAT GUN BEFORE WE LEFT MEGA NINE?
WHAT WAS THAT?
I DIDN'T HEAR ANYTHING.
IT WAS LIKE... SOMEONE BREATHING.
COME ON! YOU'RE IMAGINING THINGS.
YOU THINK?
MAYBE IT WOULD BE BETTER IF WE SPLIT UP, NOW THAT I THINK ABOUT IT.
DO WE REALLY NEED TO?
THESE OLD CARRIERS HAD TWO PASSAGEWAYS LEADING TO THE AFT SIDE ENGINE ROOM. IF WE SPLIT UP, WE'LL COVER MORE GROUND. SCREAM LOUD IF YOU SEE ANYTHING.
TEN MINUTES LATER...
HOW'S IT GOING, DARLING?
ASIDE FROM HAVING PISSED MY PANTS THREE TIMES, WONDERFUL.
KEEP AN EYE OUT.
CLUNK!
FRANK? WHAT WAS THAT?
FRANK? ARE YOU THERE? WHAT'S HAPPENING?
FRANK? SAY SOMETHING!
FRANK? ANSWER ME!

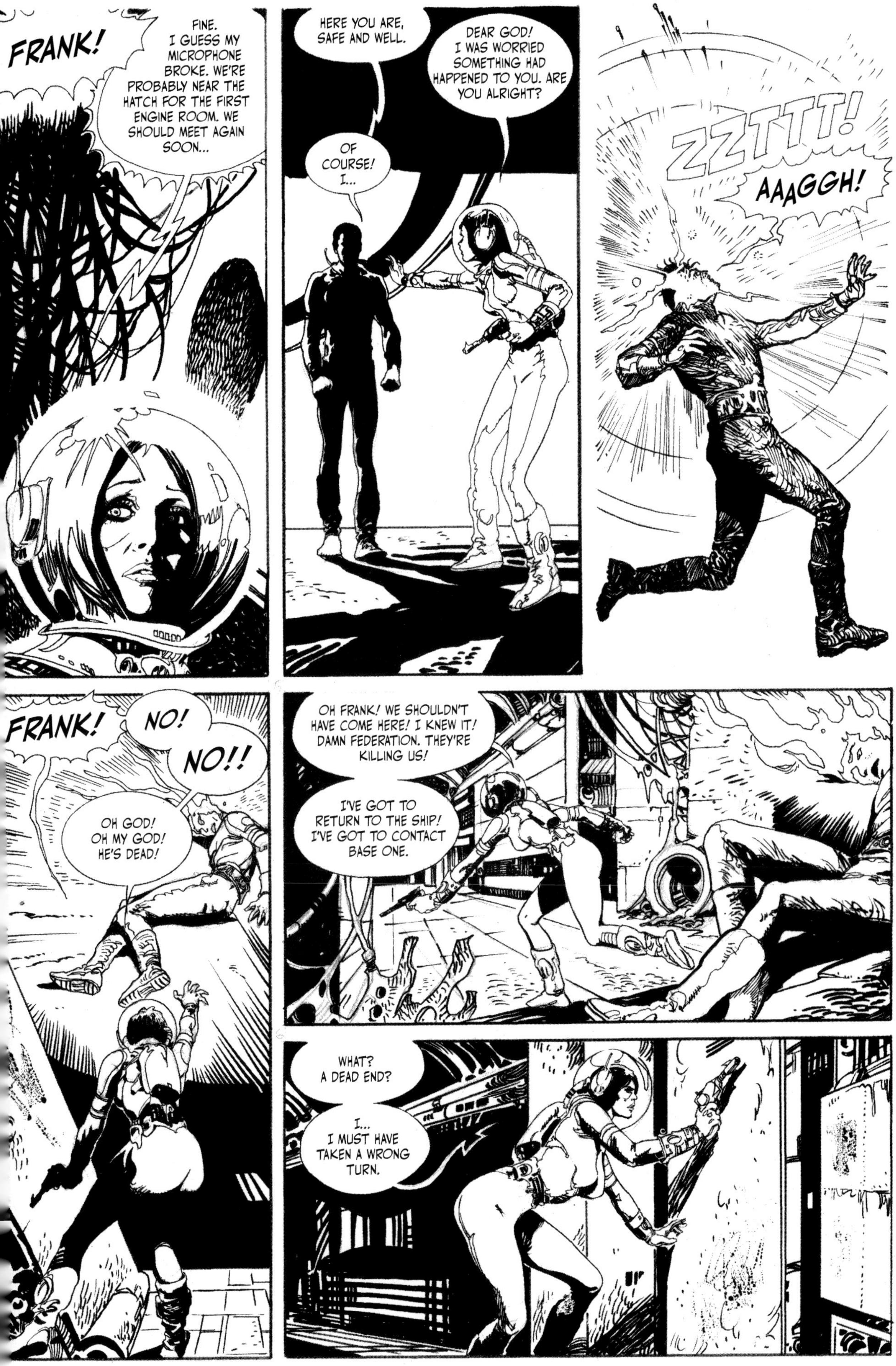
FRANK!
FINE. I GUESS MY MICROPHONE BROKE. WE'RE PROBABLY NEAR THE HATCH FOR THE FIRST ENGINE ROOM. WE SHOULD MEET AGAIN SOON...
HERE YOU ARE, SAFE AND WELL.
DEAR GOD! I WAS WORRIED SOMETHING HAD HAPPENED TO YOU. ARE YOU ALRIGHT?
OF COURSE! I...
ZZTTTT!
AAAGGH!
FRANK!
NO!
NO!!
OH GOD! OH MY GOD! HE'S DEAD!
OH FRANK! WE SHOULDN'T HAVE COME HERE! I KNEW IT! DAMN FEDERATION. THEY'RE KILLING US!
I'VE GOT TO RETURN TO THE SHIP! I'VE GOT TO CONTACT BASE ONE.
WHAT? A DEAD END?
I... I MUST HAVE TAKEN A WRONG TURN.

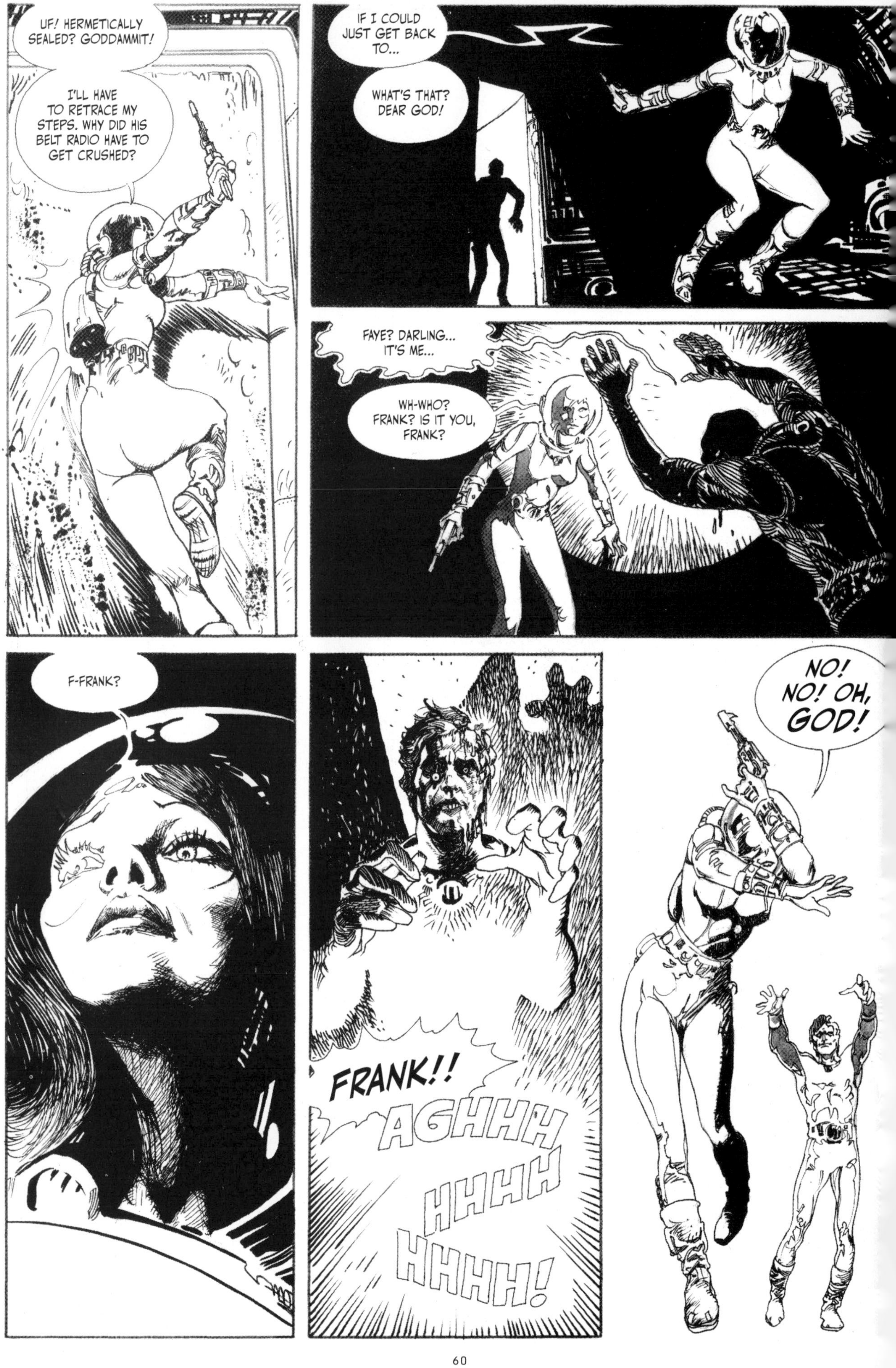
UF! HERMETICALLY SEALED? GODDAMMIT!
I'LL HAVE TO RETRACE MY STEPS. WHY DID HIS BELT RADIO HAVE TO GET CRUSHED?
IF I COULD JUST GET BACK TO...
WHAT'S THAT? DEAR GOD!
FAYE? DARLING... IT'S ME...
WH-WHO? FRANK? IS IT YOU, FRANK?
F-FRANK?
FRANK!!
AGHHHHHHHHHHHH!
NO! NO! OH, GOD!

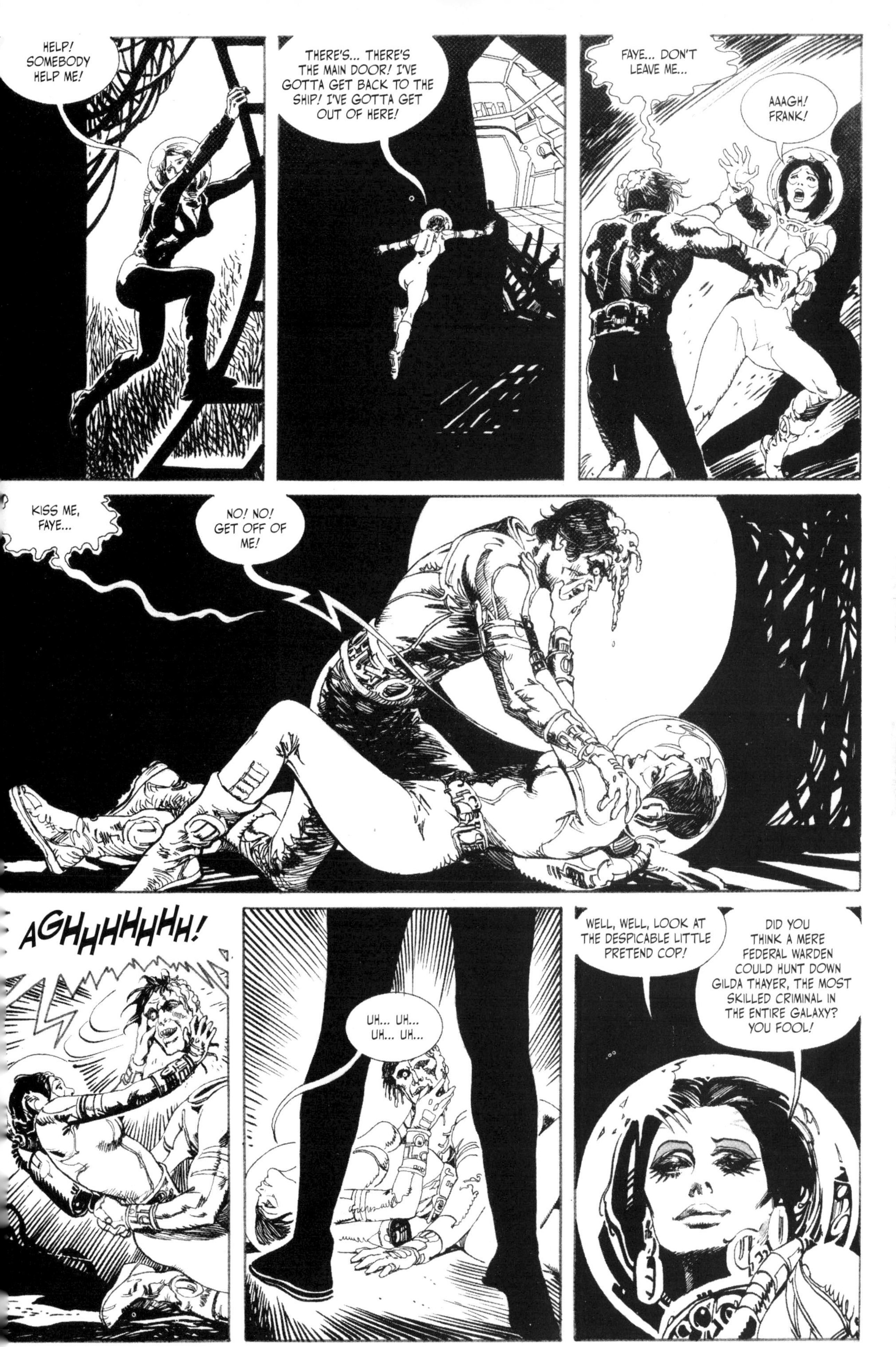
HELP! SOMEBODY HELP ME!
THERE'S... THERE'S THE MAIN DOOR! I'VE GOTTA GET BACK TO THE SHIP! I'VE GOTTA GET OUT OF HERE!
FAYE... DON'T LEAVE ME...
AAAGH! FRANK!
KISS ME, FAYE...
NO! NO! GET OFF OF ME!
AGHHHHHHH!
UH... UH... UH... UH...
WELL, WELL, LOOK AT THE DESPICABLE LITTLE PRETEND COP!
DID YOU THINK A MERE FEDERAL WARDEN COULD HUNT DOWN GILDA THAYER, THE MOST SKILLED CRIMINAL IN THE ENTIRE GALAXY? YOU FOOL!

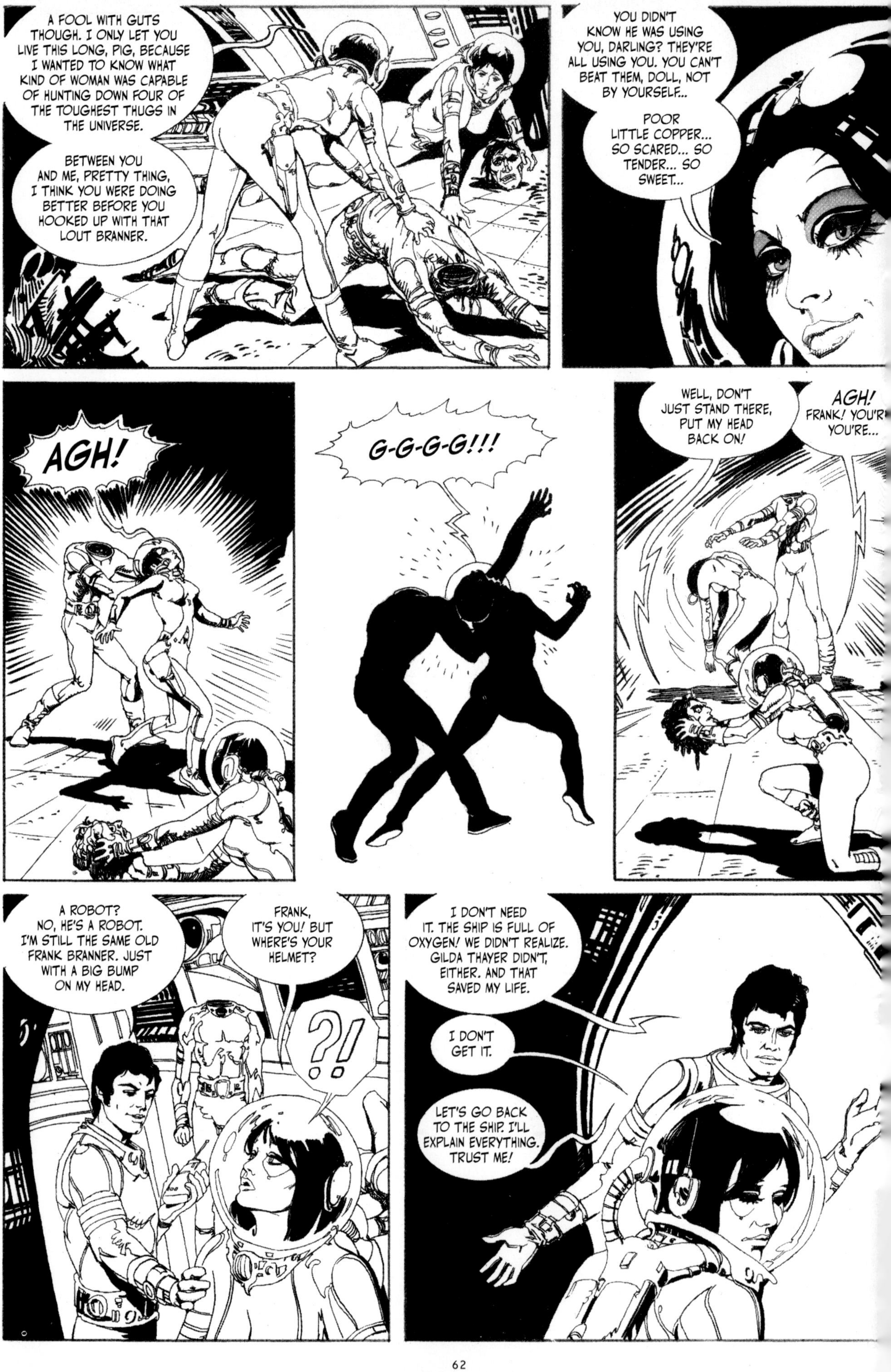
A FOOL WITH GUTS THOUGH. I ONLY LET YOU LIVE THIS LONG, PIG, BECAUSE I WANTED TO KNOW WHAT KIND OF WOMAN WAS CAPABLE OF HUNTING DOWN FOUR OF THE TOUGHEST THUGS IN THE UNIVERSE.
BETWEEN YOU AND ME, PRETTY THING, I THINK YOU WERE DOING BETTER BEFORE YOU HOOKED UP WITH THAT LOUT BRANNER.
YOU DIDN'T KNOW HE WAS USING YOU, DARLING? THEY'RE ALL USING YOU. YOU CAN'T BEAT THEM, DOLL, NOT BY YOURSELF...
POOR LITTLE COPPER... SO SCARED... SO TENDER... SO SWEET...
AGH!
G-G-G-G!!!
WELL, DON'T JUST STAND THERE, PUT MY HEAD BACK ON!
AGH! FRANK! YOU'R YOU'RE...
A ROBOT? NO, HE'S A ROBOT. I'M STILL THE SAME OLD FRANK BRANNER. JUST WITH A BIG BUMP ON MY HEAD.
FRANK, IT'S YOU! BUT WHERE'S YOUR HELMET?
?!
I DON'T NEED IT. THE SHIP IS FULL OF OXYGEN! WE DIDN'T REALIZE. GILDA THAYER DIDN'T, EITHER. AND THAT SAVED MY LIFE.
I DON'T GET IT.
LET'S GO BACK TO THE SHIP. I'LL EXPLAIN EVERYTHING. TRUST ME!

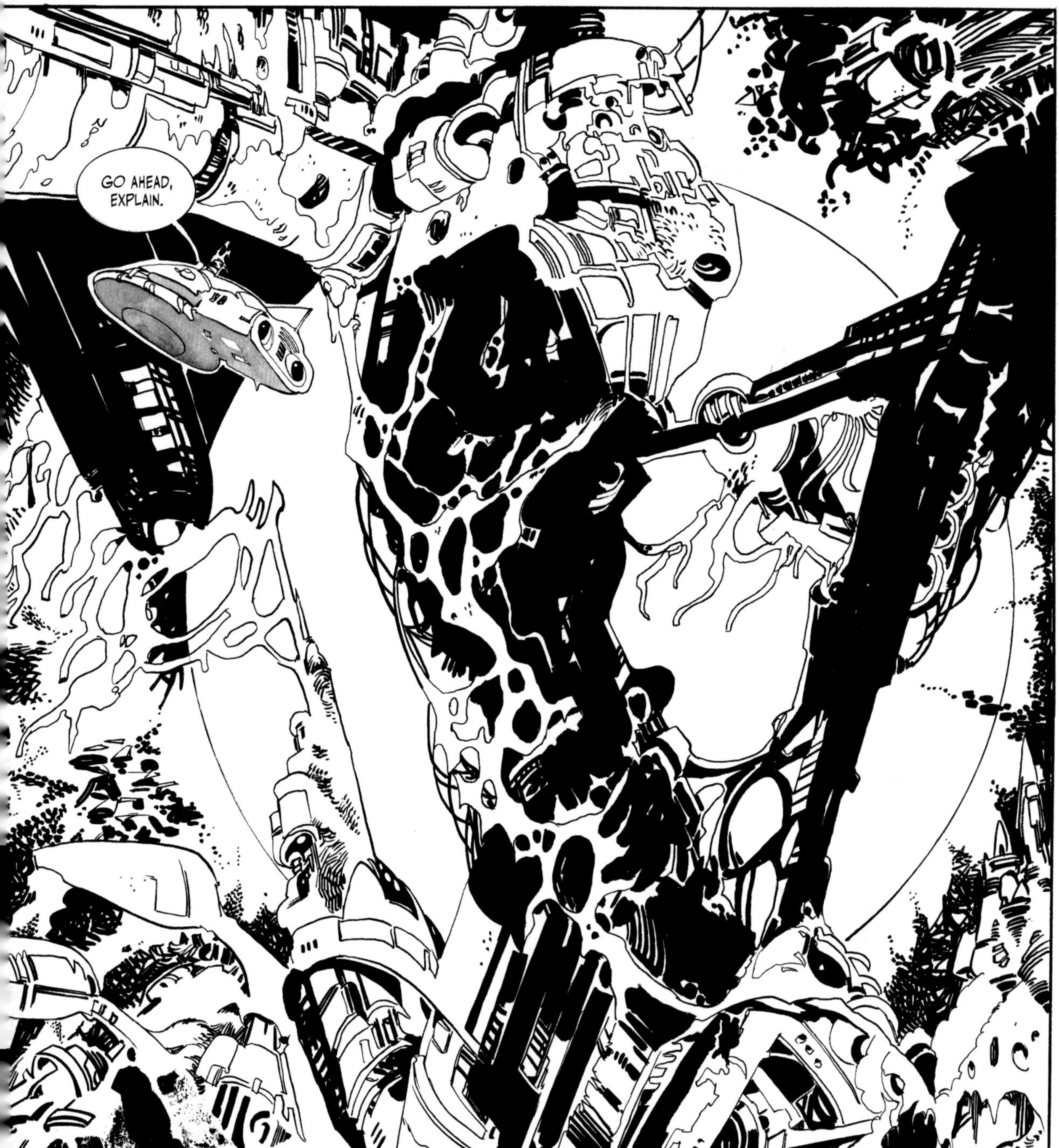
GO AHEAD, EXPLAIN.

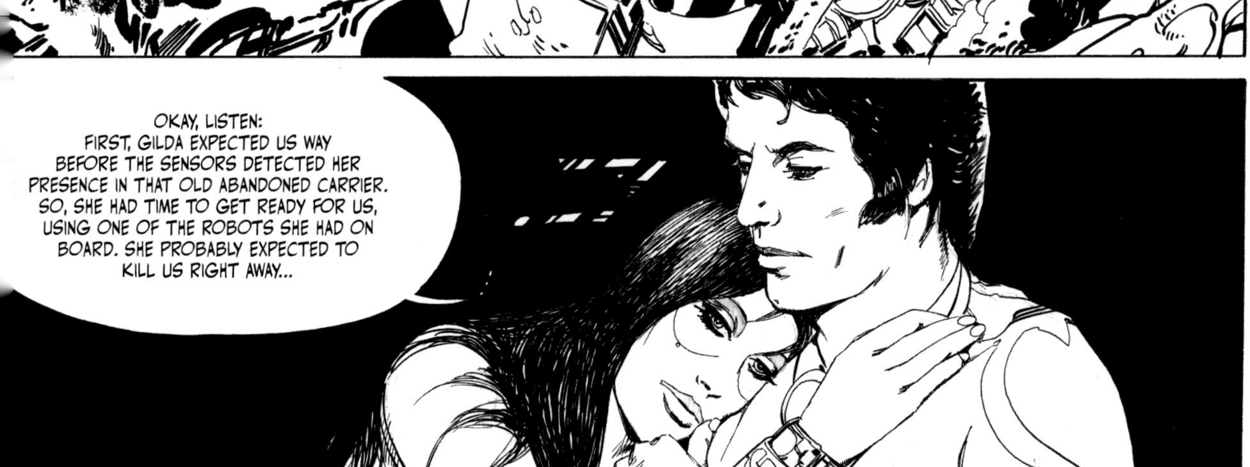
OKAY, LISTEN: FIRST, GILDA EXPECTED US WAY BEFORE THE SENSORS DETECTED HER PRESENCE IN THAT OLD ABANDONED CARRIER. SO, SHE HAD TIME TO GET READY FOR US, USING ONE OF THE ROBOTS SHE HAD ON BOARD. SHE PROBABLY EXPECTED TO KILL US RIGHT AWAY...

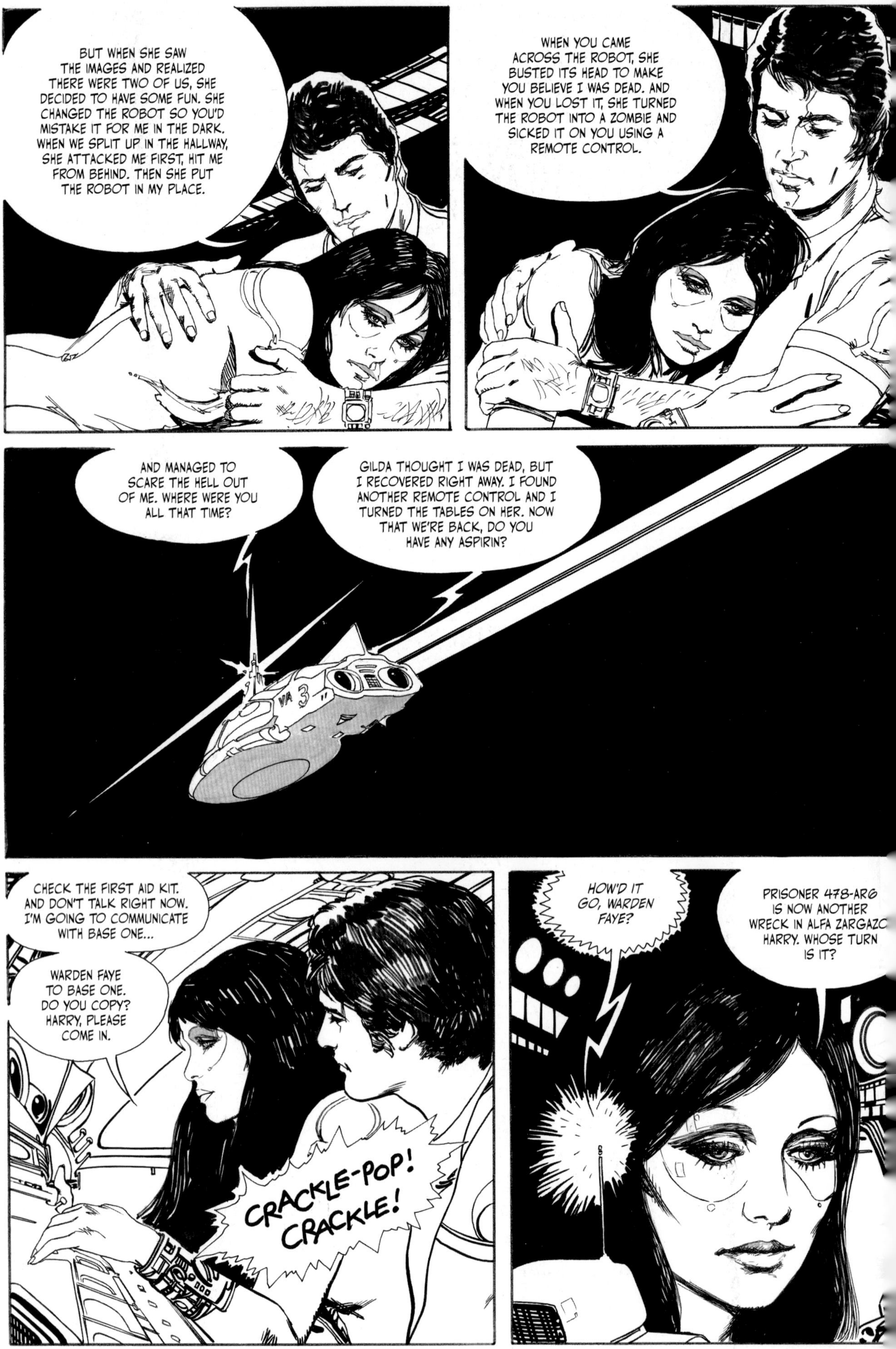
BUT WHEN SHE SAW THE IMAGES AND REALIZED THERE WERE TWO OF US, SHE DECIDED TO HAVE SOME FUN. SHE CHANGED THE ROBOT SO YOU'D MISTAKE IT FOR ME IN THE DARK. WHEN WE SPLIT UP IN THE HALLWAY, SHE ATTACKED ME FIRST, HIT ME FROM BEHIND. THEN SHE PUT THE ROBOT IN MY PLACE.
WHEN YOU CAME ACROSS THE ROBOT, SHE BUSTED ITS HEAD TO MAKE YOU BELIEVE I WAS DEAD. AND WHEN YOU LOST IT, SHE TURNED THE ROBOT INTO A ZOMBIE AND SICKED IT ON YOU USING A REMOTE CONTROL.
AND MANAGED TO SCARE THE HELL OUT OF ME. WHERE WERE YOU ALL THAT TIME?
GILDA THOUGHT I WAS DEAD, BUT I RECOVERED RIGHT AWAY. I FOUND ANOTHER REMOTE CONTROL AND I TURNED THE TABLES ON HER. NOW THAT WE'RE BACK, DO YOU HAVE ANY ASPIRIN?
VA 3
CHECK THE FIRST AID KIT. AND DON'T TALK RIGHT NOW. I'M GOING TO COMMUNICATE WITH BASE ONE...
WARDEN FAYE TO BASE ONE. DO YOU COPY? HARRY, PLEASE COME IN.
CRACKLE-POP! CRACKLE!
HOW'D IT GO, WARDEN FAYE?
PRISONER 478-ARG IS NOW ANOTHER WRECK IN ALFA ZARGAZO HARRY. WHOSE TURN IS IT?

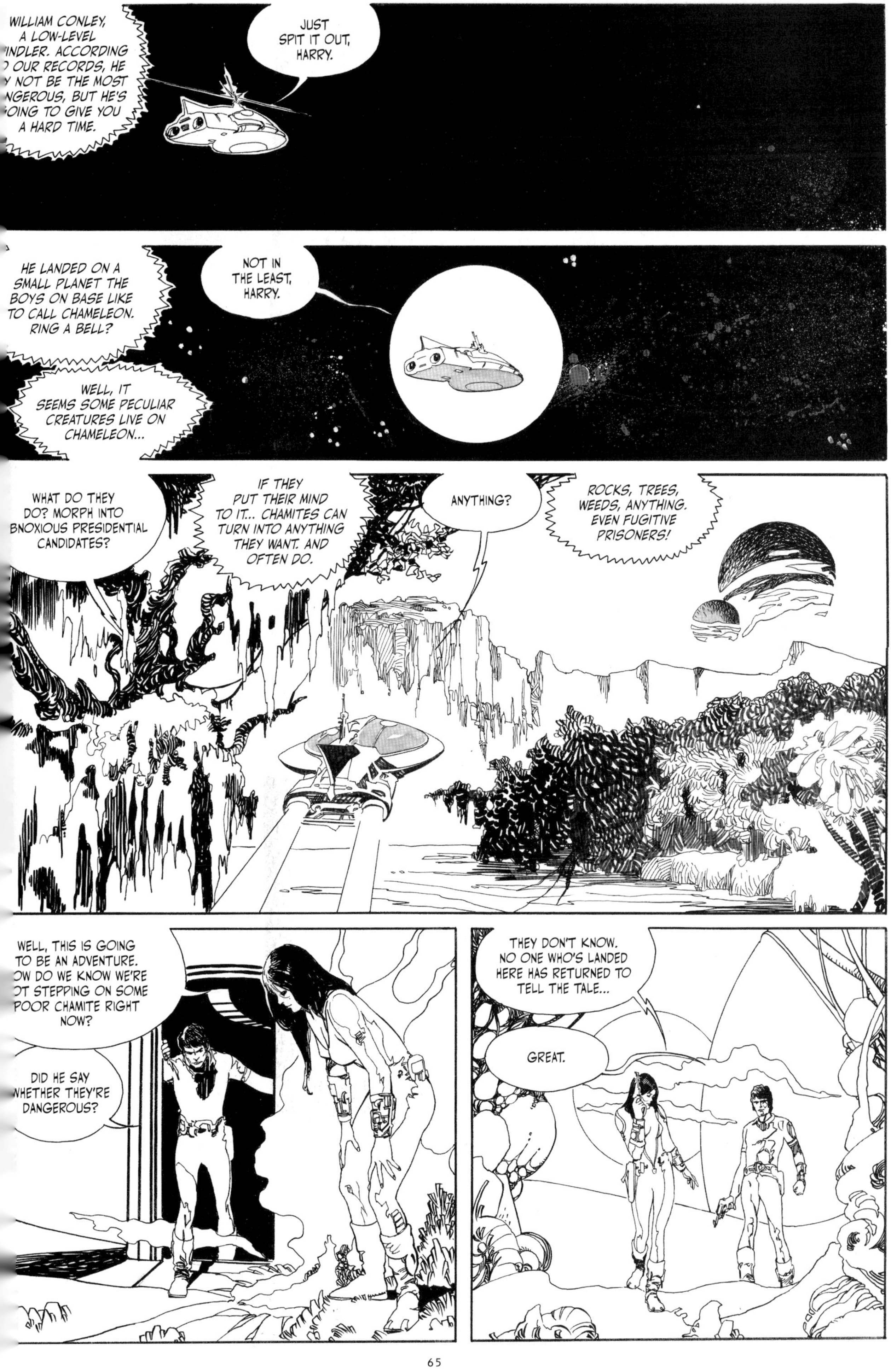
WILLIAM CONLEY, A LOW-LEVEL INDLER. ACCORDING O OUR RECORDS, HE NOT BE THE MOST NGEROUS, BUT HE'S OING TO GIVE YOU A HARD TIME.
JUST SPIT IT OUT, HARRY.
HE LANDED ON A SMALL PLANET THE BOYS ON BASE LIKE TO CALL CHAMELEON. RING A BELL?
NOT IN THE LEAST, HARRY.
WELL, IT SEEMS SOME PECULIAR CREATURES LIVE ON CHAMELEON...
WHAT DO THEY DO? MORPH INTO BNOXIOUS PRESIDENTIAL CANDIDATES?
IF THEY PUT THEIR MIND TO IT... CHAMITES CAN TURN INTO ANYTHING THEY WANT. AND OFTEN DO.
ANYTHING?
ROCKS, TREES, WEEDS, ANYTHING. EVEN FUGITIVE PRISONERS!
WELL, THIS IS GOING TO BE AN ADVENTURE. OW DO WE KNOW WE'RE OT STEPPING ON SOME POOR CHAMITE RIGHT NOW?
DID HE SAY WHETHER THEY'RE DANGEROUS?
THEY DON'T KNOW. NO ONE WHO'S LANDED HERE HAS RETURNED TO TELL THE TALE...
GREAT.

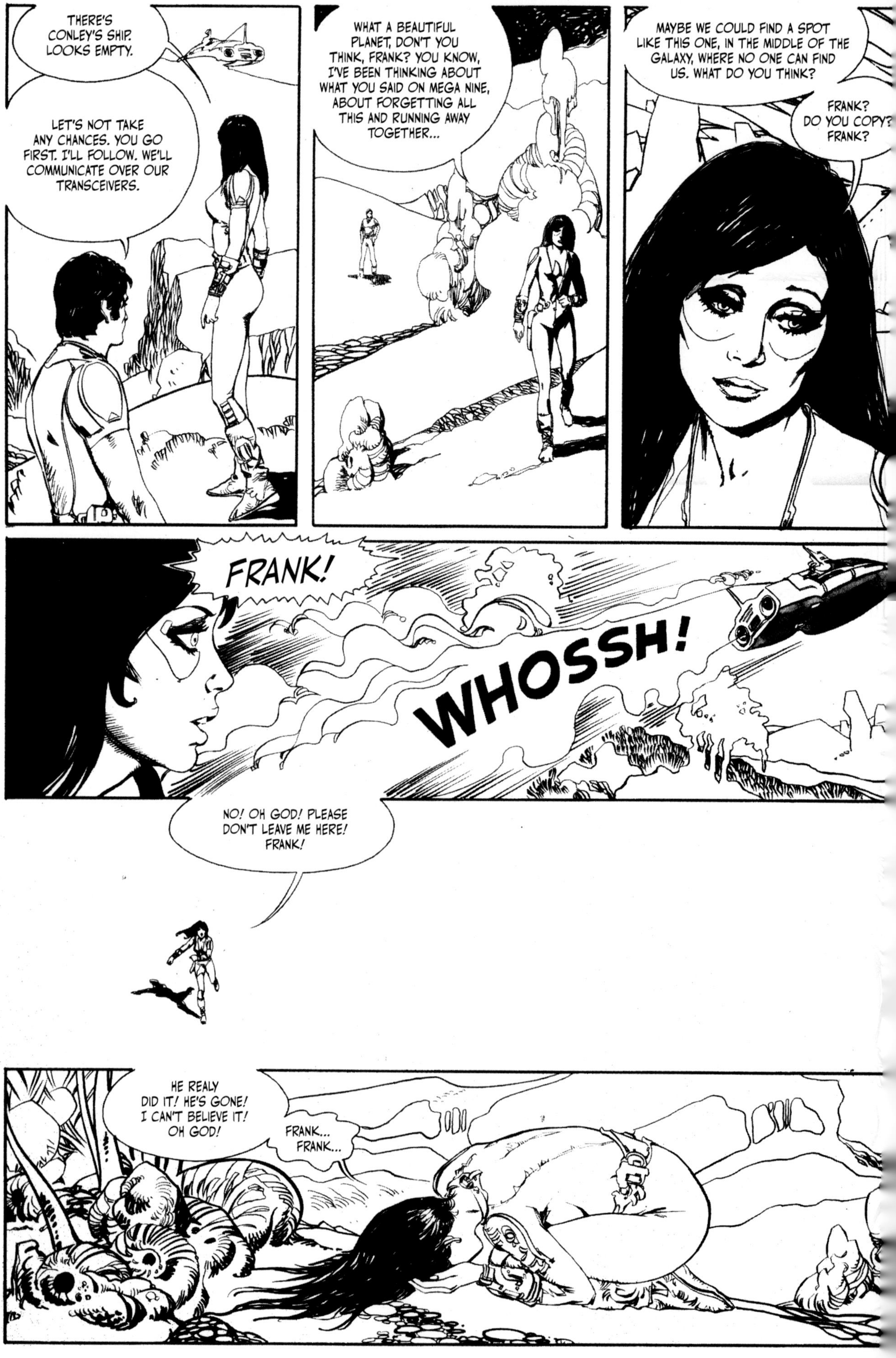
THERE'S CONLEY'S SHIP. LOOKS EMPTY.
LET'S NOT TAKE ANY CHANCES. YOU GO FIRST. I'LL FOLLOW. WE'LL COMMUNICATE OVER OUR TRANSCEIVERS.
WHAT A BEAUTIFUL PLANET, DON'T YOU THINK, FRANK? YOU KNOW, I'VE BEEN THINKING ABOUT WHAT YOU SAID ON MEGA NINE, ABOUT FORGETTING ALL THIS AND RUNNING AWAY TOGETHER...
MAYBE WE COULD FIND A SPOT LIKE THIS ONE, IN THE MIDDLE OF THE GALAXY, WHERE NO ONE CAN FIND US. WHAT DO YOU THINK?
FRANK? DO YOU COPY? FRANK?
FRANK!
WHOSSH!
NO! OH GOD! PLEASE DON'T LEAVE ME HERE! FRANK!
HE REALY DID IT! HE'S GONE! I CAN'T BELIEVE IT! OH GOD!
FRANK... FRANK...

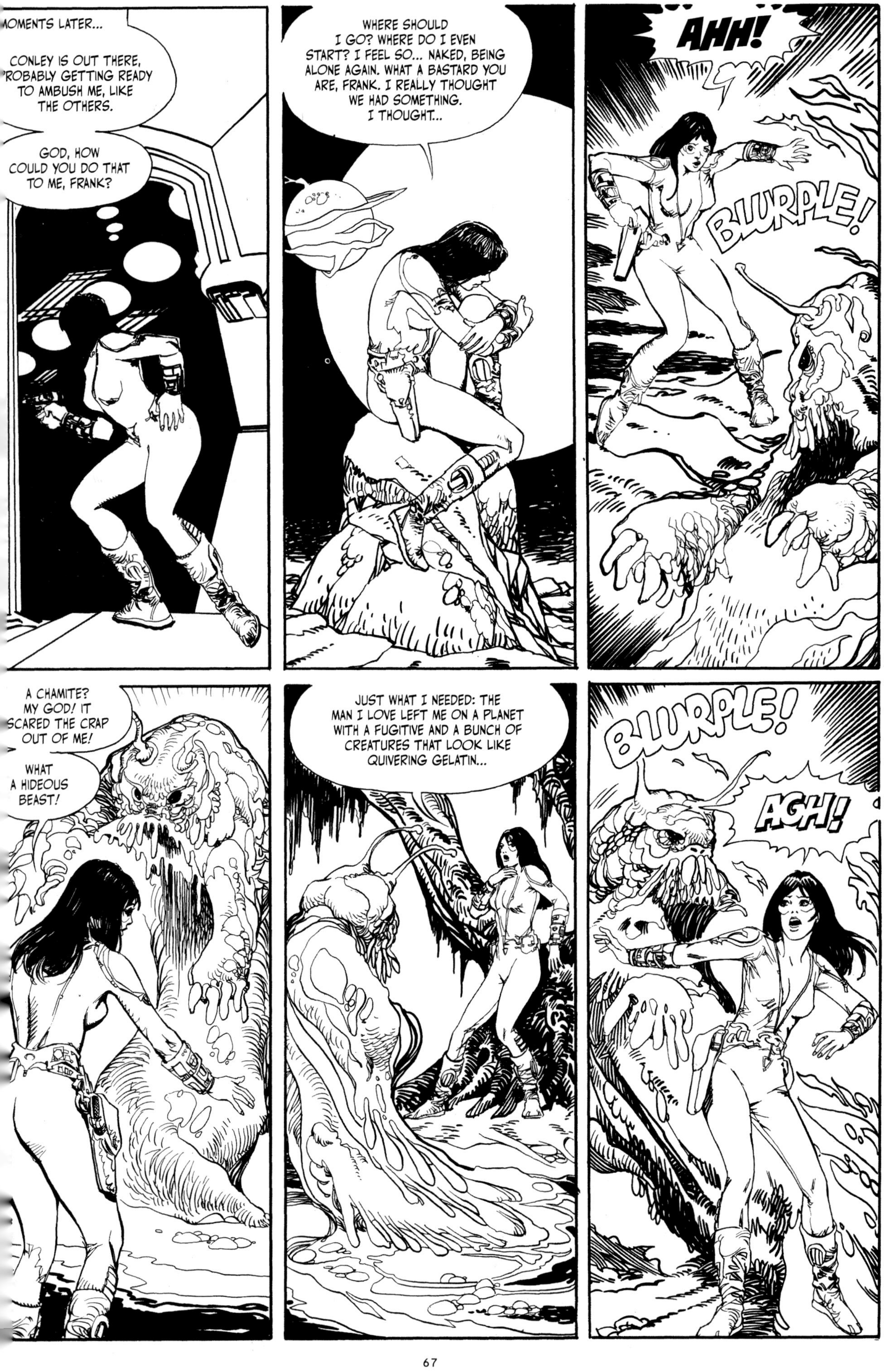
MOMENTS LATER...
CONLEY IS OUT THERE, PROBABLY GETTING READY TO AMBUSH ME, LIKE THE OTHERS.
GOD, HOW COULD YOU DO THAT TO ME, FRANK?
WHERE SHOULD I GO? WHERE DO I EVEN START? I FEEL SO... NAKED, BEING ALONE AGAIN. WHAT A BASTARD YOU ARE, FRANK. I REALLY THOUGHT WE HAD SOMETHING. I THOUGHT...
AHH!
BLURPLE!
A CHAMITE? MY GOD! IT SCARED THE CRAP OUT OF ME!
WHAT A HIDEOUS BEAST!
JUST WHAT I NEEDED: THE MAN I LOVE LEFT ME ON A PLANET WITH A FUGITIVE AND A BUNCH OF CREATURES THAT LOOK LIKE QUIVERING GELATIN...
BLURPLE!
AGH!

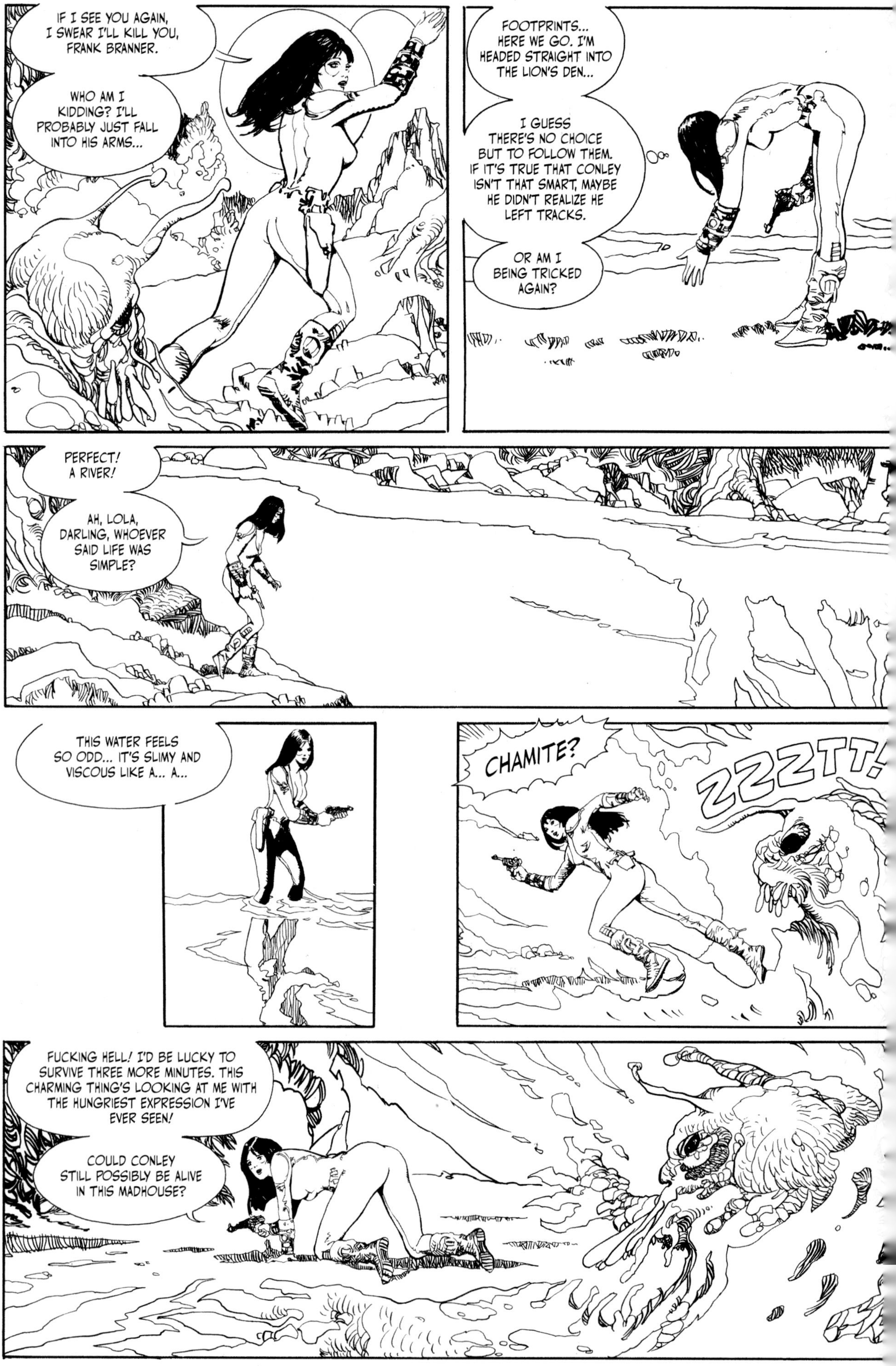
IF I SEE YOU AGAIN, I SWEAR I'LL KILL YOU, FRANK BRANNER.
WHO AM I KIDDING? I'LL PROBABLY JUST FALL INTO HIS ARMS...
FOOTPRINTS... HERE WE GO. I'M HEADED STRAIGHT INTO THE LION'S DEN...
I GUESS THERE'S NO CHOICE BUT TO FOLLOW THEM. IF IT'S TRUE THAT CONLEY ISN'T THAT SMART, MAYBE HE DIDN'T REALIZE HE LEFT TRACKS.
OR AM I BEING TRICKED AGAIN?
PERFECT! A RIVER!
AH, LOLA, DARLING, WHOEVER SAID LIFE WAS SIMPLE?
THIS WATER FEELS SO ODD... IT'S SLIMY AND VISCOUS LIKE A... A...
CHAMITE?
ZZZTT!
FUCKING HELL! I'D BE LUCKY TO SURVIVE THREE MORE MINUTES. THIS CHARMING THING'S LOOKING AT ME WITH THE HUNGRIEST EXPRESSION I'VE EVER SEEN!
COULD CONLEY STILL POSSIBLY BE ALIVE IN THIS MADHOUSE?

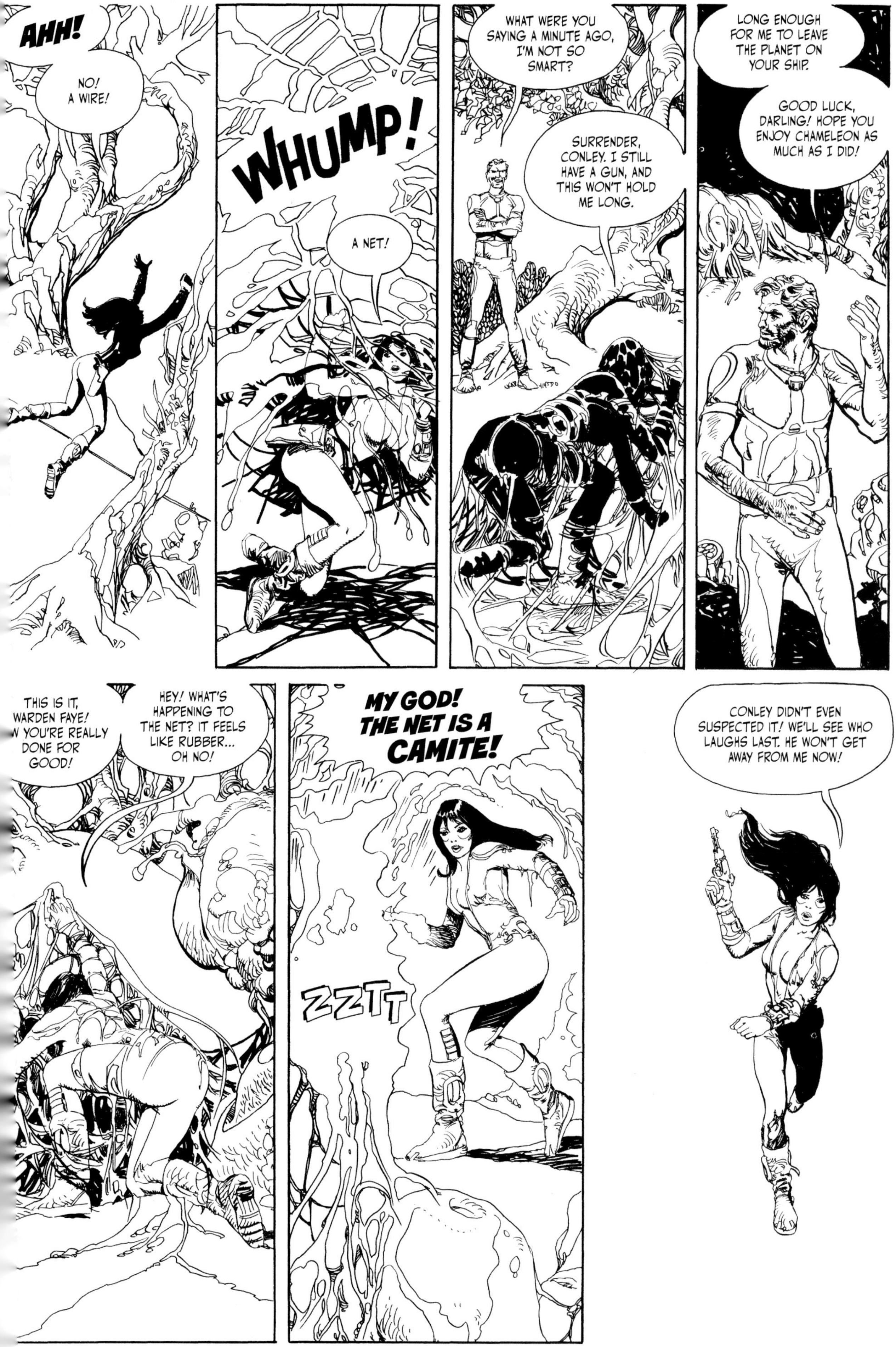
AHH!
NO! A WIRE!
WHUMP!
A NET!
WHAT WERE YOU SAYING A MINUTE AGO, I'M NOT SO SMART?
SURRENDER, CONLEY. I STILL HAVE A GUN, AND THIS WON'T HOLD ME LONG.
LONG ENOUGH FOR ME TO LEAVE THE PLANET ON YOUR SHIP.
GOOD LUCK, DARLING! HOPE YOU ENJOY CHAMELEON AS MUCH AS I DID!
THIS IS IT, WARDEN FAYE! W YOU'RE REALLY DONE FOR GOOD!
HEY! WHAT'S HAPPENING TO THE NET? IT FEELS LIKE RUBBER... OH NO!
MY GOD! THE NET IS A CAMITE!
ZZTT
CONLEY DIDN'T EVEN SUSPECTED IT! WE'LL SEE WHO LAUGHS LAST. HE WON'T GET AWAY FROM ME NOW!

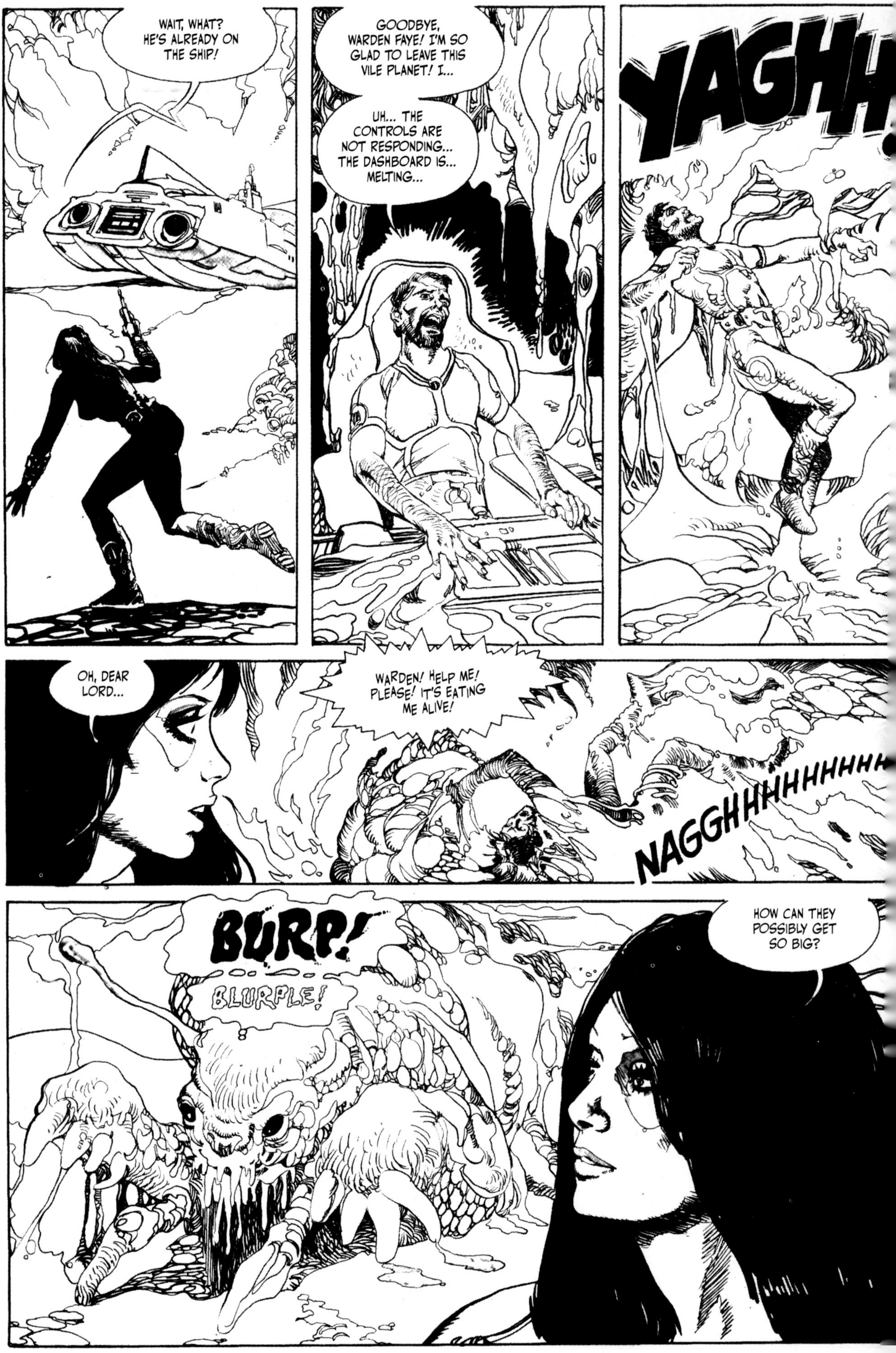
WAIT, WHAT? HE'S ALREADY ON THE SHIP!
GOODBYE, WARDEN FAYE! I'M SO GLAD TO LEAVE THIS VILE PLANET! I...
UH... THE CONTROLS ARE NOT RESPONDING... THE DASHBOARD IS... MELTING...
YAGHH
OH, DEAR LORD...
WARDEN! HELP ME! PLEASE! IT'S EATING ME ALIVE!
NAGGHHHHHHHHH
BURP!
BLURPLE!
HOW CAN THEY POSSIBLY GET SO BIG?

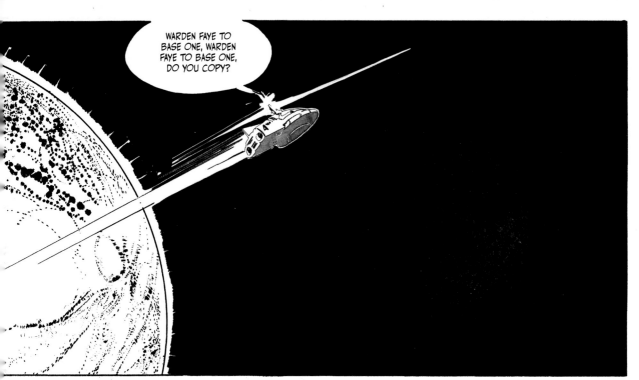

WARDEN FAYE TO BASE ONE, WARDEN FAYE TO BASE ONE, DO YOU COPY?

BASE ONE HERE. FAYE, HOW DID IT GO ON CHAMELEON?

PRISONER CONLEY IS DEAD AND... UM, BURIED. WHO'S NEXT?

OUR INSTRUMENTS DETECT AN ABANDONED SHIP ON THE PLANET. ARE YOU SURE YOU KILLED CONLEY?

BRANNER! THEY'VE REGISTERED HIS PRESENCE!

UH... YES, BASE ONE. CONLEY IS DEAD. MAYBE... YOUR SENSORS ARE FAULTY.

WE'LL DOUBLE CHECK. IN THE MEANTIME, HERE'S YOUR NEXT TARGET: HIS NAME IS STEVEN LUMIS, WANTED IN SIX SOLAR SYSTEMS FOR FOUR HOMICIDES. WE'VE TRACED HIS SHIP. IT'S HEADED TO A SMALL PLANETOID IN THE VEGA-RHAN REGION... BUT THERE'S ONE PROBLEM.

AS USUAL. WHAT IS IT THIS TIME?

THERE AREN'T SUPPOSED TO BE PLANETOIDS IN THE VEGA-RHAN REGION! NO ONE KNEW OF THIS ONE UNTIL LUMIS LANDED THERE. BE CAREFUL!

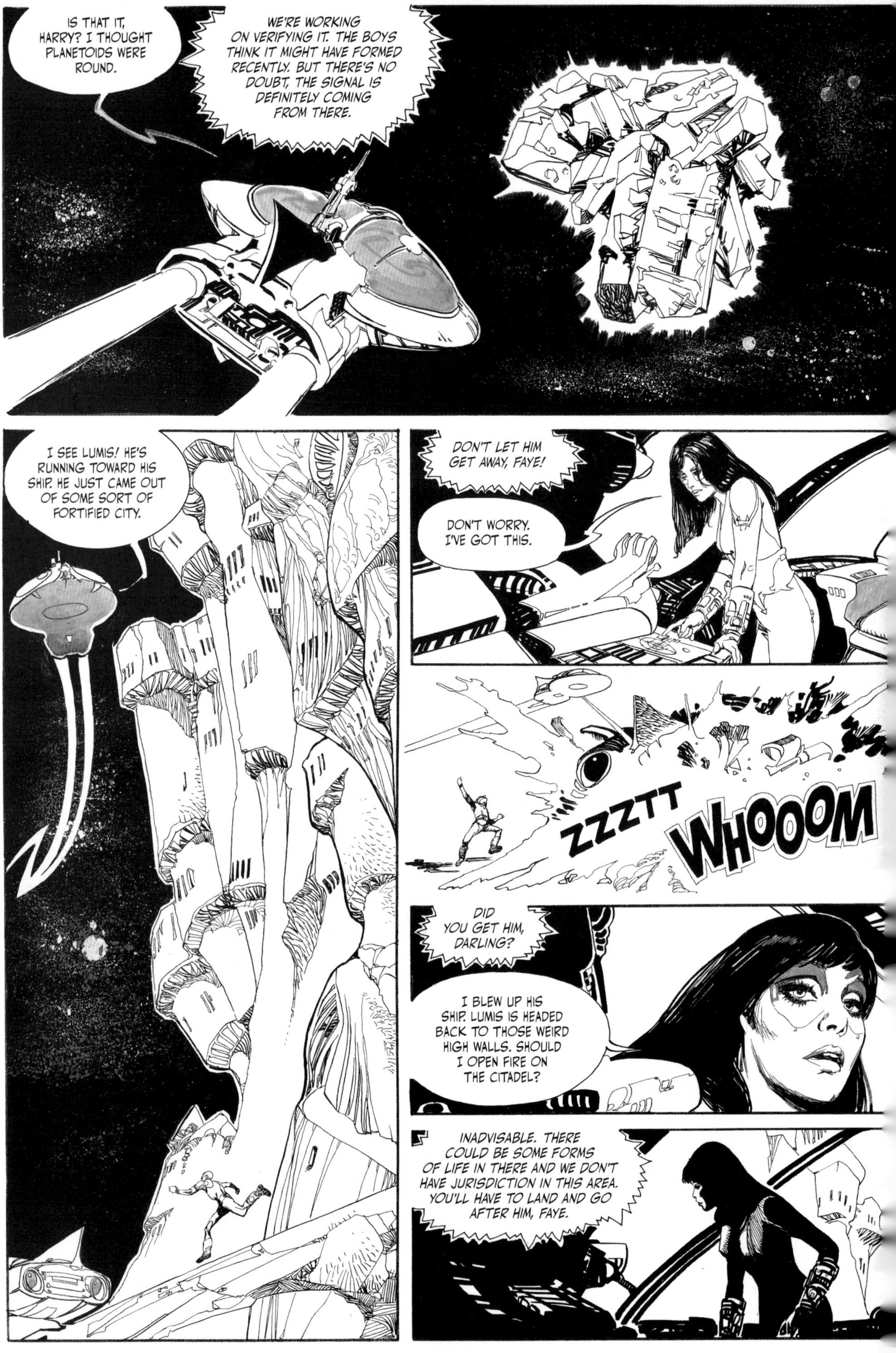
IS THAT IT, HARRY? I THOUGHT PLANETOIDS WERE ROUND.
WE'RE WORKING ON VERIFYING IT. THE BOYS THINK IT MIGHT HAVE FORMED RECENTLY. BUT THERE'S NO DOUBT, THE SIGNAL IS DEFINITELY COMING FROM THERE.
I SEE LUMIS! HE'S RUNNING TOWARD HIS SHIP. HE JUST CAME OUT OF SOME SORT OF FORTIFIED CITY.
DON'T LET HIM GET AWAY, FAYE!
DON'T WORRY. I'VE GOT THIS.
ZZZTT
WHOOOM
DID YOU GET HIM, DARLING?
I BLEW UP HIS SHIP. LUMIS IS HEADED BACK TO THOSE WEIRD HIGH WALLS. SHOULD I OPEN FIRE ON THE CITADEL?
INADVISABLE. THERE COULD BE SOME FORMS OF LIFE IN THERE AND WE DON'T HAVE JURISDICTION IN THIS AREA. YOU'LL HAVE TO LAND AND GO AFTER HIM, FAYE.

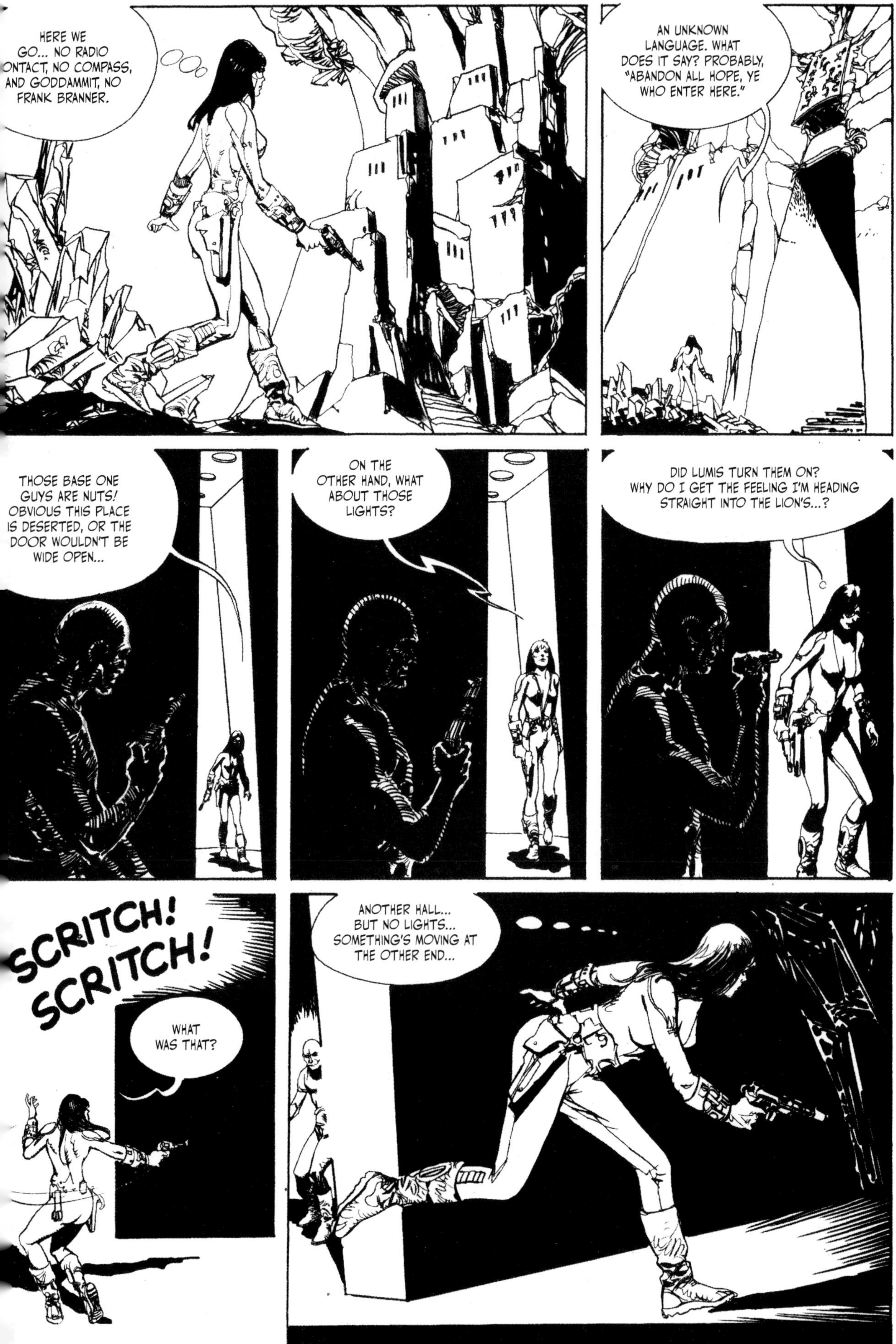
HERE WE GO... NO RADIO ONTACT, NO COMPASS, AND GODDAMMIT, NO FRANK BRANNER.
AN UNKNOWN LANGUAGE. WHAT DOES IT SAY? PROBABLY, "ABANDON ALL HOPE, YE WHO ENTER HERE."
THOSE BASE ONE GUYS ARE NUTS! OBVIOUS THIS PLACE IS DESERTED, OR THE DOOR WOULDN'T BE WIDE OPEN...
ON THE OTHER HAND, WHAT ABOUT THOSE LIGHTS?
DID LUMIS TURN THEM ON? WHY DO I GET THE FEELING I'M HEADING STRAIGHT INTO THE LION'S...?
SCRITCH! SCRITCH!
WHAT WAS THAT?
ANOTHER HALL... BUT NO LIGHTS... SOMETHING'S MOVING AT THE OTHER END...

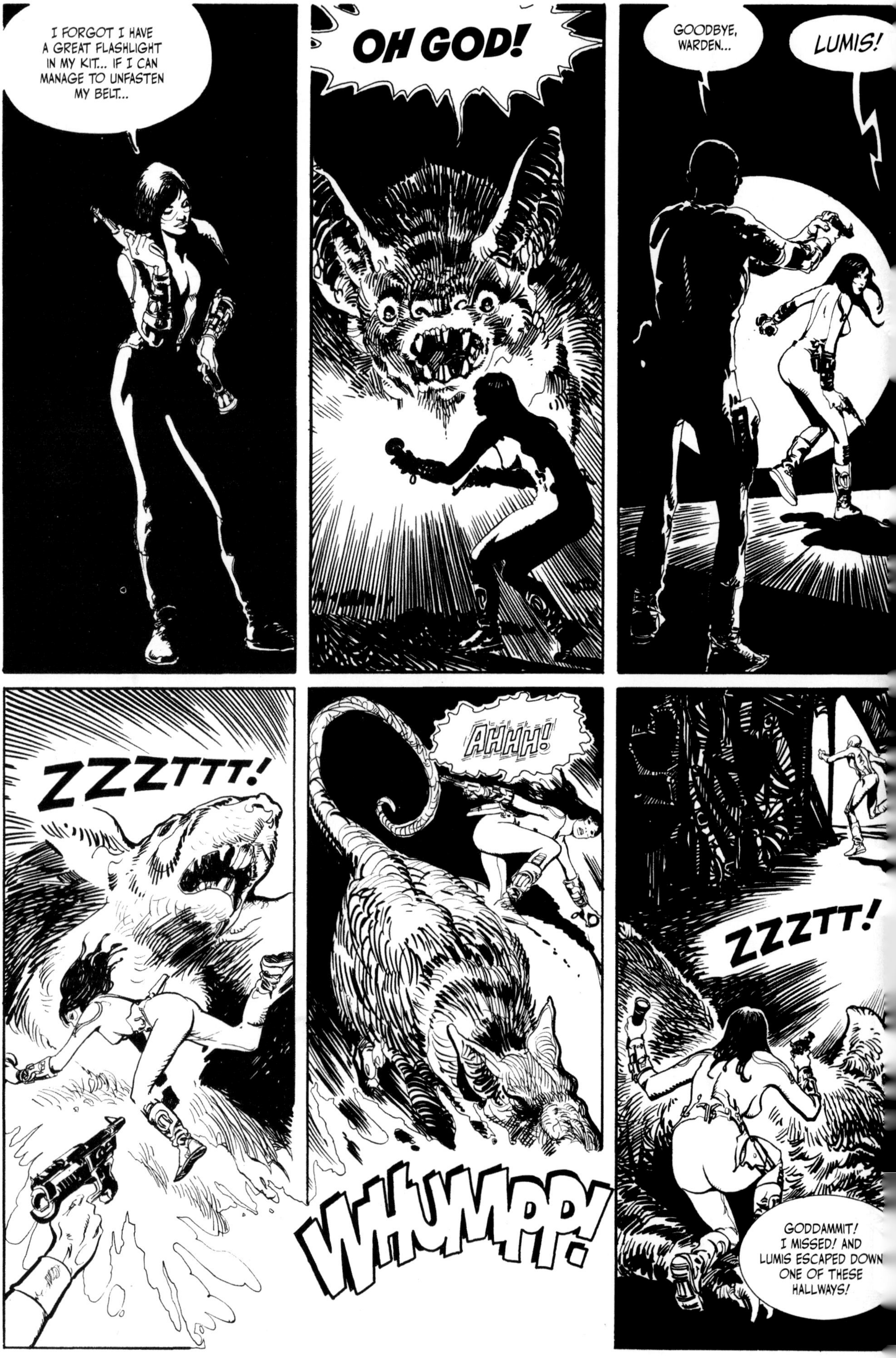
I FORGOT I HAVE A GREAT FLASHLIGHT IN MY KIT... IF I CAN MANAGE TO UNFASTEN MY BELT...
OH GOD!
GOODBYE, WARDEN...
LUMIS!
ZZZTTT!
AHHH!
WHUMPP!
ZZZTT!
GODDAMMIT! I MISSED! AND LUMIS ESCAPED DOWN ONE OF THESE HALLWAYS!

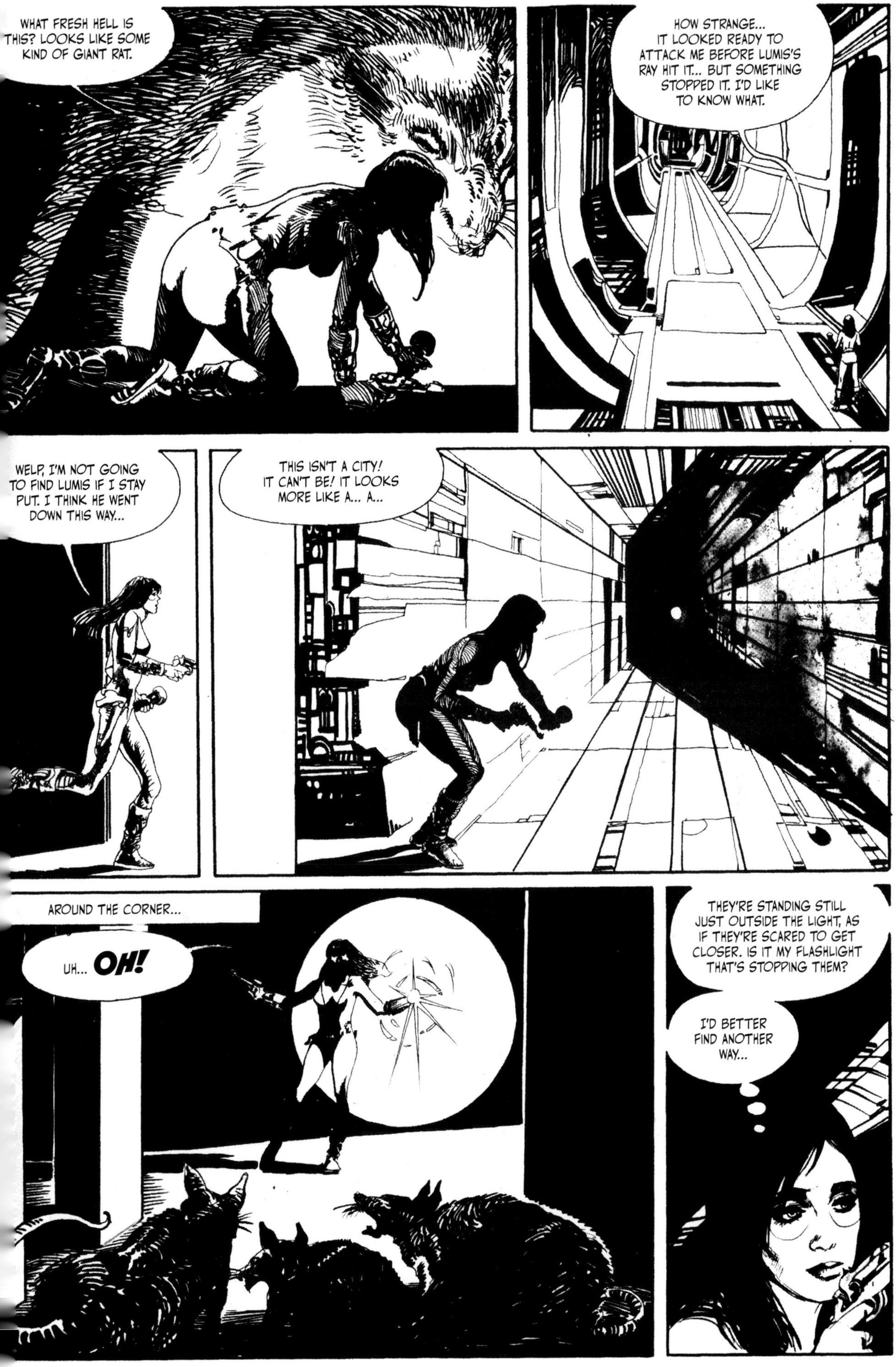
WHAT FRESH HELL IS THIS? LOOKS LIKE SOME KIND OF GIANT RAT.
HOW STRANGE... IT LOOKED READY TO ATTACK ME BEFORE LUMIS'S RAY HIT IT... BUT SOMETHING STOPPED IT. I'D LIKE TO KNOW WHAT.
WELP, I'M NOT GOING TO FIND LUMIS IF I STAY PUT. I THINK HE WENT DOWN THIS WAY...
THIS ISN'T A CITY! IT CAN'T BE! IT LOOKS MORE LIKE A... A...
AROUND THE CORNER...
UH... OH!
THEY'RE STANDING STILL JUST OUTSIDE THE LIGHT, AS IF THEY'RE SCARED TO GET CLOSER. IS IT MY FLASHLIGHT THAT'S STOPPING THEM?
I'D BETTER FIND ANOTHER WAY...

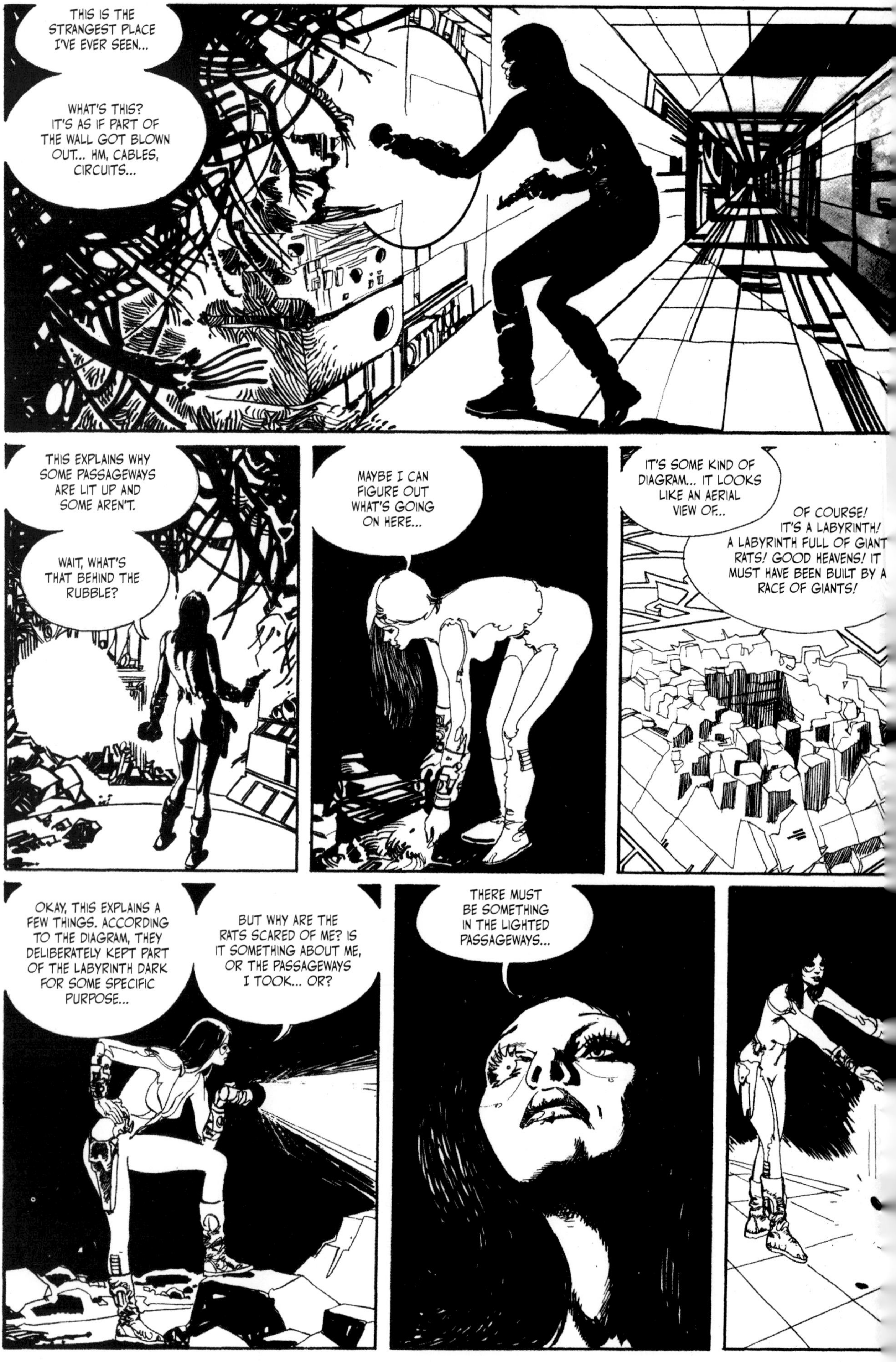
THIS IS THE STRANGEST PLACE I'VE EVER SEEN...
WHAT'S THIS? IT'S AS IF PART OF THE WALL GOT BLOWN OUT... HM, CABLES, CIRCUITS...
THIS EXPLAINS WHY SOME PASSAGEWAYS ARE LIT UP AND SOME AREN'T.
WAIT, WHAT'S THAT BEHIND THE RUBBLE?
MAYBE I CAN FIGURE OUT WHAT'S GOING ON HERE...
IT'S SOME KIND OF DIAGRAM... IT LOOKS LIKE AN AERIAL VIEW OF...
OF COURSE! IT'S A LABYRINTH! A LABYRINTH FULL OF GIANT RATS! GOOD HEAVENS! IT MUST HAVE BEEN BUILT BY A RACE OF GIANTS!
OKAY, THIS EXPLAINS A FEW THINGS. ACCORDING TO THE DIAGRAM, THEY DELIBERATELY KEPT PART OF THE LABYRINTH DARK FOR SOME SPECIFIC PURPOSE...
BUT WHY ARE THE RATS SCARED OF ME? IS IT SOMETHING ABOUT ME, OR THE PASSAGEWAYS I TOOK... OR?
THERE MUST BE SOMETHING IN THE LIGHTED PASSAGEWAYS...

IT DOESN'T AFFECT LUMIS OR ME BECAUSE WE'RE WEARING RUBBER BOOTS! THAT MEANS IF I STAY IN THE ONES THAT ARE LIT UP I'LL BE SAFE FROM THE...

PHIZZITT!

IT'S ELECTRIFIED! THE FLOOR IS ELECTRIFIED!

...RATS! BUT NOT FROM THE PRISONER! YOU'RE PRETTY SMART FOR A WARDEN, AREN'T YOU MISS FAYE?

LUMIS!

WELL, I SEE YOU BROUGHT YOUR FRIENDS...

INTERESTING CREATURES, AREN'T THEY? MY UNDERSTANDING IS THEY WERE BRED THOUSANDS OF YEARS AGO. THEY FED ON EACH OTHER. UNTIL THEY BRED A MUTANT SPECIES THAT DOESN'T NEED OXYGEN. VERY CLEVER.

OF COURSE... UH... ANY THEORIES ON THEIR ORIGIN?

CLEARLY MADE BY A RACE OF GIGANTIC BEINGS. MOST LIKELY, THEIR PLANET EXPLODED EONS AGO AND SENT THEM FLYING IN ALL DIRECTIONS. THE PIECES THAT HOUSED THE LABYRINTH AND THE NUCLEAR GENERATOR CAME OUT UNSCATHED.

THEY GAVE ME THE IDEAL PLACE TO HUNT YOU DOWN, WARDEN.

A SORT OF MOUSETRAP, YOU COULD SAY!

AND NOW, GOODBYE, MISS FAYE...

WAIT! UH, YOU WON'T GET AWAY WITH IT!

HOW ORIGINAL! I'VE NEVER HEARD THAT ONE BEFORE!

YOU'RE JUST STALLING FOR TIME. WHY? WHAT ARE YOU DOING BEHIND YOUR BACK?

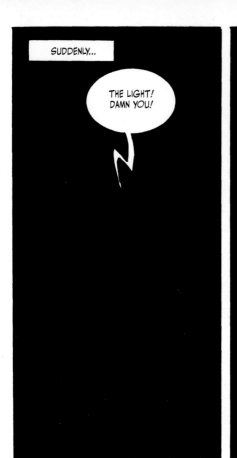

SUDDENLY...

THE LIGHT! DAMN YOU!

TURN ON THE LIGHT, GODDAMMIT! THE POWER! THE FLOOR! THE RATS ARE GOING TO...

YAGGHHHH!

NO! NO! THEY'RE EATING ME ALIVE! THE LIGHT! THE LIGHT! AGHHH!

I'M SORRY, BUT IT WAS EITHER YOU OR ME...

ENJOY, MY FRIENDS. I CUT THE POWER IN THIS HALLWAY FOR YOU... I'D BETTER GO BEFORE YOU POUNCE ON ME.

FAYE TO BASE ONE, MISSION ACCOMPLISHED. I'M LEAVING THE PLANETOID.

GOOD JOB, FAYE. WAS IT DIFFICULT?

NOT TOO BAD, HARRY. LET'S CALL IT "OPERATION MICKEY MOUSE."

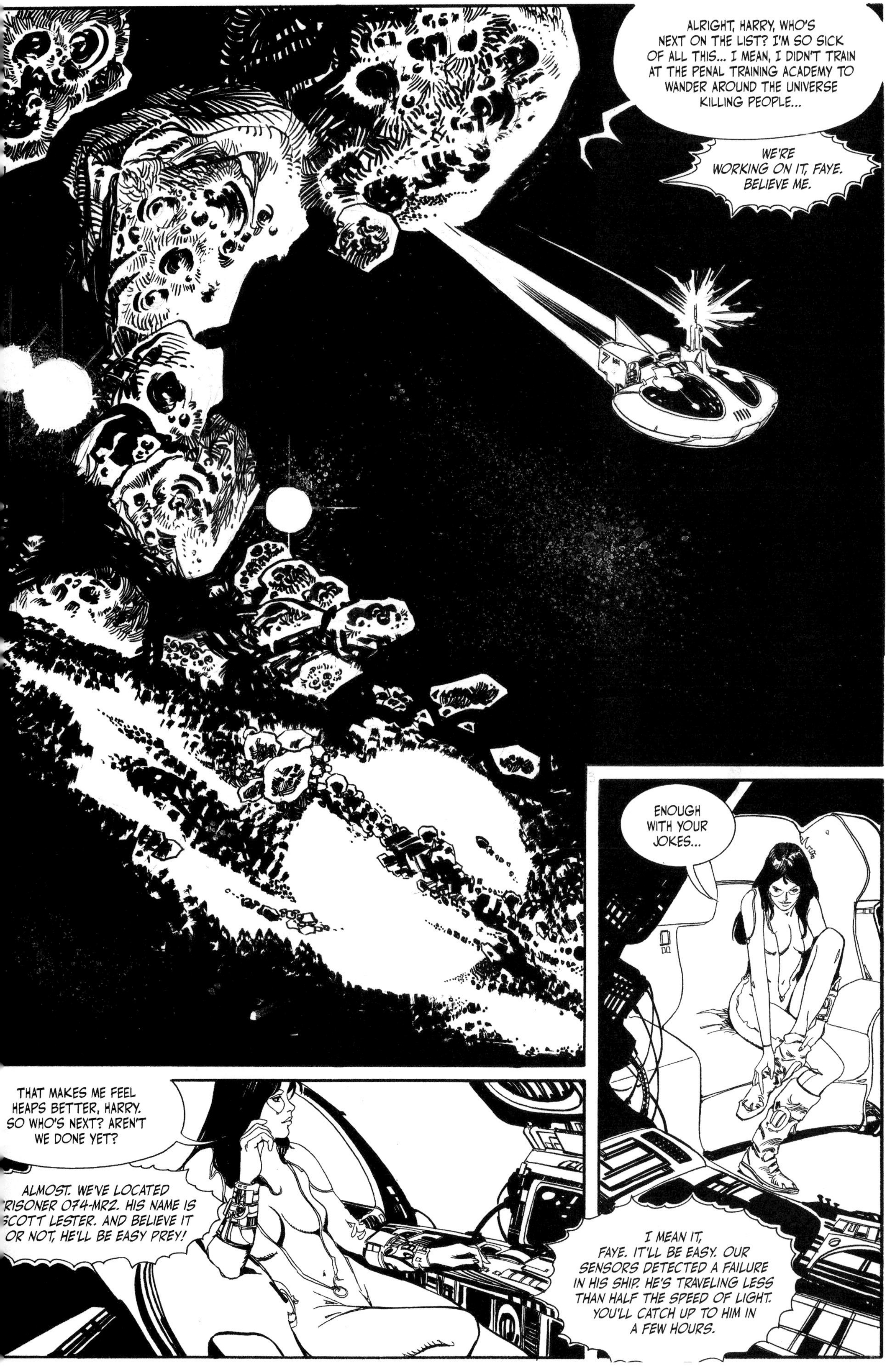

ALRIGHT, HARRY, WHO'S NEXT ON THE LIST? I'M SO SICK OF ALL THIS... I MEAN, I DIDN'T TRAIN AT THE PENAL TRAINING ACADEMY TO WANDER AROUND THE UNIVERSE KILLING PEOPLE...
WE'RE WORKING ON IT, FAYE. BELIEVE ME.
ENOUGH WITH YOUR JOKES...
THAT MAKES ME FEEL HEAPS BETTER, HARRY. SO WHO'S NEXT? AREN'T WE DONE YET?
ALMOST. WE'VE LOCATED PRISONER 074-MR2. HIS NAME IS SCOTT LESTER. AND BELIEVE IT OR NOT, HE'LL BE EASY PREY!
I MEAN IT, FAYE. IT'LL BE EASY. OUR SENSORS DETECTED A FAILURE IN HIS SHIP. HE'S TRAVELING LESS THAN HALF THE SPEED OF LIGHT. YOU'LL CATCH UP TO HIM IN A FEW HOURS.

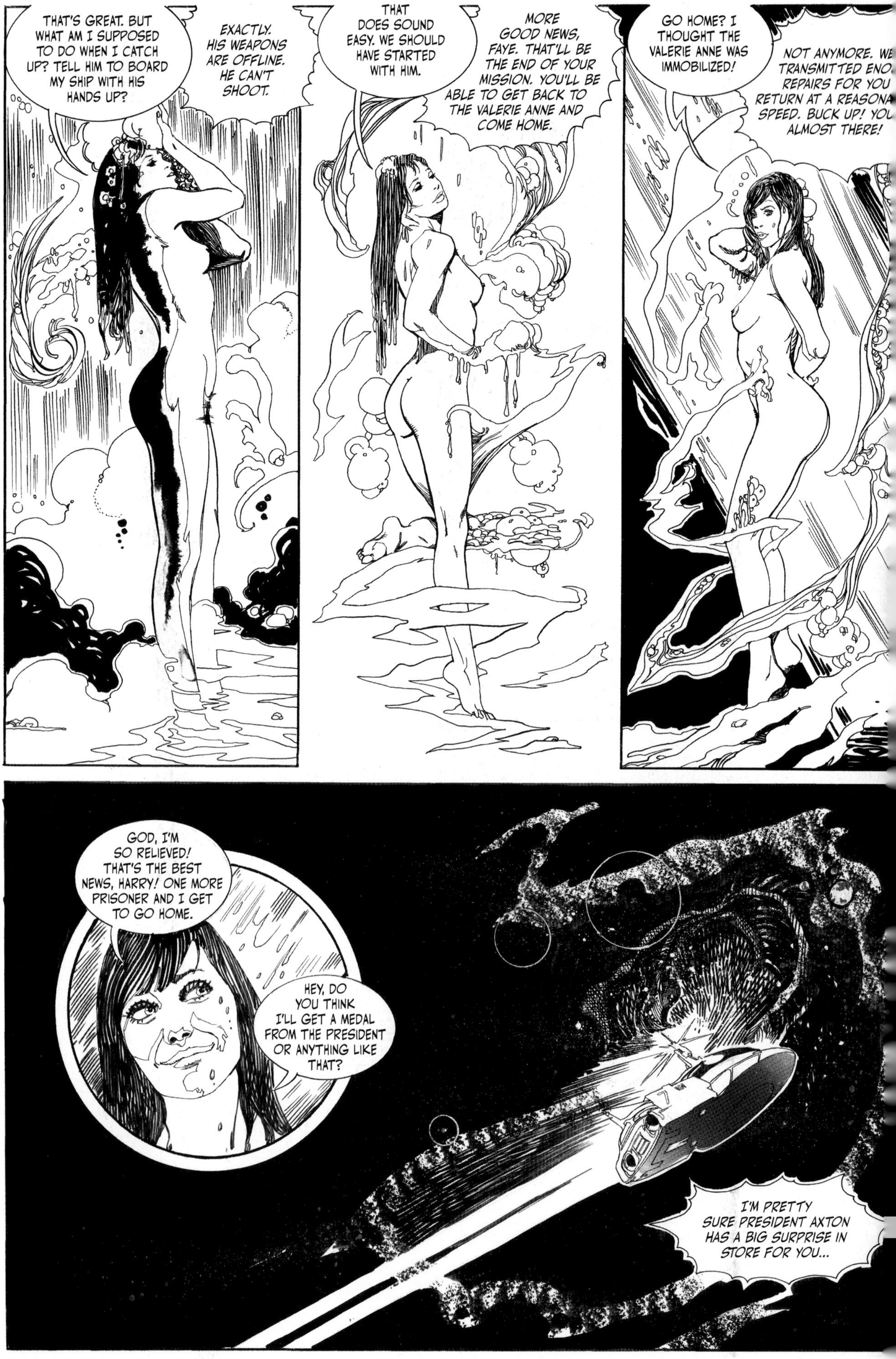
THAT'S GREAT. BUT WHAT AM I SUPPOSED TO DO WHEN I CATCH UP? TELL HIM TO BOARD MY SHIP WITH HIS HANDS UP?
EXACTLY. HIS WEAPONS ARE OFFLINE. HE CAN'T SHOOT.
THAT DOES SOUND EASY. WE SHOULD HAVE STARTED WITH HIM.
MORE GOOD NEWS, FAYE. THAT'LL BE THE END OF YOUR MISSION. YOU'LL BE ABLE TO GET BACK TO THE VALERIE ANNE AND COME HOME.
GO HOME? I THOUGHT THE VALERIE ANNE WAS IMMOBILIZED!
NOT ANYMORE. WE TRANSMITTED ENO REPAIRS FOR YOU RETURN AT A REASONA SPEED. BUCK UP! YOU ALMOST THERE!
GOD, I'M SO RELIEVED! THAT'S THE BEST NEWS, HARRY! ONE MORE PRISONER AND I GET TO GO HOME.
HEY, DO YOU THINK I'LL GET A MEDAL FROM THE PRESIDENT OR ANYTHING LIKE THAT?
I'M PRETTY SURE PRESIDENT AXTON HAS A BIG SURPRISE IN STORE FOR YOU...

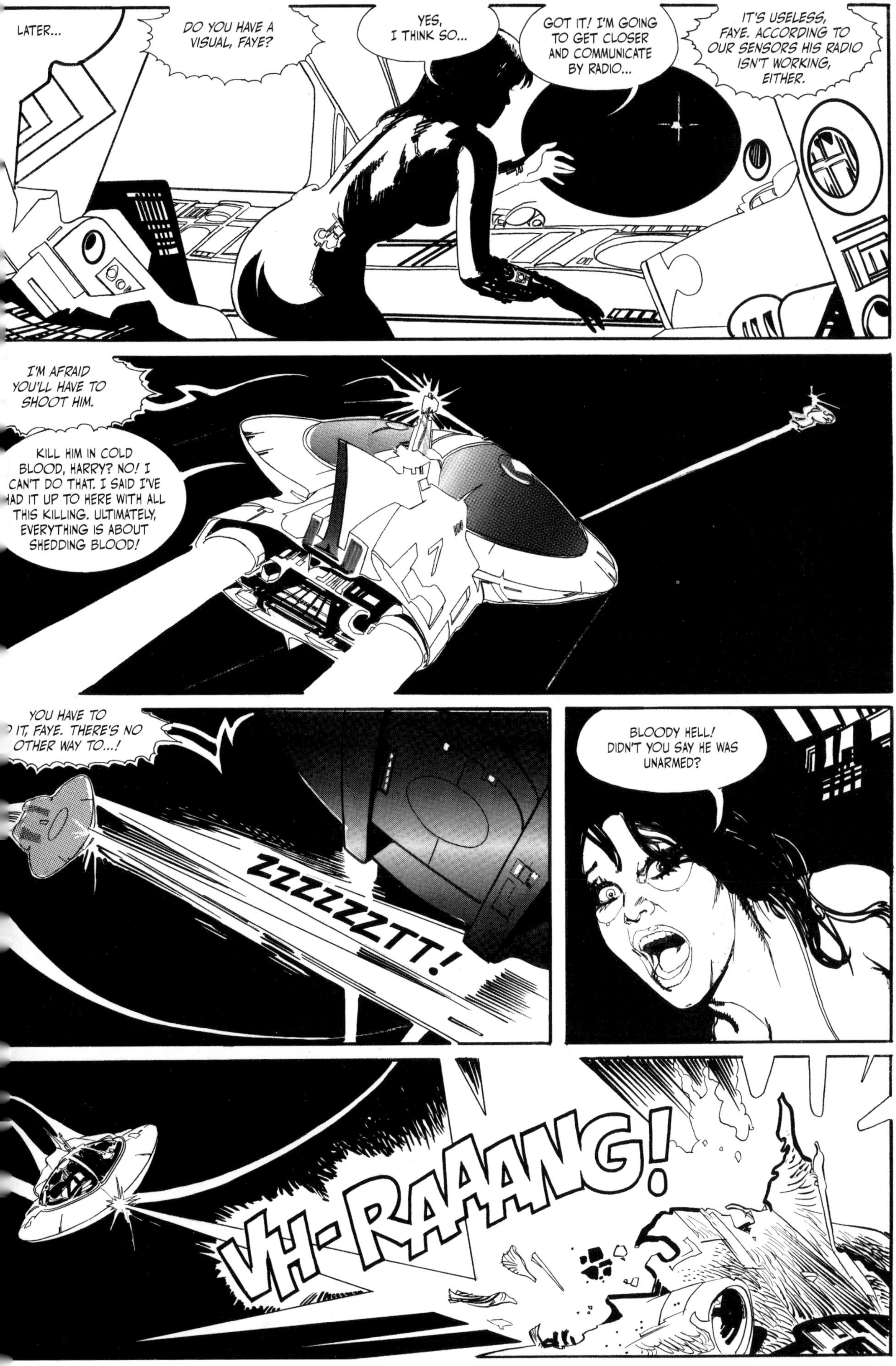
LATER...
DO YOU HAVE A VISUAL, FAYE?
YES, I THINK SO...
GOT IT! I'M GOING TO GET CLOSER AND COMMUNICATE BY RADIO...
IT'S USELESS, FAYE. ACCORDING TO OUR SENSORS HIS RADIO ISN'T WORKING, EITHER.
I'M AFRAID YOU'LL HAVE TO SHOOT HIM.
KILL HIM IN COLD BLOOD, HARRY? NO! I CAN'T DO THAT. I SAID I'VE HAD IT UP TO HERE WITH ALL THIS KILLING. ULTIMATELY, EVERYTHING IS ABOUT SHEDDING BLOOD!
YOU HAVE TO DO IT, FAYE. THERE'S NO OTHER WAY TO...!
ZZZZZZZZTT!
BLOODY HELL! DIDN'T YOU SAY HE WAS UNARMED?
VH-RAAANG!

FAYE! FAYE! ARE YOU OKAY?
BASE ONE TO WARDEN FAYE. PLEASE COME IN!
COUGH, COUGH... YES, I'M OKAY, HARRY. OH GOD! COUGH... I THINK I LOST ONE OF MY STABILIZERS. THE CABIN IS FULL OF SMOKE.
YOU DON'T NEED THE STABILIZERS UNLESS YOU HAVE TO LAND. FOLLOW HIM, FAYE. DON'T LET HIM GET AWAY!
OKAY, OKAY. DON'T BADGER ME SO MUCH, HARRY!
I'M CATCHING UP TO HIM AGAIN. I THINK I HAVE HIM WITHIN RANGE.
ATTA GIRL...
ALRIGHT, LET'S SEE HOW YOU LIKE THIS!
FIRE
SPROOOWWW
DAMMIT! I MISSED!

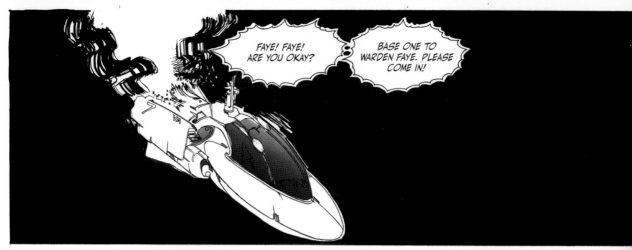

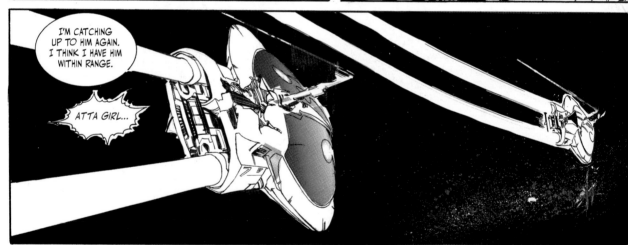

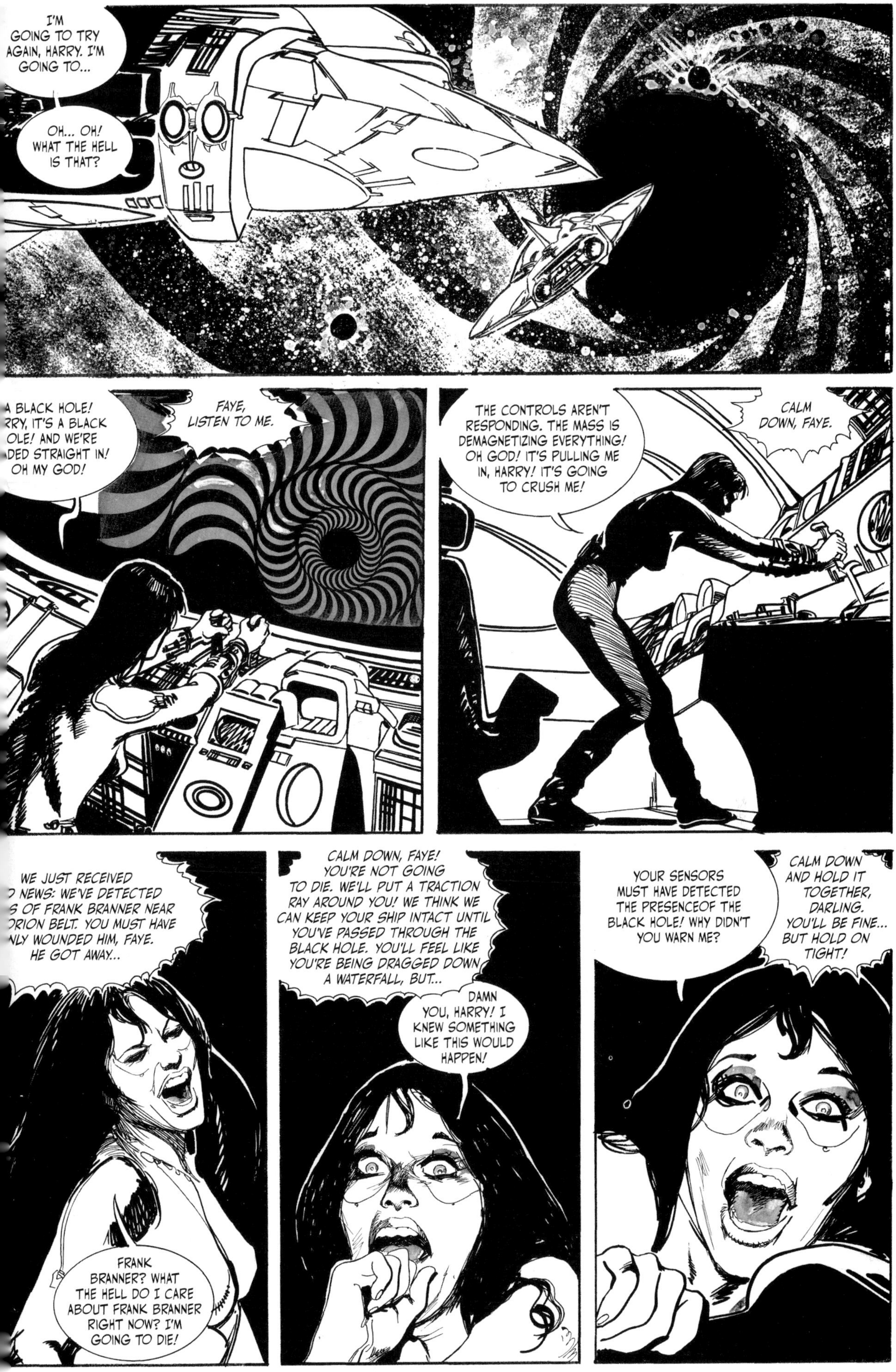
I'M GOING TO TRY AGAIN, HARRY. I'M GOING TO...
OH... OH! WHAT THE HELL IS THAT?
A BLACK HOLE! RRY, IT'S A BLACK OLE! AND WE'RE DED STRAIGHT IN! OH MY GOD!
FAYE, LISTEN TO ME.
THE CONTROLS AREN'T RESPONDING. THE MASS IS DEMAGNETIZING EVERYTHING! OH GOD! IT'S PULLING ME IN, HARRY! IT'S GOING TO CRUSH ME!
CALM DOWN, FAYE.
WE JUST RECEIVED D NEWS: WE'VE DETECTED S OF FRANK BRANNER NEAR ORION BELT. YOU MUST HAVE NLY WOUNDED HIM, FAYE. HE GOT AWAY...
FRANK BRANNER? WHAT THE HELL DO I CARE ABOUT FRANK BRANNER RIGHT NOW? I'M GOING TO DIE!
CALM DOWN, FAYE! YOU'RE NOT GOING TO DIE. WE'LL PUT A TRACTION RAY AROUND YOU! WE THINK WE CAN KEEP YOUR SHIP INTACT UNTIL YOU'VE PASSED THROUGH THE BLACK HOLE. YOU'LL FEEL LIKE YOU'RE BEING DRAGGED DOWN A WATERFALL, BUT...
DAMN YOU, HARRY! I KNEW SOMETHING LIKE THIS WOULD HAPPEN!
YOUR SENSORS MUST HAVE DETECTED THE PRESENCEOF THE BLACK HOLE! WHY DIDN'T YOU WARN ME?
CALM DOWN AND HOLD IT TOGETHER, DARLING. YOU'LL BE FINE... BUT HOLD ON TIGHT!

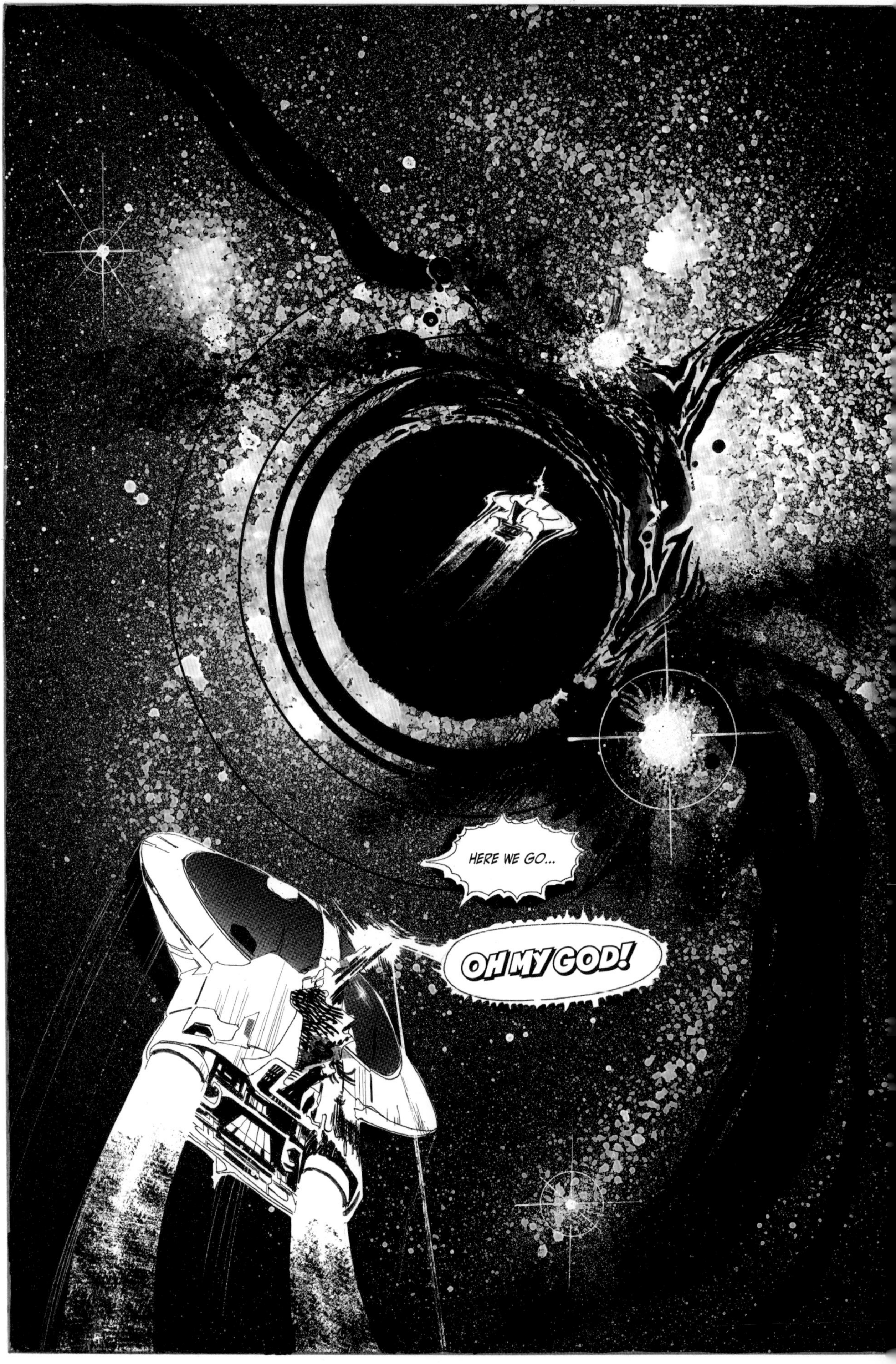
HERE WE GO...
OH MY GOD!

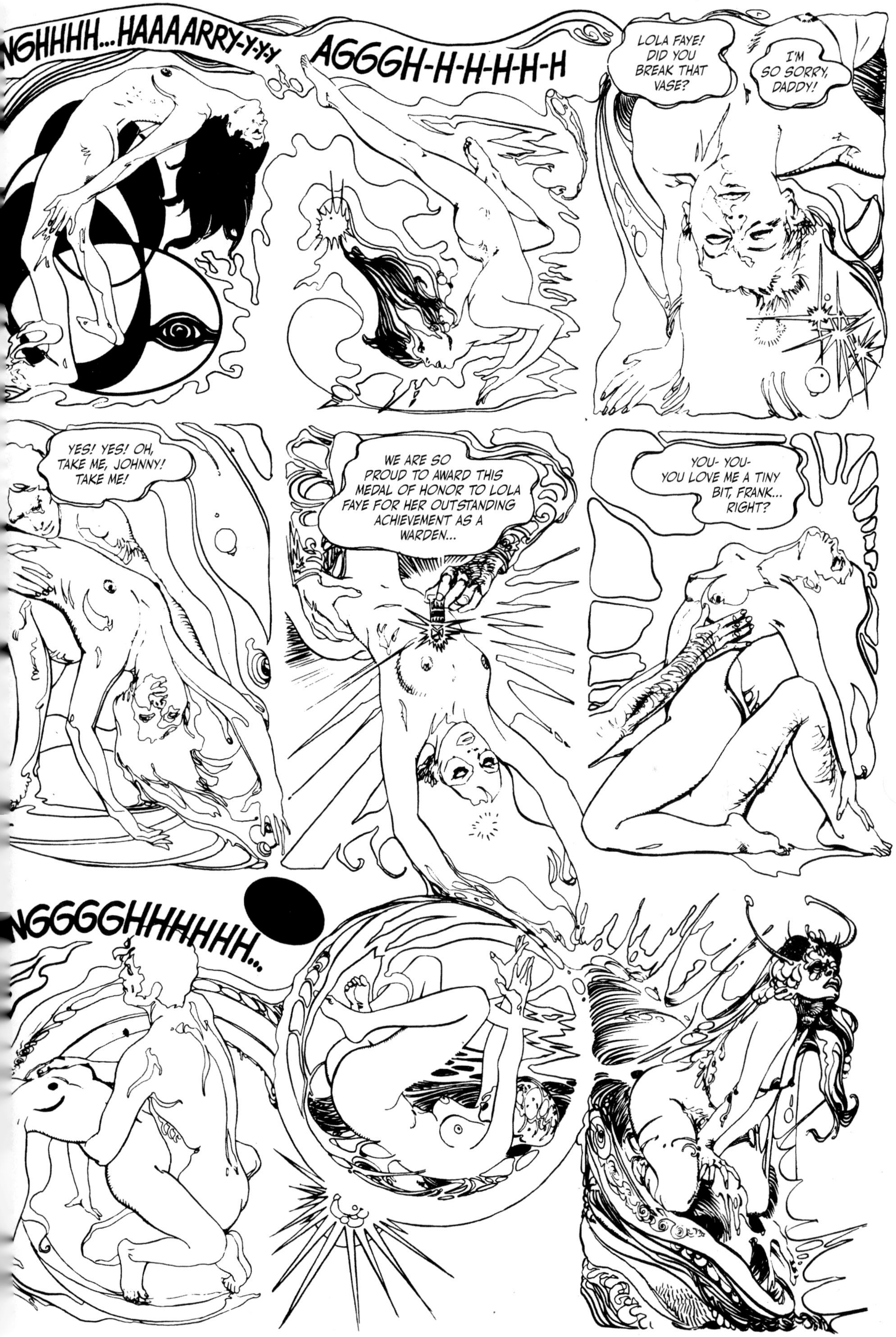
NGHHHH...HAAAARRY-Y-Y-Y
AGGGH-H-H-H-H-H
LOLA FAYE! DID YOU BREAK THAT VASE?
I'M SO SORRY, DADDY!
YES! YES! OH, TAKE ME, JOHNNY! TAKE ME!
WE ARE SO PROUD TO AWARD THIS MEDAL OF HONOR TO LOLA FAYE FOR HER OUTSTANDING ACHIEVEMENT AS A WARDEN...
YOU- YOU- YOU LOVE ME A TINY BIT, FRANK... RIGHT?
NGGGGHHHHHHH...

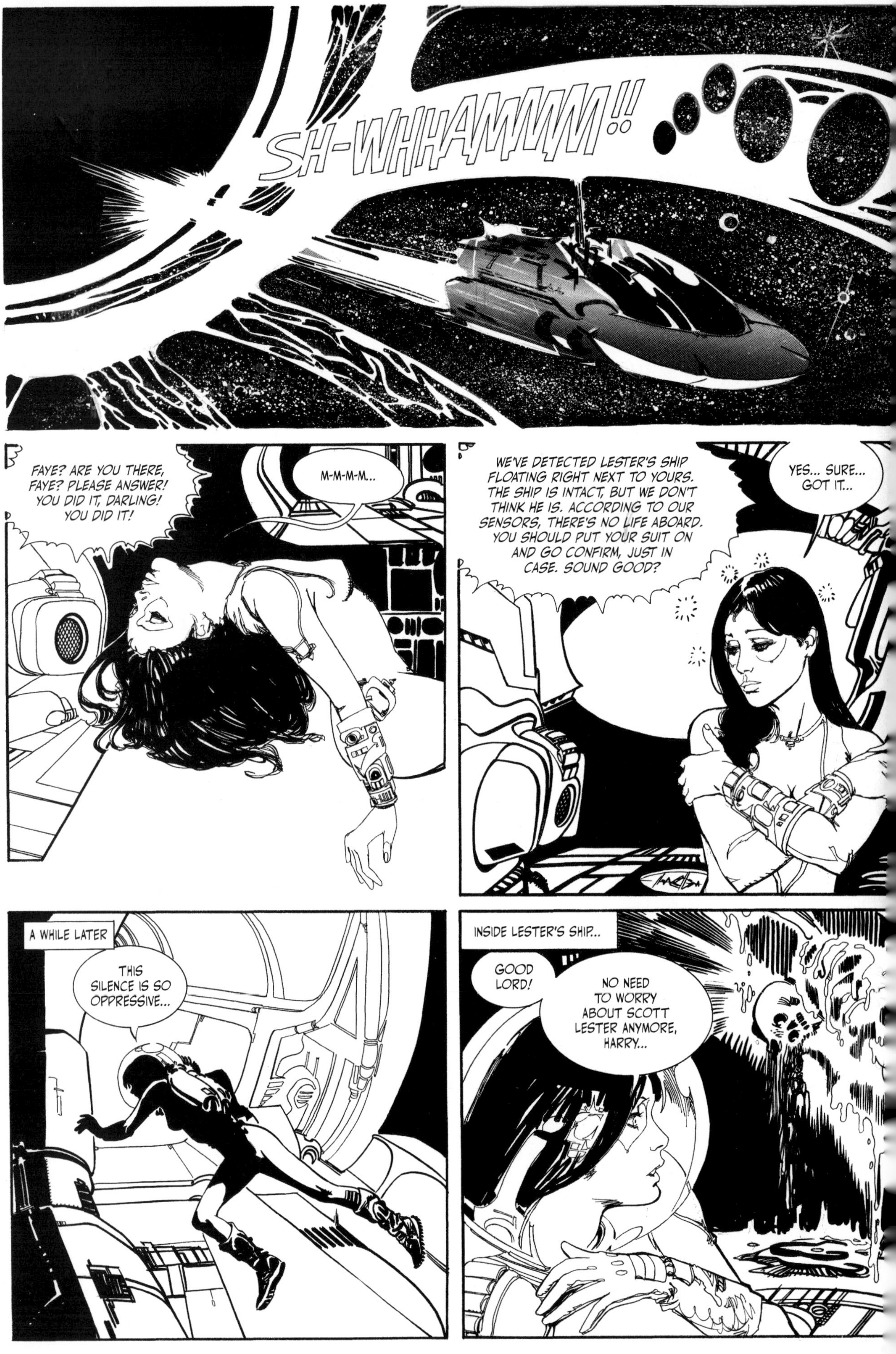
SH-WHHAMMM!!
FAYE? ARE YOU THERE, FAYE? PLEASE ANSWER! YOU DID IT, DARLING! YOU DID IT!
M-M-M-M...
WE'VE DETECTED LESTER'S SHIP FLOATING RIGHT NEXT TO YOURS. THE SHIP IS INTACT, BUT WE DON'T THINK HE IS. ACCORDING TO OUR SENSORS, THERE'S NO LIFE ABOARD. YOU SHOULD PUT YOUR SUIT ON AND GO CONFIRM, JUST IN CASE. SOUND GOOD?
YES... SURE... GOT IT...
A WHILE LATER
THIS SILENCE IS SO OPPRESSIVE...
INSIDE LESTER'S SHIP...
GOOD LORD!
NO NEED TO WORRY ABOUT SCOTT LESTER ANYMORE, HARRY...

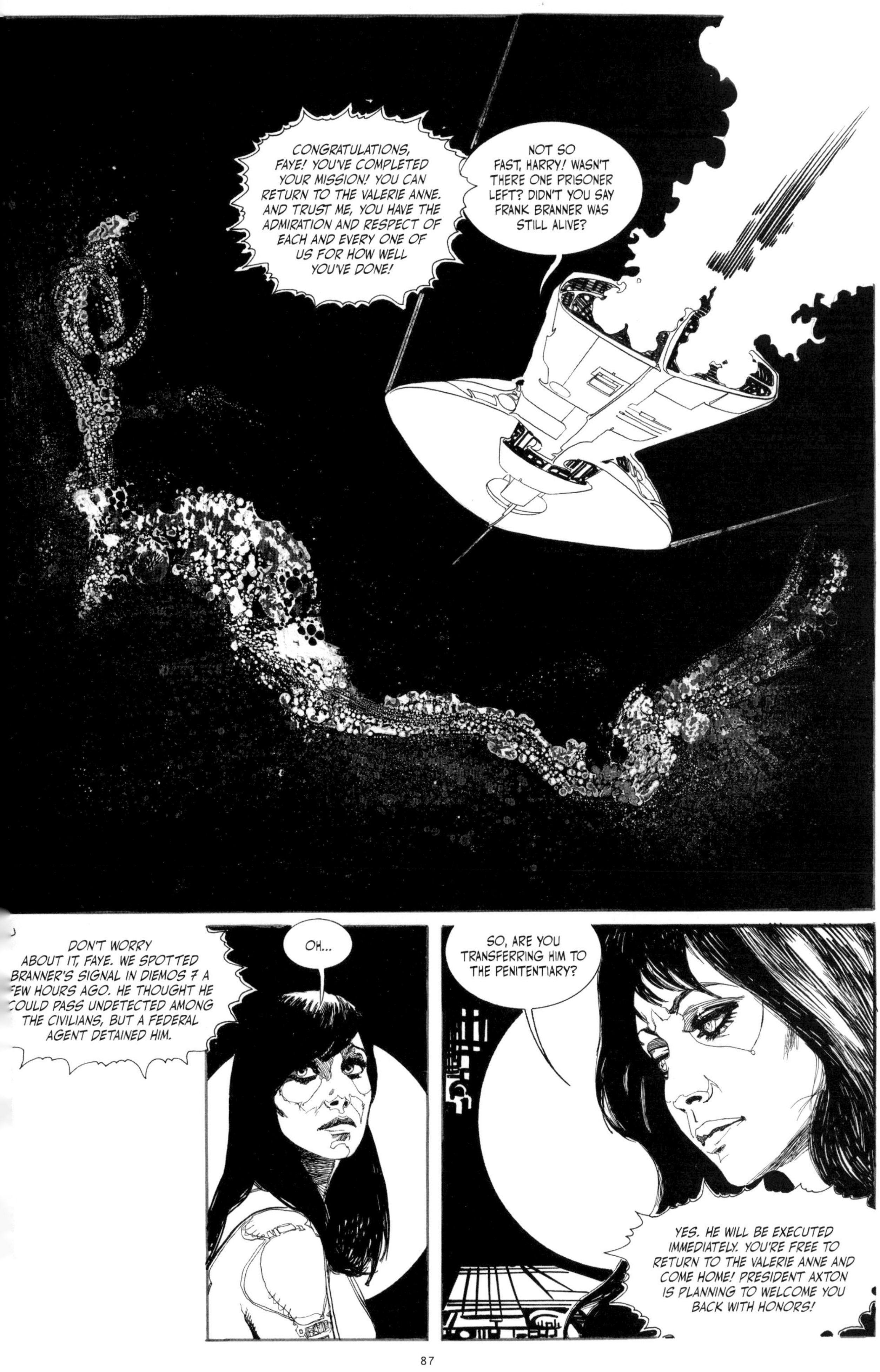
CONGRATULATIONS, FAYE! YOU'VE COMPLETED YOUR MISSION! YOU CAN RETURN TO THE VALERIE ANNE. AND TRUST ME, YOU HAVE THE ADMIRATION AND RESPECT OF EACH AND EVERY ONE OF US FOR HOW WELL YOU'VE DONE!
NOT SO FAST, HARRY! WASN'T THERE ONE PRISONER LEFT? DIDN'T YOU SAY FRANK BRANNER WAS STILL ALIVE?
DON'T WORRY ABOUT IT, FAYE. WE SPOTTED BRANNER'S SIGNAL IN DIEMOS 7 A FEW HOURS AGO. HE THOUGHT HE COULD PASS UNDETECTED AMONG THE CIVILIANS, BUT A FEDERAL AGENT DETAINED HIM.
OH...
SO, ARE YOU TRANSFERRING HIM TO THE PENITENTIARY?
YES. HE WILL BE EXECUTED IMMEDIATELY. YOU'RE FREE TO RETURN TO THE VALERIE ANNE AND COME HOME! PRESIDENT AXTON IS PLANNING TO WELCOME YOU BACK WITH HONORS!

A MILLION LIGHT YEARS LATER...
THERE IT IS, HARRY!
READY FOR TAKEOFF, FAYE! ALL IT NEEDS IS A GOOD PILOT!
DOCK ON THE UPPER LEVEL. THE SIDE WAS WEAKENED WHEN YOU COLLIDED WITH THE METEORITE...
COPY THAT.
DOCKING ACHIEVED! READY TO BOARD!
KA-CHUNK!
I'M SO READY TO GO HOME!
HARRY? ARE YOU THERE?
BASE ONE, WARDEN FAYE HERE. DO YOU COPY?
HUH? I THOUGHT YOU'D SAID THE SHIP HAD BEEN REPAIRED!
IT SURE DOESN'T LOOK LIKE IT'S IN WORKING CONDITION TO ME.
BASE ONE? DO YOU COPY?

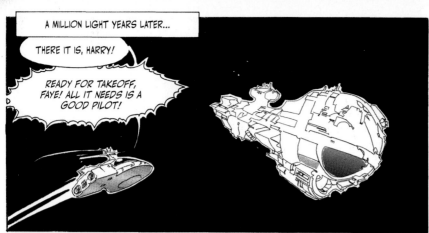

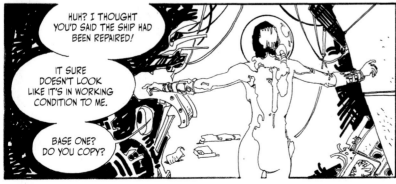

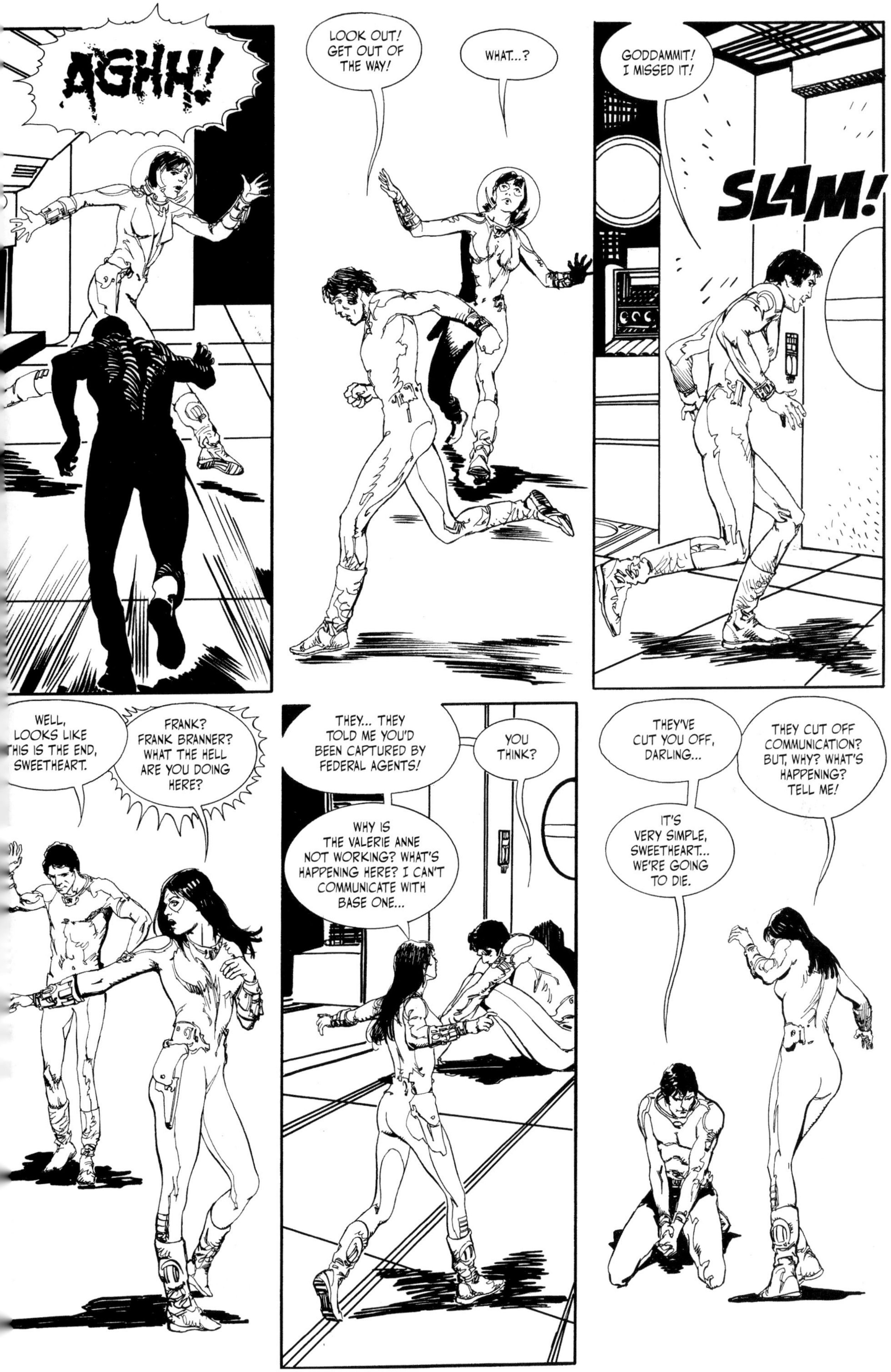
AGHH!
LOOK OUT! GET OUT OF THE WAY!
WHAT...?
GODDAMMIT! I MISSED IT!
SLAM!
WELL, LOOKS LIKE THIS IS THE END, SWEETHEART.
FRANK? FRANK BRANNER? WHAT THE HELL ARE YOU DOING HERE?
THEY... THEY TOLD ME YOU'D BEEN CAPTURED BY FEDERAL AGENTS!
YOU THINK?
WHY IS THE VALERIE ANNE NOT WORKING? WHAT'S HAPPENING HERE? I CAN'T COMMUNICATE WITH BASE ONE...
THEY'VE CUT YOU OFF, DARLING...
THEY CUT OFF COMMUNICATION? BUT, WHY? WHAT'S HAPPENING? TELL ME!
IT'S VERY SIMPLE, SWEETHEART... WE'RE GOING TO DIE.

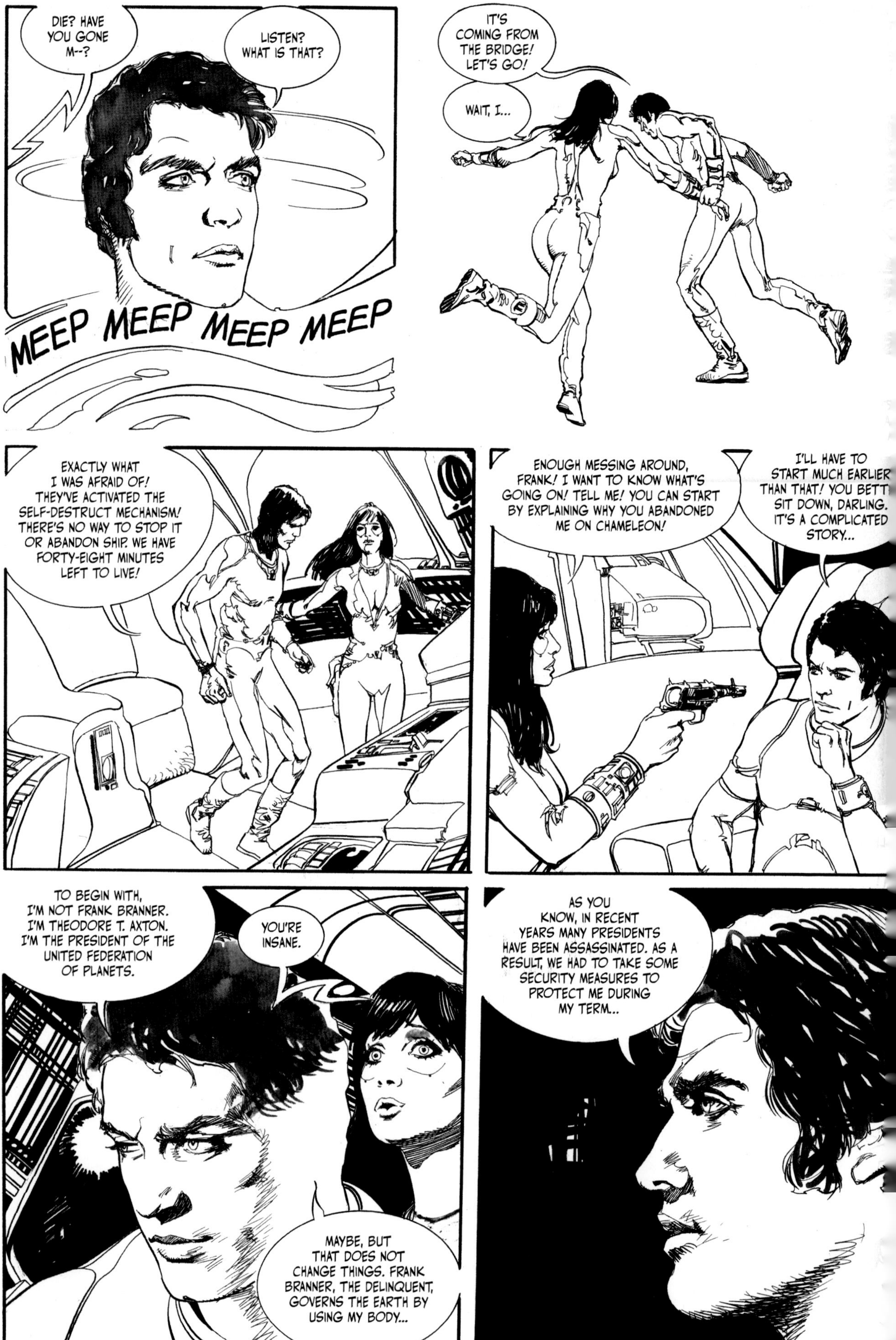
DIE? HAVE YOU GONE M--?
LISTEN? WHAT IS THAT?
MEEP MEEP MEEP MEEP
IT'S COMING FROM THE BRIDGE! LET'S GO!
WAIT, I...
EXACTLY WHAT I WAS AFRAID OF! THEY'VE ACTIVATED THE SELF-DESTRUCT MECHANISM! THERE'S NO WAY TO STOP IT OR ABANDON SHIP. WE HAVE FORTY-EIGHT MINUTES LEFT TO LIVE!
ENOUGH MESSING AROUND, FRANK! I WANT TO KNOW WHAT'S GOING ON! TELL ME! YOU CAN START BY EXPLAINING WHY YOU ABANDONED ME ON CHAMELEON!
I'LL HAVE TO START MUCH EARLIER THAN THAT! YOU BETT SIT DOWN, DARLING. IT'S A COMPLICATED STORY...
TO BEGIN WITH, I'M NOT FRANK BRANNER. I'M THEODORE T. AXTON. I'M THE PRESIDENT OF THE UNITED FEDERATION OF PLANETS.
YOU'RE INSANE.
MAYBE, BUT THAT DOES NOT CHANGE THINGS. FRANK BRANNER, THE DELINQUENT, GOVERNS THE EARTH BY USING MY BODY...
AS YOU KNOW, IN RECENT YEARS MANY PRESIDENTS HAVE BEEN ASSASSINATED. AS A RESULT, WE HAD TO TAKE SOME SECURITY MEASURES TO PROTECT ME DURING MY TERM...

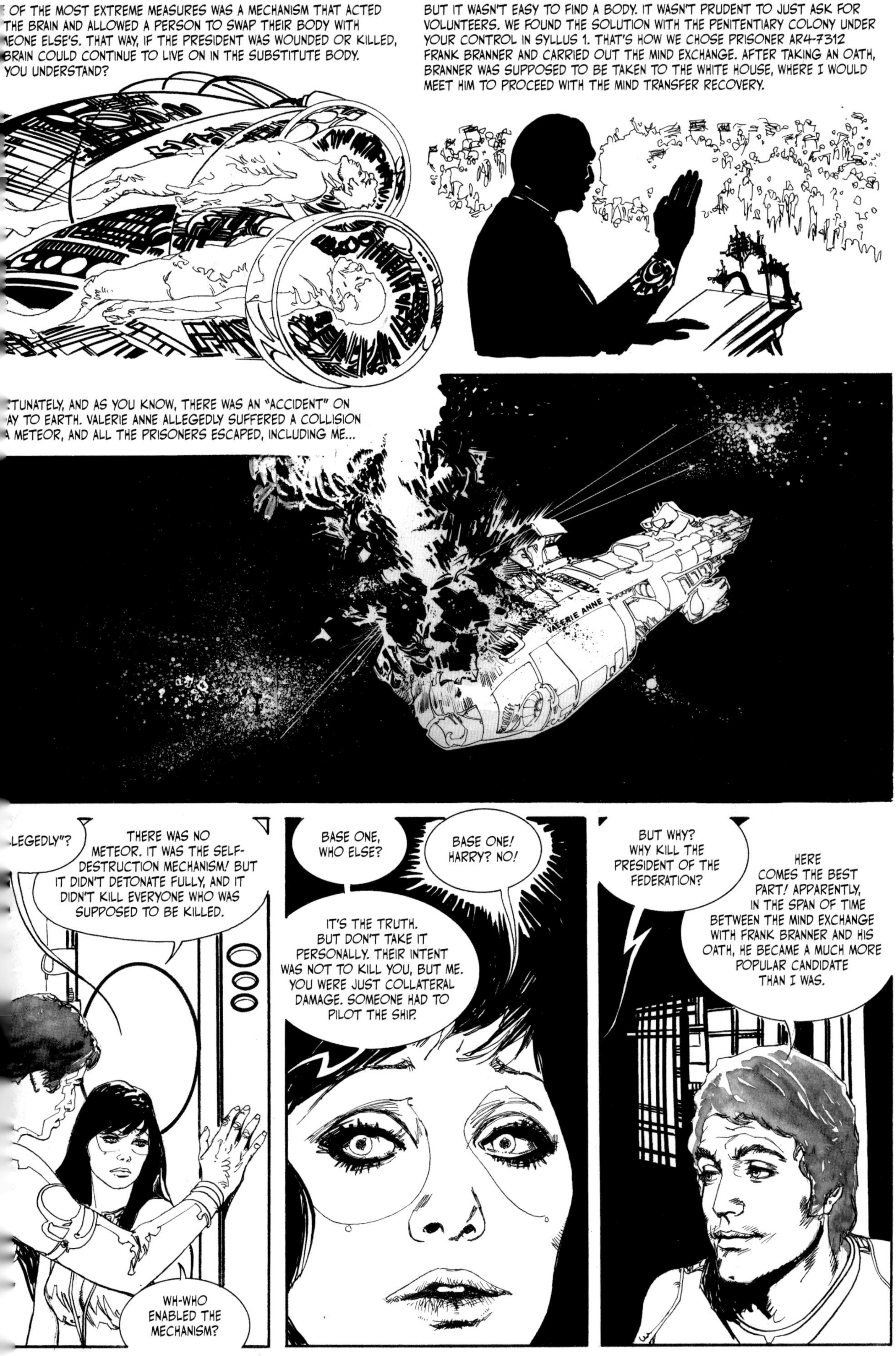

E OF THE MOST EXTREME MEASURES WAS A MECHANISM THAT ACTED
THE BRAIN AND ALLOWED A PERSON TO SWAP THEIR BODY WITH
IEONE ELSE'S. THAT WAY, IF THE PRESIDENT WAS WOUNDED OR KILLED,
BRAIN COULD CONTINUE TO LIVE ON IN THE SUBSTITUTE BODY.
YOU UNDERSTAND?
BUT IT WASN'T EASY TO FIND A BODY. IT WASN'T PRUDENT TO JUST ASK FOR VOLUNTEERS. WE FOUND THE SOLUTION WITH THE PENITENTIARY COLONY UNDER YOUR CONTROL IN SYLLUS 1. THAT'S HOW WE CHOSE PRISONER AR4-7312 FRANK BRANNER AND CARRIED OUT THE MIND EXCHANGE. AFTER TAKING AN OATH, BRANNER WAS SUPPOSED TO BE TAKEN TO THE WHITE HOUSE, WHERE I WOULD MEET HIM TO PROCEED WITH THE MIND TRANSFER RECOVERY.
:TUNATELY, AND AS YOU KNOW, THERE WAS AN "ACCIDENT" ON
AY TO EARTH. VALERIE ANNE ALLEGEDLY SUFFERED A COLLISION
A METEOR, AND ALL THE PRISONERS ESCAPED, INCLUDING ME...
VALERIE ANNE
LEGEDLY"?
THERE WAS NO METEOR. IT WAS THE SELF-DESTRUCTION MECHANISM! BUT IT DIDN'T DETONATE FULLY, AND IT DIDN'T KILL EVERYONE WHO WAS SUPPOSED TO BE KILLED.
WH-WHO ENABLED THE MECHANISM?
BASE ONE, WHO ELSE?
BASE ONE! HARRY? NO!
IT'S THE TRUTH. BUT DON'T TAKE IT PERSONALLY. THEIR INTENT WAS NOT TO KILL YOU, BUT ME. YOU WERE JUST COLLATERAL DAMAGE. SOMEONE HAD TO PILOT THE SHIP.
BUT WHY? WHY KILL THE PRESIDENT OF THE FEDERATION?
HERE COMES THE BEST PART! APPARENTLY, IN THE SPAN OF TIME BETWEEN THE MIND EXCHANGE WITH FRANK BRANNER AND HIS OATH, HE BECAME A MUCH MORE POPULAR CANDIDATE THAN I WAS.

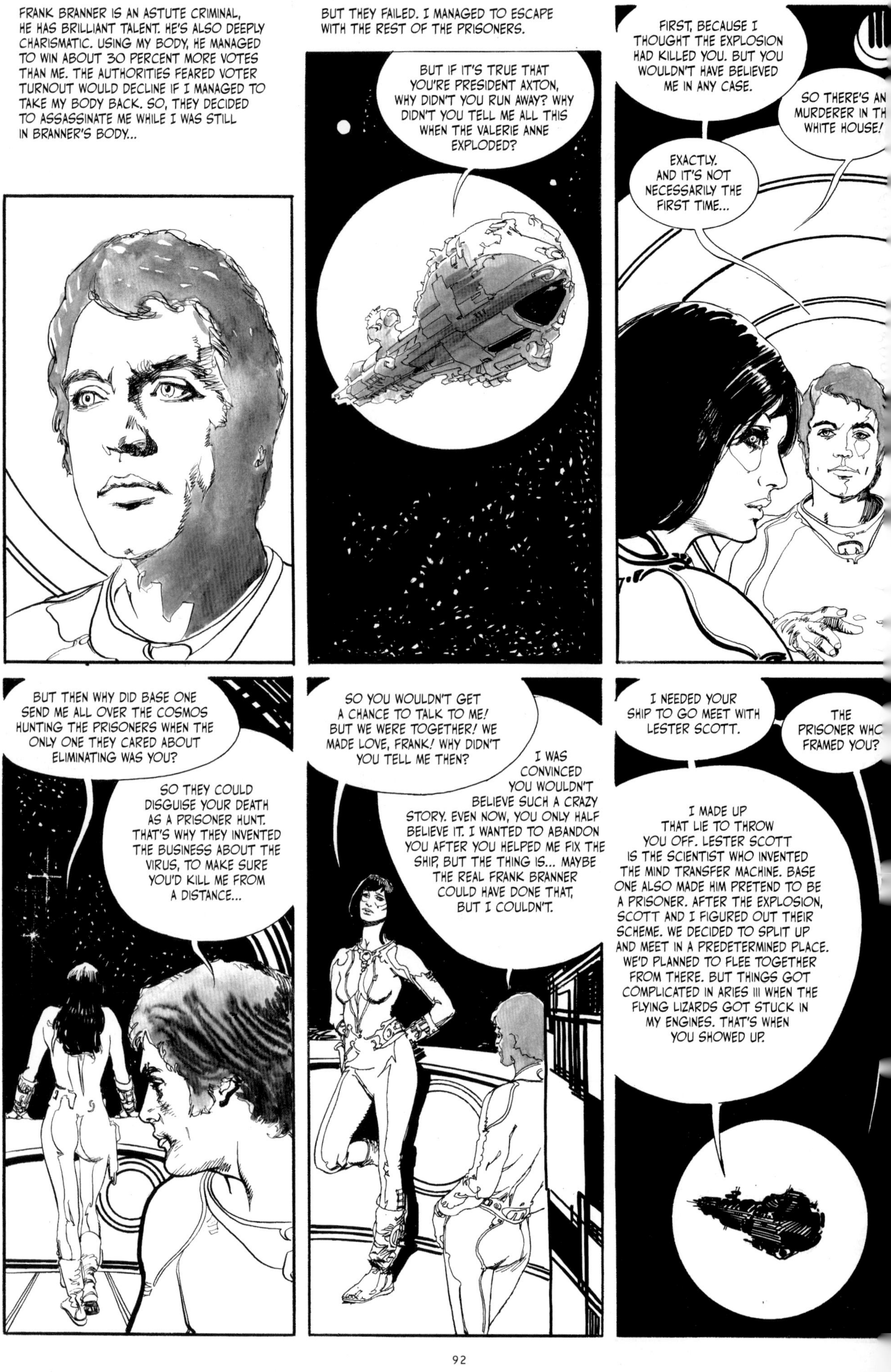
FRANK BRANNER IS AN ASTUTE CRIMINAL, HE HAS BRILLIANT TALENT. HE'S ALSO DEEPLY CHARISMATIC. USING MY BODY, HE MANAGED TO WIN ABOUT 30 PERCENT MORE VOTES THAN ME. THE AUTHORITIES FEARED VOTER TURNOUT WOULD DECLINE IF I MANAGED TO TAKE MY BODY BACK. SO, THEY DECIDED TO ASSASSINATE ME WHILE I WAS STILL IN BRANNER'S BODY...
BUT THEY FAILED. I MANAGED TO ESCAPE WITH THE REST OF THE PRISONERS.
BUT IF IT'S TRUE THAT YOU'RE PRESIDENT AXTON, WHY DIDN'T YOU RUN AWAY? WHY DIDN'T YOU TELL ME ALL THIS WHEN THE VALERIE ANNE EXPLODED?
FIRST, BECAUSE I THOUGHT THE EXPLOSION HAD KILLED YOU. BUT YOU WOULDN'T HAVE BELIEVED ME IN ANY CASE.
SO THERE'S AN MURDERER IN TH WHITE HOUSE!
EXACTLY. AND IT'S NOT NECESSARILY THE FIRST TIME...
BUT THEN WHY DID BASE ONE SEND ME ALL OVER THE COSMOS HUNTING THE PRISONERS WHEN THE ONLY ONE THEY CARED ABOUT ELIMINATING WAS YOU?
SO THEY COULD DISGUISE YOUR DEATH AS A PRISONER HUNT. THAT'S WHY THEY INVENTED THE BUSINESS ABOUT THE VIRUS, TO MAKE SURE YOU'D KILL ME FROM A DISTANCE...
SO YOU WOULDN'T GET A CHANCE TO TALK TO ME! BUT WE WERE TOGETHER! WE MADE LOVE, FRANK! WHY DIDN'T YOU TELL ME THEN?
I WAS CONVINCED YOU WOULDN'T BELIEVE SUCH A CRAZY STORY. EVEN NOW, YOU ONLY HALF BELIEVE IT. I WANTED TO ABANDON YOU AFTER YOU HELPED ME FIX THE SHIP, BUT THE THING IS... MAYBE THE REAL FRANK BRANNER COULD HAVE DONE THAT, BUT I COULDN'T.
I NEEDED YOUR SHIP TO GO MEET WITH LESTER SCOTT.
THE PRISONER WHC FRAMED YOU?
I MADE UP THAT LIE TO THROW YOU OFF. LESTER SCOTT IS THE SCIENTIST WHO INVENTED THE MIND TRANSFER MACHINE. BASE ONE ALSO MADE HIM PRETEND TO BE A PRISONER. AFTER THE EXPLOSION, SCOTT AND I FIGURED OUT THEIR SCHEME. WE DECIDED TO SPLIT UP AND MEET IN A PREDETERMINED PLACE. WE'D PLANNED TO FLEE TOGETHER FROM THERE. BUT THINGS GOT COMPLICATED IN ARIES III WHEN THE FLYING LIZARDS GOT STUCK IN MY ENGINES. THAT'S WHEN YOU SHOWED UP.

I NEEDED SCOTT SO I'D BE ABLE TO RECOVER MY BODY.

BUT WHY DID YOU LEAVE ME BEHIND ON CHAMELEON?

YOU WEREN'T IN SUCH BAD SHAPE. YOU HAD ONLEY'S SHIP. THE ONLY THING YOU NEEDED TO DO WAS FIND HIM. I HAD COMPLETE FAITH IN YOUR ABILITY.

THANKS!

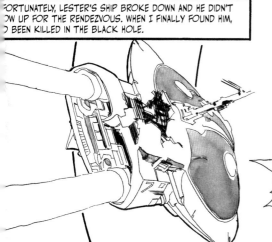

FORTUNATELY, LESTER'S SHIP BROKE DOWN AND HE DIDN'T SHOW UP FOR THE RENDEZVOUS. WHEN I FINALLY FOUND HIM, HE'D BEEN KILLED IN THE BLACK HOLE.

DEAR GOD!

I'M SO SORRY.

YOU COULDN'T HAVE KNOWN.

IF I WANTED TO RECOVER MY BODY, I'D TO MANAGE ON MY OWN. I ONLY RETURNED TO VALERIE ANNE HOPING TO A CIANOCOPY OF THE TRANSFER MACHINE THE COMPUTER'S PROGRAM.

AND DID YOU FIND IT?

EVERYTHING IS IN THIS TAPE. THE BAD NEWS IS BASE ONE KNOWS. THEY HUNTED ME ALL THE WAY HERE AND LOCKED ME IN USING THE REMOTE CONTROL FROM EARTH. THEN THEY MADE YOU TAKE THE BAIT...

AND NOW THEY'RE GETTING AWAY WITH IT! GODDAMMIT!

HOW MUCH TIME WE HAVE BEFORE THE VALERIE ANNE EXPLODES?

ABOUT FIFTEEN MINUTES...

UNLESS...

UNLESS WHAT? DID YOU THINK OF SOMETHING?

THE TORPEDO LAUNCHER! IF I COULD MANAGE TO ENGAGE A DELAYED REACTION MECHANISM...

QUICK! PUT ON YOUR SPACESUIT! IT'S WORTH A TRY!

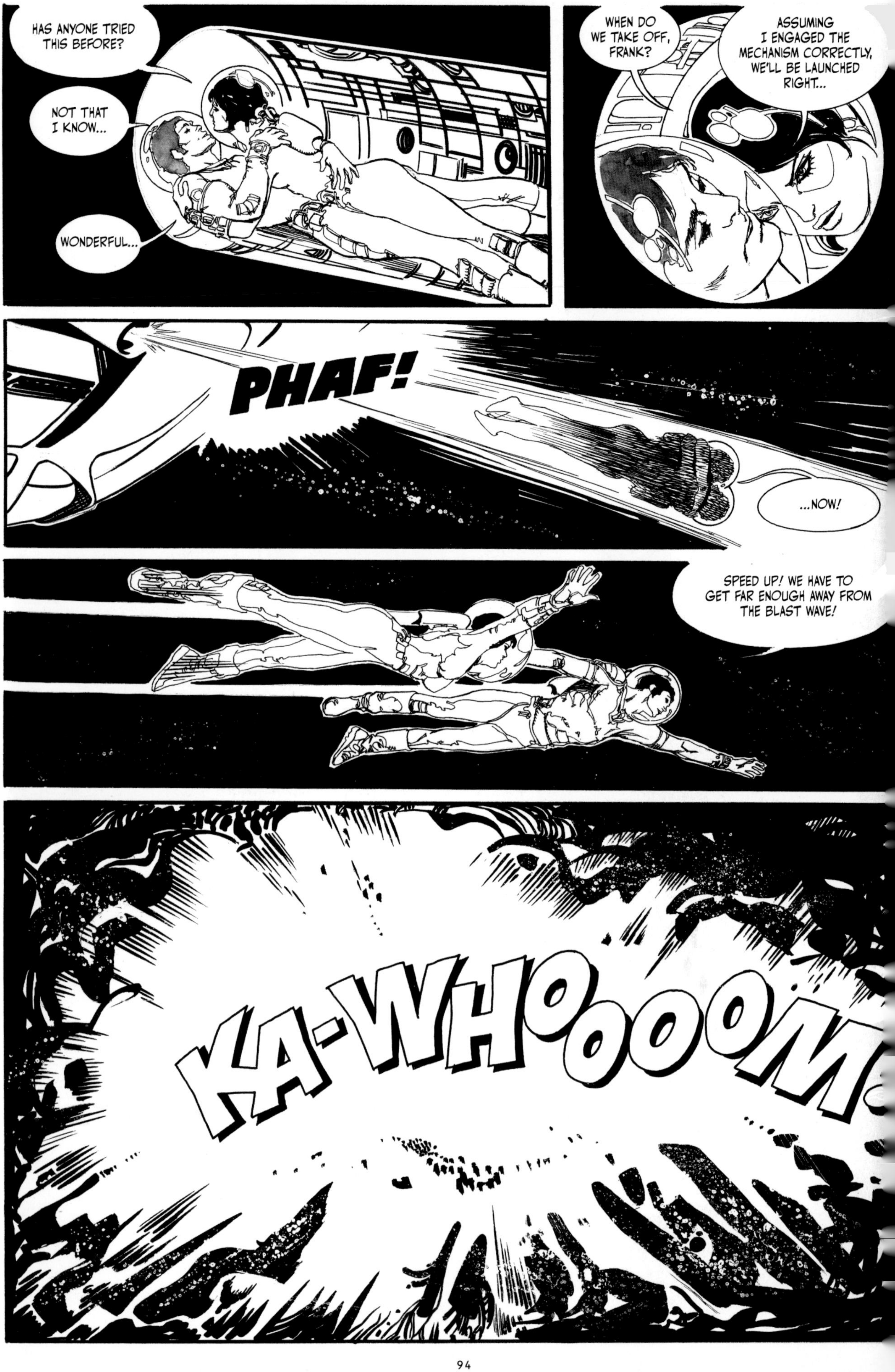
HAS ANYONE TRIED THIS BEFORE?
NOT THAT I KNOW...
WONDERFUL...
WHEN DO WE TAKE OFF, FRANK?
ASSUMING I ENGAGED THE MECHANISM CORRECTLY, WE'LL BE LAUNCHED RIGHT...
PHAF!
...NOW!
SPEED UP! WE HAVE TO GET FAR ENOUGH AWAY FROM THE BLAST WAVE!
KA-WHOOOOOM

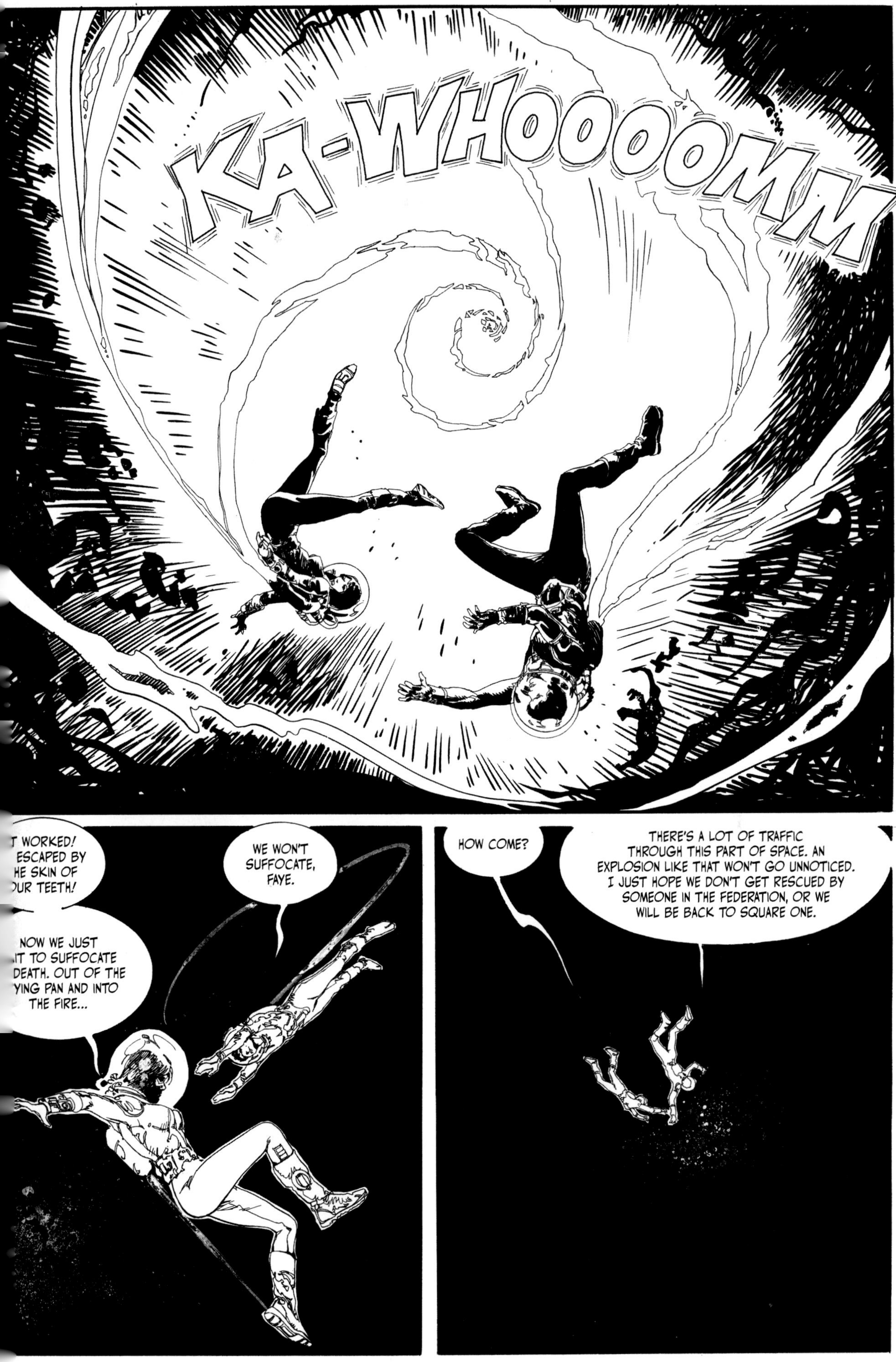
KA-WHOOOOMM
T WORKED! ESCAPED BY HE SKIN OF OUR TEETH!
NOW WE JUST IT TO SUFFOCATE DEATH. OUT OF THE YING PAN AND INTO THE FIRE...
WE WON'T SUFFOCATE, FAYE.
HOW COME?
THERE'S A LOT OF TRAFFIC THROUGH THIS PART OF SPACE. AN EXPLOSION LIKE THAT WON'T GO UNNOTICED. I JUST HOPE WE DON'T GET RESCUED BY SOMEONE IN THE FEDERATION, OR WE WILL BE BACK TO SQUARE ONE.

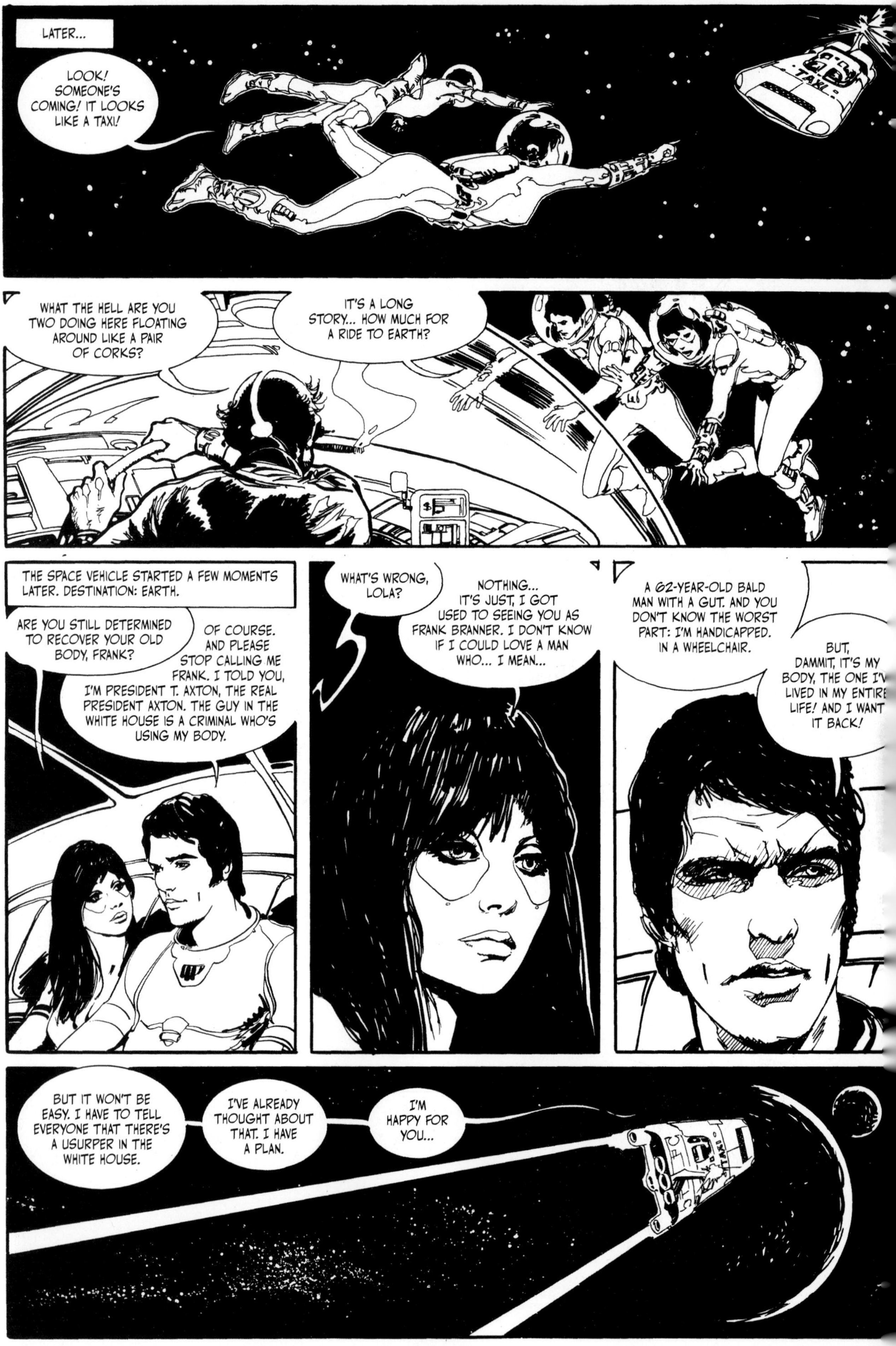

LATER...
LOOK! SOMEONE'S COMING! IT LOOKS LIKE A TAXI!
TAXI
WHAT THE HELL ARE YOU TWO DOING HERE FLOATING AROUND LIKE A PAIR OF CORKS?
IT'S A LONG STORY... HOW MUCH FOR A RIDE TO EARTH?
THE SPACE VEHICLE STARTED A FEW MOMENTS LATER. DESTINATION: EARTH.
ARE YOU STILL DETERMINED TO RECOVER YOUR OLD BODY, FRANK?
OF COURSE. AND PLEASE STOP CALLING ME FRANK. I TOLD YOU, I'M PRESIDENT T. AXTON, THE REAL PRESIDENT AXTON. THE GUY IN THE WHITE HOUSE IS A CRIMINAL WHO'S USING MY BODY.
WHAT'S WRONG, LOLA?
NOTHING... IT'S JUST, I GOT USED TO SEEING YOU AS FRANK BRANNER. I DON'T KNOW IF I COULD LOVE A MAN WHO... I MEAN...
A 62-YEAR-OLD BALD MAN WITH A GUT. AND YOU DON'T KNOW THE WORST PART: I'M HANDICAPPED. IN A WHEELCHAIR.
BUT, DAMMIT, IT'S MY BODY, THE ONE I'V LIVED IN MY ENTIRE LIFE! AND I WANT IT BACK!
BUT IT WON'T BE EASY. I HAVE TO TELL EVERYONE THAT THERE'S A USURPER IN THE WHITE HOUSE.
I'VE ALREADY THOUGHT ABOUT THAT. I HAVE A PLAN.
I'M HAPPY FOR YOU...
TAXI

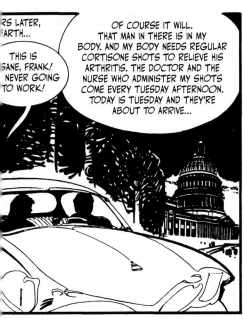

RS LATER, ARTH...

THIS IS SANE, FRANK! NEVER GOING TO WORK!

OF COURSE IT WILL. THAT MAN IN THERE IS IN MY BODY. AND MY BODY NEEDS REGULAR CORTISONE SHOTS TO RELIEVE HIS ARTHRITIS. THE DOCTOR AND THE NURSE WHO ADMINISTER MY SHOTS COME EVERY TUESDAY AFTERNOON. TODAY IS TUESDAY AND THEY'RE ABOUT TO ARRIVE...

THERE HE IS. LET'S GO!

KA-WHUMP!

HEY! LOOK OUT!

YOU IDIOT! WHY DON'T YOU WATCH WHERE YOU'RE GO- UH!

TAKE CARE OF THE NURSE, FAYE!

THIS UNIFORM'S SO TIGHT ON ME... UGH!

YES, MR. PRESIDENT.

WHEN WE GET IN THERE, DON'T SAY A WORD, JUST FOLLOW MY LEAD.

THIS DRESS S STRANGLING ME! DOOR GUARD WON'T ET US IN! LOOK AT MY BREASTS!

YOUR BREASTS ARE EXACTLY THE REASON THEY'RE GOING TO OPEN THE DOOR!

MEDICATION FOR PRESIDENT AXTON...

PLEASE, IT'S URGENT.

HOW COME DOCTOR CONLEY ISN'T HERE?

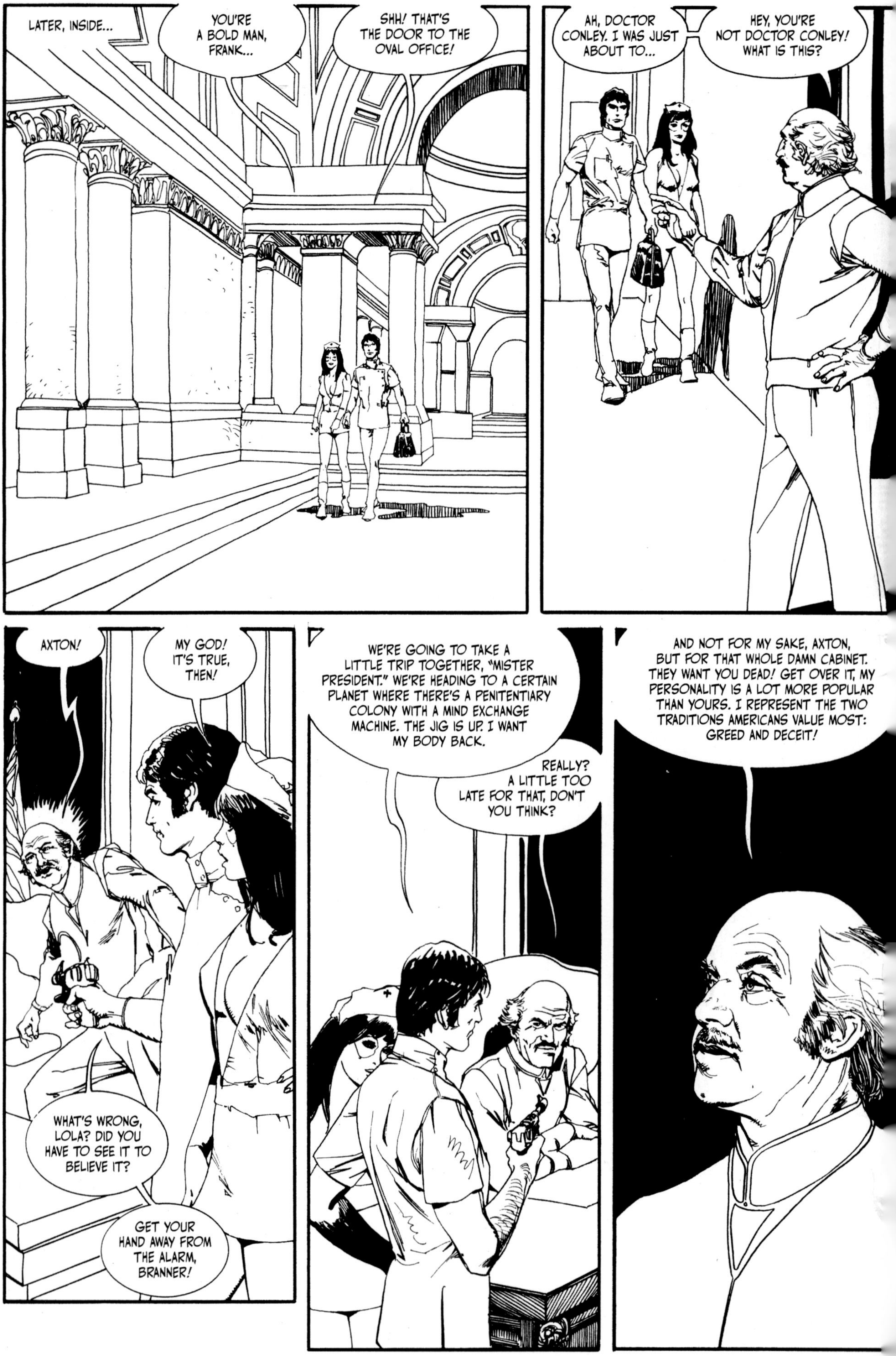
LATER, INSIDE...
YOU'RE A BOLD MAN, FRANK...
SHH! THAT'S THE DOOR TO THE OVAL OFFICE!
AH, DOCTOR CONLEY. I WAS JUST ABOUT TO...
HEY, YOU'RE NOT DOCTOR CONLEY! WHAT IS THIS?
AXTON!
MY GOD! IT'S TRUE, THEN!
WHAT'S WRONG, LOLA? DID YOU HAVE TO SEE IT TO BELIEVE IT?
GET YOUR HAND AWAY FROM THE ALARM, BRANNER!
WE'RE GOING TO TAKE A LITTLE TRIP TOGETHER, "MISTER PRESIDENT." WE'RE HEADING TO A CERTAIN PLANET WHERE THERE'S A PENITENTIARY COLONY WITH A MIND EXCHANGE MACHINE. THE JIG IS UP. I WANT MY BODY BACK.
REALLY? A LITTLE TOO LATE FOR THAT, DON'T YOU THINK?
AND NOT FOR MY SAKE, AXTON, BUT FOR THAT WHOLE DAMN CABINET. THEY WANT YOU DEAD! GET OVER IT, MY PERSONALITY IS A LOT MORE POPULAR THAN YOURS. I REPRESENT THE TWO TRADITIONS AMERICANS VALUE MOST: GREED AND DECEIT!

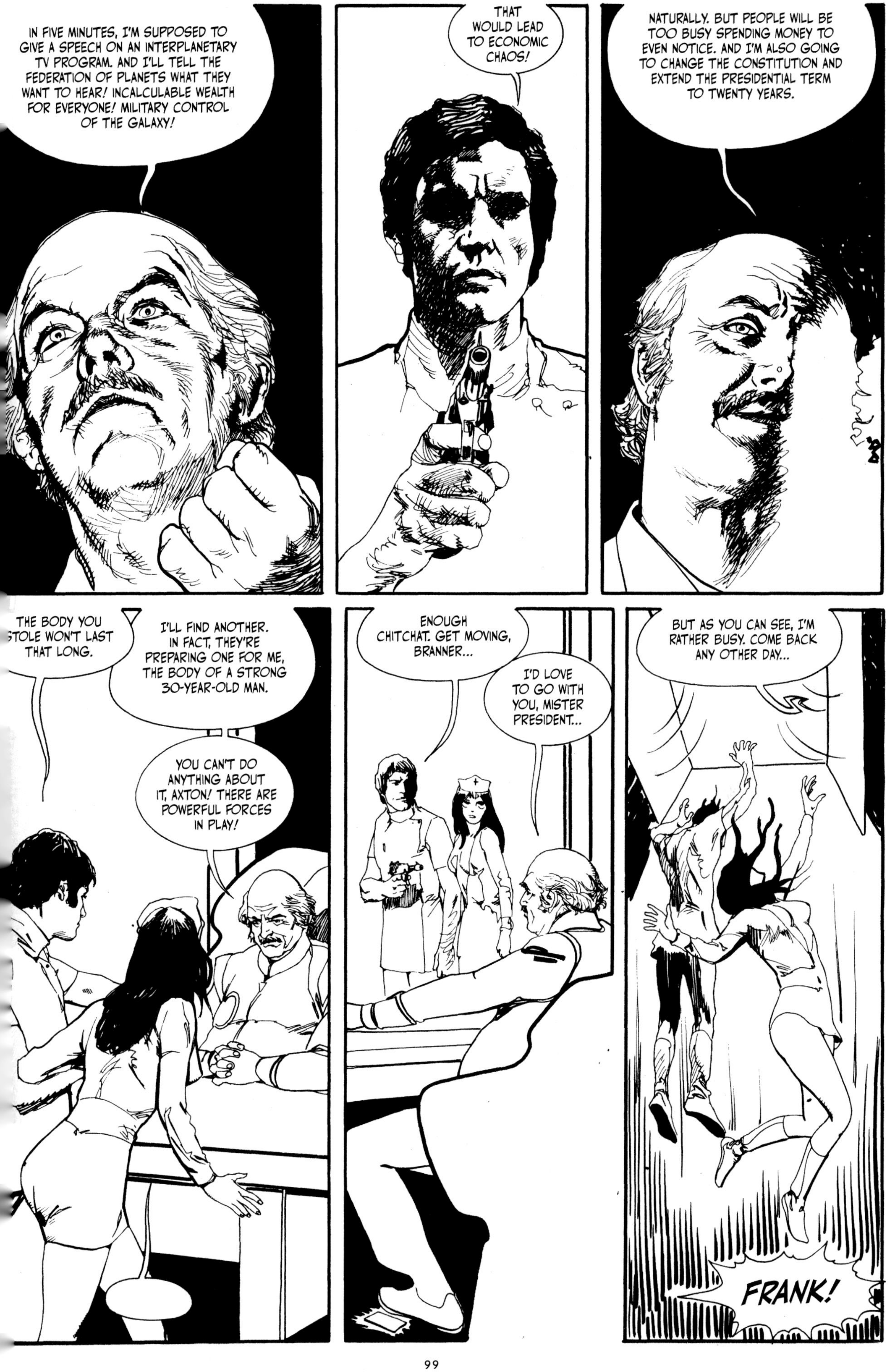
IN FIVE MINUTES, I'M SUPPOSED TO GIVE A SPEECH ON AN INTERPLANETARY TV PROGRAM. AND I'LL TELL THE FEDERATION OF PLANETS WHAT THEY WANT TO HEAR! INCALCULABLE WEALTH FOR EVERYONE! MILITARY CONTROL OF THE GALAXY!
THAT WOULD LEAD TO ECONOMIC CHAOS!
NATURALLY. BUT PEOPLE WILL BE TOO BUSY SPENDING MONEY TO EVEN NOTICE. AND I'M ALSO GOING TO CHANGE THE CONSTITUTION AND EXTEND THE PRESIDENTIAL TERM TO TWENTY YEARS.
THE BODY YOU STOLE WON'T LAST THAT LONG.
I'LL FIND ANOTHER. IN FACT, THEY'RE PREPARING ONE FOR ME, THE BODY OF A STRONG 30-YEAR-OLD MAN.
YOU CAN'T DO ANYTHING ABOUT IT, AXTON! THERE ARE POWERFUL FORCES IN PLAY!
ENOUGH CHITCHAT. GET MOVING, BRANNER...
I'D LOVE TO GO WITH YOU, MISTER PRESIDENT...
BUT AS YOU CAN SEE, I'M RATHER BUSY. COME BACK ANY OTHER DAY...
FRANK!

OW... MY HEAD! WHERE ARE WE?

IT LOOKS LIKE SOME KIND OF STORAGE WAREHOUSE...

YEAH, AND WE'RE THE MERCHANDISE.

HM. I DON'T KNOW WHY I IMAGINED IT WOULD BE OPEN. CAN YOU UNLOCK IT?

SURE. I JUST NEED TO GET UPSTAIRS TO GRAB MY GUN.

VERY CLEVER!

COME OVER HERE... DO YOU SEE THAT OPENING UP THERE? IT LOOKS LIKE A VENTILATION DUCT...

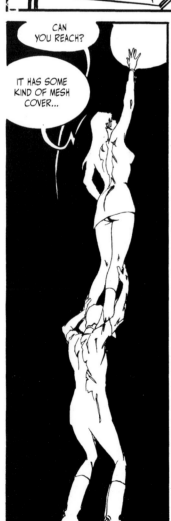

CAN YOU REACH?

IT HAS SOME KIND OF MESH COVER...

ZZAPPPTTT!

AGH! IT'S ELECTRIFIED!

NOW WHAT?

LET ME TRY. MAYBE I CAN MANAGE TO SHORT THE CIRCUIT. IT'S THE ONLY WAY OUT!

HURRY! YOU WEIGH A TON!

THERE! I OPENED IT!

UP YOU GO!

YOU DEFINITELY COULDN'T DO THAT WITH YOUR OLD BODY!

STOP MESSING WITH ME!

WHERE NOW?

STRAIGHT AHEAD, LET'S GO...

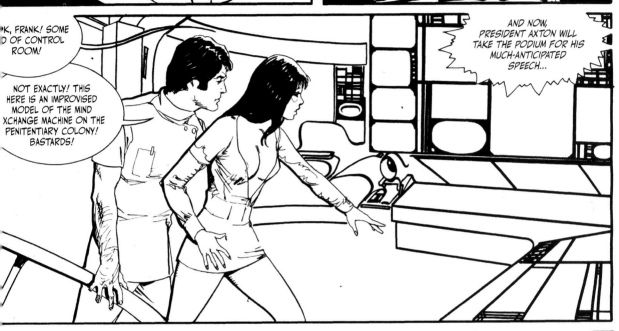

...K, FRANK! SOME ...D OF CONTROL ROOM!

NOT EXACTLY! THIS HERE IS AN IMPROVISED MODEL OF THE MIND XCHANGE MACHINE ON THE PENITENTIARY COLONY! BASTARDS!

AND NOW, PRESIDENT AXTON WILL TAKE THE PODIUM FOR HIS MUCH-ANTICIPATED SPEECH...

DEAR FRIENDS AND MEMBERS OF THE ...ERATION: I HAVE SOMETHING ...PORTANT TO TELL YOU.

OH, FRANK, WE HAVE TO STOP HIM!

THAT'S WHAT I'M THINKING! IF WE GET THIS MACHINE WORKING, I'LL BE ABLE TO CARRY OUT THE MIND EXCHANGE!

A NEW LIFE FOR THE MEMBERS OF THE FEDERATION...

AND IF I HIT THE WRONG BUTTON? YOU COULD DIE!

MY LIFE WON'T MEAN A THING IF THIS MADMAN GETS AWAY WITH THIS. COME ON!

BANG!

OH, FRANK... I COULDN'T TAKE IT IF SOMETHING HAPPENED TO YOU! I LOVE YOU!

LOLA, FOR GOD'S SAKE, PRESS THE BUTTON. THAT MADMAN IS GOING TO DESTROY THE GALAXY!

HE'S BEEN ASSASSINATED! THE PRESIDENT HAS BEEN ASSASSINATED!

LOOK, FRANK! SOMEONE KILLED AXTON... I MEAN, BRANNER!

WELL, I HAD NOTHING TO DO WITH IT!

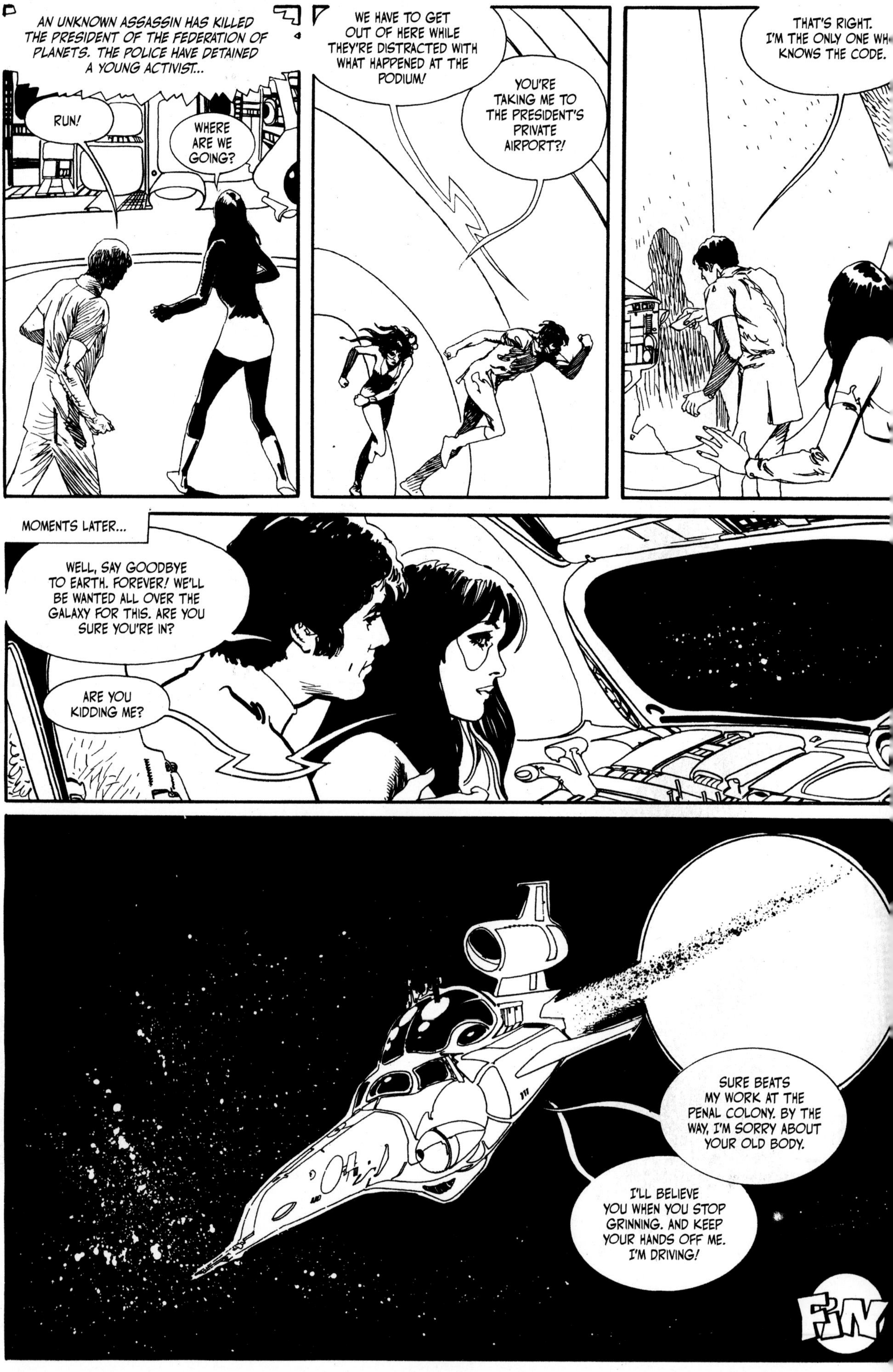
AN UNKNOWN ASSASSIN HAS KILLED THE PRESIDENT OF THE FEDERATION OF PLANETS. THE POLICE HAVE DETAINED A YOUNG ACTIVIST...
RUN!
WHERE ARE WE GOING?
WE HAVE TO GET OUT OF HERE WHILE THEY'RE DISTRACTED WITH WHAT HAPPENED AT THE PODIUM!
YOU'RE TAKING ME TO THE PRESIDENT'S PRIVATE AIRPORT?!
THAT'S RIGHT. I'M THE ONLY ONE WH KNOWS THE CODE.
MOMENTS LATER...
WELL, SAY GOODBYE TO EARTH. FOREVER! WE'LL BE WANTED ALL OVER THE GALAXY FOR THIS. ARE YOU SURE YOU'RE IN?
ARE YOU KIDDING ME?
SURE BEATS MY WORK AT THE PENAL COLONY. BY THE WAY, I'M SORRY ABOUT YOUR OLD BODY.
I'LL BELIEVE YOU WHEN YOU STOP GRINNING. AND KEEP YOUR HANDS OFF ME. I'M DRIVING!
FIN

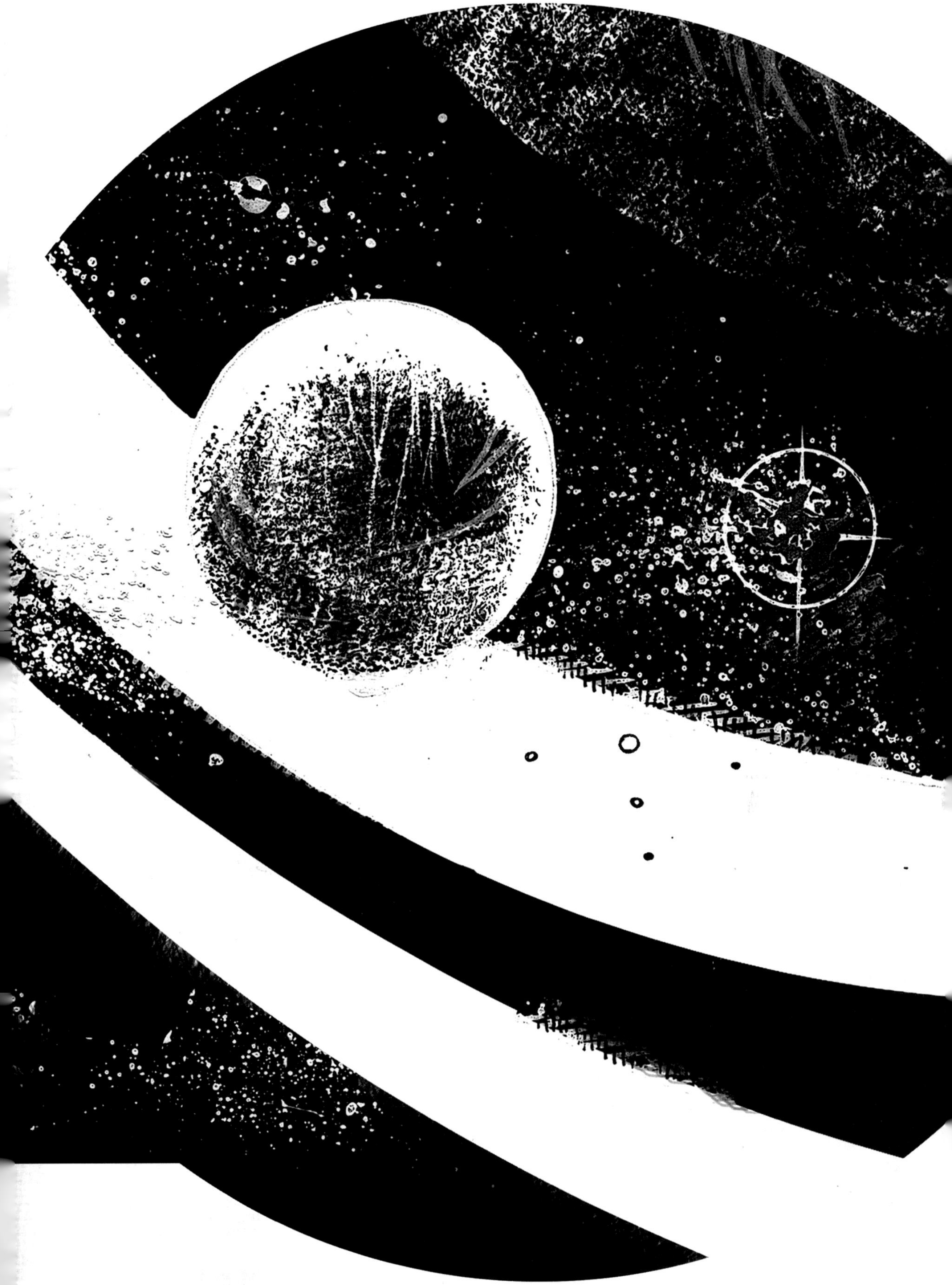

PRISON SHIP

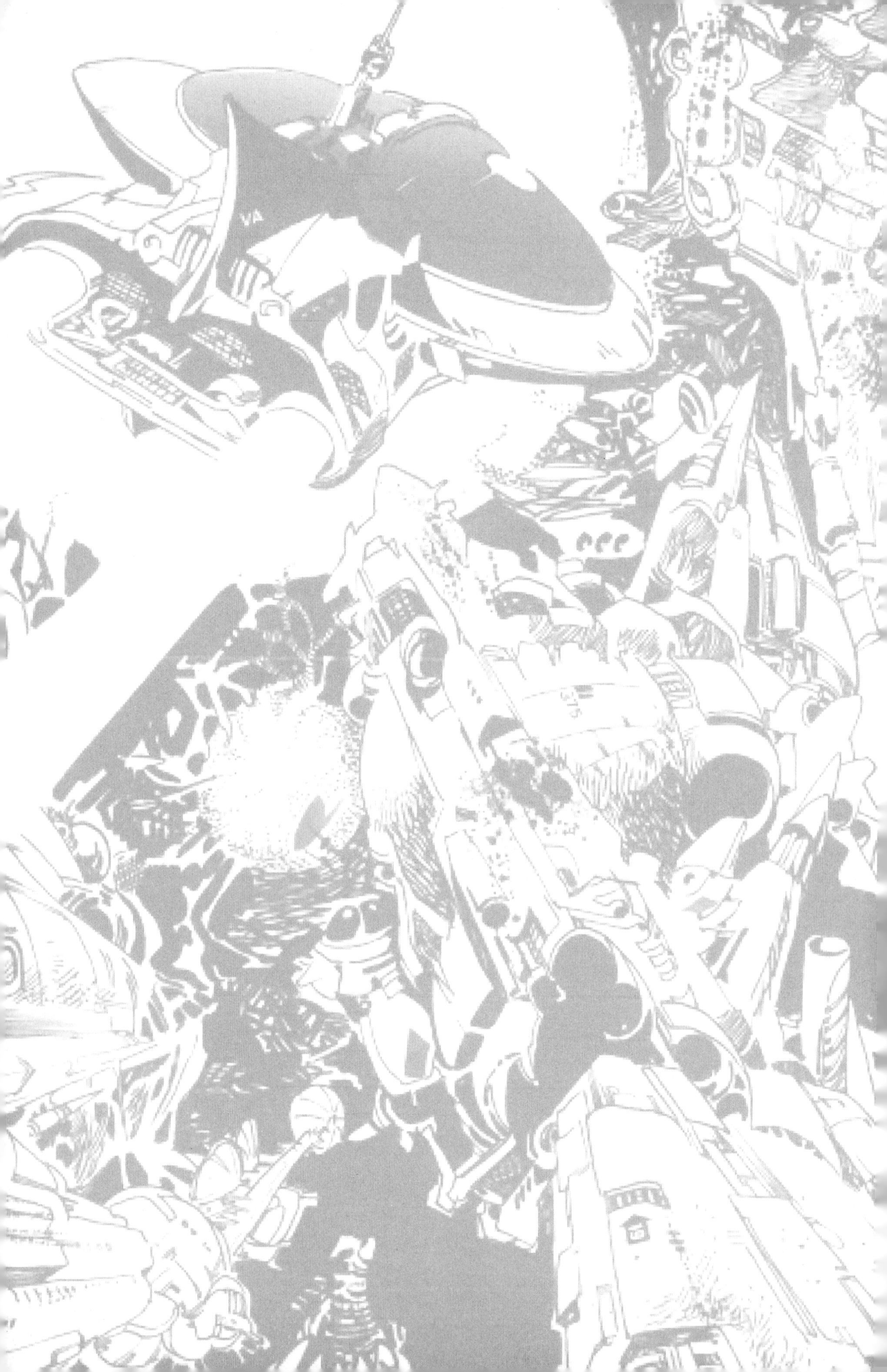